Praise for *Fire and Faith*

"This is the story of a man who championed free speech in the time of religious turmoil that led to the Hundred Years War. Despite the persecutions of John Calvin, who declared him a heretic and caused his immiseration, theologian and scholar Sebastian Castellio never wavered in his determination to challenge authoritarian claims to one truth. This 16th century tale resonates even today when free speech comes under threat again."

— **Dr. Philip Temple ONZM**, author of the Ernest Scott History Prize-winning book *A Sort of Conscience, The Wakefields.*

"Those who cannot learn from history are doomed to repeat it. The story of Sebastian Castellio has mostly been lost to the passage of time but is urgently relevant to the challenges we face in the world today. Read it and prepare to be deeply impacted by the character and vision of this man. This is timeless wisdom."

— **Craig Greenfield,** founder of Alongsiders Int. and author of *Subversive Jesus.*

"Once I started reading, I couldn't stop. I was caught up in the astonishing story of a 16th century scholar who marshaled his intelligence and courage to engage a world in which the righteous gave no quarter, but slaughtered one another in the name of God. I was captivated."

— **Dave Andrews,** author of *Christianarchy* and *Compassionate Community Work.*

"A beautiful retelling of how one extraordinary man stood against the exploding violence of 16th century Europe. Wonderful!"

— **Richard Rohr**, Franciscan priest and author of
Falling Upward.

"This is a riveting historical reconstruction of the life of Sebastian Castellio, a voice of humane Christianity in an era of relentless bloodshed undertaken by church and state. The book brings that awful era to light most vividly, and will inspire me and many others to want to honor the work of Castellio. Brilliant!"

— **David Gushee,** Distinguished Professor of
Christian Ethics and author of *After*
Evangelicalism.

"Thanks to Kristin Jack's exhaustive research and masterful storytelling, Castellio's voice can once again be heard. The timing could not be better. This book about a long-forgotten reformer has the power to spark a new, much-needed reformation."

—**Jason Porterfield,** author of *Fight Like Jesus.*

"Castellio may be one of the less familiar figures of the early Reformation, but his courageous witness to religious liberty in an era of dogmatism and persecution shines through this well-researched, creative and engaging historical novel."

— **Dr. Stuart Murray Williams**, author of *The*
Naked Anabaptist.

Fire and Faith

*The Untold Story of Sebastian Castellio's Epic
Battle with John Calvin*

Kristin Jack

This book is dedicated to all who, like Sebastian Castellio, stand against hate, violence, and oppression, advocating instead for mercy and forgiveness.

In one page of the writings of Castellio, I find more truth, more piety, and more edification than in all the books of Calvin and Beza.

— Dirck Coornhert, 1522–1590

Future generations will wonder why, after so splendid a dawn, we are forced back into such Cimmerian darkness.

— Sebastian Castellio, 1562

A man whose strength is predominantly moral exerts an influence by the mere fact that he exists, for his essence diffuses itself in ever-widening circles, spreading his convictions as ripples spread when a stone is flung into a pool.

— Stefan Zweig, on the life of Castellio

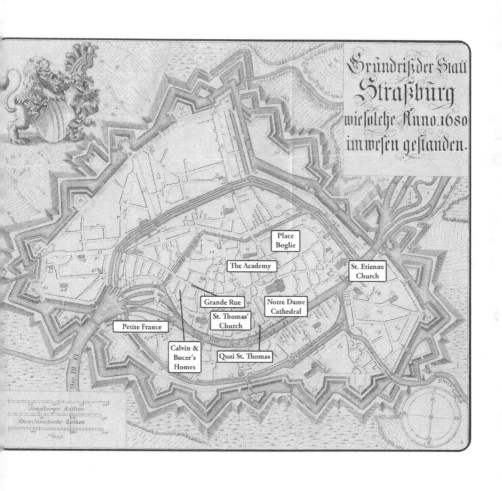

Gründriß der Statt

Straßbürg

wie solche Anno. 1680
im wesen gestanden.

Place
Boglie

The Academy

St. Etienne
Church

Grande Rue

Notre Dame
Cathedral

St. Thomas'
Church

Petite France

Calvin &
Bucer's
Homes

Quai St. Thomas

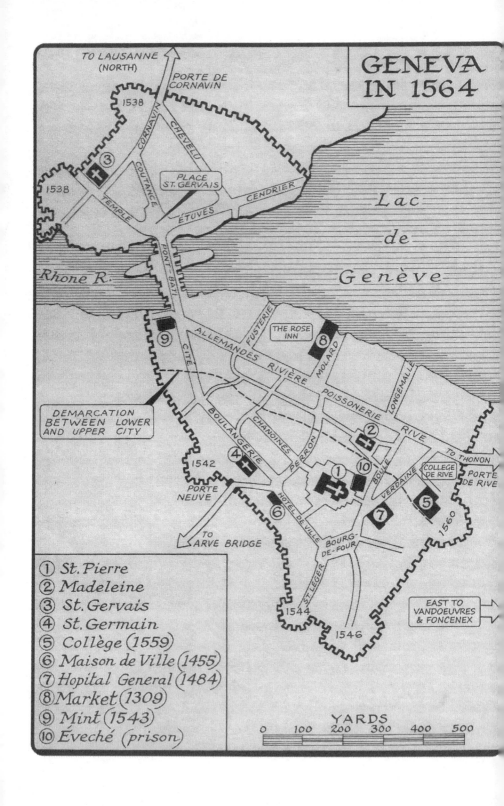

GENEVA IN 1564

TO LAUSANNE (NORTH)

PORTE DE CORNAVIN

1538

CORNAVIN
CHEVELU
COUTANCE
TEMPLE

③ ✚

1538

PLACE ST. GERVAIS

ETUVES
CENDRIER

PONT BATI

Lac de Genève

Rhone R.

⑨

CITE

ALLEMANDES

FUSTERIE

THE ROSE INN

⑧

MOLARD

RIVIERE

POISSONERIE

LONGEMALLE

RIVE

DEMARCATION BETWEEN LOWER AND UPPER CITY

BOULANGERIE

CHANOINES

PERRON

② ✚

BOULE

VERDAINE

TO THONON

COLLEGE DE RIVE

PORTE DE RIVE

1542

④ ✚

① ✚

⑩

⑤

1560

PORTE NEUVE

⑥

HOTEL DE VILLE

⑦

TO ARVE BRIDGE

BOURG-DE-FOUR

ST. LEGER

1544

1546

EAST TO VANDOEUVRES & FONCENEX

① St. Pierre
② Madeleine
③ St. Gervais
④ St. Germain
⑤ Collège (1559)
⑥ Maison de Ville (1455)
⑦ Hopital General (1484)
⑧ Market (1309)
⑨ Mint (1543)
⑩ Eveché (prison)

YARDS

0   100   200   300   400   500

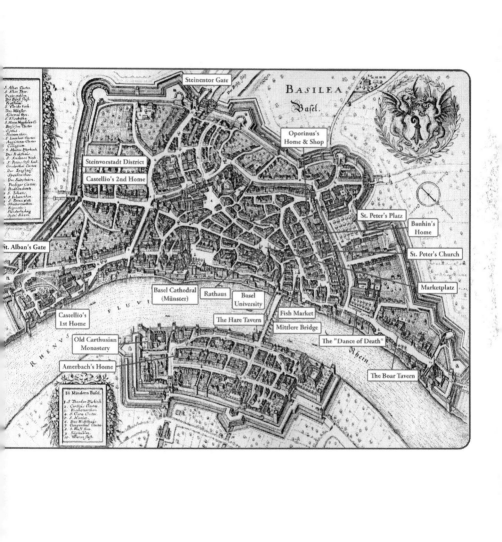

Steinentor Gate

BASILEA
Basel.

Oporinus's
Home & Shop

Steinvorstadt District

Castellio's 2nd Home

St. Peter's Platz

Bauhin's
Home

St. Alban's Gate

St. Peter's Church

Marketplatz

Basel Cathedral
(Münster)

Rathaus

Basel
University

Castellio's
1st Home

The Hare Tavern

Fish Market

Mittlere Bridge

The "Dance of Death"

Old Carthusian
Monastery

Amerbach's Home

The Boar Tavern

RHENVS FLUVI

Rhein

Contents

Author's Note

I've always been fascinated by history, particularly that seminal epoch known as the Reformation. Our forebears during that era got so much right—and so much wrong. In 2019, I found myself with far more time on my hands than ever before. I had just finished an intense medical procedure that sought to eradicate the blood cancer I was battling. For six weeks, I was in isolation and could do nothing but read. I was determined to use that time to find out as much as I could about a heroic figure who, despite the radical and prophetic nature of his life and thought, barely gets a mention in most histories of the sixteenth century. His name was Sebastian Castellio.

The more I read, the more amazed I became at this man's courage and prescience. And the more I read, the more saddened I became at how the powers that be had managed to erase his memory from mainstream history. In that moment, I resolved to write a book—not a dry historical biography—but a novel that could capture the drama, struggle and bravery of Castellio's life and times. I spent the next four years reading and researching, corresponding with scholars, and visiting the places where Castellio had lived and taught—all with the goal of learning as much as I could about the man. The end result lies before you now.

The Characters

As with many historical novels, *Fire and Faith* contains a large lineup of characters interacting with one another. With so many names flying around, it is easy to lose track of who's who, particularly if you've put the book down and come back to it later. At the back of this book, you'll find a list of the historical characters and events that appear in this story. I encourage you to flip to that section if you ever get confused about the names, actors or events you are encountering.

Chapter 1
The Burning

Basel, the Swiss Confederacy, May 13, 1559

Sebastian Castellio positioned himself as far to the edge of the crowd as he could, closest to the path that led home. He stole a glance to his left and saw anxious faces drawn with uncertainty. He and his fellow Baselers—neighbors and colleagues—had been gathered for an hour in the warm morning air, listening to speeches denouncing a man two years dead. A man they looked up to and loved dearly. Sebastian knew that almost no one—not even the majority of those on the hastily built stage—was here by choice. Each had received an order from the city's council to come. To have refused would have invited terrible suspicion. The fact that they had been summoned here by name revealed that they were already in grave danger.

In the courtyard of the Steinentor, the city's southwestern gate, Sebastian shifted his weight from one foot to the other. Against the beige wall, a timber stage had been built, now occupied by a dozen throne-like chairs. Each chair held a grim-faced patrician, all dressed in black, each man's long robe draped behind him. Jagged emotions forced their way through Sebastian's body. Fury at this macabre circus being staged for the education of those assembled. But his anger was being overwhelmed by something even more primal. A fear so palpable he felt it growing and spreading, twisting around each of his neighbors.

The last accusatory speech finished. Everyone held fast, waiting for a dead man to appear. The air about them thickened, as their breathing became heavier and each movement an effort. And then Sebastian heard it—the sound that heralded all he had been dreading: a low rumbling noise approaching from beyond the stone wall. Within a minute, the sound had grown louder and closer, a dysrhythmic *clack, clack, clacking,* a wagon's solid wheels struggling over cobblestones. Then a flicker of movement within a shadowy archway. Two workmen emerged into the sunlight dragging a load, their faces wrapped with handkerchiefs. Blinking against the bright sun, they surveyed the multitude of five hundred souls or more, many of Basel's most illustrious citizens.

One man was before the cart, pulling. The other behind it, pushing. The clumsy wooden wheels lurched over cobblestones and threatened to shake apart their pitiful burden. It seemed to take the men an age to pass through the stone gateway and into the paved courtyard on the outskirts of the city. On either side of the arch, thick rock walls extended north and south. Above rose a clock tower and turret that scowled over the unwilling city.

Between the stage and the bewildered mass of people, a heap of kindling had been assembled around a wooden post. The cart lurched forward again, until the workmen paused, as if considering how best to transfer their load and secure it to the post. They bent over the low narrow cart, muscles tense. A shudder ran through the crowd as the workmen reached into the wagon's tray and lifted out a decaying corpse, holding it by the remnants of its tattered clothes and shroud. With grunts of exertion, they tried to swing it out and onto the top of the wood pile. Though the torso moved in line with their intention, the cadaver's legs at one end and its head at the other caught on the side of the narrow cart. For a moment, it looked as though all three might fall to the ground. But with great effort and no little cursing, the two live men regained control of the dead.

It was an agonizing dance, with four attempts before, finally, they transferred the uncooperative corpse. The rotted body now lay splayed across the kindling pyre, emaciated arms, legs and head arrayed in an absurdly unnatural pose. Now came the task of tying it to the stake. It was clear the decaying mass before them was only held together by what was left of its garments. Attaching the cadaver to the post was only possible by coiling lengths of rope across its arms, its neck, its head. It was a terrible task, the body collapsing back onto the wood several times before they could secure it. Even then, they were forced to compromise, fixing the upper part of the body to the post while the lower part sank down into a bizarre semi-sitting position.

For many in the crowd, it was too much. They lowered their eyes, focusing on the ground in front of them. For others, like Sebastian, as much as they tried to look away, they could not, their wide eyes drawn to the grisly display before them. And what they saw made their blood run cold. Where the dead man's clothes had rotted, pale bone and patches of black, putrefied flesh appeared. Where there once had been a face, the lips and nose had gone, leaving a maniacal grin beneath two desiccated eyes and a patchwork of decaying skin, tufts of hair and beard, and glimpses of yellowing skull.

The dark-robed man in the center chair turned his head. With the index finger of his right hand, he signaled to a kerchiefed workman off to the side of the stage. This man, his face obscured, held a torch, the end of which had been soaked in pitch. He plunged it into a brazier of burning coals, extracted the flaming torch, then walked across to the pile of kindling and corpse. He hesitated, looking up to the cloaked figure for confirmation. That figure—a commandingly tall, severe man—gave a terse nod of his head. The torchbearer plunged the flame into the tinder, holding it there until an orange tongue began to lick its way up through the heap of dry wood. His work done, the man retreated, and the flames in the pyre began to climb, igniting the legs and feet of the dead man.

Sebastian looked down, eyes firmly upon the paving stones before him. His final act of defiance would be to refuse to witness that which they were forcing him to observe.

A loud *crack*, like a musket being fired, ended his resolve. His eyes jerked up and toward the flames. A shower of sparks billowed out of the pyre from an exploding pocket of, he supposed, sap-filled wood. In that millisecond, the image of a blazing body twitching under the onslaught of brutal heat awakened something buried deep in Sebastian's past.

He shuddered, recalling the same sight—no, far worse—more than twenty years ago. An event that had changed the course of his life.

Chapter 2
Lyon

France, 1535

Sebastian Castellio could feel himself caught up in something much greater than his own small existence. Change was storming across Europe; the old was dying and the new was being born. Religious revolution was smoldering in Germany, where Luther's arguments were demolishing centuries of Catholic hegemony, while the even more radical ideas of Thomas Müntzer were burning across Bavaria. Firebrands like Ulrich Zwingli and Heinrich Bullinger were leading similar revolutions in the cities of the Swiss Confederation. Across the Channel, England too was ablaze. Henry VIII had seized the apparatus of the Catholic Church and placed it under his own institution, the Church of England.

Sebastian's personal universe was in revolution too. Bustling Lyon was a world away from the village of his birth, Saint Martin du Frêne in French-speaking Savoy. Born in the spring of 1515, he had been named after Saint Sebastian, a Christian martyr executed twelve hundred years earlier for raising his voice against the Emperor Diocletian's persecutions.

Sebastian's childhood home had been a place of simple tasks and

simple beauty, with rolling pastures and pine-clad hills, plains
bursting with color every spring and cloaked with white each winter.
His parents, peasant farmers, coaxed a sparse living out of the land.
Loving and committed, they worked desperately to provide a better
future for Sebastian and his three brothers and three sisters. He spent
harsh winters searching every grove for firewood, followed by
evenings huddled around the hearth of their tiny cottage. He labored
long summer days beside his father and brothers, tilling fields and
scything hay. As soon as they were strong enough, each of the children went to work, toiling till their hands blistered and their bodies
ached. They learned how to hunt and fish, and how to put food on
the table through the lean winter months. Hunger was always a
threat, and Sebastian remembered the anguish on his parents' faces
whenever food ran short and thin gruel was all they could provide.
His mother and father had longed for their children to find a richer
life, one beyond mere subsistence, so they scrimped and saved to
enable them to attend the local village school. But always there was
so little, and the hope that any of them might one day find a future
beyond this was a thing they could barely dream.

Sebastian was profoundly aware that his parents had given him
many sacrificial gifts. Early, they had seen the precocious intellect in
their middle child and were determined it should be allowed to flourish. They badgered school teachers and recruited local clergy,
insisting they, too, recognize Sebastian's abilities and join those
helping him make his way in the world. Sebastian also knew his
parents had given him two other precious gifts. They had modeled
tenacity and moral strength, both of which now ran through the
center of his life like an iron rod. He could still hear his father's
words: "No matter how poor you are, you must never steal. No matter
how tempted you are, you must never lie. No matter how hard life is,
you must never give up."

After progressing as far as he could in the parish school of Saint
Martin du Frêne, his teachers, seeing his promise, urged him to
pursue a college education in the provincial capital of Lyon, even

collecting funds to make it possible. Lyon was France's second greatest city with a teeming population of 50,000, and was in many ways more progressive than Paris. Its proximity to Italy in the east and the Swiss cities to the northeast meant that many merchants and immigrants visited Lyon. The great Rhône flowed through the city, bringing people and goods from the north, while the Saône reached up toward the German border. Four times a year, Lyon hosted an international fair where goods and ideas from all across Europe were traded. War in Italy had pushed many exiles across the border, and they joined with immigrants from Portugal, Germany and the Netherlands to bring skills in art, literature, and, most importantly, printing. German arrivals displayed a particular talent for this. From the first printing house in 1470, they proliferated, attracting yet more writers to the city. By the mid-1530s, Lyon was a hub of education and scholarship, theater and art. A place where fresh ideas were tolerated with greater freedom than most other European centers.

In 1535, Sebastian Castellio came to this place of intellectual ferment, enrolling in its College de la Trinité to study classics, poetry and languages. The impressive campus consisted of three large blocks surrounding a courtyard, the back of which terminated in ramparts abutting the banks of the Rhône. It was a school of eloquence and poetry, a beacon that attracted the children of the French bourgeoise. Sebastian arrived with one set of clothes, one spare shirt, and a worryingly light bag of coins in his pocket. He'd won a small scholarship, but even so, hunger drove him in search of work that could support him while he studied. Soon his spare time was spent tutoring the children of Lyon's elite. With his physical needs met, he flourished, discovering a love of music and poetry — he had verse published in a local anthology — and even more, a flair for languages. He mastered Hebrew, Greek and Latin while absorbing Italian and passable German from fellow students.

Sebastian's early months were full of apprehension; the other students came from backgrounds that were privileged and far different to his own. Doubts assailed him as to whether he really

belonged here. But in time he was befriended by others like himself—
those more concerned with their futures than their pasts, those with
minds hungry to grow and a desire to contribute to their expanding
world. By his fourth year, his reputation for scholarship was firmly
established and he was given the task of tutoring undergraduates.
The loneliness of his early days was replaced by blossoming friend-
ships; and in particular, he grew close to two other talented scholars.
They were tutors also, one having graduated from Paris and the other
from Bordeaux, both drawn to Lyon by Trinité's reputation in classics and philosophy. One of them taught theology, the other
medicine.

Jean Bauhin was a compulsive reader and sensitive thinker. His
mind sought facts, his heart compassion, and his soul seemed
conscious of every other living creature. To walk with Jean Bauhin
was to explore creation. Every few steps, he'd stop and examine some
shrub or insect, commenting on each plant's medicinal use, or using a
small knife to clip off leaves which he'd press into his note-filled journal. He was fond of quoting Plato—"wonder is the beginning of
wisdom"—a dictum that had become his guiding light. His ambition
was to become a great physician, not one of the charlatans who sold
charms and extracted coins from the gullible, but a true healer, one
who understood the properties of every herb and tree in the kingdom.

The other man was André Zebedee, a well-traveled graduate
from the College de Guyenne in Bordeaux, who arrived in 1536, his
reputation as an exceptional teacher already established. He and
Sebastian took an instant liking to one another. The newcomer was a
little older than Sebastian, tall and square-shouldered, his serious face
dominated by two deep-set eyes of brown—caves brooding beneath
the brow of a hill. When he decided it was time to speak, Zebedee
could keep Sebastian up all night debating politics, religion and the
meaning of existence. In their first few weeks of budding friendship,
Sebastian had written a poem likening Zebedee to a subterranean
river: mysterious and dark. Only occasionally did he break through
the surface. Or that's how he seemed. A few months later, Sebastian

wrote another in which the metaphor was that of a barely dormant volcano.

Sebastian found André's smoldering intensity both attractive and frightening. With every subject they tackled—and there were many—André's thoughts churned and simmered, before pouring out of him with explosive passion. At first Sebastian had mistaken his brooding moods for reserve, but soon he came to feel the force coiled and waiting to emerge. Engaged on a matter that moved him, André was relentless. His zeal for truth was matched only by his love of intellectual freedom. And paradoxically, it was because of all these lofty virtues that Sebastian sensed danger, not just for André, but also for himself. Nine days out of ten, both men possessed calm hearts and logical minds. But if ever they believed their sense of right and wrong had been violated or their conscience assaulted, something molten moved within them. In such a moment, both these peaceable scholars could act or speak impulsively, with consequences that were hard to predict.

Among themselves, the three reveled in fierce debate not just about their studies but all the great ideas and events swirling about them. They were allies, and they were combatants, flexing their minds as they jousted over books, over Scripture, over the chess board, and over sayings of the great thinkers.

It was late afternoon. Sebastian and his two friends sat in the cool of the stone-walled library of the College de la Trinité, restless from hours of poring over colorless pages. They needed a distraction. Perhaps a few rounds of "complete the saying and say the sayer." The game was one of their favorite sports. As was typical, Sebastian launched the opening volley.

"Jean, if I were to say, 'The roots of education are bitter,' what would you say?"

Jean Bauhin responded quickly. "Oh, that's an easy one. I would quote Aristotle and say, 'but the fruit is sweet.' Now Seb, if I were to say to you that 'true wisdom comes when ...' what would you say back to me?'

Sebastian's brow crinkled in concentration. "I know this, I know this ... give me a moment ... ahh. Yes! 'True wisdom,' according to Socrates, 'comes when we realize how little we understand about life, ourselves, and the world around us.' A good saying. And tell me: was it Socrates who also said, 'It is the mark of an educated mind to be able to entertain a thought without accepting it'?"

Jean smiled broadly back at Sebastian. "Nice try, but I'm not caught by that trick. It was, in fact, Aristotle who left us that wisdom."

Jean and Sebastian preferred to plumb the classicists. André Zebedee leaned more toward the theologians. But he would often throw them a bone to begin with. "So, my learned friends, if I were to say, 'You will never do anything in this world without ...' what is this essential thing, and what is the quality next to it?"

A smile immediately spread across Jean's face. "Then I would say you are also quoting Aristotle when he advised us: 'You will never do anything in this world without courage, for it is the greatest quality of the mind next to honor.'"

Sebastian raised one quizzical eyebrow. "That was an easy one, André. Surely you can test us harder than that."

A look of mock indignation crossed André's face, followed by a mischievous smile. "Ah, a challenge. Then let us try this one: 'When you remember past events, clearly you do not compel them to have happened, and so in the same way God does not ...' what? The sayer and the saying, if you will, my clever friends."

Sebastian's eyes moved toward the ceiling, as if he might find the answer there. Jean, on the other hand, stared at his boots as he wrestled with André's riddle.

"Still unsure? Then I shall give you another hint. The speaker starts with A and is neither Aristotle nor Anselm but splits their births with his." For a full minute, silence reigned as André's two protagonists pondered this.

Eventually there came a low drumming sound as Jean's fingertips tapped on the tabletop.

"Pff. We are supposed to be citing quotes, not solving puzzles. You play with the rules of the game, I think."

"I think not," André retorted. "Actually, I chose an easy one just for you, Jean." André's smile widened as Jean shot him a look of feigned offense. Eventually he leaned back in his chair, shaking his head in defeat. But Sebastian refused to concede, leaning forward, one foot jiggling, still searching each nook and cranny of his memory.

"He starts with A, lived in the time between Aristotle and Anselm ... well then ... surely that can only have been our friend Saint Augustine! And what was it he said about foreknowledge? If I am not completely mistaken, it was: 'When you remember past events you do not compel them to have happened, and in the same way God does not compel future events to happen by His foreknowledge of them.'"

Now it was André's turn to sink back in his chair and look momentarily defeated before breaking into an appreciative chuckle. "Dear Lord ... how do you ... oh, well done, Seb, well done indeed. I think I have no option but to give this round to you."

Sebastian broke into a smile, not of triumph but admiration. He regarded his two friends as quite brilliant. Yet something else, something barely perceptible nagged at him—a sigh that warned, an intuition that forbode, hinting that all three of them would indeed play decisive roles in the vast drama unfolding all about them. And this thought sent a chill of fear and wonder down his spine.

Lyon was not insulated from Europe's torrent of new ideas, and the Continent's convulsions were more and more preoccupying their debates. They had read the words of that extraordinary Catholic thinker, Erasmus, questioning the moribund state of his own church, calling for reform and pleading for Europe to become a commonwealth built on Christian love. They'd read the books of Martin Luther calling on Christians to rebuild a church based on Scripture rather than tradition. A brilliant young French lawyer by the name of John Calvin had taken these ideas and expanded and systemized them, penning a majestic work entitled *The Institutes of Christian Religion*. It was one of the clearest and most incisive works of theology Sebastian had ever encountered. In *The Institutes*, Calvin transformed the interpretation of Scripture from the previous centuries' speculative philosophy into concrete principles. Line upon line, precept upon precept, its logic was inexorable. Moreover, Calvin's insights into both divine and human nature seemed profound. Near the beginning of *The Institutes*, Calvin had written that "nearly all the wisdom we possess, that is to say, true and sound wisdom, consists of two parts: the knowledge of God and the knowledge of ourselves." This thought alone struck Sebastian as deeper than anything he'd ever read in all the canons of Catholic Church Law.

Across France and, indeed, all of Europe, the Catholic Church banned these books, lest they corrupt the minds of the naive and rebellious. But in Lyon, with its regular international fairs and constant stream of travelers, both teachers and students had obtained copies and were discussing the ideas. Often Castellio, Bauhin and Zebedee talked long into the night trying to discern where the truth lay—and what they would do with that truth. André had even made a daring, fleeting visit to Geneva to observe its reforms firsthand.

Sebastian knew they were privileged to be living in these times where the intellectual shackles of Scholasticism, superstition and church law were fracturing under the forces of inquiry and discovery. He'd read how the Turkish sacking of Constantinople some eighty years earlier had sent Greek scholars fleeing across Europe, bringing with them a treasure-trove of ancient texts. Brilliant minds, like Erasmus's, had studied these, translating them into Latin and local vernaculars. So much that had been lost was being restored as the best of Greek, Roman, Hebrew and Arab cultures were exalted and mined. And this restoration was not just in the world of letters. Sebastian had heard of Brunelleschi, the visionary Italian artist and architect who had mastered the mysterious truths of perspective and realism. He'd heard of how the works of da Vinci and Michelangelo, combining brilliance with beauty, had exploded out of Florence. Displays of genius seemed to be breaking forth everywhere. The world was growing not only more dazzling but much larger than had ever been known before. Explorers like Columbus and Cabral had stumbled upon the New World, and Magellan upon the Pacific Ocean.

Revolutionary scientific ideas were also spreading and shaking Europe to the core. There were rumors of an astronomer in Poland with theories that would turn all understandings of the cosmos upside down. Apparently, this man, a certain Copernicus, had calculated that the known planets revolved around the sun, not the earth. If true, this would be devastating, proving Christendom's previous conception of the universe utterly wrong. It was as if Brunelleschi's insights on perspective and realism were forcing themselves, welcome or not, upon every area of life. A new light was dawning. Like Michelangelo's David, Europe was bursting forth from the rock that had bound it, into a glorious new freedom.

Sebastian knew the religious revolution hadn't started with Luther. He'd built on the work of courageous souls who'd gone before him, like the martyred Tyndale and Wycliffe, and the literary works of Erasmus. But it was Luther—so the story went—who'd been bold enough to nail his list of challenges to the church's door and demand debate. But now the revolution was gathering speed. An extraordinary cycle had been set in motion. The printing press and rising literacy were feeding a hunger for knowledge, and those who tasted of this feast wanted more. An extraordinary rebirth, a renaissance, was flowering. The scholars called it humanism—a rediscovery of the best that humanity had ever thought or created. This thought ignited a dream that the world could rise to those heights again. Perhaps beyond. It was fed by the rallying cry *"ad fontes"* (back to the sources). And daring voices, like Erasmus and Luther, were shouting the same challenge to the church: "Return to the Scriptures and their original languages." After centuries of the Bible being a closed book, the jealously guarded secret of theologians and bishops, it was now being read with fresh eyes. The clamor was growing louder and louder to unchain it, to give it back to the people.

With wonder, Sebastian could see that these turbulent currents were stirring College de la Trinité too. In classes and corridors, in taverns and hostels, heated arguments were spilling over. France was a Catholic nation, and many regarded the new religious views as heretical and seditious, attacking the way of life they had always known. Sebastian thought back to the simple faith and reassuring rhythms his parents and neighbors had lived by. Regular feast days, the stories of the saints, trust in the church for salvation. It was devout and sincere, and it had served to hold the community together through all of life's vicissitudes. And yet he knew that Erasmus's and Luther's critiques were right. Corruption tainted the church. Holy things were bought and sold. Examples abounded of prelates living immoral lives, living in opulence while the poor supported them with their taxes and tithes. At the political level, the church appeared to lust after power and wealth as much as, and sometimes more than, any king or tyrant. The Catholic Church had become a vast ecclesiastical empire. Popes lived palatially, raised armies and waged war to expand their territories. In the Americas, Catholic conquistadors backed by papal bulls were slaughtering and enslaving everything that stood between them and the gold they sought. *Surely,* Sebastian thought, *this can't be right?* Like so many others, he had begun to read and reflect on the Scriptures for himself, using Jerome's Latin Vulgate and Erasmus's New Testament, and what he read was beginning to turn his once certain world upside down. It was painfully clear that the Christian church had drifted very far from the teachings of Jesus.

Yes, he thought, *something big is happening. A revolution that will sweep up every institution—church, universities, schools, even monarchies. Something that will gather up the whole social order and shake its very foundations.* It was a fearful thought. Yet a hope also burned in him that Christendom would be shaken out of its darkness, and, as Erasmus kept pleading, into something far more noble. *And God knows*, he thought, *we need that. Everywhere we look there is war, killing and brutality; exploitation, ignorance and oppression.* But still, it was gratitude rather than despair that drove him forward. Providence had plucked him out of obscurity and poverty, enabling him to question and to learn. It was an opportunity that so many, even his own family, had never before been permitted. For centuries, the great mass of people all across Europe had been held in oppressive servitude by those above them. But he had been lifted out of this by his parents' sacrifices and by God's goodness. Surely it was his responsibility to lift others up as well. Frightening, thrilling questions now burned in his mind: *How can I join in this wave of rebirth washing over Europe? What role am I to play in this new world God is building?*

It was a Saturday afternoon late in March. Thick leaden skies had been brooding for days, but finally the cloudbanks were breaking up and winter's bitter northerlies easing. Sebastian closed the text he was reading, stretched and yawned. He'd had enough study for one day. As he surveyed the books lining the library shelves before him, Jean Bauhin stirred beside him.

"Seb, how about a walk down to Saint Paul's market? Maybe we'll see a minstrel, or find something to eat or drink, or see a bookseller with some writing tools. Look, the sun is shining! Surely a walk will do us both more good than staying cooped up within these walls."

Sebastian eyed the pile of papers on the desk in front of him and conceded. Bauhin was right. He needed to get out and clear his head. It was swirling not just with cognates of Latin and Greek but with all the theological arguments that he and his fellow students had been thrashing around these many months.

They descended the library's steps, pulling their scarves closer as they slipped past the granite balustrades and sandstone lions. A few more steps and they were through Trinité's wrought-iron gates, leaving its pale walls behind them as they strode north up the Rue Pas-Etroit and onto Rue Saint John. The sun was shining wanly out of a powder-blue sky. Here and there, they could hear the hopeful songs of birds in just-budding trees. There was a cool beauty to it all. And yet, something felt amiss. Small groups of people were scurrying along the streets, moving more quickly than usual, hurrying past them and heading in the direction they had just come. Others, greater numbers in fact, were passing them, headed north, just as they were.

Bauhin inclined his head toward Sebastian. "What do you think is up? Could there be some kind of carnival in the square?" Sebastian could do no more than shrug his shoulders. Puzzled, both men pressed forward. By the time they got to Rue Juiverie, people were calling to one another, their voices distressed. Some were shouting, "Come and see what they are doing!" Others were crying, "Leave quickly. Go home!"

Bauhin reached out and caught the elbow of an older man moving away from the square and heading south. "Monsieur, do you know what's going on? Why is everyone looking so concerned?"

The man's ash-colored mustache twitched frantically as he spoke. "They are killing them ... killing them in the square. This is not good. I don't agree with it." As soon as he had freed his arm from Bauhin's grip, he trotted on, moving as fast as his unsteady legs would carry him. The old man's message had been terse and confusing. Sebastian felt his stomach twist in an anxious knot. Bauhin's face had turned pale.

"Seb, what did he mean? Who are they killing, and why?" It was a pointless question, for obviously he knew no more than Bauhin. Sebastian was all for following the older man's example and turning for home, but Bauhin would have none of it. "Whatever is happening, we should find out what it is."

And so, despite his stomach telling him the opposite, Sebastian moved on toward Saint Paul's. By the time they reached the narrow Rue Saint Barthélemy, they had entered a stream of people moving shoulder to shoulder toward the plaza. They rounded another corner, entering the large courtyard that fronted Saint Paul's, their progress now blocked by the crowd already gathered.

Sebastian stood on his tiptoes, trying to see over the heads of those crammed in front of him. He could make out the top of three poles, but little else. Bauhin, being slightly shorter, had no hope of seeing anything, and he reached out and tapped the shoulder of a much taller man in front. "Monsieur, what is going on? What can you see?"

The tall man half turned toward them. "You missed the magistrate's speech, did you? And the bishop's little homily?" His voice was thick with contempt. "They're criminals, condemned heretics. Lutherans! And they are going to make an example of them."

Bauhin turned and looked at Sebastian, neither of them able to make sense of what they had just heard. Bauhin's eyes searched left and right, then he took hold of Sebastian's arm.

"Over here are some steps." And indeed, directly to their left, at the edge of the square, a narrow stone staircase led to the second floor of a building. People were already crowded on to its front few steps, but behind them there was space. They squeezed past and stood on the sixth step, the last one that afforded a view of the square before the staircase disappeared into the building. They looked across the heads of those huddled before them.

Three thick poles had been set into the ground. Around them, firewood had been stacked. Bound to each pole was a man. Two of them Sebastian judged to be middle-aged, late forties or early fifties. The third, the one closest to them, was much younger, even younger than himself. Sebastian was struck by how normal the three men looked. They could have been any one of Lyon's Catholic citizens. They had been stripped of their doublets and were clad in thigh-length white linen shirts. Beneath the shirts, their legs were clad in hose, and their feet were bare. The farthest man's chin was tilted upward, his eyes raised, as if looking to the horizon beyond the edge of Lyon. The second man also had his head tilted back, but unlike the first, his eyes were shut. His lips were moving, Sebastian guessed, in prayer. The third, the young man closest to them, was the most animated. His face was pale and his eyes impossibly wide, as he searched the crowd seemingly for someone to intervene. Then with a turn of his head, for the briefest of moments, his eyes fell on the stone step where they were standing. Sebastian's heart froze. In the span of a single second, their eyes locked. In that moment, it was as if all the terror coursing through the young Lutheran's heart had entered Sebastian's own.

Desperately he turned to Bauhin, his words full of fear and anger. "This can't be happening, not in Lyon. Why is no one speaking out? Why is no one stopping this?"

"Shh, be careful with your words. It's too late for that. They must have had a trial, and judgment has been passed on them. There is nothing we can do now."

Sebastian could feel himself beginning to tremble. Not from cold, but from horror mixed with anger. An energy urged him to shout, to call for a halt to this barbarism, but each time he opened his mouth, his chest and throat grew tighter. He found himself struggling to breathe.

As they watched, another character lurched from the far side of the square: a hulking, obese figure, his face masked. He carried a lit torch. He walked toward the staked man nearest him and thrust the torch theatrically at his face. The older man barely flinched, keeping his eyes unblinkingly raised. The torch bearer then thrust the flame to the base of the wood and held it till it caught hold of a yellow powder. A bitter smell filled the air. For a moment, Sebastian could taste acid rising in his throat. *Sulfur!* It was all he could do to stop himself retching. The fat man then moved to the second victim, repeating the performance as if it were a script. First the threatening thrust at the face, then plunging the torch into the yellow fuel at the base of the pyre.

Sebastian had seen enough. If he could not intervene, then he needed to flee this pantomime of justice being played out before them. He would not lend this farce his acquiescence by standing and watching. As he reached this decision, the third bonfire was lit. The young man, his head twisting from side to side, again turned in their direction, his wide eyes pleading. Sickened, Sebastian grabbed at Bauhin's shoulder. Through gritted teeth he hissed one word. "Enough!"

In terror, he stumbled down the stairs and pushed through the crowd as he made his way toward the edge of the square. He didn't know if Bauhin had followed him or not, but he would not look back. By the time he reached the place where the plaza exited onto Rue Saint Barthélemy, a blood-curdling wail pulsed through the air, echoing off the masonry on each side of the street. Before him was a sea of ashen faces, many with their hands clasped over their ears. Others covered their mouth and nose as the stench of burning flesh and sulfur became overpowering.

Sebastian felt his vision blur. His stomach heaved, and he doubled over. A stream of vomit poured from his mouth and across his boots. He smeared the back of his hand across his lips. Standing, he forced himself on. But the terrible sound behind him grew louder, taking on a fevered, hysterical pitch that no longer seemed in any way human. As Sebastian pushed past the last row of onlookers, he knew, not in his head but in his churning guts, that these cries belonged to the youngest of the three Lutherans. Clear of the crowd he began to run. He went faster and faster, terror clawing at his back, driving him down Rue Juiverie and all the way to the gates of the Trinité.

Sebastian burst through the door of his cell-like room and collapsed onto his bed, his chest heaving. For the longest time he lay there, his mind locked in a demonic loop, replaying over and over what he'd seen and heard. After perhaps an hour, there was a rap on his door and Bauhin rushed in.

"Sebastian? Are you all right? I tried to follow you as soon as I could, but the crowd kept moving and blocking me." Bauhin pulled a stool out from under the room's desk and placed it to face the bed. There was a long silence between them—even the talkative Bauhin had been shocked into an unnatural hush.

Eventually Sebastian spoke. "How does this happen when we live in a nation that prides itself on its civility and culture? How does this happen when we live in a city known for its learning and scholarship?"

Bauhin couldn't meet Sebastian's eyes. He stared at his hands as if searching them for an answer. "Perhaps we should have expected this. It has been happening in Paris and many other parts of France. This conflict between Catholicism and the new religion has been growing more and more violent, and the king has made it clear he will no longer tolerate Protestants defying his authority. We were naive to think that Lyon would be spared."

Other students at Trinité had witnessed the burnings, and that evening, it was all anyone could speak of. In every room of the college, arguments erupted over what had happened. Mid-evening, there was another knock on Sebastian's door. Zebedee joined them, carrying a candle, its light casting their faces into ghostly silhouettes.

The three men talked long into the night, Sebastian passionately denouncing what had happened as barbaric and inhuman, unworthy of a nation that called itself Christian. Bauhin, though appalled, reminded him of the great offense Protestants had given in many parts of the country. There had been reports of Protestants attacking Catholic churches and ripping out the statues of the saints, even of Mary herself. Priests and nuns had been attacked. There were even stories of Protestants defecating in the fonts that held the blessed water. Zebedee said little, listening intently as their talk ebbed and flowed between the fierce and the fearful. When Zebedee spoke, his comments were measured and tantalizing, and Sebastian was sure he was holding something back, sure that he knew more than he was willing to say. After several hours, they reached the point of exhaustion and agreed to call it a night. Bauhin and Zebedee left the room, and Sebastian slumped back on his bed. As soon as he closed his eyes, back came the images of the three Lutherans being burned and the sound of the young man's agony. That night he slept little, his heart and mind sickened by all he had witnessed.

When morning came, Sebastian's eyes throbbed and his head ached; his neck and back were locked in little spasms, his body bearing witness to his sleepless night. He forced himself to his feet, went to the small cupboard above his desk, and pulled out several books. As he read their titles, he traced the line of his unshaven jaw. He understood now that these were dangerous works to be found with, even here in Lyon. He must be much more cautious. He examined the books. Two were by Erasmus. The first was an exhortation to read the Gospels more carefully, a call to the church to leave its love of power and wealth and return to Christ's teachings. The second, his *Querela Pacis*, rebuked the entrenched European war-system, pleading with Christians to lay down their swords and, for once, act as brothers.

Another book, *On the Freedom of a Christian*, was by Martin Luther. A fourth, by John Calvin, was titled *The Institutes of Christian Religion*. These had thrilled him. They spoke of the hope of breaking free from the crippling superstitions that clung to religion, indeed all of society, like barnacles to a decrepit ship. After yesterday's events, he needed to feel this hope again. These daring thinkers had helped him to glimpse a new vision. He closed his eyes, trying to remember the words that had inspired him most.

He recalled Luther's words which had echoed around the world, or at least all of Christendom, as he'd defended himself from the charge of heresy. "Everyone believes at his own risk, but conscience must not be submitted to anyone. ... I cannot and will not recant, because acting against one's conscience is neither safe nor sound. Here I stand; I can do no other."

Luther's insistence on the priesthood of all believers—the belief that every human carried the image of God, and that every person, not just the clerics, had a holy vocation and calling—was an incendiary idea. The implications were incredible. If all stood equal before God, then all were equal before the law and before each other, whether they be king or peasant, aristocrat or pauper. Sebastian trembled as he considered what ideas like this could mean if people really believed them.

From his desk, he picked up Calvin's work and began to flick through it. Luther's words were unvarnished and direct while Calvin's were eloquent, poetic, insistent. His prose made the language sing. He turned back to the early pages. In Calvin's introductory section, there was a plea to the king of France, Francis I, begging him to allow the Protestants to practice their faith without persecution. To show clemency toward those the Catholic Church persecuted, even toward Turks and Saracens! It was a bold and audacious request. Deep within Sebastian, something stirred, and a wild thought flickered at the edge of his mind. *What if I were to seek out and apprentice myself to one of these great men, absorbing and learning all I could from them? What if I were to join them in their fight for freedom and for truth?*

He leafed through several of the tomes one more time then placed them back in the cupboard. Beside them on the shelf sat pamphlets by other radical thinkers: Mirandola's *On the Dignity of Man*, Erasmus's *On Free Will*, and tracts by Farel, Melanchthon, Zwingli and Bucer. Only a few days ago, he'd held these books as a source of intellectual stimulation, almost as if they were playthings. But now he knew that to possess them was perilous, perhaps even a death sentence. He restacked his cupboard so that the most inflammatory works were hidden behind assigned texts. He stared at the collection for a few more lingering seconds before closing and locking the cabinet door. Then, pocketing the key, he nodded his head, affirming to himself that he had made up his mind what he must do.

He needed to find these men of courage and conscience and freedom, men like Luther and Calvin, and join their cause.

After chapel the next morning, Bauhin rushed from his place to the pew where Sebastian and Zebedee had seated themselves. They waited quietly till everyone else had filed out, leaving them alone in the silence of the sanctuary.

Sebastian spoke first, whispering. "Now that the persecution has come to Lyon, I'm not prepared to stand by and do nothing. I have decided I must leave and join the Protestants."

Bauhin's face went ashen, but his reply was immediate. "No, Seb, no! It's too dangerous. You saw what they are doing to them, and have heard about all the atrocities happening in Paris. It will only be a matter of time till it's just as bad across all of France."

"I can see that. And that is why I must leave. I intend to find one of the leaders of this movement in order to learn more clearly what they teach and discover what part I can play. What is the point of all this learning if we cannot use it for good, to build a better world? What is the use if we stand dumb while men are being burned before our eyes? Erasmus thinks we are on the edge of a new age, when men will beat their swords into plowshares and treat each other as brothers. But surely each of us must play our role if that is to become a reality."

Silence fell between the three. Bauhin's head had sunk into his hands. Finally, he looked up. "I understand. What's more, I respect your decision. It is a very brave one. But for me, I cannot so easily abandon the religion of my parents and my forefathers. Nor can I abandon France. I want to stay and to work for reform within our church and within our nation. I will try to follow Erasmus's example of working for change from within." He looked across at Zebedee, who seemed lost in thought. "And André, what about you? What are you thinking?"

André looked slowly from one to the other before leaning forward to speak. "Sebastian is right. This moment in Europe's history is a critical one. The old Christendom is dying, and a new one is being born." He paused and shifted his body so that he was fully facing the others. "Sebastian, you must follow the light God has given you. Now is a decisive moment. We must all choose where we stand."

Sebastian wrapped an arm around André's shoulder and pulled him close. André Zebedee's affirmation meant the world to him. For the first time since yesterday's awful events, the churning in his stomach lightened. It might have disappeared altogether if Bauhin had stopped regarding them both with an expression that seemed to be perplexity tinged with fear.

By Monday, Sebastian had settled his plans. He had wondered about trying to find Martin Luther, the man who had sparked this whole revolution, or Bullinger—Zwingli's successor—and his even more radical followers in Zurich. He had considered the Swiss city of Basel, where Erasmus had lived his final years and where many extraordinary thinkers were based. But the idea of seeking out John Calvin had proved the most persuasive. For one thing, Calvin's first language was French, like his own, and he knew that Calvin was currently residing in Strasbourg, a free city with a lively, growing Protestant community. Other thinkers he admired and would like to speak with had also taken up residence there.

Sebastian fingered his pocket. He had managed to save a goodly purse from his private tutoring, and if he left now, it should last him till he found more work. He packed a bag with the barest essentials. He would slip out at first light tomorrow. By the tavern on the next corner was a hackney stable. He would hire a mount that would take him as far as the next large town where he would swap it for a fresh horse from stables there, and so on down the line, all the way to Strasbourg. This journey would mean ten, perhaps eleven days, in the saddle winding over rough roads, dossing in cheap inns. But now, having processed this week of horror, he was so full of yearning for what he hoped might lie ahead that he was ready to suffer any hardship in order to get there.

The next morning, before sunrise, he, Jean Bauhin, and André Zebedee stood in the courtyard of the Trinité and embraced. Sebastian swung his bag over his shoulder and turned to where a young valet waited with the horses. Taking hold of the bridle, he placed one foot in a stirrup, and lifted his other leg across the flanks of the gelding. He looked back through the pre-dawn light to where André had wrapped his arms about himself to ward of the cold. For several seconds, they simply stared at one another. He looked at Jean, who nodded back at him. Finally, he turned and gave a signal to the valet, and the pair of them spurred their horses along the path that led out of Lyon and on toward the city of Strasbourg.

Chapter 3
Strasbourg

S ebastian's journey from Lyon to Strasbourg proved less arduous than he had anticipated—surely a sign God was with him. The weather was temperate, and the rural lands he and the young valet—who he'd learned was named Hugo—passed through were a succession of fields and vineyards, thatched cottages and churches, castles and spires and towers. Lifting their eyes, they saw storks constructing nests atop roofs and in trees. Sebastian took heart from these ungainly birds that labored so diligently in defiance of gravity. He and Hugo rode on in a companionable silence, Sebastian's mind trying to calculate the cost of the choice he had made.

Eleven days and nights passed, and on the twelfth day, they entered the walls of Strasbourg, one of the prettiest cities he had ever seen. Built on the River Rhine and its subsidiary, the Ill, it was an island laced with a network of narrow streets, canals and bridges. All around were houses built of plastered cob and exposed timber beams, window boxes dripping with blood-red geraniums and petunias, white lilies, purple irises and flowers Sebastian could not put a name to.

Some ninety years earlier, a goldsmith and metalworker named Johannes Gutenberg had turned the world upside down from here.

He had combined three trailblazing creations: metallic movable type, an oil-based adhesive ink and a printing press. The process of making books, pamphlets, and posters—the very means for transmitting knowledge—had moved from costly and laborious to rapid and afford-able. Hundreds of thousands of books and pamphlets, like those he read at Trinité, were now being produced all across Europe. Most notably for Sebastian, Gutenberg had printed a run of Bibles, and soon, much to the anger of Rome, even more translations would follow in the languages of the common man and woman.

A glint of light caught his eye and snapped him out of his reverie. They had arrived late in the day. To their west, an apricot sun was setting, gilding a cathedral so vast that it took his breath away. Already he had glimpsed this city's reputed beauty. But with night falling, they decided they should find a bed. In the morning, Hugo would turn back for Lyon while Sebastian set out in search of the man whose writings had drawn him here: John Calvin.

They paused to ask where they might find cheap accommodation and received directions to a tavern called the Fleur-de-Lis, deep in a labyrinthian quarter the locals called Petite France. A stableman led them to stalls behind the inn where their horses would be fed and watered. Hugo insisted on sleeping there, too, as he refused to be parted from the mounts in his care. Among a city of so many hand-some structures, the Fleur-de-Lis seemed old and run-down. Inside, the floor's reed matting was worn and yeasty, its plaster wall peeling. But the innkeeper's greeting was welcoming and the ambience warm. Sebastian took the cheapest room on offer, a tiny attic space that contained little more than a thin straw mattress and thread-bare blan-ket. But no matter. Sebastian quickly descended into the fathomless sleep of a weary sojourner.

Sebastian woke early the next morning and wandered downstairs. He found the tavern keeper, Claude, a cheerful stub of a man with vast mutton-chop sideburns. Just as he had the night before, Claude greeted him heartily and invited him to take a seat. Sebastian looked around, taking in all he'd missed the previous evening. The space consisted of one large room. To his left, a huge fireplace sat behind a scuffed wooden bench. Above that were shelves filled with bottles, some green and some brown. In front of the bench was a line of plump oak barrels. Crescented around each, a dull stain of stale beer. The rest of the room was crowded with wooden tables surrounded by stools.

The innkeeper brought over a breakfast of bread and cheese, but instead of leaving, Claude pulled out a stool and sat down opposite Sebastian, grinning cheerfully. Sebastian was glad of the company and found Claude to be an excellent source of information.

"John Calvin? Yes, of course I know of him. Everybody knows of him! He gives lectures several days a week at the school run by Martin Bucer, who is a very good and clever man it should be said, and he preaches every Sunday at the French Protestant church. Not that I've heard him myself, but apparently, he's a wonderful speaker and a bit—what's the word?—*controversial* too. You know he came here 'cuz they kicked him out of Geneva? Well, that's our gain, 'cuz people are coming from all over Europe to hear him—young gentlemen just like you! Some dislike him, but he's good for business and good for the city, I say. Yes, it's all very good!"

That Calvin had been kicked out of Geneva was new information to Sebastian and he made a mental note to find out more. Claude, he soon realized, could easily talk on for the rest of the morning, so, having wrung from him directions to the school, Sebastian politely extricated himself and ventured out into Petite France.

As he had the previous night, Sebastian negotiated the maze of narrow alleys that surrounded the tavern before eventually finding his way onto the bustling Grand Rue. From there, he turned north along Rue Le Clerc before walking east toward Place Broglie and finally Place des Étudiants, where Claude had assured him he would find Strasbourg's academy. As the streets grew a little broader, impressive structures in various hues of stone and timber surrounded Sebastian. Occasionally he stopped to ask directions, but eventually he was sure he must be near the college—or the *"gymnasium illustre"* as the locals called it—when he rounded a corner to find himself facing dozens of young men of his own age milling outside a large rectangular building, a three-and-a-half-story structure with a pair of wide double doors set into its front facade.

He entered the large antechamber. For a few moments, he stood there, feeling overwhelmed, trying to work out what he should do next. His anxiety must have been obvious, for a voice broke through his perplexity.

"Excuse me, but you look a bit lost. Can I help you?" He looked up to see the inquiring eyes of a young man about his own age. Awkwardly, he explained his journey and his hope of meeting John Calvin.

"Oh! Ha ... well, excellent! You have come to exactly the right place." The young man introduced himself as Léo, originally of Marseilles and now a student of theology at the academy. "Of course, one does not simply march into Master Calvin's church or Master Calvin's office and demand an audience. He is an extraordinarily busy man. If he is not lecturing, he is preaching, and if he is not preaching, he is writing. No, one must make an appointment, and one must be introduced." Léo thought for a moment, his brows knitted. "I am not the man who can do that for you, but—" His face brightened. "But I know just the person who can. Come with me." With that, he headed toward the stairs on the far side of the antechamber, glancing over his shoulder to make sure Sebastian was following.

They ascended to the second floor and into a smaller foyer with hallways exiting left and right. Léo turned right then stopped at the second door and knocked. A friendly voice bid them to come in. Léo glanced back at Sebastian and smiled encouragingly, then he stepped forward. From behind a desk a stocky, broad-shouldered man rose to greet them, his square face was clean-shaven and pronounced eyebrows presided over his hooded eyes.

"Ah, Léo, it is good to see you. And who have you got here?"

"This," Léo announced, sounding like an old acquaintance, "is Sebastian Castellio, a graduate student from Lyon who has come to meet John Calvin and learn more about the Reform." The older man's face lit up, and he thrust out a large fleshy hand, enthusiastically shaking Sebastian's and introducing himself as Martin Bucer, one of the founders of the school.

Sebastian blanched. *Bucer, the famous German Reformer and former colleague of Luther.* Bucer gestured toward a small leather couch set in front of a laden bookcase. "Please, young sir, have a seat and tell me more about what has led you here." He returned to his place behind the desk while Léo excused himself from the room.

For the next several minutes, Sebastian described his studies, his mental wrestling, and ended by describing the terrible burnings he had witnessed, the event which had convinced him to come here. Bucer listened intently, occasionally making an agreeable hum or a distressed clicking with his tongue. When he finally spoke, he quizzed Sebastian on his understanding of the Scriptures and on some of the basic tenets of Protestant thinking. When he finished answering, Bucer seemed satisfied, even impressed with what he'd heard. He regarded Sebastian with a thoughtful expression before speaking.

"There is unquestioningly a place for a man of your intellect and integrity here in Strasbourg and in the Reform movement. I think God has brought you here for a purpose, and I am impressed that you have sensed the same, and by faith come such a distance. As for meeting John Calvin, yes, of course, but his schedule is incredibly busy. It will take a few days to arrange." Bucer flicked through the pages of a notebook on his desk, finally stopping on a page. "Yes, possible, possible ... the Friday of next week, in this same room, at twelve noon—sharp. You don't want to be late if you wish to make a good impression on Monsieur Calvin, let me assure you of that!"

Sebastian's heart soared, and a new sense of hope coursed

through him. As he strode back to the Fleur-de-Lis, he felt as if God might be carrying him along the boulevard.

―――――――

There were eight whole days to fill before the appointment with Bucer and Calvin, so Sebastian set to exploring this intriguing new city. Around every corner he encountered sights to capture his attention—glistening canals, grand buildings, and streets that bustled with life.

But something was missing. The heart needs more than pretty buildings to look at. By the middle of the week, he was beginning to tire of his own company and longing for a friend with whom he could share his thoughts. Evening came and he sat alone, weary from another day's walking. He sat in the dining room at the table nearest the stairs, his back to the inn's entrance. Nursing a mug of ale, he watched as Claude regaled a guest with some story or other, his wife, Evette, beside him, wiping down the bench with a cloth. Then Claude's gaze moved to the front of the inn. Sebastian became dimly aware of the sound of the inn's door opening behind him. He sighed and lifted the mug to his lips for another sip. Then, without warning, the grip of a strong hand descended on his shoulder and shook him. Startled, he swung half around, rising to confront his assailant ... and found himself looking straight into the face of a grinning André Zebedee. He forced his way fully to his feet and embraced him.

"André! In God's name, what are you doing here!"

Zebedee chuckled. "I told you I would follow once I had settled my affairs in Lyon. And then I realized: why stay in Lyon observing the death of an old religion, when you can come to Strasbourg and witness the birth of a new one?"

Excitedly, Sebastian signaled to Claude to bring another ale and two plates of food, and then he began to describe to André all he had so far discovered, including the details of his encounter with the famous Martin Bucer and the promise of his meeting with John

Calvin himself. They talked on long into the night. Finally, the sound of shifting tables and scraping stool legs interrupted them. They looked up to see Claude and Evette moving about the room extinguishing lamps and snuffing candles, wisps of smoke dancing in the glow from the fireplace. Taking the hint, they rose and dragged themselves upstairs to their rooms, agreeing to meet for breakfast at seven and, from there, to make a plan for the new day.

Over more of Claude's excellent bread and cheese, they discussed how to fill the two days that remained before Sebastian's meeting with Calvin. André was eager to explore the city, and Sebastian keen to show him all he had found. After breakfast, they set out. Beginning with the network of alleys and waterways around the Fleur-de-Lis, they strolled along the banks of canals where half-timbered homes shone in the morning sun and wooden cranes lifted loads on or off barges. They made their way around the square-towered Saint Thomas Church and set their eyes on the city's soaring cathedral, said to be the tallest building in the known world. Even from a distance it dominated the horizon, a rose-hued behemoth that cradled Strasbourg like a mother hen guarding her chicks.

They left Quai Saint Thomas and cut north through a crowded little fish market bustling with traders. The closer they drew to the cathedral, the grander its dimensions became. Now they came close enough to notice details: first, the church's pink sandstone filigree columns and figurines; then, above them, the multiple panes of the rose window.

André gasped. "It's incredible! How could they build something so huge and yet so delicate?"

They gazed at the descending strings of pink stone, so fine they could have been lacework, then rounded a corner to where Christ's passion had been carved along the western face. For fifteen minutes, they slowly rounded the huge cathedral, trying to take in all the carvings, niches and artifices, before finally entering. Inside, prisms of light filtered through enormous stained-glass windows and illuminated yet more statues and frescoes and tapestries that portrayed various biblical scenes. They circled the cavernous chamber till they came to the southern transept. Astonished, they watched as the angels and apostles whirled around the hour glass of a gigantic astronomical clock.

They made their way back outside and found the entrance to the twisting, spiraling stone stairs that ascended up and up and up, high into the spire, to a platform that looked out over the city, over the Alsace plain and toward Germany's mythic Black Forest. Dizzy and out of breath, they waited till their lungs had recovered and then descended. With one last lingering look at the biggest structure either of them had ever seen, they turned north along Rue du Dôme. Eventually, to their right, the tree-lined Broglie came into view—the plaza that contained the academy and the site of their approaching encounter with the man they longed to meet, John Calvin.

They mapped out the route Sebastian would take in the morrow. Now it was time to head back to the Fleur-de-Lis and once more partake of Claude and Evette's generous provisions.

Chapter 4
Meeting Calvin

Sebastian explained his plan for the following day to André. He would rendezvous with Bucer at noon, whereupon Bucer would take him to meet Calvin.

"Why don't you come along too. Come and meet Bucer. If he thinks it's possible, come and meet John Calvin. These are two giants of the Reformation! You've come all this way, and who knows when you'll ever get a chance to meet with such men of God again? What harm can it do?"

André shifted in his seat. "There is much in John Calvin's teaching that I agree with and admire. But not all. We may not see eye to eye. Not fully anyway."

"All the better! You can have a lively discussion and let iron sharpen iron. Besides, I would appreciate your company—your support—Zeb. I do feel a little ... daunted."

With a far-off look in his eyes, Zebedee gave an enigmatic smile. "Well, why not? It would indeed be a waste to pass up this opportunity after I have traveled so far."

The next day dawned bright and clear. They reached the academy with time to spare, so they set about exploring its numerous corridors and hallways as well as the well-kept courtyards tucked behind the two main blocks. As noon grew closer, the butterflies in Sebastian's stomach took flight then landed heavily. His thoughts raced. They were about to meet with one of the greatest minds of their generation.

He had found Calvin's writings to be so lucid and clear, so unrelenting in their lawyer's logic, that they were near impossible to resist. He forced himself to breathe deeply, trying to unknot the ball in his stomach. Zebedee was keeping his own counsel, showing no signs of anxiety, but Sebastian was sure his heart must be pounding too. With the clock in the courtyard showing five to noon, they headed inside and ascended the stairs toward Bucer's office.

At Bucer's door, they hesitated. Through a window in the wall of the corridor they could see that the hands of the courtyard clock had nearly ascended to the twelve. And then suddenly, they heard the peal of the cathedral's bell, assuring them that it was now noon. They knocked, and Bucer's voice invited them in. Sebastian pushed the door open. To his surprise, there were two men inside, their chairs pressed together. They both stood as Sebastian and Zebedee entered. One was, of course, Bucer. The other was a thin man with large, intense eyes beneath a furrowed brow; his long, thin nose gave his face a striking sense of elongation. The ovate shape of his face was accentuated by a wispy beard that extended from his chin. Physically, he was slight, but something about him emanated a sense of presence that felt formidable.

Bucer placed one hand on the thin man's shoulder and, in a mimicked French accent, declared, "Voilà! This is the young man I was just telling you about, John. He came all the way from Lyon. Sebastian Castellio and ... well, it seems he has brought a friend with him."

"Yes! Indeed!" Sebastian's stepped forward. "This is my friend and fellow scholar, also, of late, from Lyon. Please, may I introduce to you Monsieur André Zebedee, a good man whose intellect and integrity I can personally vouch for." To Sebastian's relief, Bucer smiled, seemingly not perturbed by this unexpected development.

"Perhaps today we have received two scholars for the price of one. We are indeed blessed it seems." Bucer extended an arm to his left and added, "And this, my new friends, is the man you have traveled so far to see: Master John Calvin."

Sebastian, who was standing closest, extended his hand toward Calvin, and for a terrifying second it seemed as though Calvin wasn't going to respond. His deep brown eyes focused on André, looking him up and down, appraising him carefully. Finally, he took hold of Sebastian's hand and shook it firmly, the faintest of smiles softening his lips. He then turned to Zebedee, and let out a long, exasperated sigh.

"André Zebedee." He took the measure of Zebedee for a long time before finally extending his hand toward him. "After all this time, it is good to meet you. I trust your studies are still proving fruitful?"

Sebastian's eyes widened as he stared at André, thrown by this disclosure. *André knows Calvin and never mentioned it? What other secrets does this man keep?* Even the convivial Bucer looked taken aback by this disclosure. For a moment, an awkwardness hung over the room. Sebastian swallowed hard and addressed Calvin with the title he'd just heard Bucer use.

"Master Calvin, I have read your work, *The Institutes*, and it has moved me greatly. I think it is a masterpiece of biblical exposition. Never in my life have I read anything so precise and clear. It is for this reason that we have come to Strasbourg—to learn more from you and Messieurs Bucer and Capito, and to discover where possible to lend our energy and talents to this movement people are calling 'Reformation.'"

Calvin's narrow smile widened a little as Sebastian proceeded, and it seemed he was warming to them now. He gestured for them to take a seat. As Bucer had done earlier with Sebastian, Calvin began to question who they had read, what they had studied, and what they believed about various disputed doctrines. Compared to Bucer's earlier quizzing, this was a far more thorough interrogation, both in intensity and duration, especially when Calvin came to areas where it seemed he and Zebedee held differing opinions.

For the next hour they fielded question after question concerning theology, their lives, their understanding of the political and religious situation in France and wider Europe, the academic areas in which they had excelled, and those in which they had struggled. Sebastian sensed that Calvin was calculating where—or whether—they could be of use to himself and Bucer.

The interview was exhausting, and by the end of it, both Sebastian and André felt as though they'd been rung dry, like a cloth twisted between the hands of a launder. Even Bucer looked tired, but clearly Calvin was not. The longer their discussion proceeded, the more energized he became. It appeared inquisitor was a role he enjoyed. But eventually he seemed to have heard enough. He stood up and extended his hand toward Sebastian, and then André, signaling that their time together was finished.

"Messieurs, this has been a most interesting encounter. I hope it has been so for you too. But if you would excuse us, it would be good if Monsieur Bucer and I could discuss your situation and think about what role you might have with us. If I may prevail upon you to return once more at noon tomorrow, we shall resume our conversation."

André and Sebastian were turning toward the door when, almost as an afterthought, Calvin asked where they were staying. Sebastian replied, "An inn in the Petite France quarter called the Fleur-de-Lis." He'd barely gotten the words out when Calvin's face contorted in an expression of horror.

"No, no, no. A place like the Fleur-de-Lis will not do for two respectable young men seeking to live Christian lives. We can surely do better than that. Another thing for Bucer and I to discuss. We will tell you tomorrow what we have decided."

"Oh," Sebastian stammered, taken aback. "Well, thank you ... you have been most kind."

André bowed low and let out a soft "Merci."

As they walked back to the inn, Sebastian turned to André. "So, you are an acquaintance of John Calvin and did not think that worth mentioning before now? I suppose you've been visiting Martin Luther in your spare time too?"

Zebedee's face reddened. "Sebastian, this is all new to you, but I have been studying the writings of these men ever since I was a student in Bordeaux. And not just Calvin and Luther but especially the Swiss Reformer, Zwingli. I have corresponded with Calvin, and with other Reformers too, like Bullinger and Megander in Zurich. Both Calvin and Zwingli say and write things that draw me, but I am still weighing up what I believe."

Sebastian felt a pang of confusion rising. He wondered what this new revelation might mean for their time here. André must have noticed the puzzlement on his face, for he placed a hand on his shoulder and gave him a reassuring smile.

"But like you, Sebastian, I realize that we are in the presence of great minds. As long as I am in Strasbourg, I will endeavor to learn all that I can from them."

They arrived back at the entrance to the Fleur-de-Lis, where the generous Claude seated them and placed fresh victuals on their table: ale, cheese, bread, and slices of cold ham. But in truth, he seemed more interested in hearing how their encounter with Calvin had gone than in playing the role of host. Claude pulled up a stool and pumped them with questions about their day's adventures while poor Evette scurried around looking after the other guests. When they told him how they had met with and were interviewed by not only John Calvin but also Martin Bucer, Claude was nearly beside himself. He clapped his hands together and slapped Zebedee—who was within reach—across the back. André almost choked on a piece of ham. He grabbed his mug of ale to wash it down.

Claude seemed most intrigued to know what they thought of John Calvin. He swatted aside any theological controversies they alluded to, clearly disinterested, and several times asked, "Yes, but *what kind* of man is he? I hear contrary opinions. Some say he is a good man, building God's church, and some say he's a troublemaker, destroying God's church."

Sebastian answered. "On that question, having just met the man, we can offer no firm or final opinion. But what we can say is that he is a most brilliant thinker, a great scholar, an exceptional writer, and one who is determined to restore the Christian faith to its former glory."

Nodding his head sagely, Claude muttered, "Very good, very good." Then he bid them both good night.

When they knocked and entered Bucer's study the following day, they were surprised to find only Bucer inside. After he had sat them down, he apologized on Calvin's behalf, explaining that he'd been called away on an urgent matter. "You have to understand, he has great responsibilities here, both at the church and among the French Protestant refugee community. Every time there is a pastoral crisis, he is expected to solve it. And every time there is a doctrinal dispute, he is expected to pronounce right and wrong. When he is not solving these crises, he is writing theological treatises or letters or rebuttals or preparing messages. Sometimes I worry about the toll this busyness might take on him."

He looked a little brighter as he glanced at Zebedee. "There's no rest for the righteous, it seems." He smiled at his own little joke before turning serious again. "We talked for a long time after you left yesterday, and, to be frank, we are very glad you have come. Calvin, especially, is missing the assistance of his friend Farel, who first called him to their previous work in the city of Geneva. Since their departure from that city, Farel has taken up the role of church leadership in the town of Neuchâtel. Of course, he is a frequent visitor here, but some of us have advised them not to work together for a while, not after what happened in Geneva."

He paused, looking reflective, and the two younger men exchanged a questioning glance. But before they could say anything, Bucer continued, a smile playing on his lips. "Have either of you met Guillaume Farel? Now, in his case, it's truly 'once met, never forgot,' so you'd certainly know if you had."

Both Sebastian and Zebedee shook their heads. Then André added, "I've read some of Farel's writings. They are fierce! He shows no mercy toward Catholicism, and he does not spare the mass from his denouncements."

"'The pope's an Antichrist; the mass is idol worship,'" Sebastian murmured, recalling a pamphlet of Farel's he'd once read.

Bucer responded immediately. "What else should he say but denounce the Papists and their idolatries? We are blessed in our day to have courageous preachers exposing the errors of Rome, Farel among them. Though, at times, perhaps, he mistakes himself a little too closely for one of the Old Testament prophets."

There was another pause, and now Sebastian saw his opportunity. "Are you able to tell us more about what happened in Geneva? We have heard people talking about it, but don't really understand what happened."

Bucer looked away. He seemed embarrassed. "Let me just say that each of these men is like a powder keg, but together they are like a whole armory. Best not to light the candle of argumentation when you are dealing with them, and safer still to have them working in different locations." Glancing at them, Bucer quickly went on. "But please don't misunderstand me. I greatly admire both of these fellows. Their gifts of oratory are extraordinary, and their determination to overcome obstacles otherworldly. God has used them both to advance the Reformation and break down strongholds. Calvin, in particular, is a brilliant man; he and I work well together. I think he sees me as a father figure, and he respects my opinions. This gives me the opportunity to steer his gifts away from the destructiveness of Farel into a more constructive direction. But here is our problem: this movement is spreading so very quickly that we have too few men who can lead it. Calvin feels he must do everything from reforming whole cities to correcting each wayward individual. And so I hope you, my young friends, can be a help in lifting some of this great burden off Master Calvin and myself."

Sebastian and Zebedee leaned forward, listening even more intently.

"What we propose is this: André, you are older and more seasoned than Sebastian. We are desperately short of leaders for our many new Protestant churches. And you are known to be a gifted teacher. Yet before you take up a church, we propose you stay here in Strasbourg a while more, learning from those of us a little longer in the tooth than yourself."

Zebedee nodded. "Thank you. It would be a privilege to learn from you—and from Monsieur Calvin."

Bucer's smile widened. "As for you, Sebastian ... As I've described, John Calvin is extraordinarily busy, and I haven't even told you half of it. His home is awash with students and refugees seeking him out. Several students are now living with him and Idelette, and he needs someone who can help him tutor and teach, both at his home and here at the academy. Calvin has asked that you come board with and assist him."

Sebastian stared at Bucer, blinking slowly, as if looking at a great, oncoming light. Had he heard him right? This was more than he dared dream.

Bucer went on. "I doubt if this will be a permanent arrangement. Calvin's home is more like an international boarding house really. You may need to move out and make way for other guests at some point. But, that said, ... do you accept?"

Sebastian regained his tongue, an eager 'yes' tumbling out of him.

Bucer turned back to Zebedee. "We've also found a nearby room for you that you could rent. It's close to my home and close to where John and Idelette live. This would mean we could all meet easily for discussions and to learn from one another. What do you say?"

Zebedee nodded. "I say thank you, Monsieur Bucer."

The three of them sat smiling, pleased with their new concord. And then a question occurred to Sebastian, something Bucer had said which he hadn't understood. "May I ask, who is Idelette?"

"Oh, you don't know? The great bachelor John Calvin married a month ago. He was already thirty, and it was ridiculous of him to try to cope on his own like that. Still, he took a lot of convincing, and he kept rejecting the very eligible women we suggested. Then he announced to us that God had shown him the one. Idelette is a decade older than John, a widow with two little children. Actually, Idelette and her first husband were converted by Calvin's preaching. They had formerly belonged to that sect we call the Anabaptists, but John persuaded them out of that error and into true doctrine. So, for John, considering the Bible's command to look after widows and orphans, this seemed a God-sent match." Bucer paused and cleared his throat. "Perhaps not the most romantic of reasons, but theologically very sound. And our old friend Farel came down from Neuchâtel especially to perform the marriage ceremony!"

Bucer was clearly warming to the role of storyteller. He paused and looked from Sebastian to André and back again. "Speaking of romance and marriage, how old are you two fellows?"

Sebastian's tongue got caught in the back of his teeth, so Zebedee replied. "Ah ... twenty-four and twenty-nine."

"What!" Bucer's eyes sparkled. "Then you are both more than eligible and more than ready I'd say." He chuckled. "Perhaps God has brought you both to Strasbourg for more than just spiritual reasons, eh?"

Chapter 5
Living with Calvin

If John Calvin's mind bubbled with frenetic activity, then so too did his Strasbourg home. As his writings spread and his reputation grew, students came seeking wisdom, members of the French refugee community arrived seeking aid, and notable Protestant leaders visited seeking political advice. Of course, it was Calvin's wife, Idelette, who held the place together. She was a perfect foil to her cerebral husband. She remained warm, practical and unruffled no matter who turned up needing help. And thus, she was unperturbed when Sebastian Castellio, his meager luggage in hand, appeared on their doorstep. She greeted him like a long-awaited, much-missed nephew. The distance from the Fleur-de-Lis had not been far, a walk from the center to the edge of the Petite France quarter.

Idelette brought Sebastian into the house, explaining that John was off giving a lecture that evening. As they moved along a corridor, they passed a large room with a table and chairs where several students sat studying or deep in discussion. Beyond, there were two more doors which, Idelette explained, led to the bedchambers of the servants—a housekeeper named Liesel and a valet named Chevant.

Opposite those doors was the kitchen area, and at the end of the corridor, a staircase.

They climbed the stairs to another hallway, from which Idelette pointed out doors leading to the room where three other students were staying, the room for John's brother Antoine, visiting from France, and a third room where she and John slept with her two children. A fourth door led to the room that was to be Sebastian's. It was a simple space with a small bed and a little table for study. Upon the table was a writing lectern, an inkwell, a set of quills, and a newly lit candle. A basin and jug for bathing, and a chamber pot beneath the bed completed the room's adornments.

"Now, Sebastian, would you like to come downstairs for some supper?" Idelette asked softly.

Sebastian, worried that he might be imposing, replied in the negative. "Thank you, but if I may, I'd like to retire now. Meeting Messieurs Bucer and—and your husband—made it a very big day for me. I feel I should rest."

Idelette smiled knowingly. "We shall breakfast at seven, with the Bucers and the Capitos." She explained that their home and that of the Bucers were close, fronting onto different streets but sharing adjoining gardens at the rear, a courtyard area where both households could meet and converse. "I believe your friend André will be joining us too. Just before seven, one of our servants will knock on your door to ensure you're awake. Will that do?"

"Yes, yes. That will do very well. Thank you."

Idelette retreated back down the passageway. Sebastian closed the door and removed his doublet and boots. He leaned over the desk and extinguished the candle. Stepping back, he tumbled into the bed, rapidly falling into a welcome sleep.

The next morning, as promised, a servant woke Sebastian and guided him to the table and chairs clustered in the shared garden courtyard. As he approached, Bucer rose and greeted him heartily before extending an open hand toward the one remaining seat.

"Good morning, Sebastian! Now come and give these good people the pleasure of making your acquaintance."

Sebastian smiled and took the seat next to André, who'd gotten there before him. Bucer looked around the circle of people.

"My friends, this is Sebastian Castellio, a scholar and a gentleman, and these are ..." he gestured toward the others around the table, naming them in the order they sat. "John Calvin, who you have met; Wolfgang Capito, who you have not; his wife, Brandis; my wife, Elisabeth; Idelette, who you know; and, of course, André and myself."

Each person gave a small nod of their head as their name was mentioned, the Capitos and Elisabeth also mouthing hellos in Sebastian's direction.

Breakfast consisted of two breads (a thick, grainy rye and a finer, sweetened white), two types of cheese, fresh butter and fresh milk. Food was interspersed with conversation as Bucer, Capito and Calvin reviewed the progress of the academy, debated the wider problems of Europe, and reflected on the advance of the Reformation. Occasionally, Capito and Bucer turned toward Sebastian and André to ask for their thoughts. But for the main part, Sebastian was content just to listen. He was fascinated by the Capitos, who were new to him other than by name and their reputation for kindness. He regarded the circle of friends with interest.

It was clear that the two German couples—the Bucers and the Capitos—had an easy familiarity with one another. Capito's warm, open face was dominated by large blue eyes. Sebastian knew his fame as a scholar of Hebrew and his unusually tolerant attitude toward other religious faiths. Bucer and Calvin, on the other hand, could be sharp, especially when disagreed with, but Capito always remained calm. Idelette was reserved; Elisabeth was thoughtful, but Brandis seemed to have few hesitations about speaking up. She leaned forward often, offering an opinion whenever an opening appeared. Sebastian could see that it pleased Capito when she did this as he nodded and murmured agreement. But Calvin, he thought, seemed much less impressed, pursing his lips each time she spoke.

He couldn't help but glance admiringly at Capito's wife, Brandis. She was a beautiful woman, clearly intelligent and articulate, yet there was also a sadness about her. Sebastian had heard how she'd lost two husbands to illness before meeting Capito. He wondered how anyone could cope with loss like that.

As the discussion wore on, it grew more animated. Soon it became clear that the Capitos favored bridge-building between the different Protestant groups across Europe, and even with the Catholics. But their advocation of Christian unity seemed too much for Calvin. His voice rose in challenge.

"What you ask for is impossible! Surely you can see that the Catholic Church is filled with error and superstition."

"And yet Christ prayed that we should all be one, even as he and the Father are one!" Capito retorted

Calvin's response was sharp. "But how can light have fellowship with darkness, or idols with the worship of the true God?" His voice had risen an octave, and each face was turned toward him as he continued. "Indeed, *such* corruption and *such* idolatry! And not only in the church, but in every corner of society that the Catholic Church has touched. Thus, our mission is to reform not just the church, but the whole of society. We must bring the whole of the Bible to bear on the whole of the world. We need ministers and magistrates, laymen and merchants, indeed, every man, woman and child to be zealous in pursuing holiness. The church must be purified from sin and preach the truth of God's Word! The poor must be helped. We must have just laws that are applied to all. We must have proper schools, schools that will teach children whether rich or poor, so that every soul will be educated and trained, contributing to a just society—and a just world!"

Sebastian sat upright in his seat, regarding Calvin with admiration, a sense of awe running down his spine. *This is what I was born for: to be part of such a movement, to be part of this moment in history!*

The debate flowed on, the protagonists becoming increasingly energized. Only Idelette seemed unwilling to throw herself into the fray. Finally, Capito turned to Sebastian and André, his forehead creased with curiosity. "And you two, our brightest, newest acquisitions from France, what do you say about all of this?"

André paused for thought, but Sebastian burst forth excitedly. "I agree with nearly all that I have heard you say, and especially with Master Calvin's analysis. It's true that our churches, our justice system, our schools are all in desperate need of reform. How is it right that only the rich can afford education, and that the children of the poor must languish and suffer through no fault of their own? And why has the church become so wealthy and corrupt when Christ taught the opposite? Why are we led by clerics more interested in the size of their purses than in the needs of their people? These fraudsters hide the Scriptures away, lest people read them and wonder how the Christian religion has become so ... so debased?"

"Ho!" Bucer exclaimed triumphantly. "Watch out, John. We have another French firebrand on our hands!"

Calvin regarded Bucer with one warily raised eyebrow. "Castellio is from Savoy, actually, but despite that, I will be delighted if he is indeed another reforming firebrand, willing to match his words with his actions." He turned to Sebastian. "And so, tell me: what *exactly* do you think will be your contribution?"

Sebastian swallowed hard. "I feel called to write and to teach. There I am in my element." Then, warming to the question, he went on more quickly. "I love helping people grow, to become who they were meant to be, to think for themselves. I love to see them set free from ignorance, from the superstitions behind our so-called 'tradition.' And the Scriptures—yes, all should be enabled to read and to understand for themselves what the Bible says without having to bow or scrape or go through priest or pope. I am much moved by Luther's vision of the Scriptures made available to all people, his hope that even a lowly plowboy should possess a Bible he can read and understand." Surprised, and slightly embarrassed by his own outburst, he leaned back on his stool before continuing more quietly. "I am very grateful for the opportunities I have already had in my life, and for the ones you are offering me now. Perhaps I have some small ability that I can place at your service."

"Or perhaps not so small," Capito affirmed in an aside to Brandis. "And you, André?" He looked at Zebedee.

"What more is there to say after John's and Sebastian's fine speeches? As has been said, we have had too many corrupt men leading the church, the blind leading the blind, men ignorant about what the Bible *really* teaches. So much of our religion has fallen into useless superstition and, worse than that, oppression and cruelty. My hope is to teach the Scriptures accurately, to unfold to people the truth that can set them free."

A hush descended on the group, each lost in their own thoughts. But across the little circle, Sebastian noticed Bucer and Capito exchanging smiles. He thought they seemed pleased with his and André's arrival from Lyon.

———

The following day, Sunday, Sebastian and André headed for the first time to Calvin's church. Saint Nicholas, a Gothic sanctuary built from sandstone on the southern bank of the Ill, had a congregation made up of refugees who'd fled persecution in France. The two friends were eager to see Calvin in action and hear what he had to say. They entered just as proceedings were about to begin, creeping in to the back of the crowded sanctuary. After much craning, they saw a space for them on the left of the church, four rows from the front.

As they squeezed past people, those seated in front turned to take note of the new arrivals. As much as he had come to the church to engage in spiritual worship, Sebastian couldn't help but observe that before them were several attractive young ladies, all of whom appeared to be of an eligible age. One on the very end of the row—a young woman with strikingly dark hair, plaited and coiled under a white linen coif—turned and noticed them, her eyes sparkling with interest. Sebastian saw her nudge the worshipper next to her, an equally attractive maiden, who also turned, her furrowed brow giving way to a disarming smile. Throughout the following hour, Sebastian displayed an admirable commitment to the service, giving it nearly his full attention. But out of the corner of his eye—he congratulated himself for having such excellent peripheral vision—he noticed the two young ladies from time to time as they glanced back at him and André. Whenever he looked in the other direction though, it was obvious that André—elbow on knee, chin in hand, intently listening—was focused on higher things.

Calvin was spellbinding, expertly combining passionate oratory, caustic challenge and exacting biblical exposition. But more than that, his use of intonation and rhetoric was masterful. Apart from the sermon, the dynamics of the congregation fascinated Sebastian. Nearly everyone had been displaced, having fled their homeland to escape persecution. There were whole families, but also broken families along with those who had arrived in ones and twos, having barely escaped the violence that had taken their loved ones from them.

As the service finished and the crowd departed, Sebastian found the two intriguing young ladies standing with a knot of other congregants at the back of the sanctuary. André had made it as far as the aisle at the end of the row but now turned and began to review the sermon, asking Sebastian what he thought about several points that had perplexed him. As André began peeling back the theological layers, Sebastian kept glancing toward the back of the church. At that very moment, the young woman with coal-black hair looked his way. Their eyes met. She smiled, and Sebastian felt his cheeks redden. He let his eyes drift past her, along the back wall of the sanctuary and then up to its vaulted ceiling, as if he had been doing nothing more than admiring the church's design all along. After he had completely surveyed the architecture of the church's back wall and ceiling, his eyes again drifted down to the little group at the rear of the building. This time both girls were looking in their direction, their heads cocked together in conspiratorial whispers. Sebastian's mind formed a plan: walk nonchalantly toward the door, pause and say hello, all in a very calm, dignified—yet charming—manner.

"Shall we go then?" He laid a hand on André's shoulder, gently pushing him toward the rear of the church. But André stood rooted to the spot, lost in the depths of his examination of the sermon.

"And if salvation is *completely* predestined, and if the atonement is a *fully vicarious* atonement, not leaving any work still to be done, then why does Saint Paul say, 'Work out your salvation with fear and trembling.' And what does all this say about the *vocation* that Luther says we are called to, which in and of itself must surely constitute good works? What do you think, Seb?"

"A very good point, André, and indeed, a vital question. But shall we walk and talk at the same time?" Again, he tried to steer André along the aisle and toward the exit. Only with great reluctance did André break the thread of his reflection and begin to move. But as he did so, a well-dressed matriarch in a flowing maroon gown shepherded the two girls out the church's wide entrance. Sebastian did his best to hurry André along, but it was hopeless.

"And if there is no free will, what does that say about our dignity as beings made in God's image? As creatures made only a little lower than the angels?" André was lost in a deeply reflective moment, oblivious to the urgency of the situation. By the time they reached the church's door, the little group he had been watching had disbanded across the courtyard and out onto the street beyond. Sebastian quickly moved to the corner where the church met the road. The two young women, arm in arm, were disappearing down the larger road. Behind them strode a tall young man, followed by the matriarch and an elderly man who hobbled along with the assistance of a cane, his gray hair splayed out from under a black cap. Sebastian sighed wistfully and wandered back to the church's entrance. Once more he tried to gather the thread of theological disputation André had been weaving.

The following Sunday, after the service, Calvin wanted to introduce Sebastian to certain visitors from the city of Lausanne. A long, animated discussion on the reform of churches and schools followed, and by the time it was concluded, Sebastian found that the sanctuary was empty except for themselves. It wasn't until the Sunday after that, with Zebedee distracted, that his chance finally came to speak with the two young women. After the service, they were, as usual, standing together chatting at the rear of the sanctuary. With his hands clammy and his courage wavering, Sebastian approached. Their heads were turned toward each other, deep in conversation, such that the pair did not notice him. His face flushed as he cleared his throat, and they both looked up at him curiously. He bowed slightly. The fairer of the two giggled. The dark-haired one scowled. He could feel his palms growing sweatier still.

The younger looking of the two stepped toward him, and Sebastian felt his face grow even warmer. *Should I kiss her cheek? No! Shake her hand. Quickly, before she steps any closer!* Desperately, he wiped his right palm along the hem of his doublet then extended it toward her.

She ignored it, dipping into the slightest of curtseys, then turned to her companion and called, "Genie." In response, the maiden with the dark hair joined them.

Sebastian cleared his throat and mustered all the confidence he could. "Bonjour, mademoiselles. I am Sebastian Castellio, housemate and teaching assistant to John Calvin."

The dark-haired woman gave a light curtsey, the faintest of smiles playing on her lips. "I am Eugenie Paquelon, formerly of Borbonnais, now residing here in Strasbourg."

Sebastian was captivated by her. The deep black sheen of her hair, pulled back in a French braid that cascaded down her back, made him think of cords of silk. Dark eyebrows arched over chestnut eyes. Below, full lips and an olive complexion framed her smile, one he sensed was only ever exhibited with caution.

Her companion had a fairer complexion, her countenance more open, her smile more ready, her face animated with an impish expression—as if laughter always lurked just below the surface. She reached toward Sebastian with her right hand, which he awkwardly took. For an uncomfortable moment, he wondered if he should bestow a kiss on the hand, but he settled for shaking it. Her warm hand held his for a length of time that reddened his cheeks all over again.

"I am Marie," she announced, eyes shining. "Genie's cousin and protector, also of Borbonnais."

Sebastian could see the family resemblance—the same cheekbones and high forehead—but Marie's hair was a honey-brown and her eyes lighter. She was half a head shorter than her cousin and a little younger, seventeen or eighteen he guessed.

From behind Eugenie, the tall youth he'd noticed two weeks earlier emerged. He shared the same olive complexion and dark hair as Eugenie. If anything, his eyes were darker, almost fierce. "Oh, and this is Jacques, my little brother."

Eugenie smiled as she reached up and ruffled his hair. *Not so little*, Sebastian thought, but then his gaze shifted to the maroon-gowned matriarch approaching, a reproving expression on her face. She stepped between the girls and, with a faint nod of her head, introduced herself as Eugenie's mother and Marie's aunt. Her withering glare left Sebastian in no doubt that it was she, rather than Marie, who was the protector of this family.

With some trepidation, Sebastian regarded the matriarch. Her hair was thick and gray and tied into a bun at the back of her head. Her face was deeply lined, but Sebastian could see dignity and grace there, and he was sure she must have been a beautiful woman in her younger days.

Marie was quick to rescue the situation. "Aunt Sonya, this is

Sebastian Castellio. He is living with John Calvin and helping him with his teaching at the Sturm Academy."

At the news of Sebastian's relationship with Calvin, the woman's face softened, and she allowed a smile to form on her lips. "Is that so? In that case, we are very pleased to make your acquaintance, Sebastian Castellio."

Over the next few Sundays, Sebastian pieced together their story. They were Huguenots who had fled a wave of persecution sweeping through Borbonnais. Eugenie's parents had originally been from the Dauphiné, where her father was a tailor and her mother a seamstress. As converts to Protestantism, they became increasingly uncomfortable with the large number of royalist troops stationed in the area, so they moved closer to Marie's family in Borbonnais.

Sadly, during one of the many outbreaks of sickness that had swept across Europe, Marie's family had perished. The Paquelons then took her in. But Catholic-Protestant tensions were rising in Borbonnais, too, and Eugenie's parents decided to flee to Geneva with their son and the two girls, following in the footsteps of Calvin and hundreds of others. In fact, it was Eugenie's father, Charles (the elderly, gray-haired gentleman Sebastian had seen with them that first Sunday), who had been so taken with Calvin's writings that he had instigated the move to Geneva. Not long after, they moved to Strasbourg when Calvin was exiled to the city. Marie had become their second daughter, the sister Eugenie had always longed for. The elderly Charles was in poor health these days and only irregularly came to the service at Saint Nicholas. Jacques, the strapping brother, was very protective of the two girls. Sebastian learned that he, even more than Madame Sonya, was the staunchest guardian of the family.

Sebastian found both girls delightful, and they both showed equal interest in him. Being inexperienced in affairs of the heart, he felt at a total loss as to how he should advance things. And the studious André proved to be of no help at all, claiming to be too busy with study and writing to even consider romance. He put forward the very reasonable argument that they should not consider courtship or marriage until they had real jobs and decent incomes. Sebastian was continuing to bolster his income through giving private tuition but decided André was right. Given the impasse he felt in the situation, he decided to let the matter d'amour rest.

Chapter 6
A Plague on Calvin's House

Living with Calvin had its privileges. Occasionally, he permitted Sebastian to read over a paper he had written. With each piece Sebastian read, he could feel himself absorbing Calvin's insights and the methodical way his legal mind parsed even the most complex passage of Scripture. One of the things that stood out was Calvin's genius for weaving the Old and New Testaments together, forming them into a seamless whole. This was augmented by an outstanding knowledge of the church fathers and penetrating insights into the working of European law. Of one thing Sebastian was convinced: this man was impressive.

But it was not just Calvin's work in Strasbourg that kept him busy. Bucer, one of many in Europe who still sought a path of reconciliation between Protestant and Catholic churches, played a role in setting up conferences—colloquies—that brought together leaders from both sides of the divide. When attending these colloquies, he frequently took his protégé, Calvin, with him, meaning both men were often absent from their homes and from the academy.

That year, 1540, Emperor Charles V called two pivotal conferences, bringing together some of Europe's greatest theological minds and most powerful political voices. Bucer and Calvin left for Hagenau, twenty miles to the north of Strasbourg. A month later, Calvin returned frustrated at what he saw as a lack of accomplishment, but Bucer remained optimistic. A few months later, a follow-up conference was called in the German town of Worms. Calvin attended, drawn by the possibility of working with Philip Melanchthon, Luther's brilliant collaborator. But as the months dragged on, this round of meetings also became bogged down in a morass of contentious words. Calvin returned not just frustrated but deeply cynical.

As John Calvin stalked in through the door of his house on Rue de Bouclier, Petite France, he threw his leather satchel full of papers on to the table. With Idelette out at the market, it was left to Sebastian to ask him how his time at the conference had gone, a task he approached with trepidation.

"Absurd. Pointless. These Papists are playing games with us. They are completely entrenched in their position and have no intention of moving. They are unwilling to confess that the Bible, the Word of God, is the final source of all authority for Christendom, still wanting to keep that status for the pope and his bishops. Until this changes, we will never be able to work or worship together."

But, Sebastian wondered, *why must we all worship in the same way? Why not simply commit to not attacking one another, to allow each to worship peacefully in their own way?* He knew that there were pockets across the Continent where both Catholic and Protestant churches were able to coexist. So why not make this the goal for all of Europe?

A few months later, in April of 1541, the ever-hopeful Bucer announced that he, Capito and Calvin would be attending a third conference, this time in the Bavarian town of Regensburg, two weeks away by horseback. This congress began with high hopes but once more dragged on for week after week, hardliners on both sides digging in their heels. Little was achieved to advance the cause of European peace, but John Calvin's reputation as a brilliant speaker and uncompromising negotiator rose. He'd more than held his own on an important international stage. In late October, an exhausted Capito returned, leaving Bucer and Calvin behind to continue the debate.

In October, Strasbourg was aflame with sickness and death. First came raging fever and aching head, then acute pain in all the joints. Next, the inability to hold down food or water and the vomiting of blood. Pain intensified. Lymph nodes in the groin, neck and armpits swelled like putrid fruit, engorged with bloodied pus. As pressure grew to bursting, fluid began seeping out. Boils appeared, turning the surrounding skin an angry purple. If the victim lived long enough, limbs turned black with gangrene.

One of the first to be taken was the gentle Wolfgang Capito, shortly after his return from Regensburg. Brandis nursed him for the three days it took him to die. When this news reached Idelette, she raced through the house banging on doors and urging each boarder to prepare to flee to the countryside. Sebastian hastened out of the house in search of André. As he entered the rear courtyard, he saw André moving toward him. Their paths converged at the wrought-iron table where they breakfasted.

André spoke first. "Have you heard? About poor Capito?"

"Yes, but he's not the first. They say many students at the school have succumbed too."

"I can't believe it. It's like some kind of terrible curse has fallen on us."

"I've seen something of this before, André. In Lyon, the year before you arrived. Since then, I have searched libraries and spoken with many physicians in search of an answer. The books say the first great wave of this sickness came to Europe in 1346. Witnesses spoke of galleons from the Crimea arriving in Sicily with crews either dead or near-dead. It was like watching ghost ships drifting in. Rats could be seen eating bodies on the decks. The boats were ordered to cast off and leave immediately. But it was too late. The contagion had already touched those who'd ventured too near. Within weeks, the sickness spread across Italy, France, Britain. Eventually, all of Europe. They called it the Black Death because of the color many victims turned before they perished. Some books say that, within five years, half of Europe's population had expired. The people of that time were sure the apocalypse had begun and that Christ's return must be imminent."

The look of horror on André's face had grown deeper as he listened. "But ... all of that was two hundred years ago! What does that have to do with what's happening now in Strasbourg?"

"The sickness never went away. Not really. Every few years, another outbreak would reappear in some corner of Europe." Sebastian looked André in the eyes. "The physicians say few touched by it can hope to survive. Most die within a few days."

André's face paled further. "There must be treatments. Cures. There must be ... something!"

"There are many theories, of course. Like smearing yourself with onion or garlic juice, or actually, any strong-smelling substance. Some believe that the pestilence spreads through bad air, thus an even stronger odor might defeat it. Based on this hope, some took shelter in sewers, though it seemed to do them no good. Others say that the pestilence is the result of astrological events. Others, that it is caused by witches or heretics or Jews. There have been many instances of mobs driving away—or butchering—every Jew living in their town or village, believing that would end the plague. But if you ask me, most of this is superstition, for none of it achieved anything other than cold-blooded murder."

"But in this century, here in Strasbourg, right now—what should we do, Seb? What do you believe?"

"Only one thing seems effective: isolation or quarantine. If we have any sense, we will leave while we can. I believe Antoine will lead a convoy out into the countryside this afternoon. We should go with him." André still looked horrified, struggling to take it all in.

Sebastian placed a hand on his arm. "Go gather some things into a small bag. In ten or twenty minutes, meet Antoine at the stables."

They hurried their separate ways. Sebastian reentered the house just as two other boarders headed out, kitbags over their shoulders following John's brother, Antoine. On the stairwell above, Idelette stood with the children, looking stricken. Sebastian called out to her, "You are coming now too, yes?"

Her face contorted with confusion. "I ... I can't. John is now on his way back from Regensburg, and I must wait for him." Then her chin dropped to her chest, and he had to strain to hear her next words. "Besides, one of our students has fallen ill, and our servants, Chevant and Liesel, too. Someone must stay. I cannot leave them all here alone."

Antoine looked shocked, and snapped out his next sentence. "John will be furious if I leave you behind, Idelette. You must leave now and come with us."

Idelette clenched the banister tightly. "If I leave, I condemn these three to die alone and uncared for. I cannot do that."

Sebastian froze, his eyes darting from one party to the other. Antoine turned to him, his face a picture of impatience. "Are you coming?"

Sebastian glanced back toward Idelette, the children cowering behind her skirt. "I'm sorry, Antoine. I must stay here and help. André is waiting for you at the stables. Tell him not to worry about me. Tell him to stay safe. All of you, please stay safe."

Antoine's eyes widened in disbelief. "This is absurd, both of you. You cannot stay here amongst this pestilence."

Idelette led the children down the stairs and stood them in front of Antoine. "Take the children with you and keep them well. But I must stay. I must."

The two toddlers clung to Idelette; Sebastian and Antoine had to pry them free. Antoine scooped them both up and made for the door, the children squirming and pleading to be returned to their mother.

Idelette and Sebastian each took a room—Idelette with the housekeeper, Liesel; Sebastian with the valet and Louis Feray, a student—bathing their fevered bodies with dripping rags. By the afternoon, the blood-vomiting began. To their relief, Elisabeth soon arrived and began helping them with the task of sponging bodies and emptying pails. To Sebastian's eye, Chevant seemed the most desperately ill, Liesel much less so, and Louis somewhere between. By early evening, Sebastian felt overwhelmed, yet he knew a long night still lay ahead.

Around dinner time—or what would have been, were they eating —the front door opened. Sebastian looked up.

Brandis Capito entered carrying two pails filled with water. Her eyes were red from grief, but her voice firm as she looked at Sebastian, Elisabeth and Idelette. "I have buried my dead, but while there are others still living, I must help you tend to them."

Idelette threw her arms around Brandis and held her tightly for a few moments. Brandis freed herself and instructed Idelette to take her to see the three members of the household who were still fighting for their lives.

Elisabeth led her to the doorway of the room Sebastian had been manning. She surveyed the two ailing men, then called Sebastian to her. She spoke in a calm, quiet voice. "Concentrate your efforts on Louis, for there is still hope for him. Whatever you do, keep him cool. Keep renewing your water and your cloths, and be liberal in applying them to his body. Prop both men up with pillows and cushions, for that will aid their ability to breathe." Her eyes moved once more to Chevant. He lay bathed in a thick sweat, his chest rattling with each gasp, the nodes on his neck protruding like rotting grapes. She nodded toward him. "Bathe him and keep him comfortable, but beyond that, I fear there is little more you can do."

Sebastian watched Brandis move on to the second bedroom, arriving just as Idelette staggered out. Idelette's face was red and her

littered with beds and buckets, with Elisabeth, Brandis and Sebastian sitting on the floor, all looking exhausted and shattered. Elisabeth spoke first, confirming the terrible news about Capito but assuring all the children were safe with Antoine. Idelette, she said, had been unwell but was now recovering, as was Liesel, but that death had taken Chevant and Louis Feray.

Bucer's eyes fell on Brandis. He stepped toward her, wrapped his arms about her in a bear hug. "I am so, so sorry. You have lost your husband, and the world has lost a great man."

Elisabeth spoke again. "Brandis has been a great hero. In the midst of her grief, she brought herself here and instructed us on how to care for those who were sick. If not for her, I fear more than Louis and Chevant would be dead."

Brandis shook her head, as if trying to shake off Elisabeth's praise. She looked past Bucer, toward Calvin. "John, you have had many heroes in your house these past few days, including Elisabeth, but also Sebastian, who refused to leave. All here put their lives at risk to care for others, including for your wife."

Calvin lifted his hands as if making a prayerful gesture. "Brandis, Elisabeth, and ... dear Sebastian, from the depths of my being I thank each of you." He circled the room, shaking the hand of each of them, then taking both of Brandis's hands in his. "Capito has been set free from the prison of his body now. He is free to be with his Lord." He kissed one of her hands and then went to find Idelette.

As Calvin left the room, Bucer felt Elisabeth slip her hand into his. It seemed strangely warm. Turning to the others in the room, she made them a promise: "I will call in again tomorrow to make sure everything is well, but for now, I need to be with my husband."

Sebastian took the opportunity to also leave. Even as he had been nursing those in Calvin's house, his heart had been aching with fear for Eugenie and Marie and their household. Now he moved swiftly through the deserted streets, growing more anxious with each league traversed. Everywhere were homes with sheets, table cloths or even gowns hanging from window ledges, white flags announcing surrender to the harbinger of death. He began to notice a pattern: the more densely packed homes flew the most flags. A jagged bolt of fear ran through him. Eugenie's parents were not wealthy. They rented a small ground-floor apartment in an aging stone building. He had almost broken into a run by the time he arrived. He paused, taking a deep breath before turning to look into the alley that held their home, praying that there would be no white cloth hanging from the facade.

Something between a gasp and a cry escaped him. *No!* A grubby, worn sheet—or what was left of a sheet—fluttered pathetically above the building's entrance. He threw himself against the apartment's front door, rapping it so hard he felt his knuckles bruising. Within seconds, footsteps approached, and he braced himself for the worst. The door swung open. Eugenie's eyes grew wide with shock.

"You're alive!" he cried as a dam of relief burst inside him. He moved forward as if to throw his arms around her. Her eyes widened even more as she took a step back. And in that instant, Sebastian realized he had nearly breached every protocol on how a chaste young man should behave toward a chaste young lady.

"Eugenie, I'm sorry. I do apologize, but I'm so relieved to see you unharmed by this pestilence. And Marie? Is she well?"

Eugenie recovered her composure and replied. "Yes, yes, Sebastian. We're all fine."

"Even your parents?" he continued. "Have they ... are they ... are they well? And Jacques?"

"Yes, Sebastian. It is as I have said—we are all well."

Sebastian's brow crinkled. "But I saw the white cloth above your door!"

Eugenie's face softened. "Yes, it's so sad. Our neighbors in the rooms above have lost two, both of them children, we think."

By now Marie had appeared in the hallway. Her eyes had registered surprise at finding Sebastian there, and a delighted smile broke across her face. "Sebastian! What are you doing here?"

Eugenie turned to her cousin and answered. "He was worried about us, Marie. It looks like he has run all the way here to check on our welfare."

Sebastian felt his cheeks heat. Marie intervened, her voice almost singing. "Then we are touched, and we are grateful. You are so very gallant, Master Castellio. And we, in turn, are most relieved to see that you too look well." Both girls stared at him, Marie with a look of pure admiration, and Eugenie with an expression that was much harder to read, her eyes boring into him, her mind clearly at work.

Sebastian spoke again. "Is there anything that you need? If there is, please let me know, and I will do my best. I am at you and your parents' service." He gave a small bow.

"That is most kind, Sebastian," Eugenie replied. "But we stocked up on dry goods at the start of the week. For now, we are fine."

Marie looked over her cousin's shoulder and echoed, "But that *is* most kind of you, truly it is."

Sebastian nodded in acknowledgment and began his retreat from the doorway. He took one last glance at the two cousins. Their expressions the same: Marie open and smiling, Eugenie pensive and deep in thought.

Chapter 7
Spring

So many had died that it was impossible to hold individual funerals. Instead, workers dug pits into which carts tipped multiple bodies, a process that did not allow for sentimentality. Families grieved their loved ones and life moved on, as it must.

After that grim winter came spring, and death gave way to life. Hope pushed through the soil and throbbed in the air, pulsing through each flower and trembling leaf. Those who had fled returned. On the streets of Strasbourg, courting couples promenaded, and couples carrying new life rejoiced over those imminent arrivals.

No one who knew them was surprised when Martin Bucer and Brandis Capito announced they were to wed. Their friends were thrilled. Many had heard the story of how, as she lay dying, Elisabeth had urged Bucer to marry Brandis and care for her children.

There were few sanctuaries more ornate or more grand than Strasbourg's beautiful cathedral of light and shadow. Yet beneath its vaulted ceilings and columns, Bucer and Brandis insisted on a simple ceremony in which they promised to love each other and honor God with what remained of their lives. After all, they were old hands. This was Bucer's second marriage and Brandis's fourth, each of the previous ones having ended by death. Surviving academy staff and students attended, and Guillaume Farel made the journey down from Neuchâtel to bless the union.

After the ceremony, all were invited back to the Bucers' house for pastries and sweet wine. Amid the joy, even the studious Calvin tried to enter into the spirit of things, chatting animatedly with guests. From across the room, Sebastian could see him deep in conversation with the fearsome Farel. It was hard to mistake the evangelist from Neuchâtel. He fit all the descriptions Sebastian had heard: slightly taller than Calvin, with a bony face, graying auburn hair and magnificent eyebrows that took off in different directions simultaneously. Beneath those two thickets, his eyes blazed. He threw his hands around as he talked. Sebastian noticed Calvin glance at him and then subtly extend his chin toward him, as if pointing him out to Farel. The pair continued talking for a few more minutes, then Farel started moving toward Sebastian.

Sebastian felt his stomach tighten, and he looked for an escape. Perhaps there was someone nearby whom he could engage in immediate conversation. Where was André when he needed him? He was still swiveling about, trying to find an ally, when Farel descended upon him.

"Sebastian Castellio, I believe!" His deep baritone filled the space between them.

Sebastian mustered his courage and extended his hand. "And you, sir, I believe to be the famous Guillaume Farel."

"Famous? No, no, not in any sense famous, lad. Just a humble servant of the Lord and nothing more. But you, young man, you ... I hear very good things about you indeed. A first-class scholar, and a first-rate Christian is what I am told."

Sebastian's face warmed. "Sir, I have been most fortunate to come under the influence of great men like Calvin, Bucer and Capito."

"Yes, that is true. But you have also had to make your own choices. Like leaving Lyon to come here. Like choosing to stay rather than flee when the plague struck. Our choices shape and reveal our character, and you have made courageous choices. I know he isn't one to praise you to your face, but even John Calvin has been impressed by you. And believe me, he is a not a man easily impressed."

The warm glow in Sebastian's face spread to his midriff, and he could not prevent a smile from playing across his lips. His eyes drifted across the happy crowd. How profoundly things had changed for him since leaving Lyon. His eyes settled on a corner of the room where Bucer and Calvin sat deep in conversation. Another flow of gratitude welled up in him.

The next day, he was thrilled to receive a letter from Jean Bauhin, the friend he'd left behind at Trinité in Lyon. Bauhin had gone on to complete his medical studies and, after establishing a name for himself as a man of talent, he had been taken on as personal physician to Marguerite of Navarre—the king of France's sister! Marguerite was one of the most famous and well-respected women in all of Europe, a noted thinker and author, possessing a reputation for humanity and religious tolerance. Indeed, it was widely rumored that in spite of being part of the Catholic royal family, she was certainly leaning in the direction of the evangelical faith, if she hadn't already embraced it. Many said only her broad-mindedness held her brother in check and prevented greater persecution in France.

Sebastian paused and weighed what this could mean. Was his friend, once so committed to the faith of his forefathers, now moving toward a more Protestant understanding? His eyes returned to the page. Jean went on to say that he was devouring the works of Erasmus, and that his reading of the great man's bilingual New Testament moved him deeply. Intriguing. And, lo, Bauhin was also in love and courting a young woman by the name of Jeanne Fontain! Buoyed by this news of his friend's advancements, he folded the letter neatly and placed it in his pocket for André to read later.

He then reached for a quill and sheet of paper, eager to get a letter back to Bauhin with his impressions of Strasbourg, of Calvin, of Bucer, as well as tell him all about the hardship the plague had wrought among them, careful to supply all the details he knew his physician friend would want. He wondered if he should also tell him about Eugenie and Marie and the confusion he felt over his affections toward them, but the more he tried to form the words, the more ridiculous and muddled it sounded. He signed off and sealed the letter. Hopefully within a day or two, he would hear of a rider headed for Paris who could deliver it for him.

As he readied for bed that night, he thought about the news of Jean having met the woman he wanted to marry. He was happy for Bauhin. But then his thoughts turned to his own predicament, and he sighed. Eugenie and Marie, both lovely, both worthy. How would he ever know for sure which one he was meant to pursue? Perhaps he should just trust that in his own time, in his own way, God would make it clear. With that thought, he drifted off to sleep.

Across town, in the bedroom they shared in the Paquelon house, Eugenie and Marie were talking about their dreams for the future too. As Eugenie chatted, Marie listened. Genie was clear that she wanted to marry soon and have children—lots of children! But, she declared, she was not prepared to settle for just any sort of man, nor for a marriage in which she was simply chattel.

"The man I marry must be capable of love—real love, sacrificial love—both for me and for the children we will have. I will not marry one of those men for whom business or making money always comes first and their family an afterthought. Above all, he must be kind." Eugenie, her jaw set with determination, folded her arms across her chest as she laid down her declaration.

Yes, that's exactly what I want too! Marie screwed up her brow in concentration, trying to imagine what it would be like to leave behind the life of a girl and enter that of a woman, a wife, a mother. She really couldn't picture it. After several moments of thought, she finally realized her own ideal. "The man I marry must have a sharp mind and a free spirit. He must be the kind of man that respects *my* mind and values *my* spirit. I could only respect a man who I believed respected me." She smiled to herself. This felt like a good answer.

Like his mentor, Sebastian kept himself busy. As well as helping Calvin, three other projects had become his secret passions. Because Latin was the academic language of Europe, every student had to master it in order to climb the first rung on the ladder of higher learning. This was only one of the many ways that society favored the already privileged and blocked the poor from advancing. Training in Latin began at village-school level, but even there, good texts and good teachers were hard to find. From personal experience, Sebastian knew that those books that did exist were dull and difficult. So he resolved to create a lively Latin primer, one that integrated biblical material and would be engaging and enjoyable for young minds. If he could achieve this, it would open wide the door of opportunity for children and young people like himself, born into poverty. This book would also function as a type of children's Bible. He decided he would call this primer *Sacred Dialogues*.

The other two projects were even more ambitious. In his spare hours, Sebastian furtively labored away on not one but two fresh translations of the Bible. One was a more readable Latin edition, for he knew he was not alone in finding the Vulgate's language dated and awkward. The other was a French version. His goal was to create an idiomatic version so dynamic that even the humblest French peasant would find it a joy to read or to hear. Thus far, he had kept his work on these projects all to himself, knowing that he could well end up stumbling into controversial territory.

A few weeks after Martin and Brandis's wedding, he sat in the academy library reading from the Vulgate and making notes. Bucer came to his table. "Sebastian, diligent as ever I see. May I ask what you are working on?"

Sebastian considered giving an evasive answer. *But why should I?* he thought. *And really, if I'm on the wrong track, I need to know now before I go too far. And of all people, Bucer will give me a fair and thoughtful answer.* Pushing his notes aside, he began to explain his issue with the way Latin was usually taught and his passion to see the Scriptures made available in ways that everyday people could read and understand. Then he briefly outlined the three projects he was working on.

For several seconds, Bucer simply stared at him. Sebastian's heart began to sink. Finally, Bucer found his voice. "Three works? You are working on three major works at the same time? Among all your other duties, how is this even possible?"

Sebastian suddenly realized just how presumptuous his ideas must have sounded. "Yes, you are right. Perhaps it is pride that has pushed me to embark on work no one has asked of me."

"No, that is not what I meant at all. I was struck momentarily dumb by the loftiness of your vision, but not from any criticism. This is marvelous. All of us are children of the great work that Luther started, and by this you are advancing it! Why should there be criticism of that?"

Sebastian felt a smile on his lips. He appreciated Bucer's kind encouragement. "Sir, if possible, can we keep talk of this between the two of us? It is early days yet, and it will be some time before any of this work is ready to be made public. Of the three, my work on the Latin primer is the most advanced. If I could show you that, I would be very grateful for your thoughts."

"Of course, Sebastian, of course. But remember what I said to you when you first arrived—that God may have brought you here for more than just academic advancement? You are a young man, and you mustn't spend every second of your time bent over books. You must make room for other things too."

Puzzled, Sebastian considered Bucer.

"Oh, come on, lad. Not that I notice these things myself, but my wife tells me there are a couple of young ladies you have shown a lot of interest in, and they in you. She also tells me you have pulled back the last few weeks and seem to be avoiding them now. Is this true?"

Sebastian stammered out a reply. "We met at the French church and have become friendly, but that is all. We are simply friends."

Bucer plowed on, ignoring Sebastian's awkwardness. "But you can't be stringing two young ladies along like that. It's not how a gentleman behaves. You'll have to choose one, Sebastian, to pursue."

Sebastian's face reddened. "I'm not stringing anyone along. It's just that they are inseparable, and I have no idea how to talk with one of them without the other. How does one decide, or ... or ..." He was getting himself in a tangle, and the more he talked, the worse it sounded. So he stopped.

Bucer chuckled. "Don't worry, Sebastian. I have a feeling that Brandis has decided you are her next little project, and she is an expert in these kinds of matters. I've simply been tasked with inviting you for supper tonight in order that she might discuss this very thing with you."

Sebastian wiped the sweat from his hands before he knocked on the Bucers' door. The valet, Frans, ushered him into the sitting room. They had exchanged a few pleasantries when Brandis and Bucer appeared. Sebastian swallowed hard.

Brandis spoke first. "I've asked the kitchen staff to prepare trays of food for us in here tonight. It will be less formal, and we can have a good heart-to-heart talk without being interrupted."

Sebastian was relieved to hear that and wondered if Brandis had a plan in motion for André as well.

"So, Sebastian. My spies tell me that there are two young ladies in your life, both most eligible, but it's all got a bit much for you, so you've been avoiding them the past few weeks."

He wondered who the "spies" could be. He supposed Idelette must be at least one of them.

"Yes, it's true. It has become a bit complex and confusing. I find I can't be sure what my true feelings are toward each of them—and each of them toward me. For one thing, they are constantly together ..." As his voice trailed off, he stared at his shoes, feeling defeated.

"Sebastian, if you still lived in Saint Martin du Frêne, your parents would be talking with their parents and negotiations would be already underway. But because you have no parents here, it is all a little more complicated. But take heart! Martin and I have decided to step into that role and act as negotiators for you."

Bucer gave a little cough and add, "Well, more Brandis than me. This is not really my forte, to be honest."

As if she hadn't heard, Brandis continued. "I will make an appointment with Mrs. Paquelon this week. We will compare notes, then I shall report back to you." She was warming to her work now. "But I will say this much: my spies tell me that your eyes light up most when Eugenie walks into the room."

That may be true, Sebastian thought to himself, *but I think it is Marie's eyes that light up the most when I walk into the room. Or do I just imagine this?* He groaned inwardly. *Why are these things so complicated?*

"Eugenie is also the older of the two girls, and closer in age to yourself—but I'm getting ahead of myself. I shouldn't say any more until I've talked further with the Paquelons."

That evening they ate a very pleasant meal of roast pigeon and sautéed vegetables, followed by a suet pudding. They chatted about progress at the academy and about the growing Catholic-Protestant conflict across Europe. Sebastian was relieved to find both his hosts to be people of discretion. Brandis did not bring up the subject of romance again, and Bucer made no mention of Sebastian's writing projects.

Later that week, Marie answered a knock at the door.

"Frau Bucer! What a surprise!"

"No doubt it is, Marie. I've come to speak with your aunt, actually."

"Oh, of course. Come in while I fetch her."

As Brandis stood in the hallway, Marie called up the stairwell for her aunt.

When Sonya appeared, Brandis handed her a basket of pastries she'd brought as a gift. She took hold of one of Sonya's hands in her own. "Frau Paquelon, I've come on a matter of some sensitivity." She glanced back at Marie. "Would it be possible for us to speak together privately?"

Sonya turned to Marie. "Marie, I need some vegetables from the market for tonight's supper. Could you and Genie go fetch them for me? It's a beautiful day, so take your time. Take the path along the canal."

Marie found Eugenie, and with quizzical looks, they donned their hats and gloves and took their leave.

That night, after supper, Sonya sat down with the girls and explained that they were giving their blessing for Sebastian to begin courting Eugenie, so long as Eugenie agreed.

"She is the eldest and she should be the first to leave and to marry," Sonya explained. "And with Charles so sick, it will be a relief to have another man about the house. Of course, Marie, we have hopes for you and André Zebedee, but"—she sighed—"that man is slower than a wet Sunday!"

As her aunt unfolded the story, Marie felt something inside herself trembling. It was a new sensation, something bittersweet. A uniting of joy and sadness, happiness and tearfulness all at the same time. She looked across at Eugenie, who was beaming, wearing a smile larger than she had ever seen on her cousin before. Eugenie leaned forward and embraced her mother in a crushing hug. When she disentangled herself, she glanced at Marie. Genie's smile became suddenly less certain. Then both of them clasped hold of each other, crying and hugging.

Within a few days, however, the news for Marie turned worse. A crisis had arisen in the church at Orbe. André Zebedee was to take up the arranged pastoral role. He was to leave immediately.

There was one more person whose advice on marriage Sebastian knew must be heard: John Calvin. Calvin was delighted with the news of the betrothal and firm in his counsel. Everything must be done in order and without unseemly haste. There should be a long engagement, publicly announced so that any man's objections could be raised. Only then could they move to planning a church-sanctioned wedding.

John continued to be helpful. When there was a problem with the proposed dowry—neither the Paquelons nor Sebastian had much money—he stepped in and smoothed the way. Then, without warning, he dropped in a sentence that left Sebastian bewildered.

"And if you wait, who knows. Perhaps your wedding will not be in Strasbourg but somewhere even more propitious for you."

Those last words were puzzling ones, but Sebastian was more than happy to wait and use the time to properly court this mysterious, alluring woman. He and Genie squeezed all they could into the months that followed—walks that explored each canal and bridge, along with ventures to the corners of Strasbourg they had not yet seen. One of their favorite places to spend time at was the cavernous indoor market on the Place de la Cathédrale. A wealthy merchant had turned the ground floor of his magnificent home—paneled with beautiful wooden frescoes arranged around stained glass windows—into an emporium, where all manner of goods were sold beneath its impressive stone arches.

And true to his sense of loyalty, Sebastian made sure they went to see Claude and Evette at the Fleur-de-Lis. On hearing the happy news and meeting Eugenie, Claude's quivering barrel of a body nearly exploded with excitement. Tears filled his eyes, little cries of "wonderful, wonderful" resounded from his lips, and he embraced them both. Even Evette was moved to find a bottle of wine with which to toast their future.

Each day, they made time to walk together, soaking up the beauty of Strasbourg and finding hidey-holes in which they could linger and talk. They were learning more about each other—sharing their hopes and their dreams. They both longed for the world to be a kinder place and were determined to do what they could to make it so, even if that were only within the confines of the family they hoped to soon begin. They both adored children and tried to outbid each other on how many they hoped to have.

"Five!" Eugenie declared.

Sebastian shook his head. "Seven!"

"Nine!"

They dissolved into fits of laughter, their legs, their arms, their hands, their fingers, brushing against each other, each gentle touch a reminder of the pleasure and the mystery to come. They were falling in love, and the time remaining till the sealing of their marriage vows was a vigil of yearning, one that only served to make the longing of their hearts—and bodies—stronger.

Early one morning, Sebastian received a message from the visiting Guillaume Farel to meet him in one of the offices at the academy. When he arrived, he found Farel gazing out of the windows, looking toward Place Broglie. Sebastian cleared his throat. Farel swung around, a look of great excitement lighting up his face.

"Sit down, sit down! I have great news to share—news of opportunity to further God's kingdom, and to further your own career as well." He could barely contain himself, pacing the short distance from the one end of the windows to the other. Four steps to the left, then four steps back to the right. "The city council has invited John Calvin back to Geneva to take up the role of head pastor there. And not just to oversee the churches but the educational work of the city too! I will be accompanying him initially, though I will then move to Neuchâtel to lead things there." He clapped his hands together, grinning widely as he delivered this astonishing news.

Sebastian was puzzled. "Truly, this is wonderful news. But why do you need to inform me?" His mind was whirling, trying to calculate what Farel had meant when he said this would change his own circumstances too.

Farel reached inside the breast of his doublet and pulled out a crisp rectangular envelope, which he passed to Sebastian. Sebastian's hands trembled slightly as he broke the seal. He unfolded the paper and started to read what turned out to be a letter from the Little Council of the city of Geneva. It spoke of his service and accomplishments in Strasbourg, which made him blush, for he knew he had done nothing yet. It spoke of the high praise and lofty recommendations that had been made concerning him, particularly from Guillaume Farel and John Calvin. They believed Sebastian had a great career ahead of him as an educationalist. It then went on to speak of the city's ambition of becoming one of the finest centers for classical and theological education in Europe and how their College de Rive was being prepared for this purpose.

When he came to the final paragraph, it shocked him. He read it a second time. He read it a third time, yet he still could not believe nor comprehend it. The city of Geneva, on the recommendation of Guillaume Farel and John Calvin, was inviting him to take up the position of rector of the College de Rive. He looked up at Farel in disbelief. Farel met his gaze with a burst of deep, thunderous laughter while nodding his head in affirmation.

"You'll need to get ready quickly, lad. We will provide you with transport, but they want you there by August."

Chapter 8
Geneva

Sebastian and Eugenie had only a few weeks in which to convince her parents to leave Strasbourg with them. Each of them worried about Charles's health, whether he was robust enough for the journey, but the old man rallied, determined to support his daughter's prospects. Between all of them, their possessions were few—mostly Sebastian's books and the Paquelons' tailoring material—so they easily occupied the one wagon assigned to them.

Farewelled by the proud Martin and Brandis and by the bubbling Claude and Evette, the pilgrims set off to build the city they, like Calvin, hoped would shine the light of God across a dark and riven Europe.

They passed through the regions of Colmar, Mulhouse, Basel, Solothurn, Neuchâtel, and Yverdon-les-Baine, resting overnight in each of these municipalities. They passed through farmlands and fields and orchards where peasant farmers toiled to bring in the autumn harvest before the approaching winter. They threaded their way past azure lakes and, when the skies were clear, they could see snow-capped mountains to the south, glistening and crystalline. The older Paquelons had unpacked a trunk of blankets and clothes for bedding, finding enough space in the back of the wagon to lie down, seeking some comfort as the carriage lurched over dirt roads. As often as possible, the enthusiastic Marie and Jacques rode up by the coachman, leaving the second bench seat largely for Sebastian and Eugenie.

As they swayed over yet another pothole, Eugenie leaned against Sebastian's shoulder, whispering loud enough to be heard over the stretching and creaking of the carriage's wood and leather. "The countryside is beautiful."

Sebastian gently kissed her forehead, joy threatening to overwhelm him when he considered the wonder of it all. Beside him sat a woman he loved, who shared his heart, and they were journeying to fulfill a great call. He, the child of a simple peasant farmer, had been appointed to lead a new and prestigious college. He was on his way to work alongside one of Europe's greatest theological minds. Only God could have brought this about.

After many days of lurching through hamlets and along rutted roads, they came to the ancient pilgrims' city of Lausanne, perched on the northern shore of Lake Genève. It was the last major town in which they would sleep before Geneva itself. A patchwork of hills and villas nestled against steep streets, cut in two by the River Flon which formed a gorge traversed by several stone bridges. To the east, mile after mile of terraced vineyards—now bleeding to hues of rust and bronze—clung to the slopes that cradled Genève's waters. These vineyards produced velvet wines which could be traced back to Roman times. On one of the town's most prominent hills, a magnificent cathedral towered over all else. Once famed for its intricate tapestries and statues, it had drawn pilgrims from all over Europe— that is, until eighteen cartloads of artifacts had been stripped away by Protestant Reformers. In place of religious icons, they had built a university. From now on, theology was to be learned via the mind rather than the senses.

After a night's rest in an inn named the Pilgrim's Way, they set out early on the final leg of their journey. Their sense of anticipation grew with every league, knowing that they drew closer and closer to the city they had been picturing ever since Farel had told Sebastian of his appointment. Their route now took them along the shore of the lake from Saint Sulpice to Preverenges, then through Morges and Nyon, the land flattening to reveal fields of grain and the rolling vineyards of La Côte. Finally, as dusk approached and the westerly alpine sky darkened to indigo, the silhouette of Geneva's cathedral appeared ahead of them, its three unmistakable towers guiding them toward their destination.

They left behind the verdant farmland that had accompanied them since Nyon and entered the city's walls at Porte de Cornavin, their swaying wagon passing near the Church of Saint Gervais. They crossed the Rhône on the impressive Pont Bati bridge, a vast structure of timber lined with shops and houses and mills, whose great wheels creaked and turned under the power of the river's current. Once across, they rumbled up the narrow Allemandes, lined on each side with buildings of stone and wood, then to the end of the Poissonerie Rive.

They turned right onto Rue Verdaine, and there, by the light of a coachman's lamp, they pulled up to their new home, not far from the college that was to be Sebastian's place of work. Over the last hour of their journey, dusk had been turning to night. A shroud of darkness now covered the city. The coachman passed a key to Sebastian and waited as each of the passengers dismounted. Then he turned the carriage back toward Porte de Cornavin.

Once through the door and into the house, Sebastian lit another lamp and a series of candles. It was late, and they were too exhausted to do anything other than find their rooms and collapse wearily into their beds. The older Paquelons shared one room, Marie and Eugenie another. Sebastian and Jacques occupied the third.

Geneva had a long, proud history of struggle for independence, both from its overbearing bishops and from the bordering kingdom of Savoy. At the heart of this struggle had been families who could trace their lineage in the Lake Genève region back for generations. From one such family came Ami Perrin. Though an early and loyal supporter of the evangelical preachers, particularly Guillaume Farel, he was a fiercely independent man. His highest value was that of liberty. He was a man of passion. His love of life's finer things—music and theater, choice food and wine—was uncontainable. But above all, he loved Geneva. As a leading member of the council, he had grown increasingly distressed by the city's factionalism and disorder. In an effort to see order restored, he had campaigned vigorously for the return of John Calvin.

Ami Perrin, who loved drama and grand gesture in equal measure, had volunteered to lead the delegation to bring Calvin home. And so, a few days after Sebastian had arrived, Perrin, with exaggerated ceremony, led a mounted escort into the city of Strasbourg to collect the Reformer. The triumphant cavalcade wound its way through Basel, Solothurn and Neuchâtel, showing off its prize *célébrité*, before finally arriving in Geneva. Carriages were then sent to collect Idelette and the children and bring them to their new spacious home on Rue des Chanoines, overlooking Lake Genève.

Sebastian and Eugenie set their wedding day for two weeks after Calvin's arrival. It couldn't come quickly enough for either of them. Arrangements were finalized, with Calvin delighted to lead the ceremony at the Chapel of Saint Pierre. Charles had long been working on a gown for his daughter. The bodice and arms, made of creamy silk, tailored down to a flowing caramel-colored skirt of linen. Puffed sleeves and a bateau collar edged with French lace completed the embroidered work of art.

The ceremony itself was a simple affair—the reading of the Scriptures and the signing of a legal contract before witnesses. And their nuptial party was a small and intimate gathering. After that, Sebastian and Eugenie moved into a room of their own, where finally they could know the intimacy they had longed for these past many months.

The following Monday, Sebastian rose early and made the walk from his home on Rue Verdaine to a narrow lane that ran alongside the college. The college, a former Franciscan monastery, was a capacious three-story building of chamois-colored stone with a high, terracotta-shingle roof, from which half a dozen dormer rooms showed their windows. Inside, all religious ornamentation had been stripped away, monks' cells converted into offices, and the larger spaces (the chapel and scriptorium) divided into classrooms. The spacious library had been retained, though the books on its shelves now reflected the orthodoxy of its new masters. Calvin had been so busy since his return that today was to be their first real meeting to discuss work.

Sebastian found Farel positioned on the steps that led into the auditorium. He was waving his arms as if trying to create a wind that would draw Sebastian closer. Sebastian looked up in amusement but not surprise, for he knew that the fiery preacher had been in the city for Calvin's return. Farel's face—which Castellio imagined could be frightening if arranged differently—was beaming with welcome. As Sebastian grew closer, Farel's smile grew wider. When Sebastian reached the steps, the older man thrust his hand into Sebastian's. "Welcome to the College de Rive, where God's children will be trained to do God's work. John is very eager that you should make a start, so let's not keep him waiting."

Inside, he followed Farel up the wooden staircase to the next floor. As they reached the top landing, a stout man in a blue military tunic let out a cheerful greeting, which Farel returned.

"Ah, Ami! Here is someone you must meet. This is the well-discussed Sebastian Castellio. And Sebastian, this is Ami Perrin, he who spared no effort in restoring John Calvin to the ecclesiastical leadership of this fine city. And, I might add, a man who seems to know everything about everyone in Geneva!"

The well-built gentleman with square jaw and merry eyes turned to face Sebastian, a broad grin spreading across his face. "Sebastian Castellio! Indeed yes, your name has been much discussed and your arrival much anticipated, and I, for one, am thrilled that a man of your talent has come to join us in our wonderful city. My duties have much more to do with the defense of our city and the work of the council rather than that of the college, but occasionally there is business that brings me here. If I can ever be of assistance to you, just say the word." And with that he gave a little bow.

Sebastian grinned in response to this effusive welcome. "Thank you, sir. Your name is one I have heard much mention of as well. This is a most kind offer, one that I shall keep in mind."

"Yes, yes, do that, for I mean it. And I promise to come and visit you and your family at my earliest opportunity so that I may extend a genuine Genevan welcome to them too."

"Then I look forward to that with much anticipation."

"Until then, Monsieur Castellio, adieu." Ami continued down the stairs at a waddling pace that belied his frame.

As soon as he was out of sight, Farel chuckled. "I think you will believe me when I say few in this town surpass Monsieur Perrin for bonhomie, though he is perhaps a little too fond of his wine and his parades."

"Well, his bonhomie is certainly an admirable trait," Sebastian replied. "And it helps to be welcomed so warmly to a new home."

Brief as it had been, this encounter—in conjunction with Farel's boisterous reception a few minutes earlier—had eased any doubts Sebastian had. Everything on their journey, and now in the city itself, seemed to clearly confirm that he had made the right decision in coming to Geneva. He followed Farel along a passageway off which several doorways exited. At the first door, Farel paused and waved his hand into the empty room.

"This will be your study when you are ready to move in."

Sebastian leaned past Farel's outstretched arm. It was a small, dim room dominated by walls lined with panels of dark wood. Attached to the walls were lines of empty bookshelves. Toward the wall was a dominating desk and, on top of that, a writing lectern. The window itself was a tall, narrow arch, its little panes held in place by lines of lead. The glass was dusty and dull, but through it Sebastian could just make out the shimmering water of Lake Genève. If Sebastian were to be honest, he found the room rather gloomy, but he nodded toward Farel and said, "This will do nicely."

They walked past two more doors before arriving at Calvin's office, his door ajar. Looking in, they found him arched over a desk, his quill frantically scratching away. Sebastian glanced about the room. It was very similar in appearance to his own. Farel indicated for him to enter, then stepped back into the passageway and took his leave, explaining that he had other matters to attend to.

It took several long seconds, but eventually Calvin looked up and saw Sebastian. He dropped his quill and smiled broadly. "Ah! Dear Sebastian! I apologize for my busyness and unavailability since my arrival. I have been holding continuous discussions with the city's councils, and believe me, they are not easy men to deal with. How is Eugenie? How are your lodgings?"

Calvin waved Sebastian toward a not particularly comfortable chair before pulling up another so that they sat facing one another, their knees almost touching. As soon as he took his seat, the timbre of Calvin's voice dropped, for now, it seemed, it was time to talk of more serious matters.

"We must start straight away and make up for lost time. There is so much to do, but nothing will be easy here in Geneva. French refugees continue to pour into the city, and I am expected to lead them and arrange all manner of welfare for them. Every Sunday, I will preach at Saint Pierre and Saint Madeleine. The other mornings of the week, I will lecture publicly on the Scriptures in the city auditorium. Some of the ministers here are of very poor quality and will need much training. And the town councils, despite inviting me here, are proving difficult." His shoulders shrugged, his tone becoming one of exasperation. "Nearly everything of importance that I need to do will require negotiation with and permission from them." He made a small noise, an expelling of air, something between a gasp and a guffaw, and his lips pouted.

In the pause that followed, Sebastian tried to work out if he was supposed to offer a comment or simply listen. Calvin was examining his ink-stained hands, the tips of his long, elegant fingers dark with indigo. When he looked up at Sebastian again, his mood seemed to lift.

"Now that I have finally arrived, we can all start the real work of this school. Sebastian, I hope that this college will one day rival the academy in Strasbourg, helping to mold the best young Christian minds, both laymen and ministers all across Europe. Do you still share this vision?"

Sebastian leaned forward in his seat, poised on its edge. "Yes, John, I do. And by God's grace, I will do my best to share the truth of God's Word and the wisdom of the great thinkers so that each of our students will grow and excel and take their place in the world."

Calvin nodded slowly, but his smile had evaporated. His dark eyes probed Sebastian earnestly. For several seconds a deep silence settled between them, and Sebastian could feel a heaviness descending on the room. Just as Sebastian felt he must say something —anything—to break the tension, Calvin spoke again, his voice low, the spacing of his words deliberate.

"Ours is a great cause, Sebastian, but it will not be won without struggle and sacrifice. We must gird ourselves. We must arm ourselves. We must ready ourselves for a titanic battle ahead. Many agents, human and otherwise, will oppose us and try to stop us. We fight to bring order; they fight to bring chaos. Are you prepared for such a conflict?" His voice dropped to the level of a heavy whisper. "Even now, I know for a fact that there are spies in the city, those who would sabotage our work. Among the many refugees who arrive each week, the French Crown hides Catholic agents who masquerade as

Huguenots but who report back on everything we do. Anabaptists also come, trying to hide their brazen doctrines beneath a pretense of orthodoxy. We cannot allow this. We must root them out and expel them. So, I ask again, are you prepared for such a conflict?"

Sebastian had learned that there were times when Calvin's voice had an almost mesmerizing effect, and this was one of them. The weight he had felt pressing him into the chair, the unnameable sensation enveloping him, was, perhaps, a sense of divine call or extraordinary responsibility. He felt carried along by a force over which he had little control. He blinked and whispered a barely audible, "Yes."

"Like David going into battle, God has called me to lead this great work, Sebastian, and I know that I will suffer for it. I will be attacked from many sides. My path will not be easy. I need to know that you will stand with me, support me and follow me with complete loyalty. Can I rely on you for this?"

Replying seemed to take enormous effort. There were questions he wanted to ask, clarifications he needed to seek, but the best he could do was to almost imperceptibly give a singular nod of his head.

Calvin continued to stare at him, his intense brown eyes boring into Sebastian's. For the longest time, they sat there, wordless. When Sebastian could stand it no longer, he forced himself to shift his vision. Just above Calvin's head and to the left, he became aware of a large T-shaped patch, pale against the dark paneling of the wall. The outline of where a crucifix had been ripped away. It had been replaced with a small wooden plaque upon which was written the words *post tenebras lux* (after darkness light). Sebastian's eyes shifted again, this time gazing above Calvin's right shoulder where another plaque had been affixed to the wall. It held the words of a Bible verse: "It is a fearful thing to fall into the hands of the living God."

After what seemed an age, Calvin's eyes closed. Sebastian was sure he was praying. Then finally, his eyes opened. He stood and returned behind the desk. He picked up a stack of linen papers bound together with brown string and passed them to Sebastian.

"I have written a complete list of your responsibilities. As well as overseeing the enrollment and care of all students, you will teach classes in Latin, Greek, Hebrew and French Monday through Friday and every second Saturday. You will also be expected to preach on Sundays at the small church located in the village of Vandoeuvres, about a league beyond the city's walls, as they have lacked a pastor for some time now. Take this home, read it, sign it, and bring it back with you tomorrow."

Sebastian held the pages. They really weren't many, yet he could discern a great weight in them. He felt that weight not with his hands but as if it had been laid upon his shoulders. Calvin, back at his desk, was again busily scratching away at another document, fully engrossed, as if Sebastian was no longer in the room. The meeting had clearly finished, and Sebastian was expected to see himself out.

That evening, two surprises awaited Sebastian. First, a letter had arrived from André Zebedee. It was the first he'd heard from him since leaving Strasbourg. Sonya and Marie were out strolling and Charles sleeping, so Sebastian and Eugenie retreated to their room to devour it. The first page was full of greetings and inquiries after everybody's well-being. He then plunged deeply—as only Zebedee could—into his mental wrestling with several aspects of John Calvin's teaching, specifically on the nature of the Eucharist and on the nature of free will.

Eugenie sighed. "How like André to feel that the whole world turns on answers to these kinds of questions. A few lines asking after each of us, then several pages debating theology."

Later that evening came the second treat. The delightful Ami Perrin dropped by, as promised, to welcome them on behalf of the council. Again, he was in high spirits. He brought several bottles of wine from the vineyards of Lavaux. After this pleasant addition to their supper, Sebastian sat at his desk and read through the document

Calvin had given him, while Eugenie looked on. When he came to the final page, he sat back in his chair and pursed his lips. The workload expected of him was terrific, and the annual salary far below what he had hoped for. The contract was open to the page dealing with this, and he slid it across the desk toward Eugenie. She pulled the candle closer and leaned over to read. Her brow furrowed.

"Oh!" Recovering, she added, "But it's just a start, a beginning. Once they see how good you are, they will, of course, raise your salary."

Sebastian reached out and took her hand, cradling it in both of his. "Genie, your faith in me makes me hope and believe that all things are possible. And yes, I'm sure you are right. For now, the College de Rive is struggling to establish itself, but soon it will be attracting students from all over the Continent. Good things lie ahead of us."

Their new home was small but comfortable. A study for Sebastian, a kitchen with a fireplace, and an oak table large enough for them all to take their meals together. Running from the kitchen was a narrow passageway which led to the three bedrooms. Outside the front door, stone steps ascended to the neighbor's apartment above.

They had settled into a new rhythm: Sebastian working late and rising early to ensure everything at the college was in order, while Eugenie, Marie and Sonya did the market shopping and prepared the day's food. The old market on Rue Molard was one of their favorite places to spend a couple of hours. It ran each day but Sunday. Once a month, farmers from the surrounding rural lands came to sell whatever surplus they had coaxed from the earth. Peasants, desperate peddlers, wealthy merchants, opportunistic hawkers and canny vendors were all thrown together, some selling from carts, others from baskets they carried, some from reed mats on the ground, while the most successful traded from tables and wooden stalls.

Sebastian spent long hours preparing and delivering lessons, caring for the college's students during the week and for the good people of Vanoeuvres on Sundays. It was hard, and it was challenging, but he and Eugenie kept encouraging one another to hold on to that excitement they had felt when Farel first proposed the whole incredible plan. And as Calvin so often reminded them, a great cause could not be won without courage and sacrifice.

Indeed, if he sought further inspiration, Sebastian needed only to look to Calvin. The man worked feverishly, rising to start his day well before dawn and still burning lamp oil well past midnight. Sebastian wondered if he ever slept or ate, and how he coped with the pressure of overseeing all the churches and the waves of refugees while trying to corral the councils into fulfilling his vision for Geneva. On top of this, Sebastian knew he was writing books and corresponding with leaders across Europe. The only break he got was when he traveled to attend important conferences. But such travel was demanding, and conferences were often filled with conflict. Every time Sebastian felt overwhelmed by his own load, he would look at Calvin's, rebuke himself for sloth, and press on.

Yet try as he might, there were doubts that he could not suppress. Some of the ministers working under Calvin were treated well and supplied with all they needed. Others were ignored, as if they had offended the Reformer, as if he'd washed his hands of them. And then there was Calvin's belief that every detail, great or small, that happened in life was prescribed and predestined by God. The more of life Sebastian saw, and the more he considered this idea, the less appealing it seemed. It was a doctrine designed, Calvin would say, to give certainty and reassurance to the faithful that they had been chosen by God. Fine enough. But in Calvin's teaching, it also meant that everyone else—the vast majority of people on earth— were "chosen" by God to be sent to hell unless they explicitly joined the Protestant cause, particularly Calvin's version of it. Increasingly, doubts and questions arose in Sebastian's mind. But these were dangerous thoughts, and even if he'd had the courage, finding a time to discuss them with his mentor was impossible. Calvin was busy with God's great work every minute of every day. And what's more, he made it clear that he had no time for doubters and their disloyal questions.

And now there was another reason for Sebastian to work hard and sink his roots deeper into Genevan soil. Not long after his move to Geneva, sickness swept his elderly parents from this world. In a brief visit back home, he had helped his family mourn them then plan their next steps. His brothers would remain in Savoy, but he'd persuaded his three younger sisters to follow him. It wasn't difficult. Tired of living in fear of persecution, two of his sisters, Etienne and Jeanette, journeyed to Geneva, accompanied by their husbands, Pierre and Evard. His third sister, Jeanne, settled with her husband, Matthieu, in the village of Gex, only a short distance from the city. To all be so close again was heartwarming, but more than that, Sebastian felt relief that he'd helped them escape France's ever-spreading religious violence and find a place of refuge and freedom.

Sebastian had been in Geneva nearly half a year when they finally received news from Zebedee that he planned to visit. A month later, as Sebastian was about to begin a class, a youth arrived and handed him a note informing him that a certain Monsieur André Zebedee had arrived by horseback and located himself at an inn named The Rose. Immediately after his teaching had finished, Sebastian hurried home to collect Eugenie and Marie, and they set off excitedly toward Square Molard and its nearby inn.

As they rounded the corner off Rivière, they could see the bustling of customers and hawkers coming and going from the Molard market. Just short of the market, hanging from an awning, a flaking sign held the image of a scarlet bloom. It marked the location of a stone-down, timber-up, three-story building. The ground floor was given over to a tavern, the next two floors to bed chambers for guests. Just inside the doorway was a vestibule furnished with two wooden benches. Eugenie and Marie took seats there while Sebastian sought out the innkeeper.

He pushed through the door of the tavern to find the owner behind a long bench, busily transferring ale from a barrel to a jug. Stepping forward he asked the man where he might find a guest by the name of André Zebedee. Nearby, a young lad—the same youth who'd brought him the note earlier in the day—was cleaning mugs.

The man laid his hand on the boy's shoulder and whispered something in his ear before turning back to Sebastian. "You wait here, sir, and my lad will fetch him for you."

The boy scampered off up a rickety staircase. Sebastian looked about him. A handful of guests—all men—sat hunched over small wooden tables, talking and drinking, the hum of conversation punctuated with revelers chuckling at one another's stories. Much here reminded him of Claude and Evette's place in Strasbourg, and he guessed André's room here would be just as spartan as there, and his pallet just as thin.

At a movement on the stairs, he looked up to see André springing down them, a grin spread across his usually serious features. Sebastian took three bounding strides and met André just as he was stepping off the final tread. He threw his arms firmly around André and swung him off the ground.

"André, how I have missed you! It is so, so good to see you."

"And you too, Sebastian. I have been counting the days until I could come here and see you. There were many delays, but as you see, here I am at last."

"We, too, have been counting the days. But come, come, more friends await you!"

He wrapped an arm across André's back and led him toward Eugenie and Marie in the sitting area. As soon as they entered, Eugenie stood to her feet and leaned forward so that André might kiss her first on one cheek and then the other. André stepped back and looked at her.

"Eugenie, you look radiant. Clearly marriage agrees with you."

By now Marie was standing too, her eyes dancing, an enormous smile on her face, her expression just short of laughter. André's focus shifted from Eugenie and, for a moment, they stood facing each other uncertainly, his old awkwardness reasserting itself. With a small giggle Marie rescued the situation, grabbing André's right hand in both of hers and squeezing it in welcome. He regained composure and leaned forward to kiss Marie on both cheeks.

Eugenie and Marie began to talk over one another, plotting where the three of them would take André to show off their new city. Though nowhere near as beautiful as Strasbourg, they had come to appreciate that Geneva, too, had its charms. By now they had established their favorite spots, like the gentle sloping streets from the college down to the turquoise waters of Lake Genève, the plateau where the triple towers of Saint Pierre Cathedral watched over Maison de Ville, home of the Grand Council, and beyond that, further to the west, Saint Madeleine and Saint Germain. The three streets, each with a square, led to the lake. And of course, the bustling market at the end of this very street and the plaza of Bourg de Four.

They decided to head for the cool, cobbled space of Bourg de Four but to do so by weaving their way through the narrow maze of streets between Madeline and Saint Pierre Cathedral, under the tall masonry facades that typified Geneva's buildings. Sebastian and Eugenie led the way, their arms linked as they forged through the throngs of pedestrians. Every few minutes, one of them would glance back to give André a commentary on their progress and whatever sight it was they were passing. Each time they turned, they hoped to see that André had taken hold of Marie's arm—or at least brushing one another as they passed through narrow alleyways and stairways threading medieval arches. But to their disappointment, Zebedee had both his hands firmly clasped behind his back, doing his best to appear more interested in the finer points of Genevan architecture than in the pretty young woman beside him.

Eugenie had packed a cloth bag with pears bought from the market that morning, and as they bit into the fruit, they began to unpack all that had happened the past few weeks. They told André the story of their long wagon journey and the sights they had encountered along the way. They compared letters they had each received from Bauhin. As in his letter to Sebastian, Bauhin had excitedly told André of his appointment as personal physician to the sister of the French king. Together they speculated on what this might mean for Bauhin's spiritual journey, for surely, he was being drawn into the company of the Huguenots. But their friend hadn't elaborated any further. Instead, and more somberly, he reported that the conflict between the Catholics and Protestants in France continued to worsen, and whatever side you were on, you had to be exceptionally careful what you said and to whom. In his last letter to André, Bauhin had wondered if he and Sebastian hadn't made the wiser decision, and he confided that he wasn't sure how much longer he could remain in France if things continued to deteriorate. Did this mean that he was weighing up whether or not to come and join them in Switzerland? They tossed these questions between them, swinging back and forth between lament over all that was happening back in France and hope for all that may still lie ahead of them.

By now it was late in the afternoon. They decided André would come with them for dinner that evening; so from the Bour-de-Four they meandered their way homeward, making sure to pass near the college so that André could see where Sebastian spent his working days.

Once home, Eugenie and Marie joined Sonya in preparing a small feast. They kneaded flour, oil and lard together, which Sonya then rolled and shaped to encase two large pies. Sebastian and André slipped into the study, eager to speculate more about the religious and political upheaval spreading across Europe. Everywhere people were embracing new interpretations of the Christian faith but encountering brutal suppression from those who feared change. It seemed nobody in all of Europe was able to find a way of compromise or accommodation between the differing views and the differing factions.

Eventually their conversation brought them to a discussion of their own roles in this tumult. André described how he had begun to align himself more and more with the teachings of Ulrich Zwingli, the famous Reformer from the city of Bern. As André grew more animated, Sebastian felt a pang of envy for his friend's surety. It wasn't the same for him anymore. The idealism he'd started out with was proving hard to sustain. "Calvin's expectations of me—indeed, of everyone," he told his friend, "seem to grow both steeper and more rigid with each passing month. Perhaps I was naive, thinking that things would be easier than this. But I have committed myself to this challenge, and I must see it through."

For a moment, André seemed to waver, as if calculating whether to speak his mind or not. Then it seemed he'd reached a decision. He looked Sebastian full in the face and spoke. "Seb, this teaching of Calvin's on predestination—how can you justify it? It has always seemed to me that free will is one of the greatest gifts that God has bestowed on humanity. Surely to be human is to choose what path we take and how we treat one another. Isn't this what it means to be a moral being? Isn't this part of what it means to be created in the image of God? And concerning the Eucharist, have Calvin or Luther really moved beyond the superstitions of Catholicism, the host magically transforming into the flesh and blood of Christ? I find myself increasingly persuaded by Zwingli's rationalism, that the idea is a *memorial* of what Jesus did, rather than a magical *replaying* of it."

Disarmed by André's frankness, Sebastian decided he would share something else that had been gnawing away at him. Briefly, he outlined an anomaly he'd noticed in Geneva. It seemed to him that there were two tiers of ministers here: those who showed loyalty to Calvin, who were rewarded with appointments to the city churches with their greater numbers and higher income; and those whose loyalty was in question, who were always sent to work with poorer rural parishes.

André turned grave. "Seb, I keep wondering why you have been sent to minister in such a small and distant village, when you are in fact far more learned than any of the other ministers in Geneva. Is it because it is in your nature to ask hard questions?"

Sebastian sighed. André had just voiced the doubts he'd tried to bury. He cared little about the minutiae of church doctrine, much of which seemed unimportant compared to the struggles ordinary people faced, but he *did* care about anything that might diminish people's dignity or their experience of God's love. He knew André was right. He could no longer hold with Calvin's doctrine of double predestination, the cruel idea that God had created some people predestined to be damned and cast into hell. Initially, he had tried not to think about it, but that solution was growing untenable. For he now thought the idea abhorrent.

But he couldn't give in to despair. He had risked much to follow Calvin this far; the thought that he may have made a catastrophic error was unbearable. And so, he rallied himself and offered an explanation—as much for his own benefit as for André's. "Perhaps it is more like an apprenticeship, that as we prove ourselves competent in a small church, we are promoted to a larger one. It cannot be easy building a structure of governance that embraces a whole city—a rapidly growing city at that. John's workload is so great it would break a lesser man. I cannot imagine how he manages it. Perhaps I need to be more patient. Once the foundations are built and everyone knows where they stand, I expect he will allow us all greater freedom in which to move. And as for the Eucharist, why can't each person be free to enter into the mystery of Christ's death and resurrection according to their own conscience? So long as they partake worshipfully and with respect, why must every jot and tittle be so prescribed?"

André nodded. "Perhaps you are right. As you know, I am sometimes prone to analyzing things more than is necessary." He brightened. "And here we are, you and I, by God's grace, playing roles we long dreamed of! Instead of nitpicking, I should be rejoicing, shouldn't I?" André's sudden change of tone lifted Sebastian's mood too. He could feel himself breathing more easily.

The rich aroma of pastry being baked now filled the house, distracting them mightily. A little while later, Marie called them to the table. They dined first on a large, sumptuous pie filled with rabbit, gravy, carrots and parsnip, followed by a second pie of apple, honey and a sprinkling of cloves. Compared to their usual fare of vegetable pottage, this was an exotic treat and a fine way to celebrate the visit of their guest!

André needed to be back in Orbe in time for the Sabbath. Early that Saturday morning he called in for one final goodbye. Sebastian and Eugenie embraced him. Then followed the awkward dance with Marie before he finally mustered the courage to kiss her on each cheek. She let out a great sigh before rallying and smiling back at him. Flustered by his own ineptness, André retreated to his horse. He tightened the saddle strap before maneuvering out to the Rue Verdaine and on toward the township of Orbe.

Sebastian had settled into his roles at the church and the college, and though it was arduous, part of him thrived on the challenge. He was a gifted teacher with the heart of a pastor. He loved languages and reveled in seeing his students learn and grow. His sisters were settling in, too, and he'd helped his brother-in-law Pierre to find a teaching-assistant role at the college. He was grateful to have them all so close now.

Somehow, Sebastian found time to keep working on the Latin primer and the two Bible translations, but of the three, it was *Sacred Dialogues*—his textbook designed to help students master Latin—that was ready for publication first. Of course, no book or pamphlet containing any religious material could be printed in Geneva without Calvin's approval. When Sebastian presented it to him to review, he flicked through it disinterestedly and seemed surprised Sebastian had bothered him with it. After all, it contained nothing that could be construed as doctrinal. But after a moment's thought, Calvin recommended several reliable local printers who he patronized, wishing Sebastian good fortune with the results.

Within a week, Sebastian was at the printing house staring in wonder at the bales filled with copies of *Sacred Dialogues* ready to be shipped to the various schools Sebastian had made contact with. And, of course, a load was taken to the College de Rive, where Sebastian was eager to begin using it with his own students.

Over the next few months, the hunger of others to use his book astounded him. The text had been pressed into service by every institution he had sent it to, and they, in turn, had recommended it to schools farther afield. More and more copies were being ordered and printed all across Europe, from Britain to Spain. Encouraged by this unexpected success, Sebastian redoubled his work on a "peoples' Bible" in colloquial French, driven by Luther's vision of rendering the Scriptures readable for even the most ordinary of folk. Folk like the simple farming families he had grown up with in Saint Martin du Frêne and like those he now pastored in the village of Vanoeuvres.

A year passed since their arrival in Geneva. They would have forgotten this anniversary had not the ever-generous Ami Perrin arrived on their doorstep one evening after supper with a round of cheese and several bottles of fine wine in hand. Delighted, Sebastian invited him in. Ami uncorked a bottle of his favorite La Côte red, toasted his young friend's contribution to the college and the city, and thanked him for his service. Eugenie was not much for wine, and after a little polite conversation, took herself to bed. As the two men sat at the kitchen table and supped, Sebastian lifted the cup to his lips, his eyes shining. He had grown unaccustomed to praise or thanks, but tonight they were welcome visitors to his home.

Sometime deep into the second bottle, Perrin's merry mood grew dark. His brow creased and his face clouded over as he stared at the red liquid he gently swirled at the bottom of his cup. "Sebastian, do you mind if I share something with you?"

"Of course not, Ami. You may discuss anything you like with me."

Perrin, cautiously at first, but with increasing intensity, began to disclose what was troubling him. Something, he believed, was amiss in the city of Geneva—an air of malcontent growing thicker with each passing month. Over the past few years, he had witnessed this small municipality burgeon, its population swelling with successive waves of refugees from France, driven out by persecution and drawn by Calvin's writing and reputation. Hemmed in by the protective walls, houses were in short supply and the competition for places to live was creating conflict. Geneva's narrow streets were congested and growing squalid with human and equine waste. Tension was building between those, like Ami, who were able to trace their lineages here back generations and the French émigrés who were flooding in. Control of the ancient city now seemed to be at stake.

"If it were just a question of enough housing, we could perhaps tolerate it, Sebastian. But it is more than that. So many of these French arrivals come flaunting wealth. They use this wealth to purchase bourgeoise status as soon as they arrive. And you know what that means of course?"

Sebastian didn't proffer a reply. He was unsure where Ami was heading with this.

"With that money and status, they are entitled to vote, to choose who does or doesn't sit on the city's councils. This is not even a privilege every native Genevan holds. Those of us who have lived here for generations are disturbed by this. Many are angry. For we can see that control of the city is slipping out of Genevan hands and into French ones. The ministers Calvin appoints to lead the city's churches are Frenchmen too—Frenchmen who lord their superiority over the rest of us! They show us no respect! Sebastian, I tell you, the control of this city is being taken away from those who fought for her liberty and being given to the circle that John Calvin gathers around himself."

The atmosphere in the room, only a few minutes ago so light, had grown heavy. Suddenly, Sebastian wondered if Ami disapproved of him, too. For he was also a foreigner and close colleague of Calvin's. But Ami pressed on, apparently not holding Sebastian's recent arrival in Geneva against him.

"Sebastian, I would trust your opinion more than most men I have met. So may I ask you for your frank opinion?"

"I will do my best to answer you as honestly as I can."

"Then tell me: can we trust John Calvin?"

"Trust him? Whatever do you mean?"

"I mean can we trust that he has the best interests of Geneva at heart? Can we trust his leadership and the direction in which he is taking us?"

Sebastian thought long and hard about how he should reply. As far as he had seen, Calvin's morality was exemplary. He was an upright man who detested corruption. It was also true that both his temper and his tongue could be sharp, and he wasn't above ridiculing those who disagreed with him. But Sebastian was sure that Calvin was deeply committed to living by the teachings of the Bible, committed to placing the cause of God above his own desires.

"Over the past year, I have learned that John Calvin is not always an easy man to get along with. He sometimes tends toward inflexibility. But he is clearly a righteous, moral man, and so yes, Ami, I think you can trust him."

Perrin nodded with a small, sad kind of smile before draining the remainder of his cup. "I am still not completely sure of Master Calvin, but I am sure of you. If you say he is to be trusted, then I will gladly listen to that counsel." He placed his cup back on to the table, and rose unsteadily to his feet. "The hour is growing late, and I have bothered you for long enough. I thank you for your counsel, Sebastian. I'll bid you good night and let you attend to your family." He reached out his hand, and Sebastian shook it warmly.

"Thank you for these gifts, Ami. They are more than generous." He walked Perrin to the door. As the man exited, Sebastian added one last thought. "Ami, anytime you need to talk to someone about matters like these, I am happy to be your confidant."

Perrin nodded and turned away, his ample frame melting into the growing darkness of the Genevan night.

Chapter 9
Questions

C alvin possessed a genius for organization and stratagem. Like a chess master, he planned many moves ahead, seeing opportunities and traps long before his opponents did. The councils remained firmly in the hands of native Genevans, but Calvin was relentlessly building a system of governance to rival them. First, with the cooperation of Geneva's magistrates, he had called together a body called the consistory—a mix of ordained ministers, councillors and upstanding laypeople—to police the morality of Geneva's citizens. They met weekly to discuss cases of moral failure and had the power to summon individuals to give an account of themselves. Transgressors might be given a dressing down and have passages of Scripture read to them. They might be fined whatever was deemed an appropriate amount of money. They might be banned from taking communion. Or, more seriously, they could be refused entry to any of the city's churches. An excommunicant could not marry or participate in the city's business life. The only way back was for the penitent to kneel before the gathered church, confess their sin and ask for the congregation's mercy.

But some cases were so heinous, they could not be met with that kind of leniency. Murder, obviously. And adultery. The worst cases would be referred to the Little Council, where the magistrates preferred confessions. But if the accused proved evasive, torture had to be applied. Either the *estrapade* or the *grésillons* could be used. To employ the *estrapade*, the accused's hands were tied behind their back and attached to a rope strung from a rafter. The transgressor was hoisted aloft and abruptly dropped to just short of the floor. The pain was excruciating. Joints would dislocate. Confessions would follow. If that proved insufficient, the magistrates could turn to a second method. The *grésillon* was a rough iron grill placed on each side of the hands. Large screws holding the apparatus together were tightened until the agony became unbearable. The truth would always come out. If the council found the resulting story—such as one of sexual sin or religious deviance—particularly appalling, imprisonment or execution would follow.

The ability of the consistory to monitor each Genevan's life was amplified by biannual visits to every citizen's home. Ostensibly, these were pastoral visits, but they doubled as inquiries into what form of doctrine the householder held to, what type of prayers they prayed, and what form of moral laxity may have crept into their behavior. Over time, more and more officers were appointed and given greater license to roam the city's streets watching, listening and reporting back on what they saw.

The second body Calvin formed was the Company of Pastors, made up of all the city's urban ministers and those rural ministers that could make the weekly journey. Their role was to oversee the doctrine and behavior of the churches and their leaders, ensuring that each remained pure. On Fridays, they would come together under Calvin's leadership to be instructed in godliness.

At first, there seemed to be an equilibrium between these groups and the councils, each acting as a check and balance on the other. But it was obvious to Sebastian that the Company of Pastors was in thrall to Calvin. It was made up of those who preferred conformity and those cowed into submission. And of course, each minister depended on the great man's largesse for their job security.

There were exceptions however. One was country pastor and Swiss native Henri de la Mere. From the start, there was bad blood between de la Mere and Calvin.

The other exception was, of course, Sebastian himself, though it took eighteen months till this became obvious within the Company of Pastors. As he always did, Calvin opened the meeting by expositing a passage of Scripture, in this case from the book of Romans, chapter nine. Starting with the story in which Jacob steals older brother Esau's birth right, Calvin began to preach on the doctrine of predestination to which he was so fiercely committed.

"God is so completely sovereign, his will so completely irresistible, that what a man hopes for, works for, desires or chooses is completely irrelevant as regards their eternal destiny. God, from before creation, predestines some, the elect, to eternal salvation, and all others, the lost, to eternal damnation."

Sebastian shifted uncomfortably. He'd grown more and more diffident about this doctrine. The idea that God dictates every detail of every event—good or bad, propitious or evil—as if with a hand of iron and heart of stone, this he found disturbing. It seemed contrary to the character of a loving God, and contrary to the idea of justice. But despite his misgivings, this wasn't a dogma he was willing to go into battle with Calvin over. Not yet anyway. After all, philosophers and theologians had been arguing about this for centuries without any resolution.

Henri de la Mere had not reached the same irenic conclusion. At the end of Calvin's careful Bible exposition, there was time set aside for questions. De la Mere's hand slowly rose. Calvin sighed and asked him to explain his inquiry.

"Master Calvin, you say that our own choices play no role in our destiny or salvation. Can you explain, then, why it says in the book of Joshua, 'If it seems too hard for you to serve the Lord, choose you this day whom you will serve; whether the gods your fathers served or the gods of the Amorites. But as for me and my house, we will serve the Lord.' And why does it say in the book of Deuteronomy, 'See, I have set before you this day life and death, good and evil. Therefore, choose life, that both you and your children may live'? Do not these passages say we must make a choice—to choose good over evil? And does not choice imply free will or moral agency?"

Calvin's eyes narrowed as he stared fixedly at de la Mere. When he replied, it was slowly, deliberately, as one might speak when giving instructions to a simpleton.

"To the unlearned, or to those who do not know the Scriptures deeply, or who have never studied them in their original languages—to those whose grasp of God's Word is childlike—what you advocate could appear so. We can vainly fool ourselves into thinking we are the masters of our own fate when it is God, and God alone, who decides all things. But it is only our tiny, limited perspective that creates this illusion. What are we but mere lumps of clay in His hands? God, and God alone, sees all things, knows all things, decides all things."

Sebastian thought to himself, *I see why people say John is a master of debate; he has replied astutely.* He found himself hoping that de la Mere would choose caution over valor now. But no, either bravely or foolishly, he came back at Calvin once more. "But Master Calvin, surely being created in the image of God means we have been given the ability to make moral choices, to discern between good and evil, doesn't it?"

Calvin's face darkened and his jawline firmed. His words emerged sharp as razors. "Since the fall of Adam, every inclination of man's heart is toward sin and evil, as the Scriptures so clearly teach, de la Mere! You have neither the learning nor the wit to be challenging my reading of Scripture. And not mine alone, mind you, but that of Saint Augustine and all the church fathers before him."

Sebastian's brow furrowed. He knew this last point to be debatable. His mind went back to his study of the church fathers. *There are several among them who argue the case for free will, such as Eusebius and Cassian, and many of the Eastern Fathers, as Calvin surely knows.*

Clearly annoyed, Calvin pressed on, his voice rising several octaves. "When you have learned the basics of Hebrew and of Greek, then perhaps you will be ready to hold this debate with me. And then perhaps you will be fit to preach real sermons to your flock instead of feeble homilies!"

Sebastian was shaken, for he hadn't seen Calvin quite this angry before. He looked around the room. Every minister either had their eyes cast down or were staring straight ahead, as if they—not just de la Mere—had been reprimanded. Sebastian then noticed Calvin surveying the room, taking careful note of the effect his rebuke had had on each of the ministers.

"All of you, heed this warning!" he began again. "God's sovereign will is beyond human reasoning. To set our pathetic minds to the task of unraveling such mysteries can only lead us onto dangerous ground, into shifting sand. As Jeremiah says, the human heart is deceitful and depraved. Turn away from such arrogant questioning and instead be diligent to study the Scriptures, to memorize correct doctrine, and to avoid childish and destructive arguments like the one we have had the misfortune of witnessing this morning." Calvin's breathing slowed and his face softened. He now had full control of himself and, once more, of the room. "This meeting is concluded. May God give us all the wisdom to understand his Word and the humility to submit ourselves to it. Amen. You are all dismissed. Go in God's peace."

A murmur of echoed amens went around the room. Sebastian looked back at de la Mere. He looked defiant but wisely had chosen to hold his tongue. As the ministers filed out of the room, it was not peace but a deep sense of unease that filled Sebastian. He wondered about the other ministers. If they had been disinclined to challenge John Calvin before, they would be even more so now. He made a mental note to talk with Henri de la Mere when he got the chance— in a place safely away from Calvin's gaze.

Chapter 10
Things Fall Apart

The following Saturday dawned overcast and cool, dark clouds drifting over the peaks to the west of the city. The Bise—the cold northeast wind that sweeps across the surface of Lake Genève—was growing harsher as the day wore on. Sebastian would have been happy to stay home reading, keeping the kitchen fire well stoked, but he had made up his mind that he should go and visit Henri de la Mere and find out what was behind that confrontation he had witnessed at the meeting of the pastors.

Sebastian left through the Porte de Rive gate, riding astride a bay gelding named Arion from the college stables. It was his favorite horse, due to its gentle and trustworthy temperament. Sebastian wrapped his cape about him and settled into an easy cadence. At this pace, they would reach the village of Foncenex in a couple of hours. He kept a wary eye on the road ahead and on the fields each side of him. As a lone rider, he would never travel this path after dark. Stories abounded of ruthless banditry—all the worse if the thieves detected an accent and assumed their victim to be a wealthy French émigré. As he looked to the foothills on his right, he could see a fresh dusting of snow that had fallen overnight.

Soon enough, a roadside marker appeared telling him he was

about to enter Foncenex, a tiny hamlet serving the small farms surrounding it. Little cottages built of stone and mortar dotted the landscape, dirt tracks winding between them. The noise of his approach set one of the local dogs barking, an alarm soon picked up by other canine sentinels. He had passed several larger cottages on the track that served as the hamlet's main road when he finally saw his first inhabitant, a householder who had been roused to action by the noise of his dog. The man was thin and wore the dirt-stained garb of a struggling peasant farmer. Sebastian reined his horse to a stop and called to the man.

"Excuse me, sir, can you tell me where I'll find Foncenex's church and its manse?"

The man waved a bony hand toward a track leading off to the right, running down a gap between his cottage and his neighbor's. "Couple more minutes and you're there. Just look for the pile of stones."

Sebastian nodded his thanks and nursed his mount down the path. The horse slowed, stepping around large potholes filled with turbid water. As promised, a heap of rocks soon came into view. Just beyond that, a church. Or at least, what used to be a church. One of its walls had collapsed, taking a corner of the slated roof with it. Sebastian dismounted, found a tree and tied his horse to it. He peered into the small chapel exposed by the fallen wall. The elements had begun to ravage everything on one side of the building.

From around the corner of the fallen building, he could hear the sound of children playing. He turned and moved in their direction. A short walk away was a stone cottage, like the others in Foncenex, and, like the church, in poor condition. Outside stood two large apple trees. In one of these, two children perched in the limbs talking excitedly. As he approached, they waved, smiling broadly. He returned their greeting and asked, "I am looking for the home of Pastor Henri de la Mere. Am I in the right place?"

The oldest of the two children, a boy he guessed to be about ten, slipped down out of the tree and ran toward the house. "Papa, you have a visitor."

The other child, a girl two or three years younger, began her descent from a spot several branches higher. Sebastian watched her for a few seconds before asking, "Mademoiselle, may I assist you?" He stretched his hands toward her.

The child, a tiny fair-headed thing, smiled shyly and jumped into his arms. He swung her to the ground with an exaggerated grunt. "Oh, so heavy. Have you been eating those rocks from the church?"

With a giggle, the girl sprinted off after the boy, who Sebastian guessed was her brother. He followed in the direction the children had run. As he did so, he was confronted with another pile of rubble. Beside that was a boxed-off area where someone had been mixing plaster. As he noted this, a tall, thin man emerged from the broken house, a surprised smile stretching across his face.

"Sebastian Castellio! Gracious God in heaven, to what do I owe the honor that the rector of the College de Rive should visit a humble country pastor such as myself?"

"Ah, so you forget that I am also a country pastor serving the good people of Vandoeuvres?"

"So you are. Though I do hope your parish is in a better state of repair than my own." As he said this, a woman, thin like De la Mere but a full head shorter, emerged from the cottage and stood at his side. On her hip she carried another child, a little girl aged perhaps four or five. "Helene, this is the esteemed Sebastian Castellio, head of the college in Geneva. No doubt you have heard me speak of him."

Helene nodded. "Please come and join us at our table. I baked some bread fresh this morning."

They stepped inside and found stools upon which to sit. Helene sent the boy off to fetch milk from a neighbor. Sebastian guessed that, like most small villages, this one probably supported their minister with food more than with coins.

De la Mere waved his hand toward the wall. "As you can see,

things are not exactly in prime condition here. But at least we have scraped together enough to repair most of the manse."

Sebastian noticed fresh mortar holding a section of wall in place. Only a small gap remained around the timbers of the doorframe. Beside it, resting against the wall, was an old door waiting to be hinged back into place.

"Both the house and the chapel were in terrible condition when we first came here, but we have been making progress."

Sebastian was burning with questions about the dilapidation, but he wanted to start with the questions that had brought him there. "Henri, since joining the Company of Pastors I have been impressed with your courage in standing up for what you believe in and for your honesty in expressing it. Many things are happening now in Geneva that I don't understand. Your history here is much longer than mine, and I am hoping that you'll be able to help me better understand."

'Certainly, Sebastian. If I can tell you anything that is truthful and helpful, I will tell you."

"Thank you. Now, where to start?" He paused a moment before diving into the topic. "Last week at the pastors' meeting we had quite the disputation, didn't we? Yet from the start, I could see there was more going on than met the eye. It is clear to me that there is something between you and John Calvin that I am not privy to. Would you be willing to help me understand what it is?"

De la Mere regarded him carefully. "Are you sure you want to know? Your heart will rest easier if you allow me to carry this alone and will be more troubled if I share it with you."

"Since coming to Geneva, I have grown confused about many things I used to feel sure of. It's as if there are things concealed in shadows. So yes, I do want to know the truth of this matter."

De la Mere's face creased with a grimace. "This is a long and not-very-pretty story. Even prior to Calvin and Farel's expulsion from Geneva in '38, we crossed swords over the doctrine of predestination. But the final breach came when he was expelled and issued a call to all who supported him to follow him into exile. I declined, believing my first loyalty was to stay and pastor the flock the Lord had given me in Geneva. How could I abandon the people God had called me to care for, when they were struggling and so new to this faith? But in John Calvin's eyes, that represented a betrayal. Yet it was I who penned the ministers' letter begging Calvin to return to Geneva and lead the churches again. I had hoped that this would show my good faith and redeem our relationship. But when he returned to the city in '41, one of his first acts was to have me moved from my city parish and posted to this one in the village of Foncenex. I arrived to find the church and manse far worse than you see them now, essentially in a state of total collapse. This village is small and poor; they do not have the funds to repair a church."

"Or a manse. Or to pay a pastor," Helene added sadly. "We are barely surviving. But Henri refuses to leave these people without a pastor."

Sebastian was shocked. This sounded to him like pure vindictiveness. He could not believe any Christian, and certainly not John Calvin, would do this. "Have you appealed to the council for help? For funds to repair these buildings and to support your income?"

"Only every quarter for the last three years." He lowered his voice and looked around, as if he was afraid he might be overheard. "And indeed, some money has been granted, but it must pass through the hands of Foncenex's lord, Pierre Somareta. And let's just say Monsieur Somareta has sticky hands. Very sticky hands."

Sebastian groaned, his mind reeling. "And does the council know of this corruption? Does Calvin?"

"If they cared to know, they would know. After all, the evidence is all around us!" He waved his hand expansively around the room. "Somareta may be corrupt, but he knows his theology. And he knows which side his bread is buttered on. He is a fierce supporter of Calvin, praising him at every opportunity, and a furious opponent of both the Catholics and the Anabaptists, the two traits Calvin admires most in a man. He refuses to believe that Somareta is at fault and blames me for squandering the resources the council granted."

Sebastian sat in silence. This situation was much worse than he had imagined, and the implications it cast on Calvin's judgment, indeed on Calvin's character, were dark ones. There had been so many warning signs, yet he had ignored them all, unwilling to abandon the glorious vision of the reborn society that they had talked of back in Strasbourg. He tried to think of words of comfort or encouragement he could give to Henri, to Helene, to their children, but he could think of none. He wanted to at least say, "I will pray for you," but it sounded trite even as the words formed in his mind. Finally, as he readied himself to leave, he pulled his purse from his belt and placed it on the table.

"I am sorry it is so little. I didn't come prepared. But I promise you that as I have the opportunity, I will speak on your behalf in the Company of Pastors."

De la Mere's eyes widened, and he leaned closer. "No! You must not. Did you not see what he did to me at the last meeting? Have you not heard all I have just described? John Calvin is a man who sees any questioning of his authority as an act of betrayal, any challenge to his theology as an act of heresy. You underestimate the danger. If Calvin turns on you, do not imagine that your position at the college will save you, or that the other ministers will rally around you. John has such a clear vision of what the church should become ... of what Geneva should become. If a man gets in the way of that vision, he must be removed. And once he sees you as an obstacle or an enemy, there is no forgiveness and no returning to things as they were before."

His words chilled Sebastian, even as he struggled to believe them. How could all this be true of the man who had helped him to learn so much, who parsed Scripture so expertly, who wrote and spoke so movingly about the mercy of God?

De la Mere stared at the purse on the table. It was clear he was weighing up whether he should accept it or not. Perhaps sensing this, Helene reached across the table and picked it up. "My husband is right; you must be careful. If you speak out on our behalf, we will

gain nothing and you and your family will lose much. But for this"—
she held up the purse—"we thank you. Your kindness has blessed us
greatly."

Just then, their son arrived back with a jug of fresh milk, which
he carried to the table with tremendous concentration, not daring to
spill a drop. As he did so, Sebastian stood.

"I thank you for your hospitality, but I cannot stay. There are
those back in town I promised I would spend time with this afternoon. I should be going now." *And I have no desire to take what
little food you have from your children's mouths,* he thought to
himself.

De la Mere stood, too, and reached out to shake his hand. "I have
some more repairs to make before rain returns."

Sebastian winced, feeling foolish for not having offered to help.
"Ah! Laying stone! That is one thing I know how to do. Let me stay
and assist you, Henri."

"No, I have plaster enough for only one hour's work, and a
neighbor has promised to come help, as will my boy here. We will cut
this work out quickly. But with the money you have given, I will be
able to buy more plaster, and by this time tomorrow, I hope we will
have finished. People await you in town. You should get back to them.
And, my friend, perhaps it would not be good for people to see you
assisting me too openly."

Those words flooded his head with more questions and his heart
with a determination to support de la Mere even more. "I promise to
come and see you again soon. And I'd like to bring Eugenie with me.
She bakes wonderfully, and I know she would love to meet Helene
and bring some treats for your children."

De la Mere thought about this and then smiled. "Of course. We
would be delighted to see you again, Sebastian."

Sebastian walked back to his horse, moved by the graciousness
and courage of this couple. As he mounted and began to ride, the two
children ran with him as far as the village's main road and then
waved him off. His journey back to Geneva was filled with thoughts

that alternated between admiration for the de la Meres' fortitude and despair over Calvin's and the consistory's actions.

While fields and farmland flew past him on each side, Sebastian's mind replayed the conversation with de la Mere over and over again. Was de la Mere exaggerating how badly Calvin had treated him? But the evidence of the ruined church and manse seemed to testify against that. And besides, he had witnessed firsthand how Calvin treated de la Mere at the last pastors' meeting.

By the time he returned to his house, drizzle had thickened to rain. Entering his home, he shook the excess water from his cloak and hat before hanging them on a hook near the fireplace.

Eugenie and Marie were preparing a meal of pottage and sheep's tongue. As they worked, Eugenie gently probed him with questions about his morning visit to Foncenex. As calmly as he could, he relayed the story of Henri and Helene's destitution and how they'd come to be assigned to the church in that little village. With each detail he shared, Eugenie and Marie's faces clouded with consternation. When Sebastian's voice finally tapered off, the room was filled with a brooding silence.

The next day, Sunday, dawned under a cool milk-gray sky. Sebastian was riding toward Vandoeuvres to minister to the little flock there, while Eugenie and Marie had decided they would accompany Charles and Sonya to the nearby St. Pierre's. In truth, despite the danger from bandits, Sebastian enjoyed riding to Vandoeuvres. It was a chance to leave the claustrophobia of Geneva and to clear his mind. Riding through farmland, between groves of pine and spruce, gave him a sense of space. In that clean air, he could think through the homily he would deliver.

When he returned home that afternoon, he found everyone around the kitchen table. As he hung his cloak on the hook, he realized Eugenie's eyes seemed far more somber than usual.

"Is something wrong?"

Genie sighed. "This morning John preached about sin, about how we are all debauched by it—every man, woman and child. It seems we hear that every Sunday now, but today ... today he pointed his finger at some of those sitting in church, naming their sins, telling them they needed to repent. It was humiliating for them; they were in tears. It was awful."

Sebastian took a seat, and the five of them stared at one another, trying to think of something encouraging to say. Suddenly, Sonya let out a loud, "Oh!" She stood and stepped to where the dry goods sat on a shelf, then returned to the table with a letter which she sheepishly handed to Sebastian.

"This came for you yesterday, while you were out. I meant to give it to you as soon as you returned, but I forgot."

Sebastian took the letter and turned it over. "It is from my friend Jean Bauhin in France. Remember, I told you about him? The doctor? The physician to the king of France's sister, Queen Marguerite of Navarre?" Excitedly, he slipped his thumbnail under the seal. Once he pulled out the paper, he eyes devoured the words.

He summarized as he read. "He writes what a joy it has been to be in her employ, that she is a lady of letters and great intelligence, always seeking peace. But the overall situation in France grows worse. The Catholics and Protestants are at each other's throats. The persecution of those who have declared themselves Protestant grows harsher with each passing day—to the point that even Marguerite's protection may not be enough. And so ... he plans on departing France and thinks he will head to the Swiss cities—to Basel! His contacts tell him he will find much greater freedom and safety."

When he looked up from the letter, all eyes were on him. The significance of this information was not lost on anyone. If things in Geneva continued to deteriorate, they too might find themselves looking for a city to flee to.

After the others had filed to bed that night, Sebastian and

Eugenie lingered at the table, giving voice to those questions, wondering if they had a future in Geneva after all.

By Monday morning, gray rain had settled over the city like a thick blanket. As Sebastian made his way to the college, the weight that settled on him felt more than meteorological. There was a sense of dark spiritual heaviness to it as well. He sensed that a choice lay ahead of him: to submit to Calvin out of fear, or to boldly dispute with him. But refusal to submit could only have one consequence. It would turn him into an obstacle and, therefore, an enemy of the great John Calvin. He walked on, pulling his cape tighter about him, bracing against the cold, yet he could not prevent a shiver from snaking its way across his shoulders.

The rest of that week proceeded uneventfully. Several times, he and Calvin ran into each other around the college, and each time the encounter was stiffly formal, with nods of acknowledgment but nothing more. Had Calvin heard of his visit to de la Mere? Surely someone would have informed him by now.

He hated this feeling of ambiguity, this sense of waiting helplessly for something to happen. And so, he threw himself even more zealously into completing his French New Testament, for in this he found both purpose and solace. Everything else around him seemed to be falling apart, to be moving in the opposite direction to the promise of that first intoxicating energy Luther had unleashed. But with his Bible project, he knew he was immersing himself in something wholly good. With a few more weeks of work, he believed he could have the whole of the New Testament translated.

If Sebastian had been working at a furious pace before, he did so twice as much now. The cultivation of his students' minds drove him during the day and his vision of God's Word being translated into language both simple and captivating drove him by night. He longed to produce a version that sang and danced with idioms and word pictures, one that would capture the imagination of all—rich or poor, educated or not. He drew on all his experience as a master of classical literature, on all his talent as an educationalist, and poured it out on to the paper before him.

One evening near the end of that month, as Eugenie was preparing for bed, he burst out of his study and into their bedroom. She had her back to him, brushing out her hair. In the room's candle light it shone as though threads of gold were woven through the black. It tumbled down over the smooth olive skin of her shoulders, over the laundered white of her linen nightgown, falling halfway down her back. From behind, he picked her up by the waist and swung her around. A small gasp escaped her lips.

"Oh! Has my husband returned to me after all these weeks spent with his mistress pen?"

'Yes, he has. Eugenie, I've done it. The French New Testament is complete! Of course, there will be editing and proofreading, but the bulk of it is done, and on my desk lies a manuscript almost ready for print."

Over the past few weeks, Sebastian knew he had neglected Eugenie as he had labored over this work. But as they clung to each other now, sweet joy coursed between them. She let out a delighted squeal, laughing as he swung her around, even as her eyes filled with tears.

"Well done. You have worked so hard and so long on this, but what a great work God has wrought through your hand. Husband, I am so proud of you!" She pulled him closer, their lips gently brushing before locking together more passionately, sending little waves of anticipation through their bodies. They fell together onto the curtained bed, more than ready to make up for the weeks of intimacy they had forgone.

Later, as they lay side by side, whispering of their love for one another, Eugenie took his hand and guided it down to the base of her belly. "Do you feel anything, my love?"

Sebastian chuckled. "Oh, yes. Many things." He wrapped both

arms around her, pulling her close, as he began reciting from the sumptuous Song of Solomon, that poem of erotic love sandwiched between the jaded cynicism of Ecclesiastes and the tender prophesies of Isaiah.

> *O prince's daughter!*
> *The curves of your thighs are like jewels,*
> *Worked by the hands of a skilled artist.*
> *Your navel is a rounded goblet*
> *Filled with spiced wine.*
> *Your waist is heaped wheat*
> *Set above lilies;*
> *Your breasts are like two fawns,*
> *Twins of a gazelle;*
> *Your neck is—*

Eugenie giggled and took hold of his hand, moving it back to her belly. "I am so flattered that you would compare my waist to a heap of wheat, but be still. Do you feel anything?"

"What do you mean?"

She sighed. "Men! Seb, there is new life growing in me, and I can feel it."

He sat bolt upright and stared at her. "Is this true? Are you sure?"

"Yes. Two months have passed with no issue of blood, and my belly grows rounder—more and more like a heap of wheat every day. Perhaps you have noticed that I struggle to eat in the mornings?"

His face blazed. To his shame, he had been so preoccupied that he hadn't noticed.

"I've talked with Sonya, and she confirms that these signs all point to a baby. While you have been pregnant with your French Bible, our first child has been woven together in my womb!"

"Oh Genie, beautiful Genie, you are magnificent!" I would never compare my bits of paper and ink with the masterpiece you now carry." He sank down and buried his face in the crook of her neck, pulling the rest of her body tight against his. "After all this time, I had feared we might never have the joy of this moment."

It was true. They had been married three years and had not held back from acts of intimacy. Both of them adored children and longed to see their family enlarged. And yet God had not seen fit to bless them with child. Until now.

They slept little that night, chatting excitedly about the baby, whether it would be a boy or girl and what name they would choose. The next day, they arose still elated.

When Eugenie broke the news to Marie, she shared in her ecstasy, throwing back her head in laughter and declaring that she would be the world's greatest aunt to this coming child.

After church at Vandoeuvres at the end of that week, Sebastian spent the afternoon and evening putting the finishing touches on the thick manuscript. He did a final check that all the pages were accounted for and in order, then he squared them off. Through the left-side margin he made three holes with an awl, then threaded a leather string through them to hold the manuscript together. Of course, nothing could be published without Calvin's permission, so tomorrow morning Sebastian would see Calvin and lay this precious gift before him.

His sleep that night was disturbed by a vivid and inexplicable dream: Armies clashing, slashing at one another with swords; smoke and canons and flowing blood. Men burning, tied to poles, screaming in torment—

Sebastian sat up with a start, coated with a sheen of sweat, his heart beating like the footfalls of a man pursued. The vision had shocked him from sleep to wakefulness. As his eyes adjusted from the world of dreams to the monochrome reality of his bedroom, he could see through the window the first fingers of dawn tracing a pale line along the length of the eastern horizon. He forced himself to lie back down so he wouldn't wake Eugenie. He calmed his breathing, remembering that he had on his desk the treasure of a great project, a labor of love, a book that proclaimed a day when there would be no more death or war or hatred. With this thought, his body began to relax, his breathing eased, his heart began to slow.

Chapter 11
The Testament

Sebastian had finished his morning classes and by noon, he knew Calvin would have finished his second lecture for the day. Nervously, he again squared off the bundle that comprised his manuscript and then wrapped it in a cloth. The trip from his office to Calvin's was only a few yards, but today it seemed like a hundred miles.

He knocked, and back came the sound of Calvin's voice inviting him to enter. He did so. Calvin looked up, his quill poised mid-stroke over a document.

A polite smile flickered across Calvin's face. With elaborate courtesy, he gestured to a chair and asked Sebastian how he might be of assistance. Sebastian felt himself relax. Clearly Calvin was in a good mood. His night terrors were no prophecy. But even so, he decided the best way to conquer his fears would be to go straight to the point.

"I have good news to share with you, John. Great news in fact! There is a project I have been working on ever since our time in Strasbourg, but one I have mentioned to few people, as I have often feared I might never complete it. But now I have finished a significant part of it, and I want your eyes to be the first to see it."

With that he placed the manuscript, wrapped in the protective cloth, on Calvin's desk. Calvin's eyebrows arched up almost to his hairline. Clearly, he was intrigued. "Another book? A follow-up to your most successful *Sacred Dialogues* perhaps?"

"No. Far more important than that. Something that I hope will advance the cause of God's kingdom far beyond that which can be accomplished by a Latin textbook. These past five years, I have been translating Jerome's Vulgate into colloquial French, and here before you is a French New Testament, the Scriptures written for the people of the land." Despite himself, he smiled as these words left his mouth, the words "a French New Testament" filling him with pride and wonder.

Calvin flinched as if he'd been struck. His eyes narrowed, focusing on the package in front of him. Sebastian could see he was struggling with some thought. When he lifted his face from the parcel back to Sebastian, his expression had turned stern.

"You know, of course, that no religious work is to be published—or written—in Geneva without my knowledge and approval." His words came in sharp little bursts.

Sebastian's eyebrows rose. "The final authority for that belongs to the Little Council, surely."

"In matters of religious literature, they defer to me. As they should."

"Which is why I present this to you today for your perusal and approval."

Calvin's voice came back slightly louder this time. "But why have you hidden this from me until now? Why have you done this behind my back?"

"It is not like that. As this was not specific to my role here at the college, I did not see the need to bother you until it was finished."

"I will say it to you a second time: I am the man that God has appointed to lead this city, and all religious writing and publication must go through me and me alone."

"John, you make it sound like an unlawful or sinful thing that I have done. Is not our common cause to place the Scriptures in the hands of all people so that they may read its message for themselves?"

"Yes, yes, yes." His voice had an impatient air now. "But we must be careful—careful to the utmost degree possible—that any translation or interpretation of Scripture is both accurate and orthodox, free of theological innovation lest people be led astray. Any hint, any possibility of error—anything that could even lead toward error —*must* be rooted out. I have made an oath to the printers of Geneva that I will allow no work to be placed before them without having vetted it myself. They are, of course, terrified of being led into heresy, and I have promised to protect them from that danger and its eternal consequences. You should have submitted this to me long before now so that I could protect you from error too."

A sense of shame rose up from Sebastian's midriff and made his face flush. Did Calvin think this little of him as a scholar? As a brother? How had their conversation moved in this direction?

Calvin unwrapped the cloth and flicked through a few pages of the manuscript. He stopped and began reading more intently, making occasional clicking noises with his tongue. After a while, he pulled a fresh piece of paper from a drawer in his desk and began to make notes as he read. Sebastian looked on in anguish.

After perhaps ten minutes, Calvin stared back across the desk at Sebastian. He sighed loudly. "In my brief reading of your manuscript, I have already noted numerous problems that will have to be rectified. Leave this work with me and return when I call for you so we may discuss the many changes you will be obliged to make."

Sebastian considered his mentor's words before answering. "Having heard your opinion, I would like to take it back and work on it more carefully. And then would you be willing to set aside times that I may come and read it to you? As I read, I can explain not just the words, but my intent behind using each word. You could offer your suggestions as I do so."

An indignant look crossed Calvin's face. "Have you no understanding of how much preoccupies me day and night? If you want my counsel, you need to leave this manuscript with me. As I find the time, I will correct it. And you must agree to give me full control over those corrections. From what I've seen, I will need to rewrite whole passages for you." He re-opened the drawer in his desk and slid the manuscript into it.

Sebastian stared at the edge of the desk that had just swallowed his manuscript. It was as if a part of himself had just been amputated. For five years, he had labored, pouring his heart into this work, always believing that Calvin would receive it with joy. His mind swarmed with a thousand thoughts but not a single coherent word. All he wanted to do was leave, to get away. Wordlessly, he pushed himself to his feet and exited the office. He paused at the door to his own study but could not go in. He needed to get outside, out to where the air was fresh and God's light was unadulterated.

On the grounds of the college, students strolled and mingled in groups. As he passed, they nodded respectfully and smiled. Normally, he would have stopped to offer a word of greeting or encouragement, but not today. He walked quickly out on to the bustling Poissonerie Rive and then along Rue Longemalle, toward the lake, and from there eastward along the foreshore. The midday sky above him had cleared, and a cool, wintery sun hung high at his back. With each step, his shoes crunched deep into the pebbled Genève shore. Looking left toward Molard and the market street, throngs of people walked the shoreline. Beyond them stood the western frontier of the city wall, the crescent shaped barricade that hemmed Geneva against the lake. But here, near the eastern border of the city, he was mercifully alone. The lake stretched before him in a vast arc, glassy and still, reflecting the cloudless blue vault above.

Scouring the beach in front of him, he crouched and found a flat, rounded pebble streaked with soft purples and whites. Nestling it between his thumb and forefinger, he pulled his arm back then slung it out low and hard across the lake. It hit the water perfectly, glanced off its surface, then landed and skipped again. Once, twice, six more times, curving gently off to the right before disappearing. With each landing, tiny circles rippled outward, catching the winter sun in brief starry rings. He marveled at the artistry the simple act of throwing a stone could produce. Then a deeper thought struck him. *Perhaps I, too, am like that stone—small and simple. Though my words now fall on deaf ears, sinking and unheard, only God can know what ripples they will create and how long they will flow outward.*

He recalled how, when he was much younger, he had read Bonaventure's biography of Francis of Assisi, back in an age when it was laudable to study the lives of the saints, before he had progressed to more scholastic works. He had been young and impressionable, and the stories of Saint Francis had moved him greatly. Perhaps no one in Christian history had revered the God revealed in creation as lovingly as that man from Assisi. For Francis, everything he found in nature was a rung on the ladder of worship that ultimately led to the Creator. The beauty that surrounded him in his Umbrian countryside was simply a reflection, a light cast from the source of all beauty, the living God.

Francis immersed himself in nature, embracing it so fully that his soul seemed to expand beyond the edges of his own being, reaching out in communion to all else that existed. Francis came to believe that all things in creation were interconnected and in relationship with one another—brother sun and sister moon, brother air and sister water, Father God and Mother Earth. Thus, to harm one thing was to harm all things. Even these pebbles under Sebastian's feet—Francis would have felt some sort of kinship with them. He smiled at that thought as he selected another smooth stone and sent it skipping across the lake in a trail of glinting sparks, like a meteor splitting the sky.

Looking around, he found a grassy knoll a few steps away. He sat and watched and listened. High above him, the cry of a lone gull cut through the air and echoed off the lake. Further to his right, its wings spread wide, a stork glided down to the shore. He allowed the grace and harmony of creation to fill him once more. Slowly things began to come back into perspective. Calvin was just one man and Geneva just one city. He still believed that the love that flowed from the Creator of the universe was bigger than both of them. He mustn't allow anger or despair to consume him. There were other cities with greater freedoms where, one day, he would be able to print his New Testament, and perhaps be able to speak and write with freedom. He resolved that regardless of how he was treated, he would do his best to follow Jesus's example of forgiveness and love. As his head cleared, his thoughts turned to de la Mere and his family. It had been more than two weeks since he'd visited them in Foncenex.

He rose and strode back toward the college, filled with renewed conviction. The following Saturday, he and Eugenie would ride out and visit de la Mere's family with as large a basket of goods as they could buy or bake. Once there, he would find out if Henri could shed any more light on Calvin's reaction to his Bible translation.

At the end of the week, Eugenie had prepared the promised basket of pastries. As she packed them, Sebastian looked at her swollen belly wistfully. "Perhaps I should ride alone and you stay here. It's a rough road."

"Don't be ridiculous, Seb. We'll take our time. I'll be fine. I want to meet this couple you have told me about. I want to understand their story too."

The journey certainly took longer with Sebastian riding at half-pace. But when he saw how tenderly Eugenie spoke with Helene and the children, he was glad she'd come.

Around the de la Meres' table, they admired the repairs Henri had made as they ate Eugenie's baking and washed it down with milk provided by a neighbor. The de la Mere children made approving noises as they savored the treats. "I wish we could have brought you more," Eugenie said. "We were hoping that by now Sebastian's salary would have increased—"

"But it hasn't." De la Mere finished the sentence for Eugenie. "It hasn't because Sebastian is no longer a favorite. Calvin's salary from the council is five hundred gold florins a year along with gifts of fur, food, and wine. It is an income higher than most of the city's councillors receive and vastly more than rural ministers like me will ever see."

Sebastian noted the tone of bitterness in de la Mere's voice. Would he grow bitter too? As they talked, Sebastian recounted the showdown he and Calvin had a few days earlier that resulted in Calvin's crushing reaction to his Bible.

De la Mere listened intently then shook his head. "What you are trying to accomplish is a great thing, Sebastian. And perhaps if you lived in a German city, under the patronage of Luther, it would be hailed for what it is. But —and I shudder to say these words to you—I doubt if Calvin will ever allow your French Bible to be published."

"But why? I don't understand. Even if we differ in certain opinions, surely my work advances the cause we both believe in."

"There is another factor at play of which you are unaware. Calvin's cousin Pierre Olivétan published a French Bible in 1535, which, until now, has remained obscure. But before Olivétan died, Calvin promised his cousin that he would print another edition and write the foreword for it. It is to be a kind of memorial to his cousin. Given this, he will not allow yours to be published first."

Sebastian's shoulders slumped and a feeling of futility threatened to overwhelm him. "So there has been no point in him even taking away the manuscript to proof. It's all a ruse."

De la Mere gave a wry smile. "I'm sure John will find much to say about it, much to criticize, and much for you to rewrite."

"So be it. It is now clear to me that it will never be published here in Geneva, no matter what I do. But why has he grown bitter toward us both, Henri? Like you, he and I are colleagues, and once I would even have said good friends."

Henri looked out through the small window that gave the room its light. "John Calvin is one of the most complex people I have ever met. A mass of contradictions. Much of his theology is beautiful. As you know, he writes with the grace of a dove. But if he thinks you have crossed him, or if you contradict him, he will sting you like a wasp. His letters often use words like 'mercy' and 'freedom,' but he is obsessed with order. He'd willingly fill a prison with any who would oppose him or break his rules."

De la Mere shifted in his seat before continuing. "Toward those he regards as loyal friends, he is generous. But note well that word 'loyal.' Once he suspects a lack of loyalty, dark moods overtake him. He remembers every slight and every word said against him. He stews on them; his mind magnifies them. They are a piece of grit in his shoe which after a few weeks assumes the size of a stone; after a few months, that of a rock. And your greatest offense, Sebastian? Exhibiting the trait he most detests—independence of thought."

"Everywhere he goes," de la Mere continued, "Master Calvin is secure in the knowledge that he is the intellectual superior of those he meets, that there is no one who can better him in a disputation. But you are one of the few in Geneva who can match him for learning and intellect. It infuriates him that all your study has led you not to agreement with his teaching but to questioning it. Everyone else is cowed by him. Everyone except you and I. It has reached the point where everything you say threatens him. I know this road too well, for I have traveled down it myself."

Sebastian reflected before replying. "Until now, I have done my best to avoid confrontation with him. I have refrained from criticizing even when my conscience has told me I should. And today, Henri, I am ashamed that I have again been such a coward. From now on, I believe God would have me be more courageous, more true to my conscience, and more true to my friends."

A grave stillness descended on the room. De la Mere gazed across the table at his wife Helene. She, on the other hand, stared at Sebastian with an expression of either admiration or fear. Seeking reassurance, Sebastian's eyes looked to Eugenie. Her head was lowered, perhaps overwhelmed by the enormity of it all. Then he felt her hand reach under the table and find his own, gripping it firmly.

"In that case, my friend," Henri said. "Helene and I will pray for you both every day, asking God to reward your courage with his protection."

When Sebastian and Eugenie arrived home, they found that a letter from André had been delivered by a rider traveling from Orbe. Marie had received it and had been anxiously waiting for them to return from Foncenex so they could read it together. While Sonya tended to a dinner of pottage simmering on the fire, Sebastian flicked the seal open with a small knife. Eugenie and Marie gathered behind him, one at each shoulder, eager to hear whatever news André had to share.

Sebastian spread out the pages on the kitchen table, searching through them in the hope that there might be a second letter addressed to Marie. He knew she longed for this to be so. But no, there was only one letter—eight pages—addressed to him alone.

The opening page inquired after the well-being of Eugenie and Marie. After this, it quickly moved on to discuss André's situation in Orbe and the thoughts that preoccupied him there. As he read through the letter's contents, he seemed to feel Marie's heart sinking behind him. He sensed Eugenie pull her cousin closer in a half-embrace. A grinding sense of frustration grew in him. If he had the ability to reach through the letter and smack André on the back of his insensitive head, he would do it. It was obvious to everyone except André, it seemed, that Marie pined for him. He sighed, wondering if he should write back and directly confront his friend's blindness.

Marie—courageous, irrepressible Marie—broke Sebastian's spell of melancholy. Her fingertips brushed against the final page. "Look, he is beginning to study again."

It was true. The bulk of the letter contained André's reflections on his two obsessions: free will versus predestination, and the meaning of the bread and wine in communion. Three full pages were devoted to each of these themes, as if he meant to resolve centuries of wrangling with this one letter. Then came the news that he was in correspondence with teachers at Lausanne University, writing extensively to them on these same two controversies. *All very worthy,* Sebastian thought, *but my friend, I worry that you live so much of your life inside your head that your heart starves—and starves another's heart with it.*

"I am so glad that he studies again," Marie continued charitably. "Like you, Sebastian, he has a great mind. He should continue to grow it and allow himself to use all the abilities God has given him."

Sebastian turned and took hold of one of her hands. "I will write back to him at my earliest opportunity, and I will let him know you hold these gracious thoughts, Marie. And that you bless his new endeavors."

Marie returned his smile, then, without saying more, slipped out of the kitchen. A few moments later, they heard a bedroom door close.

On Monday morning, when Sebastian arrived at the college, he found a note on his desk summoning him to come to Calvin's office at noon to discuss the manuscript. He was surprised. For Calvin to have read through it that quickly, he must have committed substantial time each day to the task. *Perhaps it is true that he never sleeps!*

For the remainder of the morning, Sebastian forced himself through his classes, working hard to not be distracted by his looming meeting with Calvin. He took joy in his students. He loved their guilelessness, their idealism, their thirst to learn, and above all, their longing to make the world a better place. In them, he could see so much of himself at their age.

Whether he welcomed it or not, noon arrived as his morning classes finished. The time to meet with Calvin and receive his judgment had come. Years of labor hinged on this moment. He tapped on

Calvin's door with a strange detachment, yet inwardly his stomach churned unpleasantly.

He entered and took his usual seat. Calvin offered no salutation but immediately opened a drawer in his desk and pulled out the same cloth-encased bundle that Sebastian had given him a week earlier, its string already untied. He reached back into the drawer and pulled out another bundle of papers and placed it beside the manuscript. Sebastian watched as the fingers of Calvin's right hand descended onto the pages of his New Testament. Finally, Calvin spoke, low and persuasive. "I can appreciate that you have put a great deal of time and effort into producing this work. And I can see that you have tried to apply your unique skills as a scholar of literature into this ... this idiosyncratic style that you have employed. But what you have produced is unacceptable as a Bible translation. You have used far too much—how shall I say it?—creative license. Far, far too much. So here are my suggested changes."

He lightly tapped the second stack of pages. At a glance it looked like twenty or more sheets. Looking steadily at Sebastian, he added, "Yes, it is a lot. The issue is that I find fault with the very premise you appear to hold concerning the art of translation. Once you read the correctives I have written, I think it will be simpler for you to start over than to try and rehabilitate what you have here."

Until now Calvin had seemed far away, as if Sebastian were viewing a scene from a dream. But something in Calvin's words touched a nerve and ignited the pyre of frustrations heaped within him. Sebastian could feel his next words gathering with such force he felt compelled to stand. "I don't think you do *understand* the premise of my translation work! My aim is not to produce a literal, word-for-word translation, as if this were a textbook. In my experience, that produces something stilted and unnatural, as if listening to a foreign accent, to halting speech. Rather, my goal is to produce something that flows effortlessly in its French, that uses idioms and word pictures so natural and colloquial that any French reader could pick it up and believe that God had written it just for them. Even you yourself say that God is willing to speak to us with a lisp, as a nursing mother would to a simple babe."

"Castellio! Remember this is holy writ, God's infallible Word, His laws and commands that you are translating. This is not some piece of fluff by Catullus. We dare not change a syllable of it simply to make it more pleasant for our audience."

"I do not seek to make it more pleasant so much as to make it more understandable. And you know as well as I do that every translation requires selection and creativity by the translator, for no two languages are completely equivalent—especially when they are separated in time by fifteen hundred years and in culture by half a world."

Calvin shook his head vehemently. "Obviously! But so many of the words and phrases you have chosen are inexact ... with double meanings, in fact. The very thing we must not do is create ambiguity in the mind of the reader. The goal of doctrine is to give certainty, to remove all uncertainty. The goal of translation is precision and purity. For above all else, God is holy—pure and untainted. Such holiness cannot be mixed with the impure or the carnal. This is why the book of Leviticus forbids us to sow two types of seed in one field or to weave two types of material in one cloth. Purity must never be compromised. Mildewed clothes must be incinerated; the leprous person, banished. Thus, God's Word *must* be kept pure. Instead, you profane it, mixing holiness with fleshly metaphors and worldly language."

Sebastian felt like a cornered pugilist, heavy blows raining down on him. His mind whirled like a tempest. Calvin's rhetoric, as always, was irresistible, but he knew Scripture held another argument. His mind groped for it desperately. As he tried to order his thoughts, Calvin glared at him.

The torrent of words had ceased. In the silence, Sebastian willed his heart to be calm. As the room stilled, he inhaled slowly. He then began to speak words he would not have dared to utter even a few weeks earlier: "Yes, all that you say is true ... in the Old Testament. But in the Gospels, with the coming of Jesus, we read that Jesus lays his hands on the leper and allows himself to be touched by the woman with an unclean bleed; that he eats with the outcasts and the sinners, the publicans and prostitutes. He picks grain on the Sabbath. And his teachings—have you not seen this, John?—his teachings are filled, not with doctrine, but with stories ... stories full of *worldly* images of grain and sparrows and fish. Indeed, it sometimes seems to me that the chief teaching of the New Testament is that, in Jesus, all that was once profane can now be made holy and sacred."

Calvin leaned forward and spoke in a voice barely above a whisper. "How dangerous. How absurdly and profoundly dangerous your thoughts are, Sebastian. A liberty of interpretation as broad as this would open the door to every form of wickedness that man's depraved imagination could conjure up. You would risk erasing the line between purity and impurity"—his fingers fell fiercely on Sebastian's manuscript—"the line between truth and error. If these bizarre ideas of yours were to spread, all that we have achieved—our overcoming of the dark superstitions and untruths of the past—all of it would be imperiled." Calvin sat back. "Unless you make the fundamental changes I suggest, I can never allow this to be published."

Sebastian was sure this outcome had been decided days ago—a fait accompli—and that nothing he could say would persuade Calvin to change his mind. "I understand. So we shall have to agree to disagree. I thank you for having set aside some of your most valuable time to look at my work."

With that, he reached forward to regather the manuscript, but Calvin quickly scooped up his stack of corrections and placed them on top of the New Testament before hastily folding the cloth cover over both stacks and sliding them back across the desk to Sebastian.

That night, Sebastian pulled open a lacquered wooden trunk in his study which contained old letters and half-finished manuscripts. He pulled out as many as needed in order to make a space at the bottom of the trunk. There he placed his French translation of the New Testament along with Calvin's notes, all still wrapped together in a cloth cover. He carefully restacked all the discarded books and unwanted scribblings on top of it, until it was completely buried. Utterly resigned, he lowered the lid and turned a small key in its lock. From the study doorway, Eugenie looked on, hand on her mouth, tears silently rolling down her cheeks.

Chapter 12
Death and Fury

His work at the college was becoming more and more difficult. He and Calvin barely spoke now, looking straight past each other whenever their paths crossed. His reception at the Company of Pastors was equally icy. Nobody would speak with him. Nobody would even look him in the eye.

This dispiriting state continued month after month as the city slid into the autumn of 1542. It was an uneasy truce held intact by the unspoken rule that if neither party fired another shot, a tenuous peace could be held. But then, without warning, a far more sinister foe arrived back on the scene—a foe so powerful it would dominate both their lives for the next year and beyond.

That September, a new contagion spread through Geneva which was, like those before it, mysterious as to its origin or cure. Again, the phantom leaped from person to person, spreading fear and death in its wake. But unlike the last plague, this one, for reasons no one could explain, slew the young and robust citizens first. At the start came headaches and a griping pain in the innards, accompanied by blood-filled stool and urine. As victims deteriorated, moods swung wildly from frenzy to despairing lassitude. In the second week of sickness, lungs slowly filled with mucus until each breath became a struggle against suffocation. Mercifully, the final stage only lasted a few hours, the wretched victim drowning in their own fluids.

After breaching the city's impotent walls, the contagion spread throughout Geneva's crowded streets and homes, taking life after life. Bodies were piled outside doorways waiting for grave diggers to cart them to pits beyond the walls. Foreigners were expelled, and the city's gates slammed shut. A curfew was imposed and suspected contacts of the sick quarantined in their homes. Geneva's plague hospital—built in the Plainpalais Quarter beyond the walls and unnervingly situated between the cemetery and the site of prison executions—began to overflow with victims. The situation grew increasingly dire. Daily, hordes of the sick and dying flooded into the overstretched hospital. Inevitably, hospital workers began to succumb, falling at their posts or smuggling the sickness back into the city. In desperation, the council begged the Company of Pastors for volunteers to help run the hospital. Hastily, the ministers convened a meeting. Nearly every pastor blanched, refusing to volunteer. Calvin said he was willing to go, but both the council and the pastors declared this was impossible—his international stature made him too valuable to be risked. But surely, the council asked, there were others willing to tend to this terrified flock?

Two dissenters raised their hands: Sebastian Castellio and Pierre Blanchet. To the relief of the other ministers, Blanchet informed the council that he would become the hospital's chaplain, offering staff and patients whatever solace he could. That night, Sebastian weighed what he should do. Perhaps his experience in Strasbourg had taught and prepared him for just such a crisis. Like the other pastors, he was fearful and wanted to protect his family. But hadn't Jesus told his followers to not be afraid and that there is no greater love than to lay down one's life for others? He saw no other option.

The following day, he arrived at the hospital's gates to offer himself for service. Peering through the locked gates, he could see men conscripted by the consistory. With pale faces and wide eyes, they watched as a cart stacked with corpses lurched off toward the cemetery. Standing nearest the gate, as if on guard, was a burly officer he had seen once before, a man named Urs.

Sebastian grabbed one of the railings of the iron gate and pushed, but it did not yield. Glancing down, he noticed a chain and padlock. Urs turned toward him. "What are you doing? No visitors are allowed to enter."

"I have not come to visit but to volunteer my services. I understand Pastor Blanchet is already here. I would like to assist him."

Urs looked uncertain and made no move to unlock the gate.

Another figure approached from the direction of the hospital, his face wrapped in a kerchief. Sebastian recognized him as one of the members of the Company of Pastors, a man called Simon Moreau, one of Calvin's most loyal acolytes. Perhaps he would be more amenable to reason than the burly Urs.

"Pastor Moreau, I have come to assist Blanchet. May I enter?"

Moreau shuffled uneasily, avoiding Sebastian's eyes. "It is impossible. The company has informed the council that only *ordained* ministers may fill the role of hospital chaplain, not laypeople."

"But I don't seek a role as hospital chaplain. I simply want to help in any way I can. I have nursed the sick before—"

"No." Moreau continued to avoid eye contact. "My instructions are clear. Only ordained ministers may work here."

If the situation hadn't been so awful, Sebastian might have laughed at its absurdity. "Surely you are not serious! We both know that the hospital is critically short of help and that all the pastors have been asked to come and assist. Why would you turn me away on such a pretense?"

Moreau glared at Sebastian. "This is your whole problem, Castellio. You refuse to follow rules. You refuse to submit to those with greater authority than yourself. The rule is clear: only ordained ministers are permitted to serve in the hospital."

Sebastian stood numb and uncomprehending. He could not put a name to the emotion coursing through him. It was some combination of rage mixed with impotence. His hands clenched into fists. A fog, thick and dark, engulfed him. Had the iron gates not barred him from these men, he could not have guaranteed the godliness of his next action. But as he stood there, something caught his eye. He looked up in time to see bodies—people who had recently been healthy, young Genevans—being carried from the hospital door. The sight of their bodies—arms askew, legs dangling—being tossed into the cart, caused Sebastian to take a step backward. Urs still looked confused by the situation, but Moreau stood firm, his eyes now boring into Sebastian's. For several tense moments, they stood like wrestlers before a match, until finally, overwhelmed by futility, Sebastian turned for home.

When he reached the lane that led to his house, Sebastian chose instead to march on toward the lakefront. It proved an easy journey now that Geneva's crowded streets were so eerily deserted. Once at the lake, he had the beach all to himself. Picking up stones, he launched them at the water, as far and as fast as he could. Each toss caused him to grunt with exertion. After several minutes, his arm ached and some of his fierce energy had been expended, though not all. Anger still animated the sinews of his body, so he set off at a jog toward the eastern edge of the city, the point where the wall met the water.

After a few minutes, his progress halted. To go farther, he would have had to follow the wall back up to where it exited the city at the Porte de Rive gate. Instead, he retraced his steps to his starting point and tried to recall the sense of peace he'd often found there by the water. Perhaps the memory of Saint Francis would aid him again. After a while, pieces of a vaguely remembered story began coming back to him.

All his life, Francis had feared and loathed the lepers that roamed the streets of Assisi, their stumps extended, begging for alms. He had always given them a wide berth. But one day, not long after his conversion to the life of Jesus, Francis again noticed a leper in the distance. This time, however, instead of fleeing, he felt compelled to approach. As he drew closer, he sensed the Spirit of God urging him to throw his arms around the disfigured leper. He embraced the man, and as he did, all the repulsion he'd previously felt was replaced with an extraordinary sense of compassion. After they had parted [and Sebastian was sure this part of the story was apocryphal] Francis had turned to take one last look at the leper, only to find a completely deserted street with no one in sight.

The inference, he knew, was that Francis had encountered none other than Jesus himself, mystically hidden in the guise of a leper.

Sebastian turned the story over and over in his mind, trying to draw something from it that would strengthen him. Instead, it only increased his sense of anger toward those who, with the exception of Blanchet, refused to minister to those dying in the hospital.

Returning home, Sebastian stalked his way into the kitchen. Eugenie looked up from where she was sewing at the table. "Seb, what's the matter? You look ... angry. Did something happen at the college?"

"No, the hospital. I went to offer my services, just as the council asked. So many have died, and they have too few to care for the many sick there. Pastor Blanchet has gone, but all the others refused. Yet they declined my offer of help and wouldn't let me enter. Apparently, one must be ordained in order to help the sick recover or die with peace."

Eugenie paled and rose to her feet. She clung to him. "Please Seb, no. Promise me you won't go back there again and try to force your way in. I don't want to lose you."

"But someone must go. And surely a minister of the gospel should be among the first."

She took hold of both his hands and placed them on her belly. "This is your child, Seb. Would you make an orphan of him and a widow of me? Please promise us both you won't go back there."

Tears began welling in Sebastian's eyes, as if the day's anger was being squeezed out of him. He pulled Eugenie closer. He could feel the new life cradled between them. "Yes Genie," he sighed. "I promise."

The epidemic waxed and waned through Geneva for the next twelve months. At times, it seemed to have peaked, for how could the death toll grow any higher? Life would resume—the college, inns, and markets reopening; the plague hospital closing—only for the disease to flare up again and claim fresh lives. The worst of these rekindlings came in April of 1543, and once more the council pleaded with the pastors to supply workers. Yet again, it was only the brave Blanchet who responded. By May, his body lay cold in one of the freshly dug graves adjoining the hospital.

With this, the fear of the other ministers grew even greater. They resorted to drawing lots, then one by one refusing to go when their name was drawn. Finally, the lot fell to one who was willing, Matthieu de Geneston, a young pastor freshly arrived from France. By June, he too had perished, and his body joined Blanchet's in the cemetery.

As the death toll mounted and attempts to curb the disease failed, the council called for another urgent meeting with the pastors. It was Perrin who spoke now. "Gentlemen, terror is gripping our city and we need you to help calm it. There is wild talk of witches and sorcerers moving through the night and smearing potions laced with plague on every Genevan door. Now vigilante groups roam the streets hunting them. They seize every misfit and mad woman, labeling them a witch and hauling them off to be executed."

A pastor by the name of Bernard rose angrily to his feet. "We know you to be a libertine, Perrin, so you find excuses to exonerate these witches. Yet many of them fully confess to their crimes and so justify their executions."

"Who would not confess to some crime or other when their limbs are being broken on a rack?" Perrin shot back. "Seven men and twenty-one women have been burned alive as sorcerers and witches in our city, yet the plague rages on unabated. How many people should we torture and kill before we realize that such cruelty won't stop it? Wasn't our Reformation supposed to end such barbarism and superstition?"

The room exploded. Bernard shouted that Perrin was an unbeliever. Most of the pastors and many of the city councillors were outraged by Perrin's words. Sebastian exchanged a glance with de la Mere. To try and speak in support of Perrin would be useless in this chaos.

John Calvin rose and gestured for quiet. Eventually the room stilled enough for him to be heard. "Brothers, brothers, we must have order in our city, and we must find a balance between justice and the way of mercy. If these people have committed a capital offense and, after a thorough examination, are found guilty by our magistrates, I advise that they be beheaded rather than burned. As Christians I think we should follow this more moderate path."

Somehow, even in the midst of such horror and confusion, goodness could not be completely extinguished. That October, Eugenie went into labor. A midwife was called, and Sonya and Marie worked with her to deliver the child. As the labor pains began to climax, the elderly midwife took command and ordered Sebastian out of the house. For an hour, he paced the street waiting for the sound of the infant's cries and the jubilant invitation to reenter.

It was Marie who finally appeared at the doorway. "Sebastian, come!"

As he ascended the front step, the keen of a child reached him. Never before had he realized a child's cry could be so beautiful. He rushed to the bedroom where Eugenie cradled the baby, her hair matted with sweat.

The midwife handed a pail to Marie and instructed her to go fill it. She turned to Sebastian. "Not an easy birth, this one, but you have a daughter now."

Sebastian leaned close to the bed, a sense of awe filling him. There were still traces of blood and mucus on the child, but she was beautiful. Eugenie looked exhausted, yet somehow she smiled. "We did it, Seb. We did it!"

They named their daughter Susanna, after one of Jesus's first female disciples. She was their joy, but also their fear as they sought to shield her from the unpredictable plagues continuing to weave their baffling path through Geneva. Finally, by the end of 1543, the pestilence seemed to be abating. But it had carried away so many: farmers, butchers, market sellers, shopkeepers, wagon drivers. In their absence, food became scarce and prices rose. As inflation gripped the city, famine and hunger began carrying away those the plague had missed. Having survived the contagion, the poorest were now falling to starvation. Even Sebastian's family experienced days of hunger now. His college salary was simply inadequate. He needed more income.

What's more, Charles's health had deteriorated further, and he was now confined to bed. In truth, Sebastian doubted his father-in-law would ever rise to work again. Eugenie and Marie were doing their best to carry on his business, but they found it hard to reproduce the craftsmanship that Charles had perfected. Royalties from *Sacred Dialogues* trickled in, but it was no great amount. Since the addition of Susanna to their family, Sebastian's mind had become preoccupied with how they would survive. There was one obvious option, one he'd been reluctant to consider until now.

For the past four years, he'd been working in Vandoeuvres as a minister in every practical sense—shepherding the people, conducting weddings and funerals, preaching, counseling and consoling. Yes, a minister in every sense except one. As the incident at the hospital had painfully highlighted, he had never sought to be officially ordained. To be ordained, he'd have to submit to a rigorous interrogation of his beliefs and his interpretation of Scripture by the

Company of Pastors. He knew they would nitpick for even the slightest hint of dissent from Calvin's doctrine, and he wasn't sure if he had the stomach for that. Nor was he convinced that a concept of ordination even existed in the New Testament. It seemed to him that Protestants had slid sideways from "the priesthood of all believers" to a new type of priesthood that resulted in yet another hierarchy of the elite.

But the needs of his family had become so pressing, he had to reconsider. To be ordained would mean an increase in income. After weeks of wrestling with his conscience, he wrote letters to the council and to the Company of Pastors asking them to formalize his ordination as a minister. Within a few days, the council replied with a letter of their own—brought to the door by no less than Ami Perrin— announcing that they would unanimously endorse his ordination, commending him for the quality of his work both at the college and at Vandoeuvres. But there was more. The council was also recommending a substantial pay raise for him once his ordination was confirmed by the Company of Pastors. It was more than he had hoped for.

After Perrin's visit, he waited patiently. A week passed, then two weeks, then three weeks. Each Friday, he sat through the pastors' meeting while all manner of business was discussed. But the question of his ordination was never mentioned. By the end of that month, his patience was exhausted. Toward the end of that Friday's meeting, he rose to his feet, asking what response the company had to his request and the council's recommendation.

Simon Moreau walked to the front of the meeting to respond. It was Moreau he had clashed with outside the hospital. He knew this man disliked him and considered him a troublemaker. Sebastian felt his body go tense. He looked around the room for de la Mere. He wasn't present. He hadn't made the trip into Geneva this day.

From the front of the room, Moreau cleared his throat. "Master Castellio, a sub-committee of the company, led by myself, has indeed met to consider the application made by yourself and endorsed by the council. This led to long and difficult discussions, for as we have investigated your situation and interviewed those most familiar with your beliefs, we have noted two things which we believe constitute major errors of theology on your part."

Sebastian froze. Indeed, there were opinions he held which differed from others seated in this room. He acknowledged that. But as he rifled through his thoughts, he could think of no major area of theology where he held an unorthodox position on any issue of substance. He was nonplussed by this accusation. "Then please, Pastor Moreau, you must inform me where these areas lie, for they have escaped my own attention until now."

"Certainly. Our interviews revealed that on more than one occasion you have been heard to express the idea—to the innocent minds of your students no less—that the Song of Solomon is not, as John Calvin teaches, an allegory of Christ's love for his church. Instead, you have taught that it is primarily an erotic love poem between Solomon and one of his brides. In so doing, you drag the Holy Scriptures down to the level of profane literature. Secondly, you have been heard expressing the opinion that you follow Luther in believing that the apostolic doctrine of Christ's decent into hell and his so-called freeing of hell's prisoners is to be understood in a real and literal sense. Again, this is in dispute with the teaching of Master Calvin, who teaches that Christ's descent into hell is meant symbolically, that is, as a metaphor expressing the overwhelming greatness of his agony."

Sebastian stood to his feet. "Then you condemn me for taking the Scriptures too seriously? On both counts you condemn me for rejecting allegorical explanations, for seeing these passages as real and actual. As for the charge concerning the Song of Solomon, if people wish to read this as a divine allegory, I care little. They may do so. But first and foremost, as ministers of the Word, should we not ask ourselves about each passage's origins, the intent of its author, and the understanding of the audience who first heard it? And no, I do not believe my reading profanes the Scriptures. This poem is a celebration of the profound love and longing between two people who explore the gift God has given them. Does Solomon's Song profane divine love—or elevate the human?"

"You are saying that God's Word contains an erotic poem?" Moreau shouted. "Something that could lead us into ... temptation? You blaspheme both God and the Scriptures, Castellio!"

Sebastian cut across him, speaking even more loudly. "And as for saying that Christ's descent to free hell's prisoners is only a figure of speech, in this *you* detract from the fullness of Christ's victory over death and over the powers of evil! Christ is always seeking to set free those who suffer, those who are trapped, and those who are oppressed by the powers of evil."

Calvin now rose sharply to his feet. "Enough of your classicistic babblings, Castellio! All of the ministers here are in agreement. The Church of Geneva is under constant assault from every side: from Catholics, Lutherans, and Anabaptists; from Bern and Lausanne; indeed, from almost all of Europe. The one thing we must not allow is for God's church to be undermined from within. The last thing we need is a doubter and questioner in our midst. We must hold fast to complete unity of mind and spirit. If we allow dissent, it will weaken and destroy our church from the inside out." He shifted to face the whole room. "My fellow ministers, hear me well. The key to our survival, to both the purity and the unity of our church, is to march in lockstep with one another. This can only be achieved by discipline. Discipline of thought, speech and action. Discipline of belief and, ultimately, discipline of doctrine. If any of us lacks this kind of discipline, it imperils us all. Therefore, we must be prepared to impose discipline on weaker brothers for the sake of preserving God's true doctrine and Christ's true church."

Around the room there was a peppering of amens and some heads nodding in agreement. Others cowered, but no one spoke in Sebastian's defense. Not one.

Calvin, still commanding the room, continued. "You, Sebastian Castellio, need to learn the meaning of submission! Submission to those in the office of leadership. And submission to those whom God has appointed over you. For this is what the writer of Hebrews, in his thirteenth chapter, commands of us."

"And perhaps, John Calvin," Sebastian replied in a fierce whisper, "you should note where Jesus says, 'If any of you wants to become a leader, he must be the servant of the rest; if any of you desires to be great, he must become the least.'"

Calvin snorted indignantly. Others in the room looked horrified. No one had ever publicly criticized John Calvin like this before.

But Sebastian was not spent yet. Before he could restrain his tongue, more angry words spewed out of his mouth. "You have publicly condemned as inaccurate my reading of Scripture on two points. In so doing, you have shamed and condemned me before all those assembled here. I demand the right to a truly public hearing. I demand that you, John Calvin, and whoever else from this company would join you, debate me before all the citizens of Geneva, that they may judge for themselves, based on the Greek and Hebrew words of Scripture, which of us is more accurate in our understanding."

There was an audible gasp. What he had just suggested was unthinkable. Sebastian bent down and roughly stuffed his papers into his satchel. Calvin had not yet offered the final prayer, but he had no desire to hear it anyway. He slung the strap of his bag over his shoulder and strode from the room, moving from the shadows of the auditorium out into the bright light of the afternoon sun.

Chapter 13
The Breach

Sebastian couldn't face the idea of returning home just yet, fearful of carrying with him that which had overwhelmed him in the meeting. Instead, he swung to his left and made his way down the gentle slope of Rue Boule, followed by Rue Longemalle, as he once more sought the solace of the lakefront. A steady wind blew in from the west, strong enough to make the water choppy and unamenable to skimming stones. Yet the lake was still as beautiful as ever. He watched as vessels—both large and small—crisscrossed the water. There were skiffs being rowed, some with nets cast over the side. And off in the distance, a barque plowed a line as its sails billowed. As his eye followed the curve of the shore, he could make out the distant beige stone wall of the city's western frontier. To his right, only a few hundred yards or so away, was its eastern edge. Was it this wall that made the city feel so hemmed in on itself?

He found a handful of stones and tried throwing them across the water. But after several misshapen hops, he gave up and instead looked about for the mound of grass upon which he had meditated so many times before. He pulled his Bible from his satchel and ran his fingers over the leather cover, worn to suede by constant use. He cradled the book in his hands. He loved these Scriptures and had devoted himself to the study of them. They were some of the most beautiful and audacious thoughts ever recorded in all of literature. And more and more, he was convinced that however you parsed it or analyzed it, Christ's message was a call to love: to love God and to love neighbor. *So why then does this book also cause so much harm and give rise to so much discord and violence?* It was a bewildering contradiction that he struggled to make sense of.

He weighed the Bible in his hands then allowed it to fall open where it may. It opened to the Gospel of John. He flicked through several pages till he found the passage that had been playing in his mind—John's thirteenth chapter. He read through it slowly, meditatively. Jesus, on the night before his crucifixion, strips to his waist, dons a towel, fills a basin with water, and like a servant, washes the feet of each of his anguished disciples—even those of Judas. Sebastian imagined Jesus offering to each a word of consolation.

Then Jesus began to instruct them. "If I your leader, the one you call teacher and Lord, acts this way, how much more should you do the same toward one another?" The chapter ended with Jesus issuing a challenge so simple in its construction, yet complex in its execution. "A new commandment I give to you, that you love one another; as I have loved you, so you also must love one another. By this all will know that you are my disciples, if you have love one for another."

For many minutes, Sebastian lay in the winter sun drawing sustenance from the words, his heart calming. He began to question the wisdom of the challenge he had thrown at the feet of John Calvin. *Perhaps my words came out of wounded pride more than wounded justice? If, as Jesus says, love is the measure of all things, was my challenge to Calvin born from love?* The sun was sinking lower, and the air around him cooling. He pushed himself up from his little makeshift chapel by the lake and began to ascend the path homeward.

As he came through the door of their home, Eugenie and Marie were at the table, both sewing, while Sonya stirred a steaming pot hung over the fire. In the corner, Susanna lay in her cradle, lulled to sleep by the kitchen's warmth. As had become usual, Charles was resting in bed at the rear of the house. He forced a smile, but as Eugenie looked up at him, an expression of concern clouded her features. She rose and embraced him.

"Sebastian, are you well? Did they discuss your ordination?"

"*Discuss* would be the wrong word, I think. That they *savaged* my request would describe it more accurately."

A look of consternation spread across Eugenie's face. "But you had the full backing of the council and a glowing letter of recommendation. How could they dismiss that?"

"It doesn't matter how. If Calvin has decided against me, then it wouldn't matter how many letters of attestation I presented. The answer would still be no."

The piece of cloth Marie was working on dropped from her hand and a fierce expression erupted across her features. "That is so unfair. You are beloved by your students at the college and by the people of Vandoeuvres. You are smarter and braver and work harder than all of these other so-called ministers. This is an injustice."

Sebastian had planned to talk alone with Eugenie about what all this might mean for their future, but now that it had all come out in the kitchen, he decided to press on. "I suspect my days as a minister, and as head of the college are numbered. My relationship with John has collapsed, and I cannot see how it is to be repaired. As you know, he was appalled by my translation of the French New Testament. Today, he made it clear he is appalled by my theology in general."

Eugenie moved to Susanna's cradle, gently rocking it, her eyes dark and filled with worry. "But he and you were once such good friends. You helped nurse his household back to health when the pestilence struck in Strasbourg. How can he forget that?"

"It seems that friendship with John Calvin is a fragile thing. Its bonds hold so long as he sees you as an ally, in full agreement with his opinions. But any hint of dissent and those bonds quickly fray. And ... and today I challenged him to a public disputation." Sebastian's face flamed hot.

Eugenie gasped, and there was a clatter as Marie's scissors fell to the floor. Everyone froze, staring at him in shock. Sonya trembled as she gave voice to the fear that hung over them all. "But if you lose your work at the college, what then? How will we eat? Where will we go?"

Sebastian tried to sound confident, but the anxiety in his voice was beyond concealing. "Whenever I have needed, I've been able to find work—whether teaching or tutoring, in Lyon or in Strasbourg. And now, since I am better known and more experienced, we have no need to give way to fear. No matter what happens, we will survive this. I will provide for you all. I promise you that."

No one in the room looked consoled as they glanced at one another. Sebastian lowered his eyes to the floor. Without a further word he made his way to the rear of the house to see Charles, leaving Eugenie and Marie to resume their sewing and Sonya her cooking.

Sebastian picked his way through dinner that evening, saying little. As soon as he finished eating, he went to his study and began searching his bookshelves. If he was going to debate Calvin, he must start preparing immediately. He was sure that his command of Hebrew and Greek—and of the Scriptures in general—were good enough, but Calvin, a master of disputation, would demand more of him than that.

Late into the night he combed through his books, scribbling notes and constructing arguments. It wasn't till the small hours of the morning that he finally crawled into bed. But sleep did not come. Over and over, he reviewed the day's events and with increasing dread contemplated the debate he had proposed.

The afternoon of the next day, Ami Perrin came to meet Sebastian in his office. News of his challenge to debate Calvin had reached and horrified not just the Company of Pastors but the council too.

"Sebastian, if you go ahead with this debate, you place not just yourself but the whole of our city in a terrible predicament. As far as the council is concerned, Calvin's reputation cannot be risked. It is he who has put Geneva on the map. His international renown draws people from all over Europe, especially France. The taxes these new arrivals pay, the cost of them purchasing bourgeoise status, their businesses—all of this has enriched Geneva immeasurably. And surely you know that Calvin's reputation for debate is famous. It is said he has never once been bettered in a disputation. If he destroys you, where will you go? What will you do? You will be finished. And the alternative—if you were to defeat him—would be even worse. Do you think he would take that level of humiliation lying down? Would his supporters? No. They would make your life hell. I'm afraid that the council cannot let you proceed with this debate."

Sebastian grimaced wearily. "Don't worry, Ami. Last night I slept little and thought much. I came to the same conclusion: that no good could come of such a debate. Regardless of who triumphed, no hearts would be changed, they would only be made harder. And now, in the better light that the day brings, I don't consider any of these issues worth pitting one faction against another. I will drop the challenge."

A greatly relieved Perrin departed, taking with him news that the council would welcome.

Sebastian was sure his roles at the college and at Vandoeuvres were now terminal. Perhaps the only reason he remained in place was that Calvin had not yet found a suitable replacement. Sebastian knew his loyalty to Calvin was all but gone. He dreaded the thought of attending another pastors' meeting. Week after week he avoided it. His opinion of these so-called ministers could not fall much lower.

Increasingly, sermons preached in Geneva's churches listed individual congregants' sins and demanded their repentance. Ministers paraded about in their black robes, proud and untouchable, and it appalled him. As 1543 stretched into 1544, he, Eugenie, and Marie struggled on unhappily.

But when winter passed and spring arrived, hope arose once more. The days warmed, and there was no sign of the contagion returning, as it had done the previous two years. John Calvin circulated a message requesting that all the city pastors—including Castellio—attend the coming Friday's meeting. He indicated that he had an important message to share. Eugenie wondered aloud if the pastors might've had a change of heart about Sebastian's ordination. Sebastian found that hard to believe. *Nevertheless,* he thought, *I shall go. Each meeting could be my last, and I would at least like to be bidden farewell.*

That Friday, after his class at the college had finished, he dragged his feet across town to the doorway of the auditorium. Other ministers were filing in. De la Mere was again absent, and none of the others bothered to greet him, or even make eye contact. He made his way to an empty bench near the back of the room.

After some mundane business, Calvin rose and began by reviewing the calamitous period Geneva had passed through: the rampant sickness, death, hunger and poverty. He expressed how much stress this had caused him and how he'd been embarrassed before the council by so many ministers refusing to help in the hospital. He then began the week's Bible lesson. It was from the sixth chapter of Second Corinthians, where Paul enumerated the many struggles he'd had to endure: "Trouble, hardship, distress; beatings, imprisonment, riots; hard work, sleeplessness, hunger; all the while maintaining purity of heart, understanding, patience, kindness and love; willing to live in poverty while making others rich."

As Calvin elucidated on the passage, Sebastian felt the anger he thought he'd dealt with rising in him again. As Calvin finished, Sebastian stood to his feet.

"Thank you, Master Calvin. You have drawn the contrast between the Apostle's courage and our own cowardice very well. You have said you are *embarrassed* by it, but I think the better word to use would be *ashamed*. We should all be ashamed of the way this company has conducted itself these past two years. The Apostle lists how he has given up all things for the sake of the gospel and for the sake of those he serves. Indeed, that is what the word 'minister' means. Yet there are many in this room who live in comfort, avoiding hardship wherever possible. Paul's life was marked by sacrifice; Geneva's pastors by ease and indolence. Christ came as a servant, befriending the poor and the lame, the prostitutes and the beggars. But we wrap ourselves in black robes and ascend pulpits that we may sit in judgment, crushing people with our lists of their sin. Christ rebuked the Pharisees for heaping heavy loads on the people's backs and then condemning them when their knees buckled. But are we not doing exactly the same thing all over again?"

Calvin's mouth dropped open as he took a step forward. Sebastian ignored him and plowed on, releasing the fire pulsing through his veins. "In the passage you read, Paul spoke of *being persecuted* for his acts of faith and love. We instead have become *the persecutors*, crushing the weak and the ignorant. Surely Christ spoke of us when he rebuked the Pharisees, saying to the people, 'Do not listen to them, for they do not practice what they preach. They tie up heavy loads on people's backs, but they themselves will not lift a finger to help you carry it.'"

"Enough!" Calvin barked, suddenly bringing an end to Sebastian's tirade. His face was white with shock, his fists curled tight, his whole frame shaking. Around the room, every minister gaped, eyes wide.

"Sebastian Castellio, today you have usurped my authority for the last time!" Calvin struggled to regain his composure. "Pastors, this meeting is at an end. You may all depart now—all except Castellio, who has once more grossly overstepped his authority. Please leave."

In his haste to conclude the meeting, Calvin had forgotten to say the final prayer, but no one seemed to notice. Most of the ministers hastened to depart as instructed. Only John Calvin and Sebastian Castellio remained in the room. Calvin strode toward Castellio and stood squarely in front of him, his face cold.

"How dare you humiliate me like that before the ministers. How dare you take hold of a passage I have just elucidated and turn it back on me, implying my exegesis inadequate. For the past months, you have sought to undermine me at every turn, and you have encouraged others to do the same. Don't think I haven't noticed it, because I have. Remember Sebastian, it was I who rescued you from obscurity in Strasbourg. It was I who took you into my house, my own home, and treated you like a son. It was I who brought you here to College de Rive and gave you the chance of a lifetime. And what have you done with all of this? You have thrown it back in my face. You must make a decision. Either you learn to submit to my spiritual authority—the authority God has given me over you and all of Geneva's ministers— or I must call a meeting of the pastors and together we will decide your fate."

"And I," Sebastian shot back, "will save you that trouble. I tender my resignation as the rector of the college and as the pastor of Vandoeuvres. You will have that in writing by tomorrow. Now, perhaps, you can use your next pastors' meeting more profitably. Perhaps you can point out one another's sins rather than those that belong to people with no power of reply!"

Calvin stood aghast. For once it seemed the great preacher was at a loss for words.

Sebastian felt ill and disorientated as he drifted home. An hour ago, he had felt more alive, more courageous than ever before, a powerful new energy coursing through him. But now, he felt more exhausted than he ever had before. His thoughts, a tempest of accusations and defenses, argued to and fro: *What have I done? I've destroyed every-*

thing I ever hoped for! And then, more gently: *But what else could I have done? Had I not resigned, surely Calvin would have dismissed me, and that would have been an even more damning outcome.*

Numbly, he moved down the pathway to his home and through the doorway into the kitchen. Eugenie was gathering up a few things and about to leave for the market. She looked up at Sebastian, who was gripping both sides of the door frame.

"Sebastian! What has happened? You look terrible! Did they not reinstate you?"

It took several moments for him to order his emotions enough to reply. "No, I am not reinstated. And far from it. Please forgive me, Genie, but ... I have resigned my role at the college and at Vandoeuvres. It is over."

He expected a flood of questions from Eugenie, perhaps the tug of her begging him to undo what he'd done. Instead, she pulled him close and held him.

"If your heart has dictated that you must do this, then you have done the right thing. You have been tested over and over again and, throughout it all, have shown only forbearance and patience until now. I fell in love with you because you are brave and you follow your conscience wherever it leads. That is why I love you still today."

He returned the firmness of her embrace before stepping back so that he might look her in the eye. "But I am now without employment, without income, and without a future in this city. Genie, we will have to leave here. Geneva holds no hope for us anymore."

For several long seconds, Eugenie's gaze drifted around the room, taking in the kitchen of the house they had called home these past five years, as if she were weighing the cost of farewelling it. Then she looked back at him. "Seb, we have had many warnings that this day might come, and in my heart, I have been preparing for it. As you yourself said, your reputation as an educationalist and as a scholar has spread widely. You will find work elsewhere—I know it. You will be gathered up by someone with a more generous spirit than John's, and they will be blessed to have you in their employ."

Sebastian pulled her close once more, giving voice to the unspoken fear that hung between them. "But your parents—dare we put them through another move? Your father's legs are so swollen now that he remains abed, and every breath he takes rattles his chest. Even Sonya is growing weaker with each passing month. And my sisters—I will be leaving them too."

Eugenie nestled her forehead into the crook of his neck. "I know, I know. But what else is left for us? As you said, there is no hope for us in Geneva anymore. We have to go. Wherever it is, we will have to trust God for our provision and protection."

That evening's meal was a bleak affair. Tears and despondency accompanied the news that Sebastian laid out before them all. As he spoke, Marie and Sonya gripped each other's hand. With each word, Sonya's head dropped lower. After supper, still tearful, she steeled herself to tell Charles that another long journey lay before them.

Sebastian reviewed his situation. It was clear that he was in a precarious position but, he hoped, not a completely ruinous one. Immediately after his outburst, some of the more offended ministers had begun a call to charge him with sedition and the crime of "undermining the prestige of the city's ministers"—both serious charges under Geneva's new laws. But in his favor was the fact that he had resigned of his own free will and not been dismissed for committing any immoral or illegal activity. His academic record was unblemished, and his students and fellow staff all spoke highly of him, as did the city's councils.

He also determined to arrange one more safeguard: before placing his written resignation in Calvin's hand, he would insist that the Company of Pastors write a letter to be signed by Calvin attesting to his moral virtue and academic abilities. To his surprise, Calvin assented. He experienced a surge of relief as he collected the signed document a few days later.

By Tuesday of the following week, he had almost finished packing his books and personal items into two trunks to be moved from his office back to the house. It was a move that signaled the end of something that had once blazed with hope. An air of disbelief hung over the college, with students and staff all distraught at the prospect of losing their beloved rector.

As he placed the last of his things in a trunk, a gentle rap sounded at the door. Ami Perrin's face appeared. "Ami! Yes, please come in."

Ami entered and threw his arms around Sebastian. Sebastian untangled himself and steered Perrin to a chair. His friend's face wore a desperate expression as he spoke. "Sebastian, please, I beg you, don't leave us. There must be some way we can renegotiate this with Calvin and the council."

"No, Ami, it's too late for that. This has been building for a long time and has now reached the point of suffocation. I cannot work under John Calvin any longer. For his sake and mine, we must part ways. I must leave Geneva."

"But we need you here, Sebastian—not just at the college, but in the city. You are one of the few who has the courage to challenge Calvin, to question his actions. Your loss weakens the rest of us. What will become of us when you go? Please, do not abandon us."

A wave of guilt washed over Sebastian. He closed his eyes and tried to push his emotions aside as he thought through the situation one more time. After a few seconds, he spoke again. "I understand your concerns, Ami, and I am sorry. But it is now untenable for me to live here, perhaps even dangerous if I stay longer. I cannot take back my resignation, and there is no one in Geneva who would dare employ me now, as well you know."

Perrin went silent for a few moments. "Yes, of course, you are right. Things are growing more dangerous for many of us ... for any who would question Calvin's teaching or his methods. When I brought John here five years ago, I never imagined it would come to this. I feel so full of regret now, Sebastian. What have I done to Geneva? All the freedoms our fathers fought for have been taken away from us one by one. We had a Catholic bishop who abused us, and now we have a Protestant one." With this he buried his head in his hands.

Sebastian reached out and gripped Ami's forearm, wanting to transmit a sense of solidarity.

Eventually Perrin looked up, a brave smile on his lips. "Wherever you end up, please let us keep our friendship alive. I value your thoughts greatly. I would like to write to you, and I ask that you honor me by writing back."

"Of course, Ami. It would bring me great joy to do that." A fresh surge of emotion welled up inside him. "You, Ami, have been a genuine friend and support to me here in Geneva. I will never forget it."

They exchanged embraces once more before Ami left the room.

Chapter 14
Sebastian's Journey

Since the pastors' meeting, Sebastian had spent each evening with Eugenie and his in-laws agonizing over what to do next. By the third evening—Sunday—they had come up with a plan that seemed the most workable. They still had no idea where they were going next, and it seemed cruel to drag Charles and Sonya from city to city while they searched for refuge. Instead, they agreed Sebastian should ride ahead. As soon as he had secured employment and accommodation, he would come back for Eugenie and the Paquelons. He would head for Lausanne first, where there was an academy similar to Geneva's college, a place he held out great hope of finding employment. From there, it would only be a short trek to Orbe, where André might have connections that could help him. At the very least, André would provide the kind of listening ear he longed for.

They went over and over the route Sebastian should take and where he could stay. Eugenie chewed her bottom lip as they discussed the plans. Then she broke into the conversation. "Promise me you will always be off the road by sunset, and that you won't stop to rest anywhere that looks dangerous or where strangers could hide. Every week in the market there are stories of those who have been robbed on the roads north of here—robbed and beaten … and worse."

"Genie, you know how those market gossips love to tell stories, adding more color with each rendition. Some of those tales are the same incident retold for the dozenth time but with enough change so that it sounds like a fresh crime has been committed each day." Noticing a flash of indignation in her eyes, he quickly went on. "But of course, I will be careful—very, very careful. I promise."

He placed his hand over his heart and stared into his wife's eyes. "And I promise to be away for as little time as possible. I am sure I will be able to secure work in Lausanne. If that happens, I will return here in a little over a week. I have no desire to leave you for any longer than that." He tried to sound reassuring but in the back of his mind unanswered questions rose and contradicted him. *But what if I can't find work? What if Calvin has written ahead and spoken against me? And these stories of highway robbery … it's true. I've heard them, too, from even the most sober-minded of my colleagues at the college.*

Barely three days had passed since his outburst in the Company of Pastors, and yet on Monday morning he awoke early and walked to the college stables to prepare a horse for his departure. Dawn was only just breaking, yet the young the stableboy was already there gathering fresh hay and water. Sebastian greeted him as cheerfully as he could. "Good morning, Tom. Looks like a splendid day that dawns before us, does it not?"

"Good morning, Master Castellio. Yes, another warm one I think."

Sebastian pushed open a low gate and began to attend to the horse he knew and loved best: Arion. As he saddled it, Tom cleared his throat. "Sir, … I heard … um"—Tom's face flushed with embarrassment—"I heard that you were no longer going to be working for the college."

Sebastian paused the saddling and gave Tom his most reassuring smile. He suspected Tom's question had less to do with his job security and more to do with the security of the college's horse. "Don't worry, Tom. If anyone complains, I'll take full responsibility and ensure no blame falls on you. And rest assured, I'll have this fellow back safe and sound in a few days."

Tom looked unconvinced but smiled anyway. Buckets in hand, he wandered out of the stables to fetch more water. Sebastian packed the saddlebags with the clothes and blankets he'd brought, along with extra bread, cheese and water in case something should go wrong and he was forced to sleep on the side of the road. He glanced up. The sun had breached the horizon now. The others in his house would be rising. It was time for him to return home with the horse and break bread with his family for the last time until who knew how long.

The mood in the house was somber as they ate a final breakfast together, and then, collectively as one, they gathered around Charles's bed. Sebastian led them in a prayer for protection—protection for him as he journeyed and for the others as they stayed. Returning to the bedroom, he tried to calculate how much money he should take—enough to survive ten days, he supposed; but not too much, for despite what he'd said to Eugenie, the chance of being robbed out on a lonely track was real. What's more, he needed to leave sufficient funds for Eugenie to feed the five lives in her care here in Geneva. He numbly shifted coins back and forth between the two purses, unsure how to split their meager savings. Finally, he made his decision and stuffed the majority of coins into the bag he would leave behind.

With a heavy heart, he made his way back to the kitchen then out of the house to where the others had gathered. He and Eugenie clung to each other, whispering to one another of their hopes for the future and how they would celebrate it when the time came. Again he promised that he would keep himself safe and would return to her as soon as he could. When they finally let go of each other, Marie was there, holding Susanna in her arms, her eyes brimming. Sebastian stepped forward and kissed both Susanna and Marie on their foreheads.

"You will take care of my two girls, won't you Marie?" he whispered. She nodded her head, her bottom lip caught between her teeth.

He checked the firmness of the saddle strap and the balance of the stirrups one final time. Placing one foot in the closest stirrup, he swung the other leg up and over Arion's back. Arion had carried him faithfully to Vandoeuvres many times, but this trip would be far more demanding. He leaned down and ran his hand along the length of the gelding's neck, noting the thickness of the ligaments and muscles. Then, after a click of his tongue, he used his knees to urge Arion forward. After a few paces, he looked back at Eugenie, Marie and Susanna, all standing as forlorn as mourners at a graveside. The sight broke his heart. He snapped his eyes back to the front and concentrated on negotiating Arion through the comings and goings of Rue Verdaine, then onto the road that would take him north.

It was late summer. As he passed through the Porte de Cornavin gate, already the air around him had lost its cool night edge. Reassuringly, a warm south wind blew from the direction of the Mediterranean. The breeze would be at his back, at least for this leg of the journey. His route would be a reverse of the course he had run five years earlier, passing through the towns of Versoix, Nyon, Rolle and Morges. This, too, should have been reassuring. But the hours of that first day seemed to stretch out before him as if he was trying to ascend Mount Olympus. Between the daytime heat and the cadence of his horse, each passing mile lulled him deeper into rumination. Over and over, he replayed events in his mind, retracing all that had led to this outcome. Should he really have resigned? Should he have spoken out as boldly and brusquely as he had among the pastors? The whole of the past three years had seen a falling apart of his friendship with Calvin, but how could he have conducted himself differently? Calvin's answer to that question would have been "with complete loyalty." But is it right to show such unquestioning deference that you ignore rampant injustice and silence the voice of your conscience?

He began sinking into a new level of despair, his thoughts alternately accusing and acquitting him. He seemed powerless to halt the slide. A great heaviness lay on his shoulders and chest. He grieved for the loss of a mentor and friend, the great John Calvin, and he grieved for the loss of a hero, a symbol, a leader. He mourned the loss of the vision they had shared and of the God-given call that had brought him to Geneva. He fretted over the crumbling of a career that five years ago had seemed meteoric in its rise, but now lay in pieces. And worst of all, a deep emptiness resided in him where an exuberant faith had once burned.

Something of his first love, his first hope, his first idealism had been torn from him. Where once he had believed with a passion that all things were possible—that he and Zebedee and Bauhin had been chosen, like Luther and Calvin, to bring forth light and sweep away darkness—he now saw how naive his thinking had been. He had failed to foresee that reforming one aspect of society would inevitably lead to the destruction of other worthy parts. And then, there was the most bitter lesson of all—how easily human sin taints even the best of human intentions. Calvin heartily preached that doctrine, and now Sebastian finally saw it for himself. As his mind tangled itself up in these debates, his awareness of time and space receded. Every time he rewound the past, searching for clues and alternatives, he unintentionally allowed Arion to slow to the gentlest of ambles.

As the temperature continued to rise, he was grateful to have the lake at his right-hand side, close enough to water his horse and refill his canteen. The first two nights he stayed in the cheapest inns he could find in the villages of Versoix and Rolle—so long as there was a stable to house Arion and provide him with fodder. But he was running almost a full day behind schedule now. Late on the third day of his journey, after passing through fields and orchards heavy with ripening fruit, he approached the small village of Saint Sulpice, nestled close to the shore of the lake. Twilight was already descending. He would have to rest here for the night before pushing on to Lausanne. Just ahead of him, a small creek passed through a stone viaduct running under the road. He crossed the viaduct and led Arion off the road. They followed the stream's course along the edge of a well-grassed orchard. As the trees began to thin, a man came into view, gray-haired and dressed in the thick jerkin of a farmer. He walked toward them carrying a wide basket crammed with the season's first apples. On either side of him stood two large dogs, their ragged coats a patchwork of black, white and tan, their attention on him watchfully.

Sebastian eyed the dogs nervously. *Some kind of mountain hound. Loyal. Protective.*

"Sir!" Sebastian called. "I have ridden from Morges. May I water my horse here and cross your land?"

The man looked him up and down, studying the dust-covered state of his clothes and his horse. The two hounds stood absolutely motionless, their attention completely fixed on the intruder, as if waiting for him to make a false move. "And where would you be headed then?"

"Lausanne and then Orbe, in search of work."

The orchardist nodded, a sympathetic expression crinkling the skin around his eyes. "I claim ownership of this land but none over the lake. Water your horse and let him make use of the grass. Stay as long as you need. This close to the village, we have few highwaymen to worry us, and my dogs will cheerfully take a bite out of anyone they think is up to no good."

Noticing Sebastian's nervous glance at the hounds, he continued on. "But now that they've seen me talking to you and noted the scent of your horse, you'll be fine." The man placed his basket on the ground, selected a large red apple from the top, and lobbed it gently to Sebastian, who gratefully caught it. "May God protect and guide you on your journey, friend."

The man regathered the basket and, with dogs in tow, headed back the way Sebastian had just come. Sebastian heeled Arion forward. As they approached the lake, he noticed how the creek spread out into muddy braids and tiny pools, brackish and weedy. He came to the lake's edge, to a place where the gelding could easily step down and find ease to drink.

Out on the lake, the last fishermen were pulling in their nets and returning to the nearby port, which Sebastian knew to be Les Pier-rettes. As the sun sank lower, the lake slowly caught fire with golds and russets bleeding against each other, shimmering with each ripple of water. The warm breeze still blew from the south, laden with sweet aromas from the nearby orchards. Sebastian tied Arion to a fallen log, using enough rope that the horse could reach the water on one side and grass on the other. As he seated himself where the meadow's edge merged with the narrow beach, his eyes fell on a little pool that had formed between rocks at the foreshore. A strange, darting movement caught his attention. He adjusted his position to see better, taking a couple of steps then lying with his chest on the pebbly shore. This new perspective revealed a cloud of midges, tiny black dots dancing over the golden water. Between them, a large dragonfly zig-zagged back and forth with incredible precision, seizing each midge one by one.

He held himself motionless, trying to discern the colors of the jeweled insect. After a while, the dragonfly, apparently sated by its efforts, settled on the crest of a rock only inches from Sebastian. He stilled his breathing, afraid he might startle the creature back into flight. Now still, it was magnificent, its body a swirl of iridescent blues and greens edged with black. The colors grew more striking toward its head, where enormous eyes glistened with metallic hues. The motionless wings, previously invisible, were four exquisite ellipses stretched out and marbled with tiny black veins. The legs upon which it rested resembled fat, black sacking needles.

Sebastian held his position until the sky had so faded that all before him merged into a uniform gray. He heaved himself up and ambled back toward Arion, who whickered in acknowledgment. Gently, he undid the saddle and stirrups, pulled off the saddle blanket and bags, and lifted the bridle and bit over Arion's head. Rummaging through one of the saddlebags, he found a brush and began combing the road dust from the gelding's neck, back and flanks. Once done, he cleaned his hands in the lake. Finally, he turned his attention to the gifted apple, savoring its sharp flesh and sweet juice. When he had devoured three-quarters of it, he offered the thick core to Arion, who enthusiastically consumed the remainder.

The warmth of the day still held, sustained by the southern foehn breeze sliding over the Alps. The lamps of Saint Sulpice, only a couple hundred meters away, glowed from various windows. No doubt somewhere there, for a coin or two, he could rent a room. But instead, he pulled a blanket from his pack and curled his body into the long meadow grass, letting himself be lulled to sleep by the last of the songbirds. The gray sky eased into black. Somewhere behind him, an owl's questioning lingered in the growing darkness. Between the weariness of the long road and the heaviness of the thoughts that had dogged him, sleep did not tarry long. As his eyelids closed, the last thing he saw were a million stars burning like pinpricks against the black velvet sky.

A swelling chorus of bird song—thrushes, larks, magpies—woke him well before dawn. The day was still a pale mauve, slowly brightening to a silvery alabaster in the east. A few paces away, he heard Arion tugging at mouthfuls of grass. As his eyes adjusted to the light, he fumbled with the saddlebag he'd used as a pillow and found a chunk of bread. It had grown hard. It took some work to rip a piece free then for his teeth to work it into a paste. He pulled out his canteen and washed the pulp down in several swallows. He yawned and stretched his arms, his shoulders and back, unknotting from the contours the earth had pressed into them. It was not the softest mattress on which he'd ever lain, but somehow yesterday's burdens had lessened, and he had woken refreshed.

Arion whickered again as Sebastian approached him. The horse exhaled a warm breath that smelled of the grass and its sweet dew. Sebastian placed the saddle blanket, followed by the saddle and stirrups, on the gelding. Once the bridle was on, Arion was prepared for this day's leg of the journey. Sebastian was sure that they were only a few hours short of Lausanne, if both he and the gelding could maintain a crisp pace.

The next two hours were spent riding hard. He could feel Arion beginning to tire, and it was with relief that they entered the old city of Lausanne. Several weeks before, on a whim—or more accurately, on a fearful intuition—he had written to the head of the Lausanne Academy, inquiring as to whether there were any positions available that might suit him. The academy had not written back, but the delivery of letters was an unpredictable thing. Perhaps they had yet to find a rider traversing the required circuit. Or perhaps the letter had even passed him on the road while he was lost in thought, mentally replaying his rift with Calvin.

He crossed one of the magnificently constructed stone bridges over the River Flon and wound his way through the patchwork of villa-clad hillsides till he located the Pilgrim's Way—an inn he knew that could supply him with a fresh horse for the next leg of his journey. Today, he would inquire at the academy in person, asking if they had received his letter and what their reply might be. Tomorrow, he would travel the distance to Orbe, hopefully with good news to share with André.

After washing himself and putting on fresh clothes, he left his room on foot and ascended the first of the three slopes on which Lausanne was built. In his satchel, he carried the letter of attestation that he had persuaded Calvin and the council to write for him. The five towers of the city's magnificent cathedral dominated the horizon ahead of him. It was toward the cathedral that he moved, knowing that the academy was part of the complex of buildings surrounding it.

As much as he had enjoyed Arion's companionship, it felt good to walk and stretch his own legs. He traversed streets lined with impressive stone architecture—everything seemed so much bigger and more spacious compared with Geneva—till he found himself almost upon the cathedral. He pushed aside the desire to explore the church's interior, knowing he'd already lost much time. He should make haste this morning. Just beyond the cathedral, he entered a large building crammed with rooms and inquired whether there was someone he could speak with about positions at the academy. A secretary offered him a seat and went off to find the man who led their theology faculty.

Within ten minutes, he returned with that man in tow. "Welcome to the Lausanne Academy," said the strikingly handsome man with a close-cropped beard and a kindly face. "My name is Pierre Viret. And you are?"

Sebastian's eyebrows rose. He knew this name well. Viret was one of the founders of this academy and a writer whose theology he respected. "My name is Sebastian Castellio, until recently rector of the College de Rive in Geneva. Some weeks back, I sent a letter inquiring after a position here. Have you received it?"

An expression of discomfort crossed the man's face, and he regarded Sebastian regretfully. Quickly, Sebastian unstrapped his satchel and extracted the letter of attestation from Geneva.

But before he could hand over the document, the man replied, enunciating each of his words very carefully. "So you are the infamous Sebastian Castellio? Yes, we did receive your letter, and also reports of your troubles in Geneva. Indeed, we have been well-informed about all of these things and more. Our sources tell us that you are a first-rate scholar and a warm-hearted pastor but, unfortunately, an unreliable and querulous theologian. For these reasons, we have been advised not to offer you a position here. I am very sorry to have to tell you this after you have made such a long journey."

Sebastian stood stunned, his letter hanging unopened in his hand. "Advised? May I ask, advised by whom?"

A flash of embarrassment crossed the man's face. "I am sorry Monsieur Castellio, but I am not really at liberty to say. Perhaps sometime in the future we would be in a position to offer you a role here, should circumstances change. But at this time, it would be impossible."

"I see." A crumbling hope cascaded through Sebastian's body. Viret reached out to shake Sebastian's hand.

"I am truly sorry. May God provide for you as you seek a position elsewhere."

Sebastian replaced the letter in his satchel then shook the proffered hand clumsily as he fumbled with the bag's buckle. "It appears that voices and forces stronger than you and I are at play here." He waited for a confirmation, but there was none. "Still, I thank you for your time, sir. It was good of you to meet with me."

Sheepishly, Viret stepped aside as Sebastian departed the room. As he left the building, again the desire to enter the cathedral took hold of him. He longed for a place to sit and be still and seek solace. But then he realized that it would almost certainly be full of students listening to a lecture parsing some jot or tittle of Reformed doctrine.

With a sigh, he wandered back to the inn and took some time in his room reading a few Psalms—dwelling on whatever words of comfort he could glean from them. When he'd regathered himself, he packed, paid the innkeeper for his room, picked up Arion from the stable, and departed. His only other stop was at a market near the edge of town, renewing his supply of bread and cheese to sustain him on the next part of his journey to Orbe.

Much of the morning had already gone. Now he would have to ride hard to make it to Orbe before dark. Fortunately, Arion seemed refreshed and up for the task. He stopped only once, pausing at a roadside stream long enough for the gelding to drink and feed on the grassy verge while he consumed a small portion of his own provisions.

As he had predicted, it was late in the evening and darkness was falling as he approached the outskirts of Orbe. The town was an ancient Roman outpost strategically positioned at a crossroads, the arms of which ran off to each of the cardinal points—one from the Jura Mountains to the Alps, and the other from the Rhine to the Rhône rivers. At the settlement's gate stood a watchman. Sebastian asked him for directions to the town's church and manse, where he knew he would find André Zebedee.

André's home fronted directly on to one of the town's grander streets. Sebastian dismounted and rapped on the front door of the manse. A valet, a young man of about eighteen, answered the door while holding a lamp in his left hand. Sebastian explained who he was and who he sought, while apologizing for the lateness of his visit. Within a few seconds, the valet had returned with André, who threw his arms around his old friend.

"Sebastian! I had heard you were on the move, and I wondered if you might privilege me with a visit. And here you are. Wonderful!"

André ushered him in while directing the valet to take the horse to the church's stable. Sebastian hastily rescued his saddlebags before following André in to the house. The manse was spacious and comfortable, and André had the look of a man who was prospering.

André directed his friend to one of the home's guest rooms, where he could wash himself and then return for a late supper if he wished. Sebastian indeed did wish. In fact, he was famished. There was still some capon and vegetable stew remaining from André's evening meal and Sebastian helped himself to a good-sized plateful. Between mouthfuls, he explained the twists and turns that had launched him on this journey.

As his story unfolded, the expression on André's face grew more and more angry. Finally, with a look of disgust, he sank back in his chair. "I knew it would come to this. Do you remember, Sebastian, that on my last visit I spoke of my misgivings over the way Calvin was implementing his reforms? The way he ruled his churches, indeed the whole city? And everything I have heard since only confirms those misgivings. It's as if he must have control over everything and everyone around him."

"Yes, André, your intuition was correct. But I ... I think for too long I was blinded by my loyalty to him, and by my longing for the vision we once shared."

"And so, what now?"

"I seek employment in another Swiss city. This morning I met the head of theology at the Lausanne Academy. He said perhaps in the future something would be possible, but—"

"No, they will never give you a position there. You must know that the academy is under the control of Calvin's followers. Seb, you continue to underestimate Calvin's power and influence, for it now extends well beyond the confines of Geneva."

Sebastian nodded, his heart sinking. So many fears he'd pushed down now rose to the surface, turning his thoughts into a tangled web of self-doubt.

André brightened both his face and his voice. "You could stay here and work with me. I would gladly half my salary from Bern and split both the role and the income with you. I know that you are an excellent pastor!"

"That is very generous, André, it really is. But you know neither of us could live on half a minister's salary, especially as I now support a family of five. No, I will ride on to Neuchâtel, to visit the school there and inquire of Farel. If that fails, I'll go on as far as Basel and seek a role in the university. People talk of that city as being one of the freest in Europe, willing to tolerate all manner of fresh ideas and questions." With a wistful smile he added, "I think I could do well in a place like that."

"Yes, but be careful, Seb. Don't underestimate Calvin's influence over Farel. Or even in Basel."

No doubt that was true, but what option did he have left? He had assured Eugenie that he would find a new position within a week, two at the most, but already that confident boast was beginning to feel misplaced. Had vanity caused him to overestimate his own reputation? Or had naivety caused him to underestimate the damage his breach with Calvin would inflict on his future? Either way, he was too exhausted from this day's blows to debate it further. He knew that André would want to keep talking—and no doubt sound him out on various points of contentious theology—but his eyes were growing heavy. Tomorrow he would rise early, swap his horse for a fresh one, and press on as rapidly as he could toward Neuchâtel, some thirty miles northeast.

He apologized for being poor company and asked permission to retire. Of course, André agreed, promising to also rise early and farewell him with a hot breakfast, one that would fortify him for the next leg of the journey.

The next morning when Sebastian rose, he found the house already lit by pre-dawn lamps and the aroma of food in the air. André stood in the kitchen, a pan of sliced onion, milk, and eggs cooking over a fire as he stirred. He had already sent his valet off to swap Sebastian's horse for a fresh mount. When Sebastian tried to pay him for this, he flatly refused, claiming to be insulted by the suggestion.

After all the disappointments Sebastian had suffered these past weeks, he was touched by these gestures and the friendship that lay behind them. Perhaps André did live too much in his head and obsess over theological minutiae, but the man had a heart as loyal as any he had ever encountered. As that thought formed in his mind, he suddenly remembered he had failed to probe his friend over his feelings toward Marie. Should she keep hoping? Should she keep waiting? He'd simply been too tired last night, and all of these questions had slipped his mind. It was now or never he supposed.

As André spooned the foamy eggs onto two wooden platters, Sebastian looked around in search of inspiration. "Ah, André. It must get lonely living in this big house all by yourself, yes? And being a minister, while not having anyone to share your joys and sorrows with, that's very hard, isn't it?"

André's brow crinkled as he thought about this. "No, not really,

Sebastian. I share the house with Adam, my valet, and he's company enough for me. As you know, I love my books and the quiet in which to study them. I'm not sure I'm the marrying type, if I'm to be truly honest with you."

Sebastian grimaced. This was going to be harder than he thought. As he glanced out the window, he could see that the sky was beginning to lighten. He needed to be more direct. "André, you do realize, don't you, that Marie carries feelings for you? For her sake, I must ask you—do you have feelings for her? She waits and she waits, holding a torch for you and you never give her any indication of where your own affections lie. You are aware of this, aren't you?"

André—the normally unflappable André—was now completely aflap. His egg-filled spoon froze halfway to his mouth. Even in this dim light, Sebastian could tell his face had flushed. "Oh! Marie? Do I hold affection for Marie? Well, yes, of course. As a friend. As a brother. As ... as ... as—"

The sound of a horse's hooves rattled across cobblestones and echoed in the street outside. Adam had returned with a new mount.

"She's not looking for a friend or a sibling, André. She's looking for a soulmate and a husband, you dolt!"

From just beyond the door came the sound of someone dismounting and boots striking the ground with a twin smack.

André pushed his hands together and brought them up to his face. "I'm sorry, Sebastian. I don't know what else to say. I just don't think God made me for marriage. Not yet anyway. That's the best I can explain it."

With a soft click then a loud creak, Adam pushed open the door, a cheerful grin on his face. "Master Castellio, good morning! I think I've found you a fine-looking gelding with a courageous spirit to match. Obedient, but also ready to run when you are. They call him Veloce."

"Thank you, Adam. You have saved me much time and effort." He turned to André, gave him a slow, bewildered smile, shaking his head. "Oh André. I have known you so long, and yet you remain a mystery to me. You have heard me out, and I will push you no further concerning this. And thank you, my friend, for all of this." He swept his hand in an expansive arc that encompassed the plates, the guest room, Adam, and the gelding waiting outside.

After retrieving his kit from the bedroom, he found Veloce outside and threw his saddlebags over the gelding's flanks. Then he turned and embraced his friend one final time. As their embrace ended, André pressed a small oilcloth-wrapped package into his hand.

"What is this?"

"Something to help sustain you on your journey. Open it when you next pause to rest."

He pushed the package into the pocket of his doublet and climbed up into the saddle. "Thank you, André. Your friendship never ceases to renew my hope in humanity."

André bowed, and Adam raised his hand in a wave. And with that, Sebastian was off.

Once out into the countryside, he let Veloce gallop. As the sky lightened and the Jura Mountains loomed far off to his left, Veloce's hooves rhythmically ate up the miles. As they approached the hamlet of Montagny, the morning sun rose to reveal acre after acre of orchard and vineyard. By the time they had passed through the town of Grandson, a vista of blue water opened out before them. Lake Neuchâtel. It was a much smaller body of water than Genève but just as beautiful, its crystal waters glittering in the forenoon sun.

Around mid-afternoon—he guessed two or three o'clock—they passed through a long stretch of wood and thicket and then back into farmland. A milestone told him they would soon be approaching the village of Saint Aubin. He was beginning to feel Veloce tiring, losing the steady rhythm he had held for so long. A short rest now would strengthen them both to make more haste in what remained of the day. Not far ahead, he could see a dusty track that veered off the road and down to the lake, so he nudged the gelding toward it.

They reached the lakefront, and his horse immediately began

lapping at the fresh water. Sebastian dismounted and fetched a rope from his saddlebag. He pulled off the bridle and bit to allow the horse to feed, threading the rope through the halter and the other end around a large boulder. He found the rock's smoothest patch and sat. He pulled the oilcloth package from his pocket. A sheen of linseed coated his fingers as he unwrapped it to reveal a spoon, a small wooden box, and a letter.

The lid of the box slid open, running along beveled grooves on either side. Inside, the box was divided into two compartments by a strip of wood. On one side, a small roll of dried sausage. On the other side, a square of honeycomb, cut so that it filled the space. Sebastian looked up at the brilliant blue sky and smiled, giving thanks. Hungrily he devoured the sausage followed by the honeycomb, all washed down with cool lake water. Then he turned to the letter.

It wasn't written in André's usual impeccable hand. There were scratchings and false starts, and he guessed André had written it hastily last night, while Sebastian slept. The first two pages consisted of doctrinal arguments for free will and against predestination, and the third page contained his views on the Eucharist. The earnestness of Andrés arguments made Sebastian smile, but toward the end came the personal touch. He asked Sebastian to carry his love and affection back to Eugenie and Marie. He assured Sebastian that they were all constantly in his thoughts and in his heart.

He closed by referencing two passages of Scripture: Proverbs 30, beginning with "three things are too amazing for me," and Matthew 19, beginning with "not everyone can accept this word." Sebastian wrinkled his brow against the sun, searching his memory, trying to recall the words in those passages, but he drew a blank. No matter. Tonight, he would have time to leaf through his Bible and decode this puzzle André had set him. He tucked the letter carefully into his breast pocket. For now, he needed to be back on the road.

Refreshed, Veloce was once more able to build a steady pace. The trees lining the road fell quickly behind them. They passed through Saint Aubin, slowing enough to admire its little cottages and church, and then picked up the pace once more.

Late in the day the roadside markers began counting down the miles to Neuchâtel, prompting Sebastian to review the plan he had formed. Although unsure what kind of reception he'd receive, he wanted to meet with Farel one more time. After all, it was Farel who had first taken a shine to him and had advocated hardest for his appointment as rector at the College de Rive. Really, it was Farel who had dragged him and Calvin to Geneva in the first place. After meeting with Farel, he would try to find the local schoolmaster as well as master Latinist, Mathurin Cordier. They'd met briefly once and exchanged letters; Cordier had been very approving of Sebastian's *Sacred Dialogues*.

Soon Neuchâtel came into view. The setting sun cast amber hues across the vista. The Jura ranges loomed over one side; the lake stretched out on the other. Every building glowed in the evening's falling light, but two large structures at the heart of the hamlet especially drew Sebastian's attention: the castle, after which the township was named, and the nearby church. Sebastian threaded his horse past day laborers and marketers wandering home, keeping his eyes fixed on the twin spires of the house of worship. He entered the cobblestoned street overshadowed by the church and dismounted. Outside, a well-dressed couple conversed by a large notice board. He waited for a few seconds before interrupting.

"Excuse me. I seek the Minister Guillaume Farel. Do you know where I might find him?"

The woman looked up at him uncertainly, but the man replied. "At his home, I would imagine, which is not far from here." He pointed down the street. "Turn left at the next corner, then look for Rue de la Collégiale. Farel's house is number ten, I believe. The old canon's residence."

Sebastian gave a small bow and strode in the direction indicated, leading Veloce by the reins. The directions had been simple enough, but implementing them proved more difficult in the evening's fading light. Finally, he arrived in front of another impressive stone building, one that seemed far too big for just one man. He looked up at its array of windows. Might Farel offer him a bed for the night? If he could save a few coins instead of paying for a guesthouse, that would be most helpful. He stepped to the door, took hold of the brass knocker, and rapped it twice. After a short wait, a valet—judging by the man's attire—answered.

"Yes? May I help you?"

"Indeed, I hope so. I wish to meet with Guillaume Farel. Is he in?"

Through the gloom, the man gave both Sebastian and his horse a questioning look. "Who may I say is calling?"

Sebastian realized that he must look a sight, both he and Veloce standing there covered in dust from the road. He wished he'd found a place to wash and change. "Castellio. Sebastian Castellio. Tell him I bring greetings from Geneva."

"Oh! Please wait, and I will tell him."

The valet departed back inside the house, so Sebastian looked for a post to hitch Veloce to. He settled for a bollard a few steps from the house. No doubt Farel would have access to stables. He hoped to be invited to secure the horse overnight there.

An interminable length of time seemed to pass before the valet returned. Sebastian thought it must have been close to ten minutes. When the man finally reappeared, he looked flustered.

"I'm terribly sorry sir, but my master is indisposed and unable to meet with you. He says he has many pressing duties he must attend to tonight."

Sebastian could sense the embarrassment in the valet's reply. As the man closed the door, Sebastian interjected. "Then would you be kind enough to point me in the direction of an inn or a guest house? I am in need of a bed for the night, and my horse is in need of a stable."

The valet seemed eager to help. "Of course. Not far from here, two streets away, there's an inn called The Eagle, which is well-known and of good repute. It has stables, and I'm sure they could offer you a room, sir." He stepped out onto the street and pointed the way, adding more detailed instructions. Sebastian thanked him and climbed atop the gelding. They trotted off in the direction indicated.

At The Eagle, the innkeeper was a chatty character, full of questions as to where Sebastian had come from and where he was going. But Sebastian was in no mood to talk. He paid the man for his room and stable, then retired as soon as he could. The custodian had already placed several tallow candles in Sebastian's bedroom. By their guttering flame he laid his saddlebags down and pulled out some more bread to chew on. The inn sold better food downstairs, but he needed to be careful now. His purse was shrinking with every stop he made. He sat on his bed and pulled one of the candles closer.

From his satchel he extracted several sheets of paper, a little bottle of ink, and a set of quills. He should write notes to Eugenie and to his sisters. Tomorrow, he would look for a rider headed for Geneva who could take the letters. He sat at the small, uneven table the room provided, trying to think of what to write. After a few minutes, he sighed, folded up the papers and placed everything back in his satchel. Perhaps tomorrow something good would happen, and he'd have better news to pass on then.

That night he slept uneasily, his dreams plagued with images of rejection and failure. When dawn's light finally broke, he awoke exhausted. His mind slowly adjusted to where he was, and he forced himself upright. Groggily, he toileted and washed. After shaking the dust out of his clothes, he pulled them on and made his way downstairs. The innkeeper, who was setting up for the day, asked if he would like to have some breakfast prepared. He declined, knowing he had to make his purse last longer than he originally planned for. Instead, he asked the innkeeper for directions to the school. He also asked advice on the best route to Basel and how long it would likely take to journey there. He was told to make for Olten, which would be a few days' ride, then head north to Liestal and on to Basel. He slid another couple of coins across the table to pay for the hire of a fresh horse, then returned to his room and packed as quickly as he could.

It was not far to the school, and he easily found the head teacher, Mathurin Cordier, in his office. But Cordier was unexpectedly cool and their meeting disappointingly brief. He reminded Sebastian that Neuchâtel's school, like its church, was fully under the control of Guillaume Farel, and that both owed a debt of loyalty to John Calvin. He could give him no leads as to where he might find a teaching position. Sebastian slowly walked away from the school, his anxiety and his hunger both weighing heavily. The day was still early, but Basel was many miles north of here, and it was now imperative that he leave for that city as soon as he could.

It took four days of hard riding to reach Olten, passing first through the towns of Bienne, Solothurn, and Aarwangen. Following the River Aare, he rose each day before dawn and found no rest till well after sundown. He had been determined to make the long stretch from Olten to Basel his final day on the road. He had risen in the small hours of the morning and persuaded the stable-keeper to let him leave, despite daylight still being an hour away. But then rain began to fall, lashing him full in the face as he left the town's outskirts. Hard dirt roads, which had allowed him to move swiftly up until now, became slick with mud. In places, small quagmires formed, forcing him to slow and guide his mount around them. Dark, sodden spruce trees loomed over him, and above them stretched a brooding sky of cold lead. His hope of a swift final leg was fading as quickly as the daylight.

Late in the day, the bedraggled horse and rider struggled into the little town of Liestal, still half a day short of Basel. Sebastian and his mount were both exhausted and in need of food and warmth. The market and most of the settlement's stores had closed for the day, but its inn was well lit with lamps. An overwhelming sense of relief swept over him as he dismounted under the inn's wooden awning. The innkeeper had seen him arrive and kindly sent a young man out to lead the horse around to the stables. Sebastian shook as much water as he could off his saddlebags, cape, and hat before entering the refuge of the tavern.

After being shown to his room, he pulled on some dry clothes, then returned to the dining room where the innkeeper had lit a fire. He helped Sebastian lay his wettest garments on a frame which they hoisted above the mantle of the fire. Sebastian was grateful for these small mercies—and for the hot pottage and mug of warm wine that came next. As he pulled out his purse to pay for his and his horse's keep, he was confronted by the pitifully small number of coins that remained. His purse was almost empty. Anxiety clenched at his stomach. He *must* reach Basel tomorrow, and he *must* find work there immediately.

At first light, he rose and made his way to the stables. To his relief, yesterday's rain had subsided. On the eastern horizon, a pale sun was already working hard to break through a sheet of cloud. He hit the road hard and fast, once more galloping northwest toward Basel. Like yesterday, the way beyond Liestal was cloaked in forest both left and right. Yet that which had seemed so foreboding the day before, now glinted with hope, the new sun glancing off dewy leaves and branches. Within a few miles, woodland gave way to farmland then a sprinkling of tiny hamlets. He slowed his horse as they maneuvered around wagons and carts, all making their way toward the famed city of Basel.

Soon the road ahead began to broaden, and the number of carts and horses increased. Peering westward, he could see the outline of buildings, the haze of smoke from chimneys. He quickened the horse's stride. As they rounded a gentle bend, a stone tower loomed ahead. As they drew closer, it became apparent it was a gate—Saint Alban, he would later learn. It was a square tower that rose above a broad-arched opening. He had reached the city's great eastern entrance.

A couple of watchmen eyed him as he approached. Passing under the gateway's portcullis he entered the outskirts of Basel—its fields of farmland dotted with new buildings. All around him, homes were in the process of being built. As he rode forward, he noted the laborers working each side of the road—some leveling the ground for foundations, others mixing plaster; some sawing beams of wood, others using rollers and levers to move blocks of stone into place. Just ahead of him, a cart had stopped along the side of the road to unload a pile of sand and rock. He slowed and hailed one of the workmen.

"Excuse me, sir, can you point me in the direction of the university?"

The man paused from raking sand out of a wagon and thrust a thumb over his shoulder. "Just keep your eye on those two spires. That's Basel Münster. Once you're there, keep heading down Augustinergasse, which runs alongside the river. The university is only a few minutes beyond the cathedral."

Sebastian nodded his thanks and heeled his horse forward. A thrill of anticipation ran through him. This famous university, where Erasmus himself had once taught, was the oldest in the Swiss Confederation, established over eight decades earlier. But as he drew ever closer, doubts flooded his mind as he began to worry that they, too, would not give him work. He tried to push these fears down, for he had no other option. He had to go forward. He had to ask. His belly ached with hunger; his purse hung limp and near empty. He had abandoned his wife, his child, and his elderly in-laws back in a city that seemed to despise his very name. *But surely*, Sebastian thought, *God in his mercy will soon turn my fortunes around?*

Chapter 15
The Last Coin

Basel was a city of plazas and fountains, great sandstone buildings, fortressed city walls and portcullises. The old town was situated on the bend of the River Rhine, just where it widened and turned northward. At its center stood three grand structures: the cathedral (known as Basel Münster), the university, and the red-hued townhall.

Near the center of town, a block from the cathedral and opposite the town hall, Sebastian found a guesthouse with a stable. As he entered, a small sign inside the door informed him that the establishment belonged to Herr and Frau Lüdi. He haggled with them over the price of his stay. After finally convincing them to accept his price, his heart began to haggle with God. Paying for the room and stable had left him with only one solitary coin in his purse. A few short weeks ago, he had ridden out of Geneva full of confidence—or perhaps, he now thought, pride. But now, he'd been reduced to penury.

He washed and changed into the cleanest clothes he could find in his saddlebags. He emerged from the guesthouse, blinking in the bright sunlight, trying to reorientate himself to his new surroundings. He walked toward the townhall—or Rathaus, as Frau Lüdi had called it—slowing to note its deep red stonework and golden spire. From here, she had told him, it was only a short walk to the cathedral, and from there, only a few more minutes north to the university. Off to his right, he could hear gulls crying and see carts laden with goods heading toward the river's edge. After a few more minutes, the university came into view.

It was an impressive building of four stories, its honey-white stone reflecting the morning sun. As he approached the entrance, he paused, breathing deeply, willing his heart to calm. He sought a man he'd never met before by the name of Oswald Myconius—a famed theologian reputed as being a fair man who sought reconciliation between the various faiths. Myconius was chair of New Testament studies at the university and, until recently, the cathedral's preacher.

Sebastian stepped into a large foyer that had smaller rooms situated on either side. Tentatively, he moved toward one of these rooms, where a young man was busily sorting papers on a desk. The fellow, whom he assumed was some kind of secretary, looked up.

"Good morning, sir! How can I assist you?"

"My name is Sebastian Castellio, formerly rector of the College de Rive in Geneva. I seek to meet with Master Myconius, if at all possible."

The young man cast his eyes up and down Sebastian and frowned. "Do you have an appointment? Is he expecting you?"

"No, I'm afraid not. But I have traveled a long way, and it is a matter of some urgency."

"I see. I can't promise you anything, for Master Myconius has a busy morning. But I shall go and inquire as to whether he has a few minutes to spare you. Please wait here." The secretary scurried off and up a wide staircase that split the center of the foyer.

Sebastian stayed in the room but watched as students ambled along corridor or stood conversing in small groups. He looked down and realized again how disheveled he must look. With the cuff of his doublet, he began polishing his road-worn shoes then smoothing down his hose, wrinkled as they were from the saddlebag. By his left calf, he noticed a tear in his legwear and tried to push the ragged threads back into place. He had just stood up, tugging as he did so at his doublet to straighten its creases, when out of the corner of his eye he noticed the young administrator returning. At his heels was a much older man, completely bald on top but with a long graying beard that hung halfway down his chest. As they drew near, the younger man stepped aside and the bearded figure reached toward him, his eyes twinkling and his hand outstretched.

"Master Sebastian Castellio, I believe. To what do I owe this visit?"

"Master Myconius. A pleasure to meet you. Perhaps before now you have heard no news of me, so allow me to introduce myself." Sebastian immediately began to rifle through his satchel, looking for the until-now useless letter of attestation from Geneva. To his relief, Myconius happily accepted it and began to read. Sebastian watched as the man's eyes scanned down the page, seeming to take careful note of the signatures at the bottom. His head gently nodded, as if in approval. He handed the note back.

"I know a little of your reputation, and I had heard that you had run into trouble with the powers that be in Geneva. Yet this letter mentions little of that, speaking well of your scholarly attributes, which I will say pleases me. I grow so weary of the way we abuse each other over every perceived difference in belief. But tell me: why have you come to Basel, and why have you sought me out?"

His tone, Sebastian thought, was direct but kind. Sebastian himself had long since passed the point of subtlety. He had made up his mind to be as direct as possible.

"As you may have heard, certain differences of opinion between myself and the church in Geneva made my position there impossible to maintain. I now seek a new position, perhaps teaching languages or classical literature. I am given to understand that this university encourages a greater latitude of personal thought and inquiry than is permissible in Geneva, so I have come to ask whether or not there may be a position for me here."

Simple enough words, but they carried the sum of all the hopes that remained in him. Myconius's brow furrowed, and his hand stroked the side of his temple as if searching for an answer there. This went on for what felt like a full minute, the twitching of the man's eyebrows giving the impression he was locked in a debate with himself. Finally, the older man broke his silence.

"I have read your work *Sacred Dialogues*, a masterful piece of pedagogy that hints at what you are capable of as a scholar. Yet apart from that, I know almost nothing about you or your work, other than the recommendation in that letter. Normally, we do not take to our faculty those who have not previously studied and graduated from here or held a high ecclesiastical position. The exceptions are those who have produced work of such exceptional quality it cannot be ignored. Like Erasmus, obviously." He paused and again raised his hand to his temple. "I am so sorry, Master Castellio. We have no posts open at present, nor am I in a position to create one for an unknown quantity such as yourself. Were you to settle in Basel and study here or publish more works of quality—like *Sacred Dialogues*—well, who knows what would be possible? But for now, no, I have nothing I can offer you."

A great pressure gathered in Sebastian's chest as Myconius spoke. Now it flowed to his stomach and gathered in a pool of growing despair. This had been his last hope. He had run out of options. He had not a single idea left as to what he should do next.

The young secretary reappeared and reminded Myconius that he was due in another part of the university. He took hold of Myconius's arm and began to lead him away, but as he did so, the old man paused and looked Sebastian up and down. His face clouded with an expression Sebastian interpreted as sympathy.

"Good luck to you, Master Castellio. I am sure something will open up soon for a man of your talents." And then, seemingly as an afterthought, he asked, "By the way, where are you staying while in Basel?"

"In a guesthouse near here, owned by the Lüdi family, sir."

Myconius nodded, his expression more sympathetic than ever. But just as he looked like he was about to say more, his secretary tugged at his elbow, whispering loudly, "We must hurry, sir. Your lecture should have started by now."

Myconius nodded again, and the pair of them shuffled off down one of the great corridors.

———

Sebastian staggered out of the foyer, aware that he did not know a single other soul in all of Basel who might help him. Something cold and hard rose and swelled, taking him over. Loneliness. Hopelessness. As he dragged himself across the town's cobblestoned streets, he missed the turn that would have taken him to the guesthouse, so he began to wander aimlessly.

Twice he came across plazas with water fountains and benches arranged for the benefit of the weary. At each plaza he sat, staring down at the gray cobbles, up at the milk-white sky, and across at the Münster's spires. As he looked around, he prayed for inspiration. But he heard no voice of counsel and felt no hand of guidance.

His mind began to descend into a tangle of half-baked plans. As soon as one vague idea formed, he would tear it down as impractical or impossible to implement. Thoughts stumbled and tumbled one after the other, each more desperate than the one before. Anguished, he pushed himself to his feet and tried to find his way back to the guesthouse. By the time he found it, it was as if a searing tangle of hot embers had formed in his head.

He entered into an empty downstairs lounge and made his way to the far side of the room, where he slumped into a chair and buried his face in both hands. For several minutes, he sat still, trying to force his mind to come up with a scheme, an idea—anything. He had no work and no prospect of work. He was hungry and virtually penniless. The ride home would take at least two weeks. He had already been gone much longer than planned, and he knew that, by now, Eugenie would be sick with worry, terrified that he had been robbed and killed on the road.

Finally, after his thoughts had spiraled around the same course for the hundredth time, he remembered the building sites he'd noticed on the outskirts of town. They looked busy. Perhaps they would take on another pair of hands. He knew the pay would be a pittance, and that it would take months of struggle to save the money needed to return to Geneva. Eugenie would be distraught. It was a poor option, but the only one he could see left to him.

A faint creaking caused him to look up. The door had opened and a large man with a great tawny beard peered directly at him. He had a pleasant, open face and eyes that burned with curiosity. "Master Sebastian Castellio? Would that be you?"

Sebastian hesitated before replying in the affirmative. The broad-shouldered stranger smiled, and with a long stride, he stepped across the room, his right hand extended to shake Sebastian's. The bearded figure arranged himself into the velvet upholstery of the chair next to Sebastian's.

"My name is Johannes Oporinus. I am a classicist, printer, publisher, and bookmaker. Not long ago, a young man—the secretary of Oswald Myconius, in fact—came to my shop to tell me that a very talented Latinist was in town and looking for work. And here I am—a publisher of Latin works with orders piling high and in great need of another proofreader and translator to assist me. I know your talents are greater than this, but would you consider coming under my employ and filling this role for me?"

Sebastian wanted to weep. All the tension, the fear, the anxiety, the frustration that had built up over these past few days seemed to burst out of him like steam from a kettle. But instead of weeping, he heard himself laugh out loud. Johannes Oporinus! The Oporinus famous all over Europe for producing Versalius's *The Fabric of Human Anatomy* and its hundreds of detailed drawings, considered to be a medical and artistic masterpiece for the ages. If the danger of being thought mad hadn't prevented him, he would have thrown his arms around this man.

Before he could reply, Oporinus continued. "As a fellow Latinist, I am familiar with your *Sacred Dialogues* and have indeed used it with students myself. By the way, well done, sir. It is a beautiful and clever composition. Now as to my terms. My business is well established but is subject to frequent changes in demand and in fortune. I have yet to build up capital, so the pay won't be much. But I do expect the business to grow and become more profitable in time. Are you interested?"

"Master Oporinus, I will be honest with you. You have found me down to my last coin, and a long way from the wife and child that I love and have left behind in Geneva. For two weeks I have been on the road searching for work and praying for God's guidance. It seems, sir, you are the answer to my prayers. You appear before me this morning like a great angel!"

Oporinus leaned back in the chair and let out a deep roar of laughter of his own. "I have been called many, many things before, but never an angel. And while not wanting to contradict you, I feel perhaps it is you who has been sent as an answer to my own urgent needs. When can you start?"

The rest of the morning was spent in negotiations over what was to be paid and when. Sebastian explained that he had left Geneva with the plan of finding work and then returning to bring the rest of his family back to live with him. Oporinus estimated he had two weeks of urgent work that needed Sebastian's attention. After that, Sebastian should return to Geneva to fetch his kin. Oporinus generously agreed to pay him not only for those two weeks but to pay him in advance for another two weeks' work, giving him just enough to return to Geneva and travel back to Basel with his whole family.

The two men lunched together, leaving Sebastian's belly filled for the first time in days. Then Oporinus led him through a maze of backstreets toward the print shop located in the ground floor of his home.

Upon rounding a narrow street lined with houses and shops, Oporinus stopped in front of a stocky, three-story block. The one belonging to Oporinus was painted white, the walls punctuated with large windows, each containing multiple smaller square panes. On each side of each window, gray shutters formed a frame. Oporinus entered an ornate carved doorway which led into a large room, something between an office and a studio, filled with clusters of tables and chairs. Large cupboards lined the walls. To the right, a staircase led to the floor above. "Up there," Oporinus said, "is my apartment."

But straight ahead of them was a plastered wall with a door at its center. Sebastian thought he could hear people talking and equipment clattering on the other side. Oporinus crossed to that door, beckoning Sebastian to follow.

Behind the wall and door was a small hall filled with printing presses, tables, benches and more cupboards. Around each press and each table, two or three men worked setting type, inking presses and carrying paper. Sebastian thought he counted twenty men at work—maybe more. Some looked up at the new arrival, eyeing Sebastian with curiosity and Oporinus with expectation.

Oporinus clapped his hands until all eyes turned toward him. He then beckoned the men closer. "Gentlemen, I want to introduce you to Sebastian Castellio, a marvelous scholar whom God has sent us from Geneva. From now on, he will be helping us with our work."

With warm smiles, each man stepped forward, shook Sebastian by the hand, and offered him words of welcome.

By early afternoon, Sebastian was sitting at the front of the shop proofreading his way through a stack of manuscripts. He smiled, still marveling at the morning's events. Yet even so, his thoughts kept worrying their way back to Geneva and those he'd left behind. By late afternoon, he'd exhausted the stack of papers Oporinus had given him to proof. He raced back to the guesthouse determined to write those overdue letters, euphoric that he finally had good news to share. Oporinus had told him he knew of a mail carrier who, in two days' time, would ride to Lausanne and Geneva. Truly, his fortunes were finally turning.

For the next two weeks, time and emotion seemed to flow at two different paces. The days were happy ones, preoccupied with the business of translating and proofing for Oporinus. But once the day's work had finished, nights stretched out interminably, his mind fretful over what might be happening back in Geneva. Had sickness returned to the city? Would the ministers and consistory prove themselves vindictive and find fault with others in his family? Eventually the fortnight passed. Sebastian feverishly packed his saddlebags and provisions for the long journey home.

Chapter 16
Two Mysterious Letters

Night followed day, and day followed night, a succession of inns and guesthouses, each leg beginning before sunrise and ending beyond dusk as he retraced the roads back to Geneva. But this time, there was a lightness to the journey. A weight had been lifted from him. It made the miles pass more easily. And despite his yearning to be home, it was cheering to see the same tavern keepers and stable hands a second time and to share good tidings with them. Even the thought of being reunited with the horses who had served him so well lifted his heart.

In Neuchâtel, Sebastian traded horses for Veloce, and then made for Orbe, where he longed to spend one night sharing his news with André. After the move to Basel, who knew when they would be able to meet again? And indeed, their second reunion proved just as wonderful as the first. Their evening together was overflowing with good food, good wine, and good conversation. André was familiar with Oporinus's reputation for intellectual curiosity and believed that Sebastian would thrive beside such a man. André also reminded Sebastian that Oporinus had learned his trade from perhaps the greatest bookmaker in all of Europe: Johannes Froben, close friend and publisher to Erasmus himself.

"We've both read the Latin and Greek New Testament that Froben produced, and it is majestic, yes? This is the quality of print you will be surrounded by, Seb!" Then a particularly serious look clouded his features. He leaned close. "You know, don't you, that three years ago, Oporinus had a copy of the Turk's holy book, *the Koran* translated into Latin and printed there in Basel." He shook his head at the daring of it, taking another sip of wine as if to steady himself.

More and more, Sebastian realized just how great an act of providence it had been that led him to encounter Oporinus. His fortunes had changed so dramatically, he could scarcely believe it. And now this food, this wine, and this time with his good friend filled him with a warmth that had been sorely missing these past many weeks. They debated philosophy and theology. They talked of fate, of free will and God's goodness. It was almost as if they had been transported back to their college days in Lyon. It was well into the night when, with great reluctance, Sebastian called their conversation to an end, knowing that a long day of riding awaited him in the morrow.

As he unsteadily wove his way to the guest room, he had to acknowledge that he had drunk more than would be considered seemly in Geneva. *Well, what of it? There are times to mourn, and there are times to rejoice. And I'm sure that he who had produced such volumes of sweet wine for the wedding couple in Cana would agree with me!* He sat on his bed and with some effort, pulled off his riding boots, almost losing his balance. He had just got the second boot off when there was a tap on the door.

"Are you asleep yet, Sebastian?"

"Yes, fast asleep, but dreaming that someone knocked on my door!"

"Apologies my friend, but I have something to give you to take back to Geneva, and I don't want to leave it till morning in case I forget."

"Of course, of course. What is it?"

André leaned around the door. In his hand was a sealed letter. In contrast to only a few minutes earlier, he looked sheepish and unsure of himself. He passed the letter to Sebastian, who turned it over in his hands. It was unaddressed.

"Since your last visit, I have thought much about our discussion concerning Marie and my duty to make clear to her my feelings. So, as best I can, I have written down my thoughts."

Sebastian, fogged as he was by the wine, could think of nothing appropriate to say in reply. He simply looked down at the letter then back up at André and nodded. André nodded back, and, with a mumbled *good night*, withdrew to his room.

Sebastian rose and placed the letter on top of an oak cabinet, dark with lacquer, set along one wall. For a moment, he stared at the letter, noting the neatness of the wax seal. It reminded him of something. Yes—that first letter André had given him all those days ago, the one with the Bible verses. He searched through the pockets of his doublet until he found it, still neatly folded. He took it out, examined it, and placed it on top of the one he'd just received. Then he laid his doublet over both of them. He returned to bed. In tomorrow's light, if he remembered, he would look up those biblical references and solve the puzzle André had set him. It was one of the last conscious thoughts he had.

He awoke groggily to the sound of pots and pans clanking. He forced his eyes open, trying to remember where he was. The bed was near a window. He turned toward it. Outside, shafts of sunlight slanted across a small garden. As his mind slowly put these pieces of information together, he sat bolt upright, realizing that it was well after sunrise.

He had overslept.

He staggered out to the kitchen where André was, once more, beating eggs and milk in a pan.

"Sebastian, you're finally up! It's not like you to miss the dawn. But we had something of a late night last night, didn't we?"

Sebastian suppressed a groan before answering. "Indeed, we did. I had planned to be on the road well before now."

"You'll make better time on a full stomach. I've already sent Adam off to fetch your mount. We'll eat breakfast together and then you'll be on your way."

Obediently, Sebastian sat. Once André had filled his plate, Sebastian consumed it rapidly. Little conversation passed between them. It was as if they had used that all up the night before.

Just as he was chewing on his last mouthful, the sound of a horse approaching the house grew more distinct. Anxious to be moving, Sebastian quickly regathered his things from his room. He pulled his boots back on, threw his saddlebags over one shoulder, and reached out with his one free hand for the two letters and his doublet. Clumsily, he sent the envelopes spinning to where the back of the cabinet met the wall. On his second attempt, he managed to scoop up the letters and doublet, and then hastily tried to push the letters into the doublet's breast pocket.

André accompanied him to Arion—the beloved horse Sebastian had ridden from Geneva. After throwing his saddlebags over Arion's flanks, Sebastian then pulled on his doublet while the ever-helpful Adam checked the straps, stirrups, and bridle. He and André exchanged one final embrace. Then he was off, driven onward by his hunger to be reunited with Eugenie and Susanna as quickly as possible.

Chapter 17
The Return to Geneva

Late on the morning of the third day since leaving André's, Porte de Cornavin gate came into view. Sebastian dug in his heels and urged Arion forward. His longing to hold Eugenie and Susanna again—and to see Marie and Sonya and Charles—had grown with every league traversed. So many days away, nearly thrice as long as he had predicted. And though he returned with good news, part of him felt guilt-ridden for having abandoned them so long.

Sebastian dismounted at the gate to their little home, his riding boots clomping loudly as he sprang down onto the large gray flag-stone. He'd only taken a couple of steps when the front door flew open and Eugenie raced toward him. She threw herself into his arms. Sebastian enfolded her, cradling her to himself. Her whole body shook and the sound of her gentle sobbing tore at his heart.

"I am so sorry, Eugenie. I never meant to be away so long. So many events conspired against me. So many plans failed. But take heart, for I believe I have secured a future for us in Basel. Or at least the beginnings of a future."

Eugenie continued to cry. He pulled her closer, hushing softly against her ear. "Shh, sweetheart. It's a wonderful city. I am sure we can be happy there. All that worries me is Charles's health and how hard the travel will be for him."

As he said this, Eugenie's sobs intensified, bubbling against his chest. After a while, her crying stilled. She lifted her face. "After we got your letter, I wrote back straight away but couldn't find a rider for days, so you never would have received my letter. Papa—he passed away only a week after you left us."

"Oh, Lord, no! And I was not here to help or comfort you. I am so, so sorry, Genie. Sonya and Marie—are they within?"

"Yes. Mama has taken it hard. Marie spends much of her time trying to encourage her to be strong and to keep going. But now my mother sickens too. She barely eats. She has been taking strange turns in which she loses the power of speech and her body grows weak. Everything here has been so hard since you left."

He felt worse than ever about his long absence and was determined he must make up for it somehow. "To lose your soulmate after so many years together, this breaks the heart and often seems to sicken the body. I should go to Sonya, but first I must see Susanna and hold her."

He tethered Arion, then Eugenie led him into the cottage. Marie sat at the table trying to focus on the sewing before her. Next to her, Susanna slept quietly in her bassinet, a fire warming the room. Marie rose. Sebastian embraced her. Marie's eyes were damp with emotion.

"Marie, forgive me. I failed you all in your hour of need."

"There is nothing to forgive. You were doing what you had to do. We knew that. But it is so good to have you back."

He glanced across at Susanna. He longed to reach out and gather her up, but she looked so deeply asleep that he forced himself to resist that urge. Instead, he moved on to the back of the house, where Charles had lain for so long and where Sonya now lay. As he entered the room, he noticed the dark rings under her eyes, how much she'd aged, how thin she'd become. He knelt beside her and placed his hands on each of her frail arms. He leaned forward and kissed her cheek.

"Good mother. I am so sorry for your loss, and so sorry I have not been here to comfort you. I ask your forgiveness for this."

Sonya looked at him with watery eyes and gave a weak smile. She reached out a trembling hand and stroked the side of his face. He took hold of the hand and brought it to his lips, kissing it gently.

"Life has been hard for all of us these past months," he told her. "But now a door has opened to begin a new life in the city of Basel. Everything will be easier for us there, I promise."

Sonya nodded silently, but not as if she'd really understood. Eugenie and Marie had entered the room behind him. Marie spoke. "Eugenie read your letter to us. You really had to ride as far as Basel? As we will too?"

"Yes. For weeks it seemed as if the whole world stood between myself and any employment. The news of my disagreement with Calvin has spread far and wide. That did not play in my favor."

Eugenie spoke up. "But this Oporinus sounds like a good man, and one who encourages freedom of thought. Does the whole of that city?"

"Perhaps not the whole but enough that we shall be safe there. Many are fleeing to Basel from all over Europe in order to escape persecution. For the most part, they are welcomed warmly." He looked at Eugenie with great tenderness. "We shall be able to build a happy home and make a family there."

⁂

That evening over supper, he recounted every twist in the road, every character encountered, and every setback that had seemed fatal until the eleventh hour and that serendipitous meeting with Oporinus. But of course, the meeting they were most eager for him to recount was his time with André in Orbe. As he spoke of his friend's goodness to him, he saw Marie's eyes shine with longing. Suddenly, he remembered the letter. He reached inside his doublet, pulled out a letter, and placed it on the table.

"I almost forgot—André has written a letter for me to pass on to you, Marie."

Her eyes kindled with hope. He picked up the letter to pass it over to her, but something was wrong. There should have been two sealed letters in his pocket, not just one. He reached back inside his doublet and felt again. It was empty. He picked up the letter on the table. It was the first of the two André had given him, the one accompanied by the lunch box of meat and honey. He blinked, trying to think where the second could be, mentally retracing his steps on the morning he left André's house.

It came back to him with terrible clarity: He had been rushing to get on the road after oversleeping that morning. He had fumbled with the letters, accidentally pushing them toward the back of the cabinet they had been laying upon. On his second attempt, he had thought he'd gathered them both up and slipped them into his doublet pocket. But to his horror, he now realized that he must have pushed one of the letters completely off the cabinet and down the gap between it and the wall. Marie's letter now lay hidden there, to be found goodness knows when.

Marie was still looking at him expectantly. He glanced down at the letter on the table and remembered that its final page was composed entirely of André's warmest thoughts and prayers for Eugenie and Marie. It wasn't *the* letter, but it was a good letter, full of warm encouragement. It would do until he could contact André to send the other. He picked off the relevant page and passed it across to Marie.

"I'm afraid to say there is another which I have left behind, and which I will ask André to forward. But in this one, he greets you with great affection and prays for you to be blessed in all that you do."

Marie picked it up and began to read with a curious expression. Then she excused herself and retreated to her room. As she stepped away, Sebastian remembered those Bible verses which he still hadn't looked up. Fortunately, he could still recall the references. He promised himself he'd locate and read them before going to sleep that night.

————————

As he and Eugenie got ready for bed, he did just that. The first passage was from near the end of the book of Proverbs, chapter 30. It read:

> *There be three things which are too wonderful for me,*
> *yea, four which I know not: The way of an eagle in*
> *the air; the way of a serpent on a rock; the way of a*
> *ship in the midst of the sea; and the way of a man*
> *with a maiden.*

Well, Sebastian thought to himself, *that's enigmatic. But at least it's poetic, and still might give Marie some hope. Perhaps he seeks to woo her with poetry.*

Heartened, he turned to the next passage, the one in the Gospel of Matthew, and read it over. As he did so, his heart sank. He could barely suppress a groan. *André, what are you thinking? And, Castellio, what were you thinking, passing this on to Marie without checking it first?*

The passage in Matthew read:

> *For there are some who are eunuchs, which were born*
> *so of their mother's womb; and there be some*
> *eunuchs, which be gelded by men; and there be*
> *some eunuchs, which have gelded themselves for*
> *the kingdom of heaven. He that is able to*
> *receive this, let him receive it.*

This passage was also enigmatic, and yes, perhaps even poetic. But as to giving Marie hope? No, it did not do that. Eugenie was sitting on the end of the bed, brushing out her hair. She looked at him as he closed his Bible.

"Is everything well, Sebastian? You look ... puzzled."

"That letter I passed on to Marie at supper—I fear I may have caused her even more pain and confusion by giving it to her. I need to ask André to write to her again, though whether that will help the situation or not, I cannot say."

He snuffed out the two candles that lit the room and slid into bed. Nothing was more welcome than the warmth of Eugenie's embrace after all these weeks away.

The next day, Marie seemed sadder than ever, and he was sure he'd contributed to it by passing her that accursed letter. He would write to André explaining what had happened and begging him to find and forward that second letter as soon as possible. Or, if it couldn't be found, to compose another.

Sebastian visited each of his sisters, telling them of his imminent departure and imploring them to write often. There were tears, but everyone knew that there was no other option but for him to leave Geneva.

Sebastian was eager to get on the road as quickly as they could, but Sonya's health was deteriorating, and the thought of making her travel right now was untenable. Of course, there were also the parishioners at Vanoeuvres to meet with and say farewell to. Over the next three weeks, Sonya's condition worsened. Turn after terrible turn, she was steadily robbed of her strength. Deep into that month, she fell into a fitful sleep from which she never woke.

They buried her beside Charles in the Plainpalais cemetery. Eugenie and Marie grieved deeply, but as Sebastian contemplated the grueling journey that lay ahead of them, he wondered if God hadn't granted them another mercy. With Sonya and Charles gone, there was nothing to keep Marie in Geneva. Eugenie begged her to come with them, an adventure to which she readily agreed.

Before they departed, however, a letter arrived. Eugenie and Marie gathered around Sebastian to find out who it was from and what it said. "It's from Jean Bauhin," Sebastian declared, turning the envelope over before going back to the letter. "But this has not been sent from France. He says that the violence, the hatred, it all grew too much. He left Paris to find a place of greater safety and freedom."

Sebastian's voiced tapered off, his eyes hungrily consuming the letter. A little gasp escaped his lips.

Harrumphing impatiently, Eugenie gripped Sebastian's shoulder and shook it. "For goodness' sake, tell us where he has gone Sebastian!"

Sebastian looked up, and a smile spread across his face. "He left France two months ago and is traveling east to the confederation of Swiss cities." He paused again, his grin widening. "He intends to settle in the city of Basel."

Chapter 18
Basel

In the northwest corner of a land dominated by towering mountains and a vast river, Basel was a kind of crossroads, situated where the frontiers of Switzerland, Germany, and France touched. Through it, the snow-fed Rhine formed a highway down which people and commerce flowed from the Alps through Austria, Germany, and France before reaching the great Dutch delta and exiting into the North Sea.

It was a city of grand buildings, the most famous of which was the university, an institution that attracted scholars from across the Continent. The city, as Sebastian was learning, was a place that seemed open to new ideas. As both the Reformation and the backlash against it spread, Basel provided a place of refuge for those Protestants fleeing Catholic persecution in Italy, Spain and France. These immigrants fueled the booming paper mills and print shops, and those who could work silk created the bindings that the resulting books necessitated.

Basel was now a hub of literature and art, one of Europe's most cosmopolitan centers. Great painters like Dürer and the Holbeins along with musicians like Virdung and Glarean were drawn there.

Poetically, Erasmus had said of the city, "I seem to live in a place of the Muses."

It was to this haven of thought and word that Sebastian brought his weary family in the spring of 1545. Their first task was to find a house to rent, one that their dwindling resources could be stretched to cover. With Oporinus's help, they secured a small home in one of the narrow lanes of Saint Alban, just inside the gate, among a throng of paper mills and mill workers near the Rhine.

Oporinus's life had not been without suffering. He had been married and widowed three times. Yet somehow, he remained genial and went out of his way to introduce Castellio, Eugenie and Marie to his circle of friends. These were a remarkable collection of people, both locals as well as those drawn from all across Europe. Included among them was the renowned legal commentator and jurist, Bonifacius Amerbach, who fascinated Sebastian all the more because he'd been a close friend of Erasmus and was now the executor of his estate. Amerbach had fought to reopen the university after the chaos of the early years of the Reformation and had saved many artworks from Protestant destruction. His home was filled with the paintings of the Holbeins, the books of Erasmus, and hundreds of other remarkable pieces.

Sebastian had often dreamed of meeting the legendary Erasmus, but he had passed away nearly a decade earlier. In Bonifacius Amerbach, he had the next best thing, a friend who was intimately acquainted with Erasmus's thinking. On top of serving as professor of law at the university, Amerbach was also legal advisor to the city's councils.

Clearly, much of Basel's intellectual and religious openness was due to Erasmus's legacy. It was almost as if the great scholar's spirit still hovered over the city, embracing the refugees and dissidents who arrived there. The early Protestant Reformers had tried mightily to turn Erasmus from his Catholicism, but he stood firm and claimed neutrality in their wearisome religious squabbles. Despite defying their efforts at proselytization, when Erasmus died, the city fathers buried his body with honor in the city's Protestant cathedral.

Oporinus introduced Sebastian and Eugenie to those he knew among the community of Italians, dissidents who had been hounded into exile by the brutal Roman Inquisition. They were led by Pieto Perna, a noted printer and scholar, and Celio Curione, a brilliant linguist now professor of rhetoric at the university. Remarkable, too, was the eccentric Gugliemo Grataroli, a talented physician with a vast personal library that ranged from astrology and alchemy to physiognomy, much of which he had translated or authored himself. He was a master apothecary with a reputation for brewing unique potions and effecting remarkable cures. When the other Italians spoke of Grataroli, it was in hushed tones, for he had suffered for his conversion to the Protestant faith. His time on the rack had left him with a limp and a haunted look, his darting eyes constantly on the lookout for unnamed dangers. If any among them had reason to fear and loathe the Catholic religion, it was he.

And then there were the curious band of refugees from the Netherlands, led, he was told, by a dazzling businessman and artist called Jan van Brugge. For several weeks Oporinus had been saying, "You must meet Jan van Brugge" or "Wait until you meet Jan van Brugge." Sebastian was thoroughly intrigued. But with the Dutchman away on business, it wasn't till weeks later that this much anticipated meeting happened.

One mid-morning, while Oporinus was at the back of the print shop showing an apprentice how to operate the press, and Sebastian was at the front proofing texts, the front door swung open and in stepped a towering figure of a man, dressed as splendidly as anyone Sebastian had ever seen. He was easily six foot or more, with flaming red hair spread across his broad shoulders, and a magnificent red beard combed to part in the middle. Hanging from those big shoulders was a cloak of vivid scarlet wool and beneath that, a jet-black

doublet and white shirt with ruffled collar. It wasn't Sebastian's practice to look a man up and down, but he simply couldn't keep his eyes
from feasting on this man's appearance. Even his tights were of a rich,
tawny hue, stretching out from a paneled skirt of gold and maroon, all
exquisitely tailored and embroidered. About his neck was a scarf of
dark blue silk and on his head a black felt cap that perfectly matched
his doublet. As the man's eyes fell on Sebastian, he broke into a huge
smile and his whole face shone as if lit from within.

He took great loping strides across the shop toward Sebastian, his
hand thrust out before him. For a moment, a bizarre thought flashed
through Sebastian's mind that he, a small drab dinghy, was about to
be overrun by a galleon flying along under full sail. He swallowed
hard and stood—the top of his head reaching, perhaps, the man's chin
—and extended his own hand, which the newcomer gripped and
pumped exuberantly.

"Hello! So good to meet you! I am Jan van Brugge, a friend of
Master Oporinus. Is he in?" Van Brugge's voice had the deep timbre
of an orator, and his words were laden with rich *r*'s and soft *t*'s,
stretched with elongated *s*'s—an exotic accent that was new to Sebastian. And perhaps there was a slight lisp within his intonation too? If
so, it didn't detract from the quality of his speech. Instead, it
somehow lent it a sense of greater warmth.

Oporinus's voice boomed from the back of the shop. "Is that you I
hear, Jan? Have you returned to us?"

Van Brugge's face lit up again. "Ja! It is me!"

Oporinus appeared, and the two men embraced, a bear hug so
enthusiastic it left Sebastian feeling glad he hadn't been caught
between them. The smiling Oporinus gestured with an open hand
toward Sebastian.

"Jan, meet my latest colleague, Sebastian Castellio. He is a great
scholar, driven out of Geneva by John Calvin."

Sebastian's cheeks flushed at this unnecessary detail, but before
he could say anything, van Brugge snorted, as if Calvin's name was
both amusing and exasperating to him. "Better off here in free Basel

than in that prison camp I would say, Master Castellio. Basel's only short coming is that not enough people here speak good Dutch, which as we know is the language of heaven."

The two big men laughed as if this was an old joke. A quip of this sort would have been considered unseemly in Geneva, and some minister or other would have been quick to rebuke. *Everything* in Basel was different.

Over the next few weeks, he met the rest of van Brugge's Dutch entourage—his wife, Dirkgen and their children, including his enigmatic son-in-law Nicholaas van Blesdijk, who was married to Jan's daughter Tanneke. Like her mother, Tanneke was dark haired and dusky skinned, while Nicholaas was tall and craggy. As much as Jan van Brugge was exuberant, his son-in-law was serious. His long nose, sharp cheekbones and intense, knowing eyes could have been carved out of granite. He was a man who seemed to never stop observing or calculating.

Over the coming months, Sebastian discovered that as well as being an artist, van Brugge was an original thinker who traded ideas—including his own idiosyncratic thoughts on religion—with correspondents all across Europe. He had two secretaries: his son-in-law Nicholaas and the extraordinarily taciturn Hendrich van Schlor. Van Schlor was a squat, jowly kind of man who seemed to be stuck permanently in a sulk.

As Sebastian got to know the Netherlanders better, it became apparent that Nicholaas was far more than just a secretary. He was a writer and thinker in his own right too. His Latin and German were superior to van Brugge's, which was perhaps why he kept him so close, for they seemed almost inseparable. But as interesting as these characters were, Sebastian had never met anyone as charming—and intriguing —as Jan van Brugge. Apparently, the magistrates and city councillors of Basel had thought so too. According to Oporinus, when van Brugge and his fellow refugees first arrived, the city officials interviewed them and offered them citizenship immediately. Oporinus said he'd never seen this happen so quickly before or since. It would seem the wealth they had brought with them from the Netherlands was not something the council could ignore. The van Brugges had bought three properties: a large townhouse called the Rote Haus, near the river; a spacious four-story manor named the Spiesshof, once part of the old Saint Leonhart's monastery; and a refurbished castle in the distant district of Binningen.

But even with all these new friends in Basel, there was one man who Sebastian longed to meet with more than any other—his dear old friend Jean Bauhin. With each passing week, Sebastian wondered if Bauhin had made it to the city. Finally, one day, he heard a rumor that a few months back a new French doctor had taken up residence near Saint Peter's Platz. A few days later, when he next had a day off from work, Sebastian set off to find out if this new doctor was indeed Bauhin. He had to pass through the fish market with its ornate fountain adorned with carvings of saints and angels. A few blocks farther on, he spied Saint Peter's Church. An alley led him upward toward the church's white stone walls. He emerged out through an archway opposite a park filled with trees. This was the landmark he'd been seeking—Saint Peter's Platz.

Of course, Sebastian thought to himself. *Where else would Bauhin locate himself but next to a woodland full of botanical treasures?* Bubbling with excitement, Sebastian crossed the carriageway, now more certain than ever that he would soon be reunited with the gentle, compassionate Jean.

He rounded a corner to find a large block of homes. On the wall outside the second doorway, a brass plaque read: "Doctor Bauhin." Jean had indeed made it to Basel! Set into the stone wall was a dark blue door, and in the center of the door, a heavy brass knocker. Eagerly, he rapped and waited. But there was no response. He rapped a second time, a little harder. More moments passed. He was about to knock a third time when the door opened a crack, and a woman's face—or at least half her face—appeared.

Sebastian's words came in a rush. "Oh! Madame! I am looking for Monsieur Jean Bauhin—I mean, Doctor Jean Bauhin. I am a friend of his. Please tell him that Sebastian Castellio has arrived from Geneva and awaits him on the doorstep."

The older woman with graying curls tucked beneath a scarf pushed the door open wider. An apologetic expression filled her face. "Sir, I am so sorry. This is his residence, but he and the family are away in Bern. They won't be back for several weeks. I am caring for the house while they are gone."

Sebastian tried to hide his disappointment. "Ahh. I see. Well, when he returns, please tell him that I—that Sebastian Castellio called and looks forward to seeing him. You may tell him that I am living in Saint Alban and working with the printer Johannes Oporinus."

"I will, sir, I will. You can be assured of that."

A month later, the door to the print shop opened. Staring into the sun, it took Sebastian several seconds to recognize the person who stood before him. But once his blinking eyes adjusted, he was on his feet in an instant, throwing his arms around his friend.

"Jean! Finally, you're here! Ah, my friend, how good it is to see you again after all this time."

"As soon as I got back, Gudrun, my cook informed me of your call. But even in Bern I heard rumors that a talented scholar and Latinist had come from Geneva to Basel and was working with Oporinus. I hoped it might be you. And indeed, I now see with my own eyes that it is most certainly you!"

For a good hour they chatted, catching up on the news of each other's family, on their mutual reasons for moving to Basel, and on André Zebedee's latest correspondence. Soon, Bauhin apologized, explaining that he had to go and see a patient. But before leaving, he invited Sebastian and Eugenie to come for supper that night. Bauhin was bursting to introduce them to his wife, Jeanne, and their young son, who they had also named Jean. Sebastian smiled. Jean always did have a gift for poetic alliteration!

That evening, they shared a wonderful meal while they heard the story of how Bauhin had established his medical career in France and of the privilege it had been working for Queen Marguerite of Navarre before they had been forced to flee the growing religious violence in Paris. Now in Basel, Bauhin's practice was flourishing. In a short time, he had established connections all over the city with men and women, lowborn and high, and all manner of nationalities.

Bauhin also related to Sebastian more about Oporinus's background, information that left Sebastian with even greater admiration for his employer. The big man had been a well-trained classicist and had held a significant post teaching Greek at Basel's university. Four years ago, he had resigned in order to set up his printing and publishing business. It seemed Oporinus's heart was to make knowledge as widely available as possible, a passion that had led him to forsake a secure academic career for the riskier business he now pursued.

With each passing month, Sebastian and Eugenie's circle of friends in Basel grew wider. Through Oporinus, they were introduced to the city's religious dissidents. Through Amerbach, to the city's scholars and academics. And through Bauhin, to many of Basel's leading families. Eugenie got on easily with Jeanne Bauhin and with Dirkgen too. Each of them came from different cultural and religious backgrounds, but what they had in common was intellectual curiosity and a thirst to learn. Sebastian could sense that a long sought after contentment was beginning to form within him. Perhaps he had finally found a place among kindred spirits.

Sebastian began taking classes at the university in Greek, a language he loved. He hoped to one day teach at Basel's university, and having graduated from the institution would certainly help. With each passing day his mind came more alive, fed by his studies and by his work. Oporinus had him translating ancient texts and editing theological reflections. Of the latter, much of it was provocative enough that it would never have been allowed to be published in Geneva. Even in Basel there were, of course, limits as to what could be printed. The city's Reformed Church looked longingly at the greater order imposed in Geneva and despairingly at the seeming disorder of Basel. More and more, they nagged the council and Martin Borrhaus, the university's rector, to clamp down on those they perceived as being given too much latitude. Borrhaus was a man with a wide heart, but now that the council had appointed him the city's chief censor, he kept a careful eye on the printing houses, ensuring they never strayed too far from the new orthodoxy.

Yet even as Sebastian rejoiced in being able to stretch his mind once more, other struggles remained. He quickly realized that all was not as it should be in Oporinus's business. The man was a visionary, courageously taking on work no one else dared to. But sometimes he lacked prudence, and several of his grander ventures failed. The work he provided for Sebastian was either feast or famine, and in the weeks when work dried up Sebastian and Eugenie would find themselves cast back into anxiety, unsure of how they would pay for their next trip to the market.

So, just as he had done in Geneva and Strasbourg, Sebastian sought out tutoring work to supplement his income. Bonifacius Amerbach was so impressed with Sebastian's abilities that he took him on to tutor his son Basilius. But finding teaching work beyond this proved difficult. As a student, he had picked up languages easily, but something about Basel's version of German confounded him, and his accent marked him out as a foreigner. To make ends meet, Marie and Eugenie found tailoring work, they grew their own vegetables, and Sebastian fished in the rivers. He also fashioned a grappling hook and dragged lumber and driftwood out of the Rhine with which to cook and warm their home. There were times after heavy rains when fallen trees flowed so thickly that the council paid townsfolk to remove these hazards from the water. All these extra endeavors were helpful, but there were still nights Sebastian lay awake, anguished by his inability to provide more for his family.

On one particularly cold and sleepless night, an idea came to Sebastian, one which he'd fleetingly entertained back when he first came to Basel. The next morning, he rose early and set out for the fields at the edge of town where new houses were appearing. There, he beseeched a foreman to take him on as a laborer. The next weeks were spent digging foundations, mixing plaster, dragging stones, and re-honing the carpentry skills he'd once practiced. As a child, he'd been taught there was nobility in earning your living by the strength of your hands. During the fallow seasons, his father had many times sought income as a day laborer, and Sebastian and his brothers had often accompanied him. Even now he found something deeply satisfying in this kind of work—a balance to the mental cogitation that otherwise preoccupied him.

On one of those afternoons, when driving sleet put an end to work for the day, Sebastian returned home and found himself fossicking through his trunk of old papers. He pulled out several half-finished manuscripts, including the Bible translations that had fallen dormant in Geneva. In some mysterious way, the mix of physical work and Basel's atmosphere of freedom was reviving his dream of rendering the Scriptures into language that ordinary men and women could understand. With renewed strength, he threw himself into the project. Within a few months, he'd published the first five books of Moses in picturesque Latin, followed by a poetic version of the Psalms. Sebastian Castellio's translations of the Bible—one into Latin, the other into French—had resumed. What's more, with an avenue for his creativity now restored, Sebastian began to not just translate other works, but to also compose poetic verse of his own. Oporinus published his poetry, framing it with some of the most beautiful calligraphy seen in Basel.

During their first months in Basel, Eugenie and Sebastian kept a wary eye on Marie, worrying about the toll of her unreturned affection for André. Ever since Sebastian had handed her that unfortunate letter, she had grown quieter and her infectious laughter a less frequent visitor. Several times, Sebastian had written to André, begging him to write another letter to Marie in place of the one he had lost. And for an equally long time, André had not responded. When he finally did, it was one of his long, awkward missives confessing how hard he found it to discuss such things and how he didn't have it in him to write the same things again.

As much as he loved his old friend, Sebastian found it exasperating that he would leave Marie—indeed all of them—hanging like this. He talked it over with Eugenie, and they agreed that she would take Marie aside and convince her to move on from this unrequited love.

The next day, a cooling breeze met the women as they strolled past the cathedral and turned into the marketplatz with its bustling stalls of food and flowers. They wandered through little boutiques and greeted shop owners they'd grown to know. They picked over tables of produce and haggled over prices. Once both their baskets were filled, Eugenie slipped an arm through Marie's and led her toward the red sandstone facade of the Rathaus. Pausing in the shade of an archway, Eugenie turned to her cousin.

"Dear cousin, you must forgive my boldness but ... but I think it's time for you to forget about André. You have given him more than enough time to prove himself, and he has failed you. There are other men more deserving of your love than he has shown himself to be. Marie, you must shake yourself from whatever hold he has on you and reclaim your heart, so that you might give it to someone more worthy."

Marie's eyes misted over, and she spoke hesitantly. "I know you are right. For such a long time I have been waiting, holding out hope, but, well, it doesn't matter anymore." She lifted a hand and smoothed moisture from the corners of her eyes. "I have you and Sebastian and

Susanna, which is more than some people ever have, and for now, that is enough for me."

A year after their arrival in Basel, the sixty-two-year-old Martin Luther passed away in Germany, leaving Philip Melanchthon to carry his work forward and John Calvin as the most famous Protestant name in Europe. Sebastian spent a long time pondering this, wondering what it would mean for the future of the Reformation and all that it had promised. Not many days later, a letter arrived from Geneva. A glance at the seal revealed the sender as Ami Perrin. Intrigued, Sebastian sat down at the kitchen table with Eugenie and Marie, having offered to read it aloud to them.

Since leaving Geneva, this was the first they'd heard from Ami, and if anyone could give them a clear picture of how their former home was faring, surely it was he. The letter began with warm greetings and wishes for their good health and an update on his own family. It was all very congenial—until Perrin started to confide his anxiety over what was becoming of Geneva and his fears for the future.

Sebastian gasped. "Listen," he said to the women.

> *The consistory has issued a decree banning parents from giving nonbiblical names to their children. Many feel deeply grieved at not being able to pass on names long used by their family. The consistory has even issued a list of permitted names drawn from the Bible. On top of this, they have intensified their crackdown on frivolous amusements— no musical instruments are permitted in church and no one is permitted to dance—not even within their own home.*

"Are they expected to do nothing but attend John's sermons every hour of the day? I hadn't realized that God's kingdom was meant to be like a prison." Sebastian looked up to see Marie's pout.

"Perhaps they do." Sebastian continued, summarizing this time. "Perrin says they are planning a ban on bright clothing and coiffured hair, for these are now regarded as displays of 'vanity and ostentation.' Ah! And to counter the sin of gluttony, they are writing regulations that will eliminate feast days from the calendar. Moreover, at any meal the number of courses is to be limited. Already most of the former holy days have been abolished. Only Christmas remains, for the people refuse to give it up. But Calvin is pushing hard to have that banned as well. Ami says there are still those, himself included, who fight for liberty. Yet Calvin's followers grow ever-stronger and the balance of power is increasingly with them. He fears what this could mean for the city of Geneva. He ends with a lament for all those who have been expelled from the free city his forefathers fought for. 'It is tempting,' he says, 'to flee as you have done. But I cannot. I will stay and fight for Geneva's freedom so long as I have breath.'"

Sebastian put the letter down on the table, and they sat in silence. Eugenie spoke first. "This is all so harsh. These are educated men, men who claim to follow Christ, called to make decisions in the best interests of the whole city, but instead they seem determined to crush the spirit of those living there. Has some kind of sickness overcome them?"

Sebastian stared at the pages of the letter. In a voice heavy with regret he said, "Yes, truly I think it is some kind of sickness—the sickness that occurs when law triumphs over grace and power triumphs over love. Like Ami, I despair as to where this all will end."

Once more, they were silent, each wrestling with what this letter might portend. Finally, Eugenie gave voice to what he imagined they were all thinking. "Then I, for one, am glad we escaped Geneva when we did."

Some six months later, a second letter arrived from Perrin. Anxiously, they gathered around the table to hear Sebastian read. Once more, he intended to summarize as his eyes scanned the page. But this time, Perrin dispensed with nearly all opening pleasantries and plunged immediately into a story of anguish Sebastian felt he could only read verbatim.

The council has passed a law making it an offense to criticize any of the city's ministers. The number of people being sent to prison and executed is continually rising, and I feel powerless to stop it. Our friend Pastor de la Mere has been thrown into prison for challenging the consistory over the treatment of a citizen called Pierre Ameaux. Ameaux, captain of the armory, criticized Calvin as a dictator and spoke against the doctrine of predestination. The council intended to fine him, but Calvin insisted on more. Ameaux was forced to strip, don a hair-shirt, and walk a circuit of Geneva begging for forgiveness at every crossroads. When de la Mere called this an abuse of power, he was removed from his position as a minister and thrown into prison. And now—the Lord protect me!—the eye of the consistory has fallen upon my own family. Two months ago, Geneva sent me on a diplomatic mission to the court of Henry II in France. A great honor, I thought, and one that made me believe my position in the city was secure. But in my absence, a war was waged on my loved ones. My wife, Françoise, was accused of dancing at a wedding.

Sebastian's brow furrowed as he read the next few sentences to himself before looking up at Eugenie and Marie. "It appears that proud, fighting spirit runs on both sides of Ami's family. Listen to this:

> *When the consistory dragged my wife and her father before them, she refused to beg for mercy. Instead, she argued with them, insisting that neither music nor dancing could be called a sin and thus she had nothing to repent of!*

Eugenie let out a gasp. Marie cried, "Good for her!" Sebastian plunged on.

> *Of course, our friend Calvin was enraged by such defiance, and the following Sunday, he thundered from his pulpit against the evils of those who indulged themselves in debauchery and merrymaking and those who defied godly authority. He called for my wife and my father-in-law to be cast into prison immediately. Thus, cornered by Calvin's sermon, the consistory had no option but to try and prove their authority.*

Sebastian's voice trailed off. Eugenie grabbed his arm and shook it. "Seb! Tell us!"

Sebastian flinched, finding it hard to tear his eyes away from the page even for a moment. "Of course, of course. Sorry.

> *When news of this dire situation reached me in Paris, I made haste to return, arriving just in time to intercede for Françoise and for her father, reminding both council and consistory of all my family has done for the city, both now and in the past. I managed to persuade the council to not proceed with the imprisonment, which infuriated Calvin and*

his supporters even more. In retaliation, they accused me of treason, claiming I had misrepresented the city's interests in France. The following Sunday, Calvin gave another sermon saying all those who followed me, the so-called enfants de Geneve, should be hung.

Sebastian swallowed hard, glancing up at Eugenie and Marie before returning to the letter. "Ami calls the situation 'a mess, a terrifying mess,' but he believes he still has enough support on the council and in the city to fight this charge off. For now. He finishes by expressing his disbelief at how so many have fallen under Calvin's spell."

As he reached the end of the letter, Sebastian exhaled slowly. A sense of shock had enveloped the three of them.

It was Marie who broke the silence. "We must pray every day for the safety of Ami and his family as well as your sisters and their families, Sebastian."

Sebastian and Eugenie nodded their agreement, knowing they had little else they could offer their loved ones still in Geneva.

Chapter 19
God Has Given

I n the middle of 1548 came signs that Eugenie had fallen pregnant again. That blessing came with new fears too: aches that gripped her abdomen; pain that stabbed her back; days when she spotted blood; and nights when her head pounded as if, she said, a small hammer had been taken to it.

Sebastian and Marie fussed over her, not allowing her to carry anything heavier than a loaf of bread. They made sure she got the best of their food, especially during their weeks of scarcity. But as her nausea worsened, she struggled to keep down even the little she ate. They engaged a midwife, and Bauhin himself called regularly, but the elixirs he prescribed seemed to make little difference. The baby was due late in the third month of 1549. As that date approached, Eugenie was instructed to stay in bed while the others tended her as if she were a princess.

The labor pains arrived in the second week of March, just as a cold sun was setting to the west of the city. Marie pushed Sebastian toward the door and instructed him to wait outside in the gathering night. The midwife, Éleana, arrived with a young assistant, an array of herbs, and a stack of cloths to wipe away Eugenie's sweat. As night deepened, the contractions grew in intensity, seizing Eugenie as if they would cut her in two. More blood appeared on the bed sheets, and the midwife's face grew anxious. She sent her assistant off to fetch Bauhin, but she returned unable to find him. Eugenie writhed with each wave of pain now, and Marie, her eyes wide with apprehension, stepped out of the house and told Sebastian to go find Bauhin immediately.

It would have been swifter for Sebastian to have hired a horse from a local hackney, but fear had replaced thought so he plunged on foot through Basel's darkening streets, panic driving him. Blindly, he ran along Saint Alban's Vorstaad and the Rittergasse, out onto Rheinsprung, past Saint Martin's, through the platz, along Stadenhaus and through the fish market toward Saint Peter's Church. His lungs heaving, he crossed the final road leading to the Hebelstrasse and threw himself against the Bauhins' sturdy door. A maid answered, frightened. She called for help. Madame Jeanne came to explain that Bauhin was treating someone on the far side of town. His chest thumping, Sebastian garbled a description of what was happening and begged her to send Jean as soon as he returned.

Sebastian ran back the way he'd come and was about to re-enter their narrow lane when a scream split the air. Even from a distance he recognized it as Eugenie's. His blood ran cold. As he drew close to the house, Marie emerged with Susanna in her arms, their little girl distraught.

"Where is Bauhin?" Marie demanded, her face ashen.

"Attending someone else, but he will come as soon as he can. What's wrong, Marie? Tell me."

"The baby must be turned, for he is facing the wrong way. The midwife is trying, but she is not strong enough. She has called for another midwife to come, but we need Bauhin. I need to help her, too, but this is no place for Susanna. Or you. Take her somewhere else."

Another agonized scream arose from the house. Sebastian's stomach turned. A look of even greater fear shone in Marie's eyes, her pupils wide and black. She pushed Susanna into his arms. "I must help them. Please, Seb. Please get Bauhin."

Sebastian staggered a few steps into the street with Susanna—whimpering and calling for her mother—in his arms. Roused by the commotion, several neighbors had come out onto the narrow lane to see what was happening. Next door lived an older couple, the husband a papermaker in a nearby mill. The man's wife was kindly, and she and her daughters, Alise and Katarina, had often helped them in the past. Sebastian thrust Susanna into the woman's arms.

"Please, good mother, look after my daughter. I have to go and fetch help."

Once more, he set off running toward Bauhin's house. In his panicked search for a shortcut, he took two wrong turns and had to turn back again. He was losing his head. He knew this second visit was likely futile, but once more he threw himself against the Bauhins' thick wooden door, thumping it with the heel of his hand. Again, Madame Jeanne appeared and swore she'd send her husband as soon as he returned. As he turned to leave, he saw Madame Jeanne's hands rise to cradle both sides of her face.

He ran back toward home. His frantic journey had served no end, but still, doing something, anything, was better than waiting, than being tormented by Eugenie's screams. He entered the narrow street and heard no sound. Hope began to rise. Had the crisis passed? But then a low, rising wail grew and grew until his skin prickled and flowed with sweat. On and on it went, the tortured rhythm of a moment of silence followed by a steady ascending cry.

The road filled with more neighbors, all asking what was happening. Sebastian stood numbly among them, his arms wrapped about himself, rocking and swaying. His legs barely held him upright. With each chilling scream, neighbors ushered their children back indoors, while those nearest plied him with unconvincing assurances.

It could have been one hour or two—for he could no longer keep track of time—when suddenly, he heard the sound of hooves clattering across stone and turning into their little street. Bauhin! Sebastian rushed to him as he dismounted from his horse.

"I have been with another patient who was very unwell. As soon as I returned home, I rode here as quickly as I could. But understand this, Seb, I am no midwife. I have never attended a birth."

He thrust the reins of the horse into Sebastian's hands. "Take care of this." He snatched his satchel, bounded up the steps, and charged into the house. A few minutes after Bauhin entered, Marie came out. There was blood on her hands.

"It's not good Sebastian. It's not good. We can't turn the baby. Eugenie is suffering terribly." A strange gasping sound forced its way out of her. She bit her bottom lip and seemed to pull herself back together. She looked at him with a terrible fierceness. "You must pray. Pray for us and for Genie. We are doing our best Sebastian, but—"

She turned and hurried back into the house.

Sebastian felt the blood drain from his head and a wave of nausea rise in his stomach. He was sure he would fall, but he held hard to the horse's reins, leaning his shoulder against the beast's flank. He stared at the house in confusion for a minute, both he and those gathered around him terrified by the cries coming from inside. A neighbor by the name of Daniel stepped out of the crowd and came alongside him.

"I reckon it's not doing you any good standing here. Look, there's a stable only a block away. I'll bet they'll put the horse up there for gratis, given the situation. Come on, I'll help you." He wrapped a strong arm around Sebastian's shoulders and led him down the street, the horse's reins still clutched in Sebastian's hands.

Sebastian was in a daze as his neighbor led him to the stables that backed up to an inn near their home. After they negotiated for the horse to be lodged, it was clear Daniel wanted to prevent Sebastian from returning home, perhaps convinced he'd be better off staying out of earshot. But Sebastian refused. The two of them began a fearful march back the way they'd come. They arrived in time to hear a terrible, low-pitched cry from the house—not so much a scream as a deep, whole-bodied groan. It seemed to go on forever. Sebastian fell to his knees in the street. Burying his face in his hands, he tried to pray. But the only words he could find were, "Have mercy, *please*; have mercy, *please*; have mercy." Over and over again, he prayed these words.

And then the screaming ceased.

After what seemed like endless minutes, there came a new sound. Softer and higher. A cry, not so much of pain but of bewilderment and demand. The unmistakable keen of a baby. Sebastian lifted his face and looked to the house, hope and wonderment ebbing back in to his heart.

A figure appeared at the door. No, two figures. Marie, her apron and sleeves covered with blood, and in her arms, a bundle wrapped in clean linen. Sebastian staggered to his feet and moved closer. The bundle was pink and blue, bruised and bloodied, but breathing and making small movements. Alive.

Sebastian stared at Marie, his face imploring her to say the words he longed to hear—that Eugenie was fine. His heart hung in the abyss between fear and hope. Marie's eyes pooled with tears. They flowed down her cheeks. She looked utterly lost.

"I am so, so sorry, Sebastian. We tried everything, but we could not save her. Genie has gone. She didn't— "

No. He hadn't heard correctly. It wasn't possible. Bauhin wouldn't let that happen. Marie wouldn't let that happen. God wouldn't let that happen. He burst past Marie and into the house. He raced through the kitchen, toward the room where Eugenie had given birth, their bedroom in which they'd lain together to make the child that Marie now held. He tried to push his way through the doorway as Bauhin was exiting. Like Marie, Bauhin's hands and forearms were covered with blood.

He caught Sebastian by the shoulders and held him there. "Dear Sebastian, I tried everything I've heard and read, everything the four of us knew, but it was impossible. I'm so sorry my friend, so very sorry."

Sebastian heard the words as if they were far off, as if he were overhearing a conversation between two strangers on the far side of a vast room. He had to get to Eugenie. He pushed Bauhin away and lunged toward the bed. The midwives were gathering sheets stained with blood. They had found a clean sheet and pulled it up to Eugenie's neck. She lay there more pale than he'd ever seen her, her head tilted back, her eyes half closed and half open, as if staring up at the ceiling. No! They were wrong; she was still alive, and he knew it. He threw himself upon the bed, embracing her, shaking her, calling her name over and over.

Great sobs began low in his stomach, building force as they moved up his chest, before erupting from him as wails, so deep and powerful, they caused his entire body to convulse. He buried his face against hers. How long he lay there weeping, he could not tell. But eventually he felt Bauhin's gentle grip on his arm.

"Sebastian, she is gone. She goes to be with God now. But you have a beautiful, healthy son waiting in the next room, waiting to feel your touch. This child will need all of your love and attention. Come and see your son now. Please."

Sebastian sat up but remained on the edge of the bed staring down at Genie. Her hair, so black and beautiful against the white of the pillow, was matted across her face, held there by her sweat and his tears. Tenderly, he brushed the tendrils from her cheeks. He leaned forward one more time and kissed her, his lips brushing gently against hers as they had done so many times before.

Bauhin gripped him by the arm, lifted him, and led him toward the door. "Come, Seb. Come and see your beautiful little boy."

In the kitchen stood Marie, tears still flowing freely down her face. As Bauhin and Sebastian approached, she moved toward Sebastian. Wordlessly, she passed the babe to him, making sure he had embraced all of the little bundle before letting go. When Sebastian looked at his son, something moved deep inside him. The child had a little shock of dark hair, with well-defined eyebrows and lips. He looked like Genie. Sebastian lifted him up to the crook of his neck and clung to him tightly.

"Come," Bauhin whispered gently. "Come and stay at my house for what remains of this night. You are exhausted and in need of rest. Let me take you home with me, then I will return and work with these midwives to prepare Eugenie's body for burial. I promise you, we will tend to her with the utmost care on your behalf."

"No," Sebastian spoke with a new determination. "Marie and I must do it. We must, for we are her family, those she loved, those who loved her. I thank you for your kindness, Jean, but it is our task to prepare her for her final journey."

He glanced across the room at Marie, who nodded. She turned to look at Bauhin. "But what we do need you to do, Jean, with the help of these midwives, is find a nurse who can suckle this child, for it is urgent that he has the nourishment of a breast now."

Bauhin reentered the bedroom. Éleana, the older of the two midwives, emerged and approached Sebastian. "Sir, I will take your baby to a nurse. I promise we will keep him safe and fed tonight and bring him back to you tomorrow."

Hands trembling, it took all of his strength to hand the baby over to her. Bauhin touched his shoulder. "It's a good solution, Seb. I will accompany her and make sure all is in order."

The second midwife came out of the bedroom carrying two pails of bloody water. She left the house. Bauhin spoke again, his voice still hushed. "When this midwife returns with the fresh water, please let her and Marie wash and prepare Eugenie's body. The birth was harsh and caused her much damage. There are things you should not see, things no husband should see. It will be your job to bathe her face and her hands, to talk to her and pray for her as she makes her journey from this place."

Sebastian nodded. He was numb, but he could appreciate the cruelty that Bauhin was shielding him from. And so, for the next hour he sat in the kitchen while the two women tenderly attended Eugenie. Finally, Marie came to lead him back to see his wife. As they entered the room, the two midwives slipped out and into the night.

He took hold of Eugenie's right hand—so cold—and squeezed it, whispering to her of his love and his lostness, promising her he would protect Susanna and their baby boy and never let any harm come to them. Marie, on the other side of the bed, held Eugenie's other hand. With silent tears she joined in the eulogy, the love poem they were both composing for her. And so it went on for the rest of the night, the two of them holding vigil, companioning each other and Eugenie's spirit as it began its last journey.

It wasn't until dawn's light entered the room that Marie asked, "The baby. What name will you give him?"

He blinked slowly, as if trying to remember something said a long time ago. "We chose a name should this be a boy. Nathaniel. It means 'God has given him.'"

Chapter 20
Tenderness

After the funeral, nothing seemed real. The necessity of talking, the necessity of eating, the necessity of rising each day and dressing—they seemed hollow, meaningless tasks. And yet they had purpose because of the necessity. Susanna still needed to be fed and clothed, held and loved. The wet nurse had moved in with them, and Nathaniel, after initial struggles, was now feeding hungrily and thriving.

Without Marie, Sebastian would have been completely lost. Tears came easily to both of them most days, but Marie proved the stronger of the two. It was she who knocked on his bedroom door and urged him up each day. It was she who worked tirelessly to prepare meals for him and for Susanna. And it was she who kept telling him to be strong and to be the best father he could be, because that's what Eugenie would have wanted, and because that's what was needed of him. She invoked Eugenie's name often, as if she were still a presence living with them. When he tried to say her name, a great swelling gathered at the base of his throat, making it hard for him to speak.

Bauhin dropped by often to check on them, especially on Nathaniel, who, of course, held a sacred place in his heart. On one of these visits, he asked Sebastian if he'd heard the latest news from Geneva.

"What news, Jean?"

"John Calvin's wife passed away a couple of weeks ago. After a long illness apparently."

Sebastian's eyes stung. Despite his friction with Calvin, he had always admired Idelette—her kindness and gentle warmth. And perhaps his own loss had widened his heart to enable him to feel for John's loss.

Marie, standing near, cradling Nathaniel, said, "That's so sad for John. What will happen to Idelette's children now, I wonder?"

Bauhin bowed his head, as if realizing he had simply added to the sadness his friends were carrying.

Life went on like this for weeks until, somehow, the fog began to lift. Sebastian first noticed it one evening just before Susanna's bed time, when Marie was playing a game with her in the kitchen, a game that involved clapping in time to a rhyme. On the third time the sequence broke down, Marie buried her face in her hands in mock despair, and Susanna giggled. It was the first sound of happiness that he could remember hearing for the longest time. Susanna turned toward him and smiled. The purity of her face, the innocence of her eyes, melted something inside him. He smiled back at her. In another corner of the room, the wet nurse sat near the fire with Nathaniel, who fed contentedly. It dawned on him right then that he had been given more blessings than many men knew in a whole lifetime.

That Marie would continue to live in the same house as Sebastian, Susanna, Nathaniel and the nurse went unquestioned by all who knew them. Certainly in Geneva, it would have been seen as immoral, and the consistory or Company of Pastors would have stepped in. But here, their friends rallied around with gifts of food and words of solace that spoke only of love. Marie had once said she would be the best aunt the world had ever seen, and she seemed determined to live up to that pronouncement. Sebastian was grateful that Susanna had Marie there to comfort her, to fill some of that terrible abyss ripped open by Eugenie's death. But as the months crawled past, he began to realize something else, something mysterious and unexpected. Day after day, Marie was also beginning to fill the aching, lonely chasm in his own heart.

He had always thought of her not as a cousin by marriage but as his sister and friend. But now, as they worked together to build a home filled with tenderness, friendship no longer described the bond that grew between them. After supper and once Susanna was in bed, the nurse would leave to tend to her own family. And as the frequency of Nathaniel's feeds decreased, Sebastian and Marie found themselves alone together more and more. Often, the two of them would sit at the table and try to make sense of their new lives.

For three months, they dwelled in this liminal space between death and life, until finally Sebastian became sure of what his heart was telling him: he must choose life. And so, by the light of the kitchen's candles, he asked Marie to marry him. Her lips parted, and she gaped back at him, eyes glistening in the flickering luminescence, her pupils deep as coal-pits. Immediately after the words left his mouth, Sebastian wanted to take them back. He could see a look of confusion and shock on her face at his outlandish proposal. A new wave of fear washed over him. After the tragedy of Eugenie's death, he had finally found a kind of happiness, a kind of stability. Had he now jeopardized that with his foolish words? Reflexively, he stood, wanting to apologize, wanting to turn back time, if only by a few minutes.

Marie stood too. She stared at him with all the intensity of one trying to unwrap a mystery or solve an old puzzle. Noiselessly, she moved around the table, sliding her right arm around his waist and her left under his shoulders. She leaned in against him, enfolding him in an embrace so intimate they now formed one shadow in the dancing candlelight.

Clinging to each other, their bodies began to tremble as they both wept for all they had known and lost and now might find together. The candles on the table had burned to stubs by the time their tears ceased flowing. Marie finally looked into Sebastian's eyes and whispered, "Yes. Of course, the answer is yes."

In late summer, they held a simple wedding service and made public the cords that bound them, cords of love and pain and sacrifice. All their new friends were there, embracing them with their best wishes and bathing them in their prayers. Even André came, making the long trip from Orbe. He was, as far as anyone could tell, genuinely happy and at peace with this new union, blessing them with both his presence and his words.

As with every new union, awkwardness was to be expected. Marie had never lain with a man before, and Sebastian had only ever known intimacy with Eugenie. But they found their hunger for oneness overwhelming, a tension that demanded release. Marie made up for her inexperience with a tender responsiveness that took his breath away, and he, after all the months of pain and sadness, was fed by a spring of new energy in which they both took joy.

Chapter 21
Rumor and Mystery

Of all their new friends, the van Brugges gave them the most comfort. Dirkgen and Tanneke drew close to Marie and embraced her. Jan was ever willing to share his theological insights with Sebastian, thoughts which ranged from the brilliant to the baffling. Sebastian soon realized Jan was a mystic, a man who talked about God as if he were an intimate friend or lover. He began to reflect on Jan's faith and how it compared to the faith of a very different man he knew: John Calvin. That's when a realization slowly dawned in Sebastian's mind, one that he found disquieting: What we bring to the Scriptures shapes what we find there. Jan approached God as an artist; John as a lawyer. Sebastian knew there was an ancient Latin phrase for this concept: *Quidquid recipitur ad modum recipientis recipitur* (We receive things not as they are but as we are).

If a gardener and an engineer were given the Bible to read, he wondered, *what different treasures would they find hidden in its pages?*

More and more, Sebastian grew intrigued by the way that beauty and spirituality were woven together in Jan's life. Not many weeks after their wedding, Jan invited him and Marie to lunch at his impressive manor house, the Spiesshof. As they chatted and waited for the food to be served, Sebastian's eye caught a disk of colored glass hanging in one of the windows, dancing in the sunlight. Enchanted, he asked Jan if there was anything else of his work he and Marie might see. Jan thought for a moment, and then beckoned for Sebastian, Marie and Dirkgen to follow him.

They proceeded down a hallway to a door where Jan beckoned them to cross the threshold. Sebastian drew a deep breath as the miasma of paint and oil washed over him. Jan maneuvered his way around tables and easels toward a vast canvas propped against the wall. As Sebastian drew closer, an intricate pattern emerged from the canvas: a plane of symmetrical, semi-circular cells drawn in a deep indigo ink, rather like the scales of a fish or the tiles of a roof. There were hundreds of them, all almost identical in dimension, fanning out wider and wider as they moved across the canvas. Over them had been swirled watercolors in several shades of blue—from azure to turquoise to amethyst. Running around the edges of the canvas was more ink-work forming borders in an intricate geometric design. At the far right edge was the outline of a naked male—two in fact, mirror images of one another, one up, one down, a band of blue, shimmering like water, separating them at the knees. One figure had a hand reaching to the left, the other a hand to the right. A slash of vermilion red ran through both figures.

"What do you see?"

Sebastian leaned forward then stepped back, trying to get a sense of perspective. "The bulk of it seems to be a close-up view of a creature of great beauty and symmetry. A giant fish? The wing of a bird? A dragon, perhaps?"

"Form, as always, is in the eye of the beholder. When I ask Dirkgen, she sees a web rather than a creature." Jan smiled. "I call this piece *Knowledge, Will, and Imagination*—"

"Oh," Sebastian interjected, mystified.

"By which I mean God's knowledge and our will as they dance together and unfold through time and space."

Sebastian examined the canvas again. "And these images?" He pointed at the two male figures.

"The two Adams. Alpha and Omega. The beginning and the end. He who was and is and is to come."

A wave of unknowing rippled through Sebastian. Other than the painting being beautiful, it made no sense to him.

Jan gave a soft chuckle. "I'll show you."

From a nearby bench, he used his hand to smooth the creases from a large sheet of paper. On the same bench, he found a quill and an inkpot. "Philosophers are always debating the question of free will and predestination. If God is everywhere and all knowing, then surely everything we do is ordained and predetermined by him, yes? Thus, some even say that human beings are no more than puppets on a string, dumb marionettes for God to play with. Others argue no, we are creatures made in God's image, co-creators with him, endowed with the freedom to make choices, especially moral choices. Like Christ, we could quote the psalmist and say, 'You are all gods,' to which the writer of Hebrews added, 'And made only a little lower than the angels!' But how do we resolve this battle between free will and predestination, between man as puppet and man as artist?"

Unsure if his friend posed a rhetorical question or not, Sebastian attempted an answer. "As you may know, Augustine draws a distinction between foreknowledge and predeterminism." He peered at the painting again. "But how this signifies that idea?" He shook his head.

"Here, look!" Jan leaned over the bench and in the left-hand margin of the new page he drew three symbols, like stars, each a third of the way down. "These are decisions you have to make. Perhaps something simple like whether or not to go to the market, whether to buy apples or pears, or which route to take to get to the market: the main street or the back alleys. Perhaps the decision is about something much more important like whether to marry Hilda or Freda or Eva. Or whether to take a great risk and offer your life for a noble cause. Anyway, to keep it simple, let's say in this case you start with three decisions—as shown by these stars—and ever after have two possible choices."

From each of the three stars he drew two semicircles, like large C's, with each of the C's large enough that their arms touched the one above to form a single column. "But now from here, whatever choice you've made reveals more possibilities and choices. We'll keep it simple again. Say you have to make only two more choices: whether to eat the fruit raw or to cook it; whether to have children or not." From the two horizontal tips of each initial C, he drew four more semicircles that touched each other. "And of course, each of those choices has led you down a different path, a different destiny, and created new and different possibilities and choices. Perhaps even a different world."

He drew five more semicircles on the tips of the three newest C's, so now there were twelve in all. "And now yet more choices, more paths, other destinies." And again, he added semicircles to the tips of the last five C shapes, creating a column of six more. To them he added a column of seven more. And on and on it went across the page. Even though Jan's hand was moving rapidly, Sebastian marveled at how precisely he formed each figure. The rows and columns of scales marched across the page, fanning out from left to right until the whole of the sheet was full. "Of course, it is so much more complex than this, as we nearly always have more than two choices to make. And we live with the consequences of every other creature's choices too. But I think you can see what I mean by all of this, yes?"

"To be honest, not exactly, Jan. Other than that, you have created an exquisite design."

"I'll explain. As we go through life, it feels as if time moves from left to right, from start to finish, and that decisions unfold step by step, one after the other. Our minds struggle to comprehend the complex pattern that really exists. But in my painting"—he gestured toward the canvas—"where is God?"

"Outside of it, of course."

"Yes, outside of it. But also, inside of it. He's everywhere. Surely there is no place where God is not. God is beyond the canvas but also within its weave and even in the paint, for he is both the art and the artist. We look at this and we read it from left to right, step by step. But because God is both inside and outside of time and space, he can read it from right to left or left to right, from top to bottom or from corner to corner. He can even read it from inside of the canvas looking out. Every moment is now to God. For him, there is no future or past, only the present. No choice we make ever surprises God, for he could always see it as a possibility. But I don't say 'foresee' it, as there is no 'fore' for God, only the present. But"—he held his index finger aloft—"and this is important: God gives us free will, and we choose. In fact, we *must* choose. All of us are like Adam on that first morning, waking and beholding the creation, having the choice to either tend it or plunder it. To obey or disobey. Like Cain, we awake with the potential to love our brother or to destroy our brother. God knows every possible choice we could ever make and every possible consequence and destiny that could result from each and every possible choice. He *sees* it all. But he is not a puppeteer forcing us to make *that* choice or *this* choice, for there would be no dignity, no freedom for either party in that, not even for God. You remember what Augustine said, yes?"

Sebastian smiled as he remembered the quote André Zebedee had tested him with all those years ago. "'When you remember past events, you do not compel them to have happened, and in the same way God does not compel future events to happen by his foreknowledge of them.'"

"Exactly. Except I would not use the word foreknowledge. Just knowledge. Or imagination—both ours and God's. As we like to say, 'To those who believe, all things are possible.'"

Sebastian chuckled softly. In Calvin's scheme, there were only ever two fates: salvation or damnation, and humanity played no role in either. God, since before creation, had arbitrarily chosen each person's eternal destiny, and nothing anyone did or did not do could change that. This was God as puppet master, to borrow Jan's figure of speech. But here in front of him—this was God the infinite artist. "I'm not sure I understand it completely, Jan, but it *is* beautiful."

"Perhaps, but it frustrates me that with my little paints and tiny canvases I can capture so little of God's beauty. Or of the universe's, for that matter."

Just then, from off to their right, Marie's voice interrupted Jan's discourse. "Look, it's Anna!"

At the note of surprise in her words, Sebastian swung around expecting to see that a newcomer had entered the room. But no. Marie stood staring intently at another canvas propped against the wall a few feet away. A cloth covered a portion of the work, but still, the likeness was unmistakable: Anna van Berchem, the wealthy heiress who was part of the Dutch refugee community, her luminous brown eyes and high cheekbones perfectly captured. As he walked over to admire it, Sebastian felt his cheeks reddening at the sensuality of the image—Anna's unrobed shoulders, the nakedness of her breasts rendered discreet only by the wood of the lower frame. Sebastian looked back at Jan, whose face had turned red.

"Yes, of course, it's Anna! Beautiful, isn't she? And a frequent guest in our home. She is like a daughter to us, and Jan has portrayed her perfectly, don't you think?" Dirkgen beamed with pride.

"It's marvelous," Marie agreed. "You have such a gift, Jan."

Jan seemed to ignore her comment as he reached toward one of the windows and lifted a small, round glasswork that hung from the catch. Curious, Sebastian moved to stand beside him. Jan held a palm-sized disk that encased an intricately painted figurine—a woman dressed in purple, a scarlet flaming sword held aloft in one hand, the other pressing a Bible to her breast, while golden-brown hair curled and flowed like water down to her waist. Beneath her, the word *Veritas* had been painted in fine, black letters.

With a grin, van Brugge pressed it into Sebastian's hand. "It is yours, my friend."

"I couldn't. Think of all the work you have put in to it and—"

Van Brugge cut him off. "It's for you, Sebastian. A symbol of our friendship."

Marie had drawn close. "It is exquisite, Jan."

Jan was already moving toward the door, his hands raised as if fending off the praise. "Thank you, my friends. You are very generous to me. But I believe our lunch will be ready for us. Beauty may feed our souls, but it is food that sustains the body. So, come. Let's continue our conversations while we eat."

As the days passed and their friendship deepened, Jan began hinting to Sebastian that they should write a book together, yoking his spiritual flair and imagination to Sebastian's scholarship. Each time, Sebastian would raise an eyebrow and cautiously reply, "Perhaps one day, Jan." It was all he was prepared to commit himself to. As much as he loved the van Brugges, he was wary of allying himself too closely with their idiosyncratic ideas.

Moreover, the longer he lived in Basel, the more he noticed whispers and insinuations about these Netherlanders. The rumors had begun among Calvin's followers in the Reformed church, but were now spreading into the university circle as well. That dreaded word, Anabaptist, was beginning to be used to describe this little Dutch-settler community that lived so intimately and held so many things in common.

Anabaptist was a label Sebastian had come to view with great suspicion. Those who regarded themselves as orthodox, whether Catholic or Protestant, often used it to describe anyone they differed with on doctrine. He knew that hatred of this sect was one of the few things that Catholics, Lutherans, and Calvinists held in common.

Back in Geneva, whenever anything to do with the Anabaptists had come up for discussion, Calvin would quickly pour contempt on everything about the sect. They were led by what he called "hedge-preachers," uneducated men and women who—so his story went—

hid in forest and bush and, when the authorities weren't looking, leaped out to preach the gospel to whomever they could find—often the simple and uneducated. And when the poor embraced their simple message, as many did, these radical pastors would then dip them in the nearest body of water and assure them that they were now part of the new creation, the just society that God was building. Because this shadowy movement had been driven underground, identifying and arresting its leadership was difficult. But the authorities in Europe were sure of three reviled names at least. These nefarious figures were Thomas Müntzer, David Joris and Menno Simons. Müntzer had been executed at the end of the infamous peasant uprising, but Joris and Simons were still at large.

If pressed further for cause against the Anabaptists, Calvin would recount the events of 1525 and 1534—two infamous rebellions, the histories of which the respectable classes cited as warnings against allowing the poor and ignorant to interpret the Bible for themselves. Sebastian had read the horrific accounts. Begun in 1525, inspired by Luther's teachings on the priesthood of all believers and encouraged by the charismatic preacher Thomas Müntzer, peasants in Northern Germany had risen up against their feudal lords, demanding justice and rights to land. Believing that he would surely speak out on their behalf, they had called upon Luther to support them in their struggle against oppressive landlords. Luther's reply had been swift and vicious. He published a booklet entitled *Against the Murderous, Thieving Hordes of Peasants* in which he urged the authorities to "smite, stab, cut and slay these rebellious wretches." Of course, the well-equipped armies of the German princes did just that, soaking the soil of the fatherland with the blood of the dispossessed. One hundred thousand of Germany's poorest were slaughtered. For those who survived, many entered the waters of re-baptism and embraced the Anabaptist movement, which, it was now clear, possessed a far deeper vision for social equality than Luther ever had.

For the next nine years, authorities brutally suppressed both the Anabaptists and the peasants alike, determined to ensure that there were no further uprisings. But this was a fervent and apocalyptic era, and the desiccating winds of poverty, plague and social injustice created tinder-dry ground upon which every spark caught alight. Under the sway of fiery end-time preachers, an army of peasants marched on the west German town of Münster and installed their own King David, a man who ruled his new dominion with an iron fist. The leaders then declared polygamy to be lawful—in fact, to be forcibly practiced. For hadn't King David and his son Solomon had their harems? Any who dared question these divine commands soon found themselves clutching at their slit and bleeding throats.

Armies were raised and sieges mounted, but the citizens of the new kingdom were surprisingly tenacious, holding out for a full year. By June of 1535, however, their resources were exhausted, and Münster lay littered with the emaciated bodies of the starving. Finally, the besieging army, Catholic and Protestant combined, stormed the city and turned its cobblestone streets into rivers of blood. The leaders of the rebellion were publicly tortured and executed, their bodies left to rot in cages hung from Münster's Cathedral. It was a salutary lesson to all who passed by: God and his church were still to be feared. Sebastian knew that those cages still hung there, the rotting bones testifying to the folly of rebelling against those more powerful than yourself.

Because so much of his information about the Anabaptists had come to him through Calvin, Sebastian made up his mind that he should seek Oporinus's views on the matter. The master printer was one of those encyclopedic men who seemed to know at least a little something about everything. One afternoon, as Sebastian slid a final translation to the edge of his desk, his big bear of a friend entered the room from the rear of the print shop. Oporinus crumpled a white cloth between his oily hands, smearing a layer of thick, dark ink across the towel. Humming the tune of some song or other, he walked to Sebastian's desk and cast an eye over his work, grunting appreciatively.

Sebastian cleared his throat. It was a delicate topic, but knowing Oporinus was not deterred by social niceties, he plunged straight in.

"Johannes, those they call the Anabaptists—what do you know of them?"

Oporinus's thick eyebrows arched in surprise, but he hesitated only momentarily. "It seems they started out in one of our own Swiss cities, Zurich. In 1525 or so, an earnest little group was studying the New Testament and asking themselves what it meant to truly be a disciple of Jesus. As they read, they came to the conclusion that there were no examples in the Bible of children being baptized. But there were plenty of examples of adults being submerged into and rising from baptismal waters. The New Testament described baptism as the sign of beginning a new life, a marker that said the recipient desired to walk in the footsteps of Jesus. Thus, this band of enthusiasts marched down to the nearest river and started immersing one another, declaring themselves reborn. It didn't go down well with the city authorities, that's for sure. They got chased out of Zurich. Those who were too stubborn to leave were either imprisoned or drowned for their troubles. As I'm sure you know, both their beliefs and the persecution of their beliefs spread rapidly across Switzerland and Germany. In turn, they were hunted and hounded out of every place they were found, or put to death if they proved themselves stubborn. Even here in Basel, all of them were chased out in the years between 1525 and 1530, but not before many of them were drowned by the good Christian leaders of our councils and our church."

"But that seems so absurd. Why should this different understanding of baptizing cause such fear and anger among the authorities and in the church? Why kill people for such an act?"

"Think about it, Sebastian. It is no small thing. Independence of this magnitude is an affront to both church and state. Those holding onto power know they must keep total control of the sacraments, including the sacrament of baptism. By controlling the sacraments, they maintain control over how infants are inducted into the order of our society, how children are catechized and educated, how couples are married, even how the dead are buried. It is through rolls such as these that the authorities keep track of who lives where in each parish. It is how they extract taxes and tithes. It is how they conscript for their armies and, over a lifetime, how they marshal their citizens. Those who control the sacraments control the people. So of course, they will never surrender that control without a fight. As for the church, there is a double reason to fear these re-baptizers, for they question one of the church's most central dogmas."

A chill passed through Sebastian. Whether it was fear or excitement he could not tell, but he was sure that Oporinus was leading him to the brink of some new precipice.

"Augustine was one of the first theologians," Oporinus continued, "to argue the case for original sin—the idea that each and every one of us has inherited an utterly sinful nature from Adam. Others before him had postulated this as an idea, but for Augustine, it was a fact about which he was very dogmatic. And if every human, from conception, is completely tainted, then infant baptism became a necessity, the only thing that can wash away the guilt of Adam that damned every newborn. For Augustine, this was critical, for if a child —even a babe at the moment of its birth—should die before baptism, sin would take them straight to the fires of hell. With such fear hanging over them, every parent was—and is—desperate to be in the good graces of the church and its priests and sacraments. Fear is the most powerful way to control people, isn't it? But then along come these Anabaptists who don't seem to care a jot about what Augustine said. They argue for free will and that baptism should be freely chosen. You see, Sebastian? It is no small thing. It is revolutionary."

Sebastian said nothing when Oporinus finished speaking. Ideas and doctrines that had been built up in his mind over a lifetime were teetering. Oporinus was forcing him to see that the religious conflicts and persecutions raging across Europe ran much, much deeper than a simple squabble over how to interpret the Bible. It was about power and control and salvation.

"And you know about the tragedy of Münster, yes?" Oporinus

asked.

"Of course. Who hasn't heard of Münster? As far as Calvin was concerned, it was the final proof of the depravity and blood-thirstiness of the Anabaptists, the reason why order must be maintained by church and state working together and using whatever force is necessary to suppress them. And in the light of Münster, it seems true. The level of violence Anabaptists are prepared to use is terrifying, isn't it?"

Oporinus's lips parted, as if forcing a smile, though really it was closer to a grimace. He blew a hiss of air out through clenched teeth. "Perhaps, Sebastian, perhaps. But remember, history and its interpretation is always written by those who have triumphed. By those who hold power. Those who are weak or defeated seldom win the right of reply."

Sebastian's brow collapsed into a question mark as he absorbed this enigmatic reply. A dozen more questions rose in his mind. But before he could ask any of them, the door opened, heralding the arrival of an assistant from the university, come to pick up the very work Sebastian had just finished. While Sebastian showed the man some of the more contentious corrections he'd needed to make, Oporinus slipped on his doublet and left the shop.

Of all the questions swirling through Sebastian's head, there was one that troubled him most. In fact, the question had troubled him ever since his time in Lyon: how had Christianity become so violent? In the Scriptures, Jesus had taught that his followers must love and forgive their enemies, no matter how badly they were treated by them. So committed was Jesus to this ethic, that he had even forbidden his disciples from defending him with swords when a mob threatened his life. Yet every Christian sect—Catholic, Lutheran, Calvinist, and now, even Anabaptist, the very group that talked of trying to follow in Christ's footsteps—was at war and slaying one another.

Despite his discussion with Oporinus, he was no closer to discerning whether the rumors about Jan and his supporters were true. He weighed up the evidence. It was said that the majority of Anabaptists came from among the poor and dispossessed. These wealthy Netherlanders clearly did not fit that description. And if a willingness to use violence was a second feature, this Dutch party had hidden all trace of it. He was hard-pressed to name a group of people more given to kindness, gentleness, and forbearance. In contrast to most of Basel's nobles, he had never seen van Brugge with a sword strapped to his side. And as to the question of adult baptism, no one from their circle had ever raised that issue. Indeed, he had witnessed Jan and Dirkgen putting their youngest children forward to be christened in the Reformed Cathedral.

All of this led Sebastian to conclude that the rumors were false. And yet there were things that nagged away at him. The way they shared their homes and possessions and cared for one another's children—as if they were not just friends but a community of brothers and sisters. And of course, they had fled as one from the Netherlands, a known stronghold of Anabaptists. This was a mystery, one full of intrigue. There was so much about the van Brugges that he loved and admired, but his intuition told him that below the surface there were things hidden, as yet disclosed. This thought unnerved Sebastian.

After so many years of chaos and uncertainty, pain and loss, Sebastian and Marie began to marvel at how right—even tranquil— their life together felt. Yes, there were still weeks when Oporinus could offer him nothing, and he had to feed his family by hauling fish and wood from the river or by laboring on building sites. But compared to the bitterness of Geneva, these exertions seemed sweet. Here in Basel, he could fully pour himself into the passions Geneva had suppressed: laboring by day, writing by night. In August of 1551, after twelve long years, he finally completed his translation of the Bible—a masterpiece, written in the most eloquent Latin his skills could produce.

It was a striking publication, and not just for its arresting language or its clever use of maps, images and thoughtful annotations. It was also the audacity of its preface. Castellio dedicated the work to England's fourteen-year-old king, Edward VI, who had succeeded his father, Henry VIII. Despite his youth, Edward was known to be a passionate Reformer with a love for languages and theology. In the preface to his Bible translation, Sebastian pleaded with Edward to work for peace and promote tolerance toward all.

"Your Majesty," he wrote. "Do you see? Even as knowledge and the number of books in our world multiplies, the love of each toward his neighbor diminishes, with conflict between believers now more bitter than ever. Christendom slumbers in a state of darkness, still waiting for the prophet's vision to be fulfilled: that day when swords will be beaten into plowshares, and spears into pruning hooks."

With the publication of his Bible and its extraordinary preface, Sebastian Castellio proclaimed a message that had been lost for centuries: violence carried out in the name of Christ is self-contradictory. The conviction had been building in him ever since the horrors of Lyon. It had been honed in debate with Oporinus and van Brugge. It had been made more certain by every hour he spent studying the Scriptures. Finally, he was willing to say in the most public way possible that something was deeply, tragically wrong with the way Christianity was taught and practiced across all of Europe. Sebastian Castellio, the gentle scholar, had launched an attack on those who crushed others and used the Scriptures to justify it.

There was much to celebrate. His translation was being hailed by many as the most beautiful version of Scripture yet. And that spring, even as Sebastian had been applying the finishing touches to his manuscript, Marie's belly had been swelling with child. That April, blissfully unaware of all the great conflicts raging around her, little Anna Castellio entered the world. They were now a family of five. And caring for them, would consume all of Sebastian's energy for the next few years.

Chapter 22
The Tragedy of Michael Servetus

The year 1553 began with a long-hoped-for blessing, something that seemed like a miracle. Out of the blue, Sebastian was offered the chair of Greek at Basel University. For years, the case for his appointment had been building. His publishing output could no longer be ignored. His talent for translating works of antiquity from Greek to Latin could not be denied. And his Latin Bible was in high demand and praised by many. Yes, his star was on the rise. Yet he had one other powerful factor also working in his favor: Bonifacius Amerbach, the administrator of Erasmus's legacy, was a firm supporter. Bonifacius had been charged with administering the funds from Erasmus's estate to support both the poor and those scholars who "continued in the spirit of Erasmus." Sebastian Castellio, he believed, was the perfect candidate.

After eight years of poverty and anguish, of toiling over and over again, Sebastian had been invited into one of the university's most prestigious posts, though its prestige exceeded its financial remuneration. Still, it would be more than he could ever earn as a laborer or proofreader. And for that, Sebastian and Marie gave thanks to God, for their family's needs were greater than ever. Another daughter, Barbara, had arrived.

Sebastian was in high spirits, having settled contentedly back into a life of teaching. Furthermore, he had spent the past few months completing the revisions to his French Bible—which now included both Testaments—and was busy readying it for printing. One golden Friday afternoon on an uncommonly warm autumn day, a handful of teachers from the University of Basel were taking lunch at The Hare, a popular inn of stone and plaster squatting on the riverfront. For weeks now, Sebastian had kept them abreast of the progress he was making with his Bible translation. In a bubbly mood, he decided that today he would share with them the joyous news that it was now complete.

As he related the long, stumbling journey to get his French translation to this point, he grew perplexed. Those seated at the table in the tavern greeted his news, not with raised mugs but with uneasy glances in the direction of Martin Borrhaus, the university's head of theology and Basel's chief censor. Someone sitting to Sebastian's left cleared his throat and tried to change the subject. The conversation grew stilted. It limped to an awkward close. Borrhaus stood and laid a hand on Sebastian's shoulder. "Come to my office, would you?" With that Borrhaus slipped away, a little more stooped than usual.

Fifteen minutes later, Sebastian stood at the door to Borrhuas's office feeling uncertain as to why he'd been summoned. After Sebastian sat, Borrhaus outlined his dilemma. He wished to make it clear that hearing of Sebastian's new translation brought him joy, and that he held huge admiration for Sebastian's scholarship and hard work. If it was up to him, he said, it would be printed tomorrow.

Then he leaned forward, his forearms on the desk. "But it is not that simple. I am sorry, Sebastian, but we have come under enormous pressure from other Swiss cities not to allow your French Bible to be published. They haven't explained why, but they oppose it. And they stir up the councils and the church to oppose it too."

Sebastian leaned back in his chair. "When you say 'other Swiss cities,' you mean Geneva, don't you? And when you say 'they,' you really mean John Calvin, yes?"

"Yes, Geneva and Calvin. But not only him. The theologians led by Theodore Beza in Lausanne, they have been stridently against it as well."

Sebastian gave a start at the name Theodore Beza. Though they had never met, he knew the name well. A protégé of John Calvin, Beza was a fellow scholar, classicist and poet. Quite a good one too. Sebastian recalled having read some of his Latin verse and finding it very worthy.

Borrhaus's voice snapped him back into the present. "I am under a lot of pressure here as well, Sebastian. The new professor appointed to the theology department, Wolfgang Wissenburg, adheres strongly to Calvin's teachings and despises dissent. But don't be despondent. There are others of us prepared to wrestle with the council and the church for you. It may take time, but I believe your Bible will see publication. Please, take heart and be patient."

Castellio answered with a resigned nod followed by a wry smile. Even after all this time, the long shadow of John Calvin still hung over him. And the line of attack had widened. Not just from Geneva now but also from Lausanne.

Sebastian stood and thanked Borrhaus for his explanation. Then he excused himself to prepare for his next class. He descended the broad wooden staircase to the floor below, a path that would take him past the Office of Administration near the main entrance. As he neared the administration office, Jakob, a young secretary, hailed him with a piece of paper held aloft.

"Master Castellio, while you were out at lunch, a man came looking for you. A tall man with red hair. When you were not to be found, he wrote this note for you and insisted I give it to you immediately upon your return."

Sebastian took the note and glanced down at the signature. Jan had signed his name with a flourish of wide, cursive letters. Immediately his heart quickened. Jan had never come by the university looking for him before. This certainly must be a matter of some import. His eyes flicked back to the top of the page and he began to read.

> *Dear Sebastian,*
> *Come for dinner this evening at the Rote Haus. An important visitor from Geneva has come with news that affects us all. Many of us will be gathered there. Others you think of who share our thirst for freedom, bring them too. Please come.*
> *Jan*

The note was enigmatic, but its sense of urgency clear. Teaching his class that afternoon was no easy task, his mind swirling with possible meanings to be gleaned from Jan's note.

That evening, Marie and Sebastian arranged for two young women who lived near their house, Alise and Katarina, to come look after the children. Then they set out for the Rote Haus. A twenty-minute walk brought them to the door of the van Brugges' townhouse. A servant ushered them into the tiled parlor where Jan and Dirkgen were speaking with those who had already arrived. Just behind the van Brugges stood Oporinus with Amerbach and Platter, all three wearing grave expressions. Next to them stood Nicholaas and Tanneke, the heiress Anna, and some of the other Dutch refugees. Beyond them were the Italian contingent, including the animated Perna and the brooding Gugliemo Grataroli, all circled around Curione. They conversed loudly with words and gestures. To his delight, Sebastian recognized among them an old friend from Geneva days: Bernadino Occhino. Bernadino had been one of the many who had fled Italy when Cardinal Carafa took control of the Roman Inquisition in 1542. Carafa's zeal was infamous. He was known to have said, "Even if my own father were a heretic, I would gather the wood to burn him." The purges that followed Carafa's promotion were vicious, and Occhino had been wise to flee.

"Bernadino! What are you doing here?"

"Sebastian! So good to see you again. The short answer is that Curione invited me, but really my journey here has been a long one. Like you, I found Calvin's Geneva increasingly suffocating. I left not long after you did. For a while I was in Augsburg, until that city was overrun by Catholic troops. From there, I fled to England to take up a position at Canterbury Cathedral, under Cranmer. But when Mary took the throne and had Cranmer burned, I once more took flight. And now I find myself here."

Sebastian shook his head. "So they kill one another in Christ's name in England now too?"

"Yes. It seems they are no wiser than we on the Continent. But I'm told Basel is a bulwark of freedom still. Is that true?"

"It is. And we pray it will long continue to be so. Will you join those of us here who work to secure that liberty?"

"As much as I would like to, I cannot. I have taken a position as pastor to the Italian community in Zurich. I will be leaving for there in a few days."

Just then, Jan crossed the room and took hold of Sebastian's arm. Sebastian introduced him to Bernadino. The two men nodded politely to one another.

"Jan, I got your note, and so we have come. What is the purpose of this meeting?"

"I think it better you hear it yourself from the mouth of our visitor, Matteo Gribaldi, fresh arrived from Geneva."

Sebastian's eyebrows rose. *Matteo Gribaldi?* That explained the excitement of the Italians. Gribaldi, the famous Italian legal scholar, was known for his teaching all over the Continent. He authored books regarded as authoritative in the field of European law.

Sebastian tried to recall what else he knew about this not infrequent visitor to Geneva. They had met a few times back when Gribaldi lived nearby in Farges. Gribaldi had originally fled to Farges after witnessing a Protestant—a fellow legal scholar—being burned to death in Venetia. He had greatly angered the Inquisition by writing up an account of the man's life and martyrdom, arousing sympathy and causing the story to become well-known all across Italy.

Sebastian's reverie was broken by Jan's voice booming in his ear as he called the room to order, stifling the various conversations. "My friends, please, come now into the dining room where food and drink will be served and our guest awaits us."

Dirkgen stood at the doorway to the dining room, encouraging the various guests to move toward the banqueting table. As Sebastian and Marie neared her, her face lit up. She reached out for Marie. At the same time, Tanneke and Anna appeared, and two by two, arms linked, they entered the room. Marie instantly gasped.

Crossing the threshold, they stepped into a space thick with flickering lights. To their left yawned an enormous fireplace of polished stone cradling a crackling blaze. Tapestries lined each wall. In the farthest corner stood an oak cabinet filled with porcelain, and in the center of the room, a vast table laden with food. Atop the table, serving dishes were heaped with roasted meats, steamed vegetables and poached apples, pears, apricots and peaches. Beside the plates of food stood bottles of wine, uncorked, their breath adding to the room's aromas. Spaced across the table were ornate candelabras of silver. Hung at each corner of the dining room were more candelabras, their numerous flames casting alternate shadow and light. On each side of the table, a dozen chairs had been arranged. At the far end, beneath a bank of windows draped in velvet, a man stood nursing a glass of burgundy wine. He wore a smart navy-blue doublet, a crisp white shirt, and beneath that, skirts and padded silk tights of cream with blue slashes. His sharp eyes attended to each guest as they entered the room. Sebastian raised a hand. Gribaldi smiled back in recognition.

Jan went to Gribaldi, then once more addressed the group.

"Thank you all so much for coming tonight, and at such short notice. Thank you, too, to Monsieur Curione and Monsieur Perna, through whom our guest comes to be among us. And we are indeed honored to host one of Europe's greatest legal minds, Master Matteo Gribaldi, though the news he brings us tonight is not good. For that reason, Dirkgen and I ask that you be seated, that we may eat these pleasant delicacies before we are informed of other morsels, some so repugnant they may disturb our appetites."

Though the food and drink were sumptuous, the conversations were distracted as guests speculated over the purpose of Gribaldi's visit. As the main course finished, valets appeared, carrying trays filled with sweets spiced with ginger and cloves. But few seemed interested in these. Instead, they glanced in van Brugge's direction, clearly anxious to hear Gribaldi's news.

Jan stood and clinked a small spoon against a glass. Three sharp pings silenced the hum of voices. With a slight bow, he cleared his throat. "Gentlemen and ladies, I ask you to honor our guest by paying heed to the testimony he brings, and by then considering how best we might respond." Turning to the head of the table, he addressed Gribaldi: "Il Signore Gribaldi, please begin."

Gribaldi took a final sip of his wine, then rose slowly, almost contemplatively, to his feet. He stood for a moment with his eyes closed and head lowered. Then he looked up and began to speak in his rich tenor, made more resonant by the melodious Italian lilt. "My friends, most of you I have not met and do not know. But Signore Curione tells me you are men—and women—of integrity, of peace. Those who love truth and freedom and despise unjust violence. For this reason, I feel able to speak frankly among you tonight, to bring you an honest report of all that I have recently witnessed in the city of Geneva."

He paused. Took a breath. "Some of you may be aware that I live within twelve miles of that city, and passing travelers often bring with them the latest news from that town to mine. You may also be aware that I am a jurist, highly studied in matters of European law and justice. As such, news pertaining to these realms holds particular interest for me.

"Some weeks ago, a traveler from Geneva alerted colleagues of mine that a most peculiar legal case was taking place in that city. Those colleagues then quickly appraised me of the situation. Because of my past dealings with the Inquisition, my colleagues were aware that I am particularly attuned to cases of religious persecution. But to my amazement, the case they alerted me to was not another instance of a Roman Inquisition crushing dissent. No. This report indicated that a heresy trial had been initiated in the city of Geneva against a fellow Protestant, a situation in equal parts curious and trepidatious. I rode to Geneva accompanied by one of my secretaries and spent three weeks closely observing the legal process being followed. What I saw shocked and dismayed me. A prisoner was being held in appalling conditions and with no recourse to counsel—a Spanish man by the name of Michael Servetus."

The moment this name was spoken, a murmur of recognition ran among those gathered who knew the Spaniard's writings. Here and there a more indignant voice rose above the rest.

Gribaldi cleared his throat, attempting to take control of the room once more. That gesture being ignored, he simply resumed more loudly. "Yes, yes, I perceive that some of you are familiar with this man's reputation and writing, just as I was. I will freely confess to you that I have found his books both worthy and sincere, and this added to my conviction that I must try to aid him. Moreover, it seemed to me that at every turn he was being denied both due process and natural justice. The longer I observed the case, the more clear it became to me that the man's guilt—his 'heretical' view of the Holy Trinity—had already been decided in advance by Geneva's ecclesiastical and administrative authorities and that the trial, to the extent that you could call it a trial, was simply a facade by which their prior decision should be confirmed.

"I suspect all of us in this room are familiar enough with the work of the various Inquisitions to know that this is their modus operandi.

Indeed, some of us have had to flee for our lives from just such machinations. But to see the same evils repeated in a city that holds itself up as an example of Christian grace, as a ... a pinnacle of biblical scholarship, this I found most shocking. So great was my consternation that I made repeated attempts to meet with the city's chief minister, Monsieur John Calvin, that I might impress upon him the importance of following a just legal process. These requests were rebuffed, causing my agitation to grow so great that I challenged John Calvin—for it seemed to me he was playing the role of chief prosecutor as well as the city's pastor—to a public debate over the application of European and Roman law. After all, as you may know, John Calvin is also a trained lawyer. I conveyed this challenge by the way of the Small Council, the body who were 'officially' conducting this case.

"Perhaps I am a proud man, for I thought my reputation as an international jurist would afford me some standing and some protection in this matter. But that very evening, a member of the council—and from what I understand, its only dissenting member—came and warned me to flee. He said that a prison cell was already being prepared to accommodate me. That very night, my secretary and I rode out of the city with haste. We made the decision not to return to Farges but to come here to Basel, well known as the most tolerant and advanced of the Swiss cities. This is a place where, I believed, my testimony would receive the fairest hearing. I only stand here before you a free man tonight because of the warning given me by a man whom I believe some of you know"—he speared Sebastian with a direct look—"a certain Ami Perrin."

Everyone now gazed at Sebastian. Across the table, Curione was examining him with a fierce intensity. Next to him, another Italian, Doctor Grataroli, looked up one side of the table then down the other before his haunted eyes fell back upon Sebastian, his expression so piercing it was as if the physician were trying to read Sebastian's thoughts.

"Gentlemen and ladies," Gribaldi resumed, "this news I bring you is very fresh, yet time is not on our side, nor on the side of the man unjustly accused. I believe his trial will reach a conclusion within the next few weeks unless we can somehow intercede on his behalf. If not, this man of well-reasoned beliefs and a sincerely held interpretation of Scripture will be executed by fire, chained to a stake by fellow Protestants."

The room went completely still. Beside him, Sebastian heard Jan breathing hard. Out of the corner of his eye, he noticed that the Dutchman was repeatedly clenching and unclenching his trembling hands. In the awful silence, each person seemed to be absorbing the gravity of what had just been said.

And then the room erupted, a cacophony of indignation. Each person turned to his neighbor and voiced a sense of outraged justice. Sebastian could hear Oporinus, a few seats away, shouting, "Barbarians!" above the din. Many of those assembled had fled religious persecution themselves, and their anger on Servetus's behalf—and against John Calvin—was passionate and visceral.

Curione stood but had trouble making himself heard over the noise of the room. Next to him, an argument had broken out between his fellow Italians. Turning to his left and right, he gestured with his hands for quiet. After he'd made several attempts, others began to take notice. The garble of conversation subsided, and he spoke out clearly, his speech gilded in a Tuscan accent.

"Listen to me, please. Many of us in this room know what it's like to be persecuted for our beliefs and so, I have no doubt, are able to feel the anguish of this man whom Signore Gribaldi has just described to us. But we need to find a way to turn these emotions into actions that may help to see his life spared from the flames." He paused. Those gathered were hanging on to each of his words. "I have arranged for Gribaldi to address the university's head faculty and administrators tomorrow. And I have invited members of the two councils to also attend, though this initiative has not gone unchallenged. There are many Reformed ministers who speak against us and warn the authorities against any protest, urging them to put our city's alliance with Geneva ahead of all other considerations. But among us—we who have been granted this tenuous gift of liberty—surely, we can do something!" His wide eyes implored as they swept up and down those seated at the table before coming to rest on Jan. It seemed that Jan was expected, as the host, to add some more words of challenge and hope, and perhaps a call to action. But for a long minute, Jan simply sat in his chair, his head lowered, his breathing labored, his body trembling. Sebastian laid a hand on his shoulder.

"Jan, I think Curione is calling on you to speak now. Can you manage it?" Sebastian's touch seemed to break whatever spell Jan was under. He nodded, took several more heavy breaths, then pushed himself to his feet. He placed both his hands flat on the table in front of him, as if to hold himself steady. When he spoke, his voice cracked with emotion.

"We who live in Europe take such pride in calling ourselves Christians. Yet look how we treat one another. Look at how we despise any person whose opinion or doctrine differs from ours by even one shade. Look at the persecution, the burnings, the wars that rage across the Continent—so many of them in the name of Christ. How can this be? How can this be?"

A look of genuine confusion clouded his face, like that of a man who has seen something incomprehensible. "No! This should not be. This *must* not be. Now is the time for each of us to use whatever gift we possess to fight against this great evil, yes? We must ... we must ..." Clearly struggling to control his emotions, he continued glancing down at his hands then back up at those who were listening. He tried to press on, but it became clear he found the task difficult. His speech finally stuttered to a conclusion. "Please, for those of you who are able, come tomorrow to the university to hear Monsieur Gribaldi a second time. But for now, as each of us leaves this place, we must remember this man, Michael Servetus, and consider how we may act in a way to intercede for his very life."

Jan sat heavily in his chair, breathing hard, as if all the air had been sucked out of him. When he spoke no more, the earlier cacophony of earnest conversations resumed. Some stood and made their way around the table, desperate to draw more information from Gribaldi. Others made for the door, still debating as they went.

After a few minutes, Jan had regathered himself, and his sense of urgency had returned. He turned and took hold of Sebastian's arm. "Now we must write! Now we must write!"

Sebastian struggled to understand the meaning of his friend's words.

"The book!" Jan said, almost shouting. "Remember? I said we must write a book. You said, 'Yes, someday perhaps.' Well, now is the day! We must write a book to save this man and expose this evil."

Sebastian finally registered the import of Jan's words. "But Jan, you heard what Gribaldi just told us. The trial in Geneva will conclude in a few weeks. We could not possibly write a book fast enough to influence the outcome."

"Then we must start immediately—if not to save Servetus, then to save the next man they want to burn. And the one after that. Don't you see Sebastian? This could be the fate of any one of us in this room! I will write as soon as I can to the councils of all the Swiss cities —including Geneva—pleading for this man's life. But I need your scholarship, Sebastian. You read the Scriptures in Hebrew and Greek and know the works of the church fathers. You have long philoso- phized about these things. Men like Calvin and Bucer, Melanchthon and Borrhaus—they will only be convinced by scholars like you, not artisans and pastors like me. A man's life is at stake, Sebastian. And beyond that, surely many men's lives." Jan's grip grew tighter as he half rose from his seat, towering over Sebastian. "I look at your many gifts and your thirst for what is just, and I think—I think perhaps you were born for such a time as this. You must write."

Sebastian sat speechless. Inside a terrible battle raged between his heart and his head. His heart said yes, take up the cause of the persecuted, speak up for the voiceless. But his head swirled with fevered warnings.

Jan was still gripping his arm, staring at him, his delft-blue irises luminous in the room's flickering light. Sebastian felt cornered, trapped. He glanced across the table where Dirkgen, Tanneke and Anna were all deep in conversation. A worried Marie stared back at him, searching his face as if reading every crease for a sign of what he and Jan were debating. When their eyes locked, he knew she understood that he was wrestling with the weight of a great decision.

"I will think about it, Jan. I will. I promise you that. But I cannot give you an answer tonight."

Jan looked dismayed but nodded and released his grip on Sebastian's arm. By now most of the guests had made their way toward the door. Dirkgen and Jan rose from the table and moved swiftly to the parlor to farewell their guests with a final valediction. Nicholaas, their son-in-law, was still seated, caught up listening to a furious argument Curione was having with Gugliemo Grataroli, each of them waving their arms about passionately. Sebastian stood and farewelled Oporinus, Platter and Amerbach, then made his way around the table to Marie, slipping his arm through hers as she stood.

As they entered the parlor, Dirkgen stepped forward and kissed Marie on the cheek. Beside her, Jan hovered anxiously, once more grasping Sebastian by the hand and staring beseechingly into his eyes. Sebastian looked away from the towering Dutchman, lowering his gaze to the tiled floor. In anguish, he broke his hand free from Jan's clasp, slipped it into Marie's, and led her out of the house.

A half-moon had risen over the city. It lit their way as they walked home, its silvery light providing little comfort. A northerly breeze had freshened, and the day's mildness had turned to a chilly night. The streets were largely deserted, and their footsteps echoed along Basel's cobblestones. Marie broke the fearful silence. "So, Geneva has grown even greater in its intolerance, and this poor man must suffer for it. Sebastian, do you think there is anything anyone can do?"

"I don't know. But Jan is begging me to work with him to at least try."

"But how? What can you do?"

"Jan wishes us to write a book. Together. Starting immediately."

Marie's brow furrowed. He could tell her mind reeled from thinking about all the ramifications that action might produce, both good and bad. She finally gave voice to what was weighing so heavily in both their thoughts. "You, more than anyone, could write such a book. But it would be a dangerous undertaking."

"Yes, exceedingly dangerous. Many, both on the Catholic side and the Reformed side, would seek to silence the authors of such a book."

"And what answer did you give Jan when he asked this of you?"

"I said I must think about it. What he proposes is no simple thing. It could cost us everything we've gained and everything we hope for the future."

Marie held his arm more tightly and leaned into him more closely. "Then I suppose you must ask God what is the just thing to do."

Sebastian sighed deeply but didn't reply. Those words weren't the ones he'd wanted to hear.

The next day was the Sabbath. As they readied themselves for church, Sebastian gently placed his hand on the small of Marie's back. "Do you mind if I take a walk by myself later this morning? I need to go somewhere quiet where I can think."

"Oh, I see. They make you chair of Greek, and you no longer have need of church. Is that how it is?" Marie's eyes sparkled with mock challenge.

Sebastian assumed a defensive stance, raising his hands with his palms facing her. "Marie, dearest, I obviously fall short of your saintliness. However, that is not what I meant. Rather, *following* the church service I wish to find a time and place where I can be alone, not surrounded by others."

Marie, now serious, considered the question. "Alise from next door will be coming with us this morning. So yes, husband, we will manage."

Sebastian kissed her on the forehead. "As I said, you are a saint. And I thank you."

After the service, Sebastian gave Marie's hand a squeeze and took off toward Saint Alban's Gate. Exiting the city's walls, he soon found himself in the midst of farmland and orchards. Three meadows beyond the city wall, and just short of the little River Birs, a track wound off to the left and down toward the Rhine. Sebastian's shoes scuffed through a carpet of red and amber detritus fallen from the trees overhead, each footfall exposing a layer of humus and releasing more of autumn's musk. There was always comfort in this walk. He had come here often, whenever he felt the need to be alone, to probe his thoughts for their deepest and most solid convictions. He had brought his old Bible with him, the one with the roughed leather cover.

As he neared the river's edge, he turned and followed the dirt track upstream, knowing that he would soon come to the stump of an ancient beech, one he had sat on many times while looking out over the water. It was a spot hidden by the trees that stretched between its location and the road. The morning was crisp and clear. The sun had been up long enough to warm the stump but not enough to dry all the dew off it. Sebastian took a thick, linen kerchief from his pocket and completed the task.

The peace of the place slowly enveloped him as he gazed out on the ever-moving Rhine as it flowed toward the distant sea. He bowed his head and worked to recapture all the words that he could from Gribaldi's impassioned speech of the night before and from Jan's equally impassioned plea. He looked up at the river, then the sky, and silently asked for courage and guidance. A seed that had been lodged at the back of his mind now drifted toward the front. *Today, read from the first letter of the apostle John, chapter four.* It was a passage he knew well. With his thumbnail he located it, opening his Bible to the love letter written by John, the youngest of the disciples—the disciple whom, it is said, Jesus loved most. And slowly, meditatively, he began to read.

> *God is love. Whoever lives in love lives in God, and*
> *God in them. This is how love is made*
> *complete among us so that we will have confi-*
> *dence on the day of judgment: in this world we are*
> *like Jesus. There is no fear in love. Instead, perfect*
> *love drives out fear, because fear has to do with*
> *punishment. The one who fears has not yet been*
> *made perfect in love.*
> *We love because he first loved us. Whoever claims to*
> *love God yet hates a brother or a sister is a liar.*
> *Whoever does not love their brother or their sister,*
> *whom they have seen, cannot love God, whom*
> *they have not seen. For he has given us this*
> *command: anyone who loves God must also love*
> *their brother and sister.*

Sebastian read and reread the passage. He tried to absorb it the way his skin was absorbing the morning sun. He pictured himself as an empty vessel, as one encountering this ancient text for the very first time. After a few minutes the words began speaking to him with a clarity he had seldom known before. *Because God is love, we are called to love—a love so powerful it will drive out all hate, all darkness, all fear. And if anyone walks in hate or fear, it can only be because they have never truly known God's love.*

He drew in a full draft of the cool morning air, filling his lungs with its sweetness. In the distance, he heard the peal of Basel Münster's bells calling the city's faithful to its next service of worship. Below him on the Rhine, a family of teal inched their way against the current, the youngsters peeping plaintively, working to stay close to their parents. Closing the Bible and placing it under one arm, he rose and slowly retraced his steps along the riverbank, back toward home.

He knew what he must do.

Chapter 23
The Most Dangerous Book

When Sebastian got home, he found that Marie and the children had not yet returned. So he sat at his desk and formed a plan. *I will walk to Curione's house where, hopefully, I can talk with Gribaldi and get more details from him about Michael Servetus's situation. Then I will find Jan and tell him of my decision.* He paced across to the corner of his study where most of his books stood on the wooden shelves he had built. He picked one out, then another, and carried them back to his desk. *Tomorrow, when the Sabbath is over, I will search among the university's much more impressive collection. I will make it my goal to understand what the earliest church thinkers said concerning how the unorthodox should be treated and then compare it with what both Calvin and the Catholic Church are doing.*

But exactly what kind of book should he and Jan write? Of this he wasn't yet sure. He only knew it would be regarded as seditious and would place their lives at risk.

By the time Marie and the children returned, Sebastian was scratching away furiously on a stack of paper, every few seconds dipping the tip of his quill back in the inkpot. Cradling Barbara in one arm, the other children gathered behind her, Marie stood quietly as he remained hunched over his desk with open books spread around him. All of them had learned to wait patiently when Sebastian was this lost in concentration.

Finally, he noticed them standing there. He rose from his desk and gathered Nathaniel and Susanna into his arms. Marie's brow creased as she surveyed the mounds of paper and the books on the desk. "You have decided, haven't you? About Jan's proposal."

Sebastian gave her a look he hoped was more reassuring than he felt. "Yes, I have decided. I will write a book with Jan."

Marie kissed the top of Barbara's head before looking up at him again. "As I knew you would, Sebastian. As I knew you would."

That afternoon, Sebastian made the long walk across town to the northern part of the city where Curione and many of the Italians lived. He rapped on the door, and Curione's valet answered.

"Is Celio in? And the visitor from Farges, Master Gribaldi, is he here still?"

"Yes, shall I—"

"Please take me to them, for I need to talk with them."

He led Sebastian to the lounge and tapped on the half-open door. When he stepped aside, Sebastian saw Curione and Gribaldi deep in conversation. As soon as Curione saw him, he cried out, "Sebastian! What brings you here? Come and join us!"

Sebastian pulled a heavily upholstered chair over and sat by the two men. "What brings me here is a book. A book yet to be written, and one that I pray will aid this Michael Servetus that you, Matteo, told us about last night. And if not him, then every man or women after him who might find themselves in his situation. It will not be an easy undertaking, but it is one that I hope you will consider joining us in, Celio. You, me, Perna, Jan, and Oporinus."

Gribaldi was staring at Sebastian, his eyes growing more intense with each of Sebastian's words. "You do realize how dangerous such an endeavor will be, don't you? And Celio, you also?"

Sebastian cleared his throat. "Yes, Matteo, I do. Believe me, I have not made this decision lightly. But I fear my conscience will give me no rest if I refuse to heed its voice." He turned to Curione. "I know this is the first you have heard of this, so I will not press you for an answer today."

Curione's eyes searched Sebastian's. "I need to hear more. What manner of book are we talking about?"

Sebastian described the rough outline he had formed. "But before I can say any more about what we should write, I have more questions for Matteo about what is happening in Geneva."

Matteo nodded. "If I can tell you anything more, Sebastian, I will."

"Thank you. Firstly, how did this man Servetus, a Spaniard, come to be in Geneva?"

"It seems he and Calvin have a long history. They met in their student days, when they were both studying at the University of Paris. More recently, Servetus had been living in Vienne, working as a physician and living under a false name because he was hiding from the Catholic Inquisition. He had already been placed on the Inquisition's wanted list for advocating theology declared unorthodox. He began writing to Calvin, wanting to rekindle their relationship and describing his insights concerning biblical interpretation. He even sent Calvin a copy of his book called *The Restoration of Christianity*."

"If this man's ideas are innovative, I am going to guess that Calvin did not receive them well."

"Not at all well. In fact, Calvin alerted the Catholic Inquisition in Vienne that there was a heretic hiding in their midst, sheltering under a false name, and that they should arrest him."

"What?" Curione interjected. "Surely Calvin would not assist a Catholic Inquisition?"

"Not directly. He used a proxy. There was a Protestant convert in Geneva by the name of Trie. This man had a Catholic cousin living in Vienne. Apparently, the two cousins used to write one another often, baiting each other about the errors of the other's faith. Anyway, it was through this channel that Calvin sent information to the authorities in Vienne. He sent pages torn from Servetus's book and from the personal letters Servetus had sent him. I suppose he hoped that the Inquisition would take care of Servetus for him. That's how vexing he must have found the Spaniard's theology to be."

Sebastian's brow creased with even more questions. "Good Lord. How dark and conniving. What happened then? Did the Inquisition arrest Servetus?"

"Yes, and threw him in prison while they conducted a trial. Because of the evidence Calvin had sent, he was certainly going to burn on a stake in Vienne."

"But obviously he didn't."

Gribaldi shook his head. "A daring escape from the prison prevented it. Something about climbing onto a privy roof and leaping over the wall of the courtyard. From there, he made his way to Geneva."

"No! Why? If Calvin betrayed him to the Inquisition, why on earth would he then run to Geneva?"

"It's hard to fathom. Some sort of fatal attraction, some sort of fascination with John Calvin that he'd held ever since Paris. Perhaps to confront Calvin for betraying him. Or perhaps he was naive enough to think that he could convince Calvin that his own novel ideas were theologically correct after all."

"Those ideas. What are they?" Sebastian pressed. "Last night you said he held unorthodox theories about the nature of the Trinity."

"I suppose you could call Servetus a modalist. He doesn't believe that God exists in three distinct persons. Like the Jews and the Muslims, he calls this polytheism. Rather, Servetus believes that the Creator can manifest or operate in three distinct modes: as Father, as Son, as Spirit. Apparently, back in Spain, Servetus had many friends among the Jewish and Mohammedan communities, and he sought an explanation that would make more sense to them—and to him."

Curione spoke again. "This seems a minor difference to me, a matter of semantics. Would you send a man to the stake for this?"

"Minor to you and me, perhaps, but not to all. And certainly not to John Calvin. But this is not the only issue. Servetus also claims that the Bible contains no evidence for infant baptism, only for the baptism of adults. And he ardently believes God has given us each free will. In his writings, he opposes the doctrine of predestination, saying that it 'shackles God in chains while reducing humanity to a block of stone.'"

Sebastian nodded. "I see how these ideas would infuriate one as rigid as Calvin, and, in his eyes, deem Servetus deserving of damnation."

Curione interjected again. "So this man goes to Geneva to see John Calvin. He sounds foolish to me."

"Servetus is perhaps reckless, but he is no fool. Intellectually, he is quite brilliant; a noted thinker in the fields of medicine, geography, languages, and—some would say—theology. But let me continue. He came to Geneva apparently thinking that after two days he would cross into Italy and continue to work there as a physician, perhaps under another assumed name."

"But he didn't make it."

"No. He hid in a Genevan guest house called The Rose. But he forgot, until that morning, that on the Sabbath it is compulsory to attend the divine service. Not to do so would bring him under scrutiny. So guess which divine service he attended?"

Sebastian's eyes widened. "Surely not!"

"Yes, surely. Saint Pierre, where John Calvin was preaching. He was recognized. Officers were called. And he was dragged into prison at Calvin's instruction. By the time I got there, in late September, he had been in prison many weeks, living in darkness. He was without an advocate, a friend, or even a change of clothes. He was in a bad way —clothed in rags, infected with lice, freezing cold. The trial is a total farce. He has committed no crime on Genevan soil, so really they have no right to imprison him. And despite his many requests, they have allowed him no lawyer."

Curione looked distressed. "Was there no one to speak on his behalf? No one at all?"

"It seems to me that the city council and the Company of Pastors are competing to show each other that *they* are the most righteous body, the most zealous, the most willing to purge heresy from the face of the earth. The only member of either body arguing against execution was, as I mentioned last night, Ami Perrin. But there were also others in the city opposed." He looked at Sebastian. "Your successor as rector of the College de Rive, Jean Colinet, for one."

"Ah, Jean is a good man, and a brave one too."

"Indeed. He likewise speaks well of you. Concerning this case, he had accused the Company of Pastors and the consistory of tyranny and cruelty. They, in turn, labeled him a 'Castellionist' and have laid a formal charge of 'undermining the honor of Geneva's ministers.' Two others I met were also opposed. A man called Léger Grymoult, a teacher, and a Dutchman called Pieter Zuttere, a refugee from the Inquisition who is a writer and printer by trade. Zuttere told me he is carefully watching the trial and keeping a record of all that he sees. This could be very useful one day."

"Yes, I think so. But we must make haste with our own writing, for you have indicated that this trial is approaching a conclusion. I wish to go and talk with Perna, Jan and Oporinus now. I will leave you to discuss that which I have proposed. Tomorrow I will return and ask you to share your thoughts with me again, Celio."

Gribaldi reached for Sebastian's hand. "This book you are proposing—it is crucial, something Christendom needs as never before. I will be praying for God's guidance and the protection of his angels to be over you as you write."

"Thank you, Matteo. We will need that if we are to succeed."

From Curione's house, Sebastian moved on to Perna's. At the door, a servant ushered Sebastian into the home's spacious study, where he found Perna engaged in a writing project of his own.

"Sebastian! Welcome. This is a happy coincidence, for today I am translating a text from Italian to Latin. Perhaps I should get you to proof it for me while you are here."

"I doubt you need that, Pietro. Your eye is the more skilled when it comes to Italian. I've come today to discuss with you the matters raised by Matteo Gribaldi."

As Sebastian unfolded his plan for the book, Perna listened intently. When he'd finished, Perna took hold of his hand and gripped it hard. "My answer is yes. I will write with you. A man only has one short life, and if he can make it count for something important, he should seize that moment."

Sebastian's second to last stop for the day was the van Brugges' townhouse, where he planned to inform Jan of his decision. As he walked toward the Rote Haus, a cooling breeze from the Rhine struck his left cheek. It was Jan himself who answered his rapping at the door, his eyes searching Sebastian for an answer to last night's question.

"How about we sit together and make a plan for the book that God has given us to write?" Sebastian said, giving his friend a wry grin.

Jan gasped then lifted Sebastian off his feet in an embrace. "Yes, come! Let us talk!" He led the way to the great table in the dining room.

"Jan, I am a classicist and well familiar with the writings of the church fathers. Let me assemble arguments from the earliest theologians right up till the present. You concentrate on arguments constructed from the New Testament and those from natural justice."

Jan nodded. "I can do that. But I will co-opt Nicholaas to help me. He has a better command of words and language than I. Between us, it is he who is the more able scholar."

Sebastian hesitated. There was something about Nicholaas that always made him a bit uneasy. He found Jan's son-in-law guarded and hard to read.

Apparently, Jan read his hesitation. "No, really Sebastian. He is both my secretary and my son-in-law. He is completely loyal. We can trust him to do this with us, believe me."

"Then I will rely on your word. We need as many skills as we can assemble if we are to bring such a work into the world. I will visit Oporinus next. His cooperation will be essential in bringing this book to print." He and Jan agreed to meet again in the morrow, and Sebastian exited back out into the Basel streetscape.

Ten minutes later, he was at Oporinus's. He found the printer at the front of his shop, stacking reams of paper. Being the Sabbath, the presses were still, but even without a room full of workers, Sebastian pressed his finger to his lips, his words coming out little more than a whisper. "A man's life is at stake, but more than that, perhaps the future course of the Christian religion. Do we wish to see Europe turn back to the Dark Ages, a time of war and torture, when endless violence was committed in Christ's name? Or do we push forward to an age of love and mercy, toward the kingdom Jesus spoke of?"

The big man listened in silence, holding Sebastian's gaze with his own. Sebastian knew Oporinus was weighing up his commitment to truth and calculating how great a price he was willing to pay for it. Finally, Oporinus replied, "I will give you my answer tomorrow."

Sebastian could ask no more of him than that. He returned home as swiftly as he could and went straight to his desk, where he began to feverishly consult his books and jot down page after page of notes. His hand moved rapidly across the paper, ink seeping from the quill and smearing on the flesh of his palm. Several times he paused and used his kerchief to wipe away the ink before beginning again. Late in the night, he finally laid his pen down and sought his bed.

The next morning, Sebastian rose early, determined to make the fullest use of the day. He ate quickly, kissed each of the children, then gathered up his satchel stuffed with papers. As he reached the door, Marie slipped a small parcel into the pocket of his doublet. She smiled and, on tiptoes, placed a kiss on his lips. He stepped out the door and threaded his way through Saint Alban's narrow lanes, past the paper mills and the two streams that fed the mill wheels, moving westward toward the university. The winter sky was full of rose-tinged clouds, brooding low, hugging the city. Even at this early hour, the streets teemed with workers on their way to the mills, warehouses and barges. To his right, between buildings, he glimpsed the Rhine, turgid and gray as it lumbered its way toward Rotterdam. He passed the cathedral and the old Augustine cloister, now an annex of the university, before arriving at the university itself.

His class load was light on Mondays, so he knew he should be able to ensconce himself in the library without anyone searching him out. The library covered half of the ground floor on the east side of the building, its farthest wall facing over the river. Tables and benches lined each side of the capacious room. In the middle, tall wooden shelves held books by the hundreds. Sebastian loved being here, working his way through a sea of ancient, leather-bound tomes beneath the ornate ceiling of filigrees and cornices. Even the smell of the leather and ink spoke to him, reassuring him that he was a scholar, a pilgrim journeying in the flow of history, immersed in its bubbling stream of ideas. This room was a vast banquet to be feasted on. When the reforming council had ordered the closure of Basel's monasteries in the 1520s, they had seized books gathered by monks over centuries and brought them to this chamber, claiming them as prizes for the new faith.

Sebastian selected a table by a window, overlooking the river, knowing the morning's eastern light would assist his reading. No other teachers and only a handful of students had come to study this morning. He almost had the place to himself. He began to work his way along the shelves. It was a slow search, for the books had not been placed in any particular order other than chronological. Fortunately, his ability to scan the titles in Greek, Latin, Hebrew, German and Italian helped greatly as he hunted for anything which might be useful.

Within an hour, in the oldest section of the library, he stumbled upon a series of thick volumes encased in brittle leather, each embossed with what had once been deep-set, but now faded, gold lettering: *Volumen de Patres Ecclesia*. He was pleased. He had found most of a series that surveyed the wisdom of the church fathers going back to the first few centuries after Christ. He carried the books back to his table and chose the oldest first, prying open its cover, which was stiff with age. He breathed deeply, inhaling the aroma of centuries past, strangely nervous as he lowered himself into the book's antiquarian debates.

The writing was faded and difficult to make out, and much of what he encountered was irrelevant to what he sought. He found himself skipping over vast, dense passages as his eyes searched for clues as to how the early church dealt with unorthodoxy, whether it ever considered force or violence to be permissible in those cases.

It was a wearying task. So much of what he read seemed like needless flotsam, debris to be pushed out of the way as he pursued his goal. There were endless arguments over the *exact* nature of Christ—his divinity and his humanity—that went on for page after page. *If only theologians had expended as much energy enacting Jesus's teaching as they had on debating his metaphysical essence. If they had actually focused on living the life Jesus asked us to live, what a different world we might live in today! Instead, they studied the bark of each tree and forgot the purpose of the forest.* Still, as the hours passed, Sebastian began to discover small treasures, slivers of wisdom which he noted. Each time he found a gemstone, his quill slipped into the inkwell and wrote a line of script, a quote, followed by his own comment.

By mid-morning, he was wrestling his way through the words of Justin Martyr, a philosopher and convert born at the end of the first century. After wading through several pages of aged prose, his tired eyes widened with discovery. Justin had written:

> We ourselves were well conversant with war, murder and everything evil, but all of us throughout the whole wide earth have now traded in our weapons of war. We have exchanged our swords for plowshares, our spears for farm tools. ... Now we cultivate the fear of God, justice, kindness, faith ... and the more we are persecuted and martyred, the more others in ever-increasing numbers join us.

Sebastian paused and considered what was known about this man. Most of his writings had been lost to history, but a few remained, mostly pleas to the Roman emperor Antoninus to lift his harsh hand from those he was brutalizing. *And now,* he thought, *it is the church that does the persecuting and those around it who must cry out for mercy.*

He broke from his reverie and forced himself back to the book before him, working his way on through its fragile pages. Soon he found another helpful quote, this time from a noted theologian named Athenagoras. Writing just a few years after Justin Martyr, he declared, "We Christians cannot endure to see a man being put to death, even justly."

He dabbed his quill in the ink and made a copy of the reference. He continued to turn the book's fragile pages, reading the often dense and circuitous writing. He closed the cover of that volume and picked up another—one which examined the teachings of significant church leaders from the second century after Christ. His eyes were tired, but they refocused when he came to the sayings of the famed Clement of Alexandria. "Above all, Christians are not allowed to correct by violence sinful wrongdoing." Again, Sebastian picked up his pen and made a note.

He plowed on through more passages filled with instruction and admonishment, forcing himself to focus. After a while, Sebastian came to the teachings of a great African scholar by the name of Tertullian, the first theologian to write in classical Latin, a man whose father had been a Roman centurion. Suddenly, he came to a passage that stopped him. He went back and read it a second time. Simply and boldly, Tertullian stated, "It is a fundamental right, a privilege of nature, that every man should worship according to his own convictions. It is not in the nature of religion to coerce religion, which must be adopted freely and not by force."

This theologian had been a firebrand, unwilling to compromise the teachings of Jesus for the sake of conformity. Tertullian went on. "Christ, in disarming Peter, disarms every soldier." A few passages beyond that, "God puts his prohibition on every sort of man-killing by that one summary precept: 'Thou shalt not kill.' ... God certainly forbids us to hate—even with a reason for our hating—for he commands us to love even our enemies." A low whistle escaped Sebastian's lips as he made more notes.

Eventually he came to the words of one of antiquity's most famous theologians: Origen of Alexandria. He slowed, doing his best to grasp Origen's words. At one point, Origen allowed himself to muse upon how powerful the Roman Empire could become should it embrace Christianity. Thinking better of it, he then insisted, "The Gospel of peace does not permit people to take vengeance even upon enemies."

Sebastian read a few more paragraphs and was about to move on, but then froze and slowly read the words that confronted him. "Christians cannot slay their enemies nor can they condemn to be burned or stoned, as Moses commanded, those who have violated God's law." He picked up his quill and noted the passage. *This is unequivocal. How could we have missed this?*

A couple dozen pages later, Sebastian came across a section dedicated to Cyprian, Bishop of Carthage, who wrote midway through the 200s. He smiled at the ancient pastor's word play. "God designed iron for tilling, not for killing." This perceptive bishop clearly had a keen sense of irony and of the hypocrisy present in his own day and age. "Homicide is a crime when individuals commit it, yet it is called a virtue when it is carried out publicly."

Sebastian slid the ancient volume to the edge of the table and reached for another. But now, midway through the fourth century, he sensed a subtle shift away from the teachings of the previous centuries. He labored his way through more passages of abstract philosophy until he came to an extract from something called the *Canons of Hippolytus*. It seemed that by this period, it had become permissible for a Christian to serve in the military, though with a strict caveat: "A soldier of the civil authority must be taught not to kill men and to refuse to do so if he is so commanded."

After working through several long-winded passages laden with arguments over the meaning of this or that Greek and Latin word, Sebastian yawned and stretched his arms. Looking up, his eyes followed the shadows crisscrossing the library's intricately crafted ceiling. His thoughts drifted to the artisans and craftsmen who built this building all those decades ago, how hard and precisely they had to labor to produce such beauty. On a cornice to his left, a cobweb had formed. He seemed to be able to make out the movement of a tiny spider tending to its prey, binding it in a prison of silk threads. He blinked and forced his thoughts back to the book in front of him, taking stock of what he had discovered thus far. It seemed so clear to him now. The early church, in an attempt to be faithful to Jesus, had rejected violence in all its forms. Why had he never seen this before? Had it been deliberately hidden? And how was it possible that the greatest minds of the Reformation—men like Luther and Zwingli and Calvin—had been so blind to this truth?

Putting that puzzle aside, he pushed on. He was now working his way through a fourth volume. In some places, the ancient words were so deeply absorbed that the ink nearly disappeared. His eyes strained to discern them. Midday came and went without him pausing to eat. He felt himself flagging, his eyes tiring, his mind drifting. He yawned again. Marie would be preparing food for the children now. How wonderful it would be to walk home and join them! He shook his head and lowered his eyes once more, determined to press on. But soon he began to skip pages, then whole sections, eager to get to the words he'd been anticipating since arriving that morning: those of Saint Augustine, the great Bishop of Hippo. Widely regarded as the prince of theologians, Augustine's eloquence and output from the 380s onward had eclipsed all who had gone before or after him.

More than anyone else, Saint Augustine's teachings had shaped the direction of the church, both in his lifetime and in the centuries that followed, among both Catholics and Protestants. Luther and Calvin had sought to be faithful interpreters of Augustine. Indeed, some argued that Calvin's *Institutes* contained little that was original; its ideas were simply a reworking of Augustine's. For the last eleven hundred years, fidelity to the teachings of Augustine was so strong that contradicting them was equated with heresy.

More than a quarter of the volume before him was dedicated to Augustine's teaching. The afternoon's hours drifted by as Sebastian studied line after line, paragraph after paragraph, hungry for what-ever truth he might gather from the great prelate's words. He read through a précis of Augustine's *Confessions*, a deeply personal account of how God's love had captivated and transformed him. Sebastian found it peppered with pearls, poetic and moving.

> Late have I loved you, beauty so old and so new. Late have I loved you; you called and cried out and shattered my deafness. You were radiant and resplendent; you put flight to my blindness. You were fragrant, and I drew in my breath and now pant after you. I tasted you, and now I feel but hunger and thirst for you. You touched me, and I am set on fire to attain the peace which is yours.

But Augustine's tender words grew harder as he aged. With the shifting of his political circumstances, his writings increasingly obsessed not over love but over humanity's sinfulness and the fires of hell that awaited the lost. Eventually, Sebastian came to the bishop's more pragmatic works, those that focused not on Christ but on the functional relationship between a godly church and a so-called godly state. Tucked among letters to fellow bishops and civic leaders was the summary of a letter that Augustine had written to a Roman military commander. It concerned a dispute between a breakaway sect called the Donatists and the larger, more orthodox group to which Augustine himself belonged, those he called Catholic.

In his letter, Augustine urged the commander to use whatever force was necessary to bring the Donatists back into the mother church. As much as Sebastian had been moved by Augustine's earlier words, he now despaired as he followed the brittle logic of this later argument. If a Donatist were to use force against the orthodox, this, according to Augustine, would rightly be named violence. As such, it should be severely punished. If, however, the orthodox or the state were to use force against the Donatists, this, he insisted, should rightly be viewed as "discipline" and "correction." This kind of force was permissible.

A few pages later came a second blow, a sentence that chilled Sebastian to the bone. "Persecution is unjust when the wicked inflict it upon the Church of Christ; persecution is just when the Church of Christ inflicts it upon the wicked." This was pure Calvin. Pure Luther. It was as if they had taken these words of Augustine and applied them to the circumstances of their own day. Where the Donatists had stood in Augustine's day, Protestant leaders—like Luther and Calvin—had placed the Catholic Church. Of course, Catholics had done the same to Protestants. And, sadly, both groups had used Augustine's twisted logic to justify persecuting the Anabaptists.

The more he read, the more his distress grew. In Augustine's greatest and most famous work, *The City of God*, he had taken these thoughts to another level, describing how it was the church and the state's duty to work together to ensure the defense of the godly and the defeat of the wicked. The theologian employed the Latin phrase *bellum iustum* (a just war) to describe the duty of the godly state to defend itself, to defend others, and to punish the wicked. Augustine had moved well beyond his earlier teachings, indeed the church's earlier teachings, and now argued that if Christians went to war or were ordered to use violence on behalf of the state, they should not feel ashamed. They were simply doing their duty. They could retain the peace of Christ in their hearts regardless of how violent their outward actions were.

Sebastian's head swam. Augustine had overturned the consistent witness of the church fathers from across the previous four centuries, from the time of Jesus onward. *But why? And why had no other theologian challenged him on this ... this ...* Sebastian searched for the right word. *This catastrophe?*

Perhaps he'd missed something that would account for this sudden leap. He turned back to passages on the life and teaching of Saint Ambrose, the Bishop of Milan and Augustine's mentor. Soon he saw the words he'd missed earlier. Ambrose had first proposed the doctrine of *bellum iustum,* arguing that if a state conducted war in a godly way, it was not only justifiable, it was commendable. Ambrose had written that one could only praise a man who risked his life to defend his state; specifically, to defend the Roman Empire. In a work called *De Fide,* Ambrose went even further, claiming that it was no longer the spirit of the military eagle that led forth the Roman armies, but "the Spirit of Jesus himself." Sebastian shuddered as he reread that sentence.

Sebastian realized that he'd come to a pivotal time in church history. He turned a page and found a chilling new detail. In the 380s, the devoutly Christian Emperor Theodosius, cheered on by Ambrose, had passed a law empowering Roman inquisitors to root out and destroy heretics. This, he realized, was a foreshadowing of the bloody Inquisitions and Crusades that would follow. As he thought about their terrible savagery, his mind filled with dark images —torture and death, flames and bodies, screams of agony.

Sebastian shifted in his seat. Out of the corner of his eye, he sensed a small movement to his right and slightly behind him, between the shelves. Someone was watching him; he was sure of it. Slowly, he laid his pen down and pulled one of the books closer so that it covered his notes. He feigned reading, but tilted his head slightly to the right. In that direction, away from the windows, the light was dimmer and the tall shelves cast eerie shadows, making it hard to discern the real from the imagined. But then, a moment later, there it was again. A small motion. Not the bold stride of someone going about their business, but the slight shift of one standing and observing.

Sebastian sat staring at the open book before him until, finally, he thought he heard footsteps moving away. He cautiously rose to his feet. When he reached the aisle between the shelves, no one was there. He padded quietly down the aisle, emerging where it opened out on the library's darker southeastern side. This part of the chamber was empty too, but someone had lit a lamp and hung it at the end of one of the bookshelves. On the desk nearest him, he could see that a large book lay open. He stepped forward and leaned over the desk. On the left-hand page of the book was the image of a human skeleton, and on the right-hand page, discernible through the room's half-light, a grinning skull. Sebastian shivered. With both hands he lifted the tome and looked at its cover. It was a volume of Vesalius and Oporinus's famous anatomy series, *The Fabric of the Human Body*. He carefully placed it back on the desk and looked around, peering into the thick shadows at the corners of the room. No one.

He made his way back to his table, trying to convince himself that he had imagined it all, that the movement had been the trick of a lamp's flickering light. But then he reached his bench and immediately felt the color drain from his face. His eyes roamed over the collection of books before him. This was not how he'd left them. The difference was not great, but he was sure of the subtle change. The book covering his notes had been moved. An additional inch of his scribblings were visible now compared with a few minutes earlier. Once more he glanced around the library, but found it deserted.

He took stock of the situation. Even if someone had seen his notes, he was not away long enough for the person to read them all nor to grasp what he was looking for, surely? He could have been studying any issue of church history by reading these works. Even if someone had observed his day's reading, no case could be made against him simply for that. Yet now the library felt claustrophobic and unsafe. He needed to get outside, to feel the fresh air on his face. He carefully gathered up his notes and slid them into his satchel. Then he hurried toward the library's double doors that would usher him outside. He looked down to buckle his satchel, when suddenly a sharp voice made his head snap back up.

"Castellio!" it snarled. "What are you doing? Be careful!"

Startled, Sebastian took a step back and found himself staring into the face of the recently appointed theology professor, Wolfgang Wissenburg. They had almost collided at the library's doors, a spot where its broad lintel cast a dark shadow. The man scowled at him suspiciously.

"Ah, Master Wissenburg, I'm ... uh ... studying—doing some background reading."

"Greek, of course?"

"More about historical context, really. I always think if we do not learn from the light of the past, we walk forward into darkness. Wouldn't you agree?"

Wissenburg ignored the question. "I dropped into your office to speak with you this morning, but you weren't there."

"What did you want to speak with me about?"

Wissenburg's attention had dropped to Sebastian's ink-stained fingers. "I received a visit from Bürgermeister Meyer. It seems you attended a meeting a few nights ago at which an inflammatory speech was made against John Calvin and Genevan justice. I want to remind you that Geneva is our closest ally, and we share the same Orthodox faith. The Bürgermeister has given me a warning to pass on to you and van Brugge: be very careful about what you say"—he made a point of staring at Sebastian's fingers—"and what you write concerning these matters."

"Of course, Herr Wissenburg. I will take the Bürgermeister's words to heart, and I will be careful, very careful indeed."

Wissenburg said nothing but stepped aside to allow Sebastian to pass.

A cold breeze hit Sebastian as he exited the building. Goosebumps rose on his skin. His shirt, he realized, was damp with sweat. He took several deep breaths and made his way to the stone wall that lined the top of the river bank. *How had Meyer heard about our meeting? Who had told him? And was it Wissenburg I sensed watching me?* Perhaps not, for he got the impression Wissenburg had only just entered before their near collision. Besides, Wissenburg was not the type to skulk in the shadows. He was the kind who preferred open confrontation.

His racing heart began to slow. He leaned against the wall and remembered the parcel Marie had placed in his doublet that morning. He fished it out and unwrapped the cloth, revealing a small, spotty apple and a chunk of hardened cheese. There was a slip of paper there too. He opened it. A note in Marie's neat hand. He smiled as he read it.

Sustenance for my brave, handsome knight, a man of courage who fights for truth.
I love you. M.

Cheese and apple had seldom tasted so good; the tart juice mixing with the salt of the cheese made his mouth tingle. Behind him, children's squeals of delight combined with the cries of gulls hovering over the river. He turned. Three children—a boy and two girls—raced toward him, using a stick to paddle a barrel hoop along the street. The hoop crashed against the wall next to him. As it bounced up, Sebastian caught it in one hand, smiling at his own success. The children skidded to a halt only inches away, their expressions a mix of shyness and hope. It was obvious they were of one family, with similar features and long, scraggly hair.

"So tell me," Sebastian said. "For how long did you manage to keep this hoop upright?"

The tallest child, the boy who Sebastian presumed to be the oldest, spoke. "Nearly all the way along the Rheinsprung, sir!"

"What? Without getting run over by a horse and rider? Incredible. You are obviously children of great talent! However, perhaps it would be wiser to play this game somewhere safer, like Saint Peter's Platz, for example."

He handed the hoop to the smallest of the trio, a tiny girl who might have been six or seven. She smiled at him, her eyes filled with innocence. The three turned and began running up the slope of the street, headed in the direction of Saint Peter's platz. The tall boy looked back over his shoulder, and called out a thank you. Unbidden, Sebastian thought, *Surely the Lord is more pleased with the games of children than with the games of men.*

He turned to the river and surveyed the barges loading and unloading, others moving out into the current heading northward, down to the Low Countries. The Rhine rolled on, its inexhaustible flow burgeoned by the mix of rain and snowmelt from the distant Alps.

Restored, he gathered up his satchel and reentered the library. When he reached his desk, he stopped and surveyed the pile of books. Once more, he was sure they'd been rearranged. Several sat in slightly different positions from where he'd left them, but at least they were all still there. He pulled his satchel closer and thanked God he'd taken his notes with him when he left the building.

He returned to the volume he'd taken leave of earlier and began to flick his way back through its pages. It took him a few minutes to recover his train of thought, at which point he decided to work backward in time in hope of finding the first seeds of the violent theology that had appeared in the fourth century. As he reflected, it seemed clear that the justification for the church's violence had begun not just with Augustine but with his tutor, Ambrose. But why? What had given these two men the audacity to overturn the previous three hundred fifty years of Christian consensus against the use of violence?

Despite searching for an hour, Sebastian was unable to find any theological justifications for violence that came earlier than Ambrose. So he decided to resume reading forward in time. Within half an hour, he'd read to the end of the fourth century thinkers, and in another two hours to the end of the fifth and sixth centuries. But with each epoch traversed, he felt more and more crushed by what he read. There were, not surprisingly, more interminable arguments over the *precise* nature of the Trinity. Yet sadly, as time progressed, these theological disputes became punctuated more and more by violence. This harsh intolerance seemed to reach its peak in the sixth century, for here the Roman Emperor Justinian passed a law demanding that all Roman citizens be baptized as Christians or be stripped of their property.

Wearily, Sebastian glanced up at a great square-paned window that overlooked the river. It was late afternoon now, and the sky over the Rhine was darkening. He glanced across at the large clock on the library's eastern wall and pushed the books away from him. He had arranged to meet with Oporinus, Jan and Nicholaas at the Rote Haus at six o'clock. He would need to leave now if he was to make it on time.

Night was falling fast, and its chill deepening. But Sebastian was grateful for the way the cold air cut through the day's accumulated weariness. Twice he paused and peered behind him, trying to see if anyone followed. It didn't appear so. He began to feel foolish for even thinking such a thing. Surely the incidents in the library were the product of his overtired mind. He decided he wouldn't mention it to the others when he arrived.

Jan's townhouse was not far from the library. After twisting his way through a few narrow lanes, he spotted the windows of the Rote Haus glowing with lamplight. He knocked. Jan's secretary, van Schlor, opened the door. The jowly man signaled for Sebastian to enter and ushered him into the parlor, where Jan, Oporinus, and Nicholaas were sitting. He found them at the end of the enormous wooden table, the same one they'd all dined at a few nights earlier when they had gathered to hear Matteo Gribaldi speak. At each end of the table, two candles struggled to overcome the night's gathering darkness. Against one wall, a fire crackled in the grate, adding its own fitful light to the tableau.

Through the half-light, Jan's voice beckoned. "Come join us, Sebastian. Oporinus has just arrived too. Sit. Let us share what we have each discovered." The Dutchman had already spread out on the table several pages of notes. Pulling one of the candles closer, Jan began to read aloud from what he'd written. "'So, if we in Europe claim to be Christians, claim to belong to Jesus, we must of course start with Jesus's very teachings,' yes?" Without waiting for them to answer, he forged on.

"'And of course, Jesus teaches his disciples—and us—that we must love our enemies, not striking back at them, not seeking an eye for an eye, but peaceably absorbing an enemy's blows. We must offer the other cheek, offer even our coat to the one who has taken our shirt. When we are persecuted, we must return not vengeance but blessing. When we are offended, we are to extend forgiveness.'"

Oporinus held up his hand. "Whoa, Jan. I know this is what you believe, but many theologians—both Reformed and Catholic—argue that because the Old Testament laws and Moses's instructions came first in time, they are primary and the teachings of Jesus only secondary."

Sebastian interjected, "Or that the laws of Moses apply to the public sphere—how civic life is to be organized—and the laws of Christ only to the private sphere —how we each conduct our personal interactions with others, the attitudes we carry in our hearts.

Luther argued that one could faithfully worship Christ in church on a Sunday, but then on Monday, work as an executioner for the state, faithfully doing *its* bidding. He would say you must apply Christ's teachings to how you treat your neighbors and how you deal with 'spiritual things.' But in the public sphere, you must obey the laws of the state, not Jesus. Calvin has taught the same. Indeed, he has built the life of Geneva around the laws of Moses rather than around the laws of Christ."

Jan pushed himself back from the table, his voice rising. "What mental twisting these doctors of the church perform! If what they preach at us is true—that Christ is the very incarnation of God himself come upon the earth, the second person of the Holy Trinity— then surely there is no higher authority than his in all this world. Surely the words of Jesus rise above those of Moses and of the Old Testament! Yes?"

"That we should listen to he who holds all wisdom and all knowledge? Yes, I think Paul's letters and the book of Hebrews make that abundantly clear," Sebastian agreed. "At least to all except those who lead our church—and those who have led it ever since the time of Ambrose and Augustine."

Jan hadn't finished yet. "What was the attitude of Jesus toward those who were the enemies of his race?" He waited for a reply, but when the others looked back at him blankly, he pressed on. "I speak of the Samaritans! Those half-castes whom the Jews regarded as appalling heretics. Jesus makes one of these very people the hero of his most famous story, the good Samaritan. They're the hero in other stories too. And do you remember when Peter and John wished to call down fire on a Samaritan village that did not welcome them, in imitation of the Old Testament prophet Elijah? Jesus rebuked them and said, 'You know not what manner of spirit you are of, for the Son of Man came not to destroy lives, but to save them.'"

"Wait—where is that passage?" Oporinus asked, leaning forward.

As Jan searched his notes, Nicholaas answered. "The ninth chapter of Luke's Gospel."

"Underline what you have written there. This is a telling passage."

Jan smiled and shifted in his seat, clearly lifted by Oporinus's affirmation. "And there is much more! The disciples in the book of Acts are persecuted but never persecuting. Whipped for disturbing Roman peace, they refuse to back down yet never strike back. But I should stop now. Let us hear what you have found, Sebastian."

It took Sebastian a good twenty minutes to outline all his notes. His voice grew somber as he came to the teachings of Ambrose and Augustine. He described how they reversed centuries of Christian teaching on violence, defiantly insisting that force could—and in some cases should—be used to advance the position and power of the church. When he finished, he looked up at his three friends. Nicholaas was, as usual, impassive. Jan looked confounded. And Oporinus sat lost in thought, the fingers of his left hand stroking his beard.

"But why? Why did Ambrose and Augustine overturn centuries of counsel against using violence? Why did they defy what seems to be such clear teaching and clear example from Jesus and the apostles?" Jan asked.

Oporinus's fingers formed a fist which dropped to the table. "We must remember that for the first few centuries after Christ, the Christians were a tiny minority within the Roman Empire. They were savagely persecuted, seen as heretics who deviated from Roman custom, rebels who refused to participate in the empire's religious ceremonies. Yet even in the face of this persecution, their numbers grew. Indeed, it seemed that the more brutally the emperors persecuted the Christians, the more their numbers grew. For three centuries this sect was a nagging thorn in the side of each emperor, an irritant they wished to be rid of.

"But by the dawn of the fourth century, the empire was in decline, wracked by division, and under threat of invasion by the tribes surrounding it. Some blamed this chaos on the Christians and their strange religion. They were accused of weakening the empire by blaspheming its old gods and refusing to fight in the empire's defense. When we get to the year 306, a new emperor, Constantine, rises out the intrigue and treachery of Roman politics, taking the wreath handed to him by his father. Constantine could see that centuries of persecution had failed to rid the empire of these stubborn Christians. Indeed, it had only made them stronger. Moreover, Constantine had an openness to the faith. His own mother, who was dear to him, had become a Christian." He paused for thought, taking a sip of wine from the cup Jan had placed on the table in front of him.

"Constantine surveys this once great empire and sees that it is tottering, shaken by discord within and assault from without, and he realizes that something extraordinary must be done to save it. And so, if the empire cannot destroy this strange, growing religion, why not co-opt it to unify the empire and help it survive? In 312, Constantine announces that he has seen a vision—the sign of the cross in the sky—and that from now on all persecution of Christians must cease. Their faith is now welcomed, to be held as coequal with the old Roman religion. By 325, Constantine is presiding over a council of theologians, encouraging them to get their disputed doctrine of the Trinity consistent and agreed upon. By 380, under the Emperor Theodosius, Christianity is declared the official religion of the empire. Constantine, and the emperors who followed after him, start to lavish the church with property, buildings and gifts of money. They begin to grant positions of high leadership to the most cooperative of the bishops. One of the leading bishops of the time, Eusebius of Caesarea, is so swept away he writes a biography of Constantine that presents him as a saintly-warrior whose army conquers only by God's power.

"All this has been a brilliant move by the emperor for, in effect, he has now made himself the de facto head of the church as well as of the state. And for those who lead the church, they suddenly gain substantially more authority and status while at the same time witness the end of centuries of bitter persecution. Where once they had been regarded by those in power as heretics, they are now invited to help administer power. What could possibly go awry with such a serendipitous turn of fortune?"

Sebastian sensed the sarcasm in Oporinus's voice. "You, for one, don't sound convinced," he said wryly.

"The danger is so obvious," Jan interjected. "How could they not have remembered the temptation of Jesus? 'For the devil took Jesus up to a high mountain, and showed him all the kingdoms of the world, and all their splendor, and said to Jesus, "If you'll only bow down and worship me, I will give all these things to you."'"

Oporinus glanced at Jan. "Yes. That is exactly like the pact the church made with the emperor."

Sebastian's eyebrows rose, and he exchanged a knowing look with Jan.

"In that moment, the church had access to power and privilege unlike anything it had ever known before—and unlike anything, I think, Jesus ever intended for it to know. The church went from being an enemy of the state to being the state's partner in maintaining social order. For a long time, the church had forbidden Christians from enlisting in the Roman army as a soldier because the occupation was so contrary to Jesus's teachings. Admittedly, this principal had been weakening throughout the course of the third century, but within a few years of Constantine's so-called conversion, it was completely turned on its head. Soon after, you could *only* join elite Roman legions and wield the imperial sword if you were a confessing Christian." Oporinus paused and took another long sip of wine. When he spoke again, the contempt in his voice was palpable. "Jesus talked about the power of love and servanthood. Our church has instead been seduced by the love of power and privilege."

Sebastian had stared hard at his friend, as if watching each of Oporinus's words emerge from his mouth. Then he fired back a question of his own. "Do you not believe that Constantine's conversion was a true one?"

"His conversion to what?" Oporinus replied. "To being a follower of Jesus? He was on his way to battle, his legionaries armed to the teeth when he saw this supposed cross in the sky—a fiery cross and a heavenly banner saying 'Under this sign you shall conquer.' The next day he marched out to slaughter his political rivals. Does that sound like the work of Jesus to you? Throughout his reign, he crushed his enemies. He even murdered his own wife and son! From this point forth and ever after, all manner of violence, abuse, conquest, and Crusade became possible in Jesus's name."

Jan's fierce whisper cut through the room. "Then I say it was not God but the devil who sent Constantine that vision."

Sebastian spoke again. "You paint a cynic's picture, but surely good also came from Constantine, yes? Under his reign, churches, hospitals, and asylums were built. And Christians were no longer martyred. Surely this was good fruit?"

"There's no doubt that good accrued to the empire and, in the short term, to the church," Oporinus began. "But in the long term, immense harm was done to the Christian faith. It seems to me that whenever power and religion are joined, the dark underbelly of each is summoned forth. Following this so-called vision in the sky, Constantine ordered his armies to march always carrying banners painted with the cross or a Greek symbol of Christ's name. These were to be a sign of victory for them and of death for their enemies. More and more, the name of Christ became a symbol of conquest. By the time we reach the eleventh century, every crusader has the sign of the cross painted on his breast as he slaughters Muslims and Jews, pagans and Eastern Christians, women and children. Without a pang of conscience, successive waves of Crusade annihilate anyone in the path of their conquest. It was Constantine who passed the empire's first anti-Semitic laws—laws made harsher by subsequent Christian emperors. To this day, the Mohammedans think of us as 'the people of the sword,' and the Jews know us as those who have most violently persecuted them."

"Do you see how devilish the church's embrace of Constantine became?" Jan hissed. "We've turned the Suffering Servant into a killer; the Prince of Peace into a god of war. We've converted the instrument of his torture, the cross, into a symbol under which others must suffer and be murdered."

Sebastian shook his head slowly, not in denial but in sadness. "But where do Ambrose and Augustine fit into this story?"

Oporinus pondered the question for a second and then answered, "Ambrose rose to a position of political and ecclesiastical power in the generation that followed Constantine's reign, in the time of the Christian Emperor Theodosius. From the time of Constantine, the partnership between church and state—between religious power and political power—grew more and more entangled and interdependent, until they were utterly inseparable. The Roman State and the Catholic Church merged into what we might call Roman Catholicism. Yet the empire was still insecure. Enemies hammered on the gates and ambitious rivals fought for power from within. The empire remained a shadow of its former glory. There were still those who accused the Christians of being the cause of this, who agitated for a return to the old gods.

"As a bishop from a high-born Roman family, Ambrose was desperate to prove that Christians were the best possible Roman citizens and that the Christian religion was good for the empire. Above all else, he and Augustine did not wish to see the church lose its position of preeminence and fall back into the terrible persecution of the early centuries. In order to accomplish this, they were willing to abandon some of the more troublesome teachings given by Jesus and held by those who'd gone before them. In time, with Roman church and Roman state almost indistinguishable from one another—as if two branches of the same mighty tree—it simply did not occur to anyone to challenge Ambrose's or Augustine's teachings. Don't forget, those two men came to have the title *Saint* placed before their names. Their words are regarded as virtually canonical."

Once more Oporinus paused and lifted his cup, gently swirling the wine and seeming to contemplate it before his next words. "Beyond them, I would say the next most influential voice came in the eleventh century, from that other gentle saint, Thomas Aquinas.

He took up Augustine's arguments concerning a just war and went even further in justifying the persecution of heretics. He argued that a heretic *must* be put to death in order to preserve the purity of God's truth. It is from Aquinas's words that witch-hunters justify their murders. Aquinas's pen dressed cruel dogmas in virtuous clothes, as acts necessary for the preservation of social order and for the saving of the world." Oporinus lifted the cup to his lips and took another sip, letting the wine sit on his tongue, savoring it for a moment before swallowing. "But like all before and after, Aquinas was simply building on Augustine's teachings."

Sebastian bent forward, his forehead creased with concentration. A new piece of the puzzle was falling into place for him. "Yes, of course! Luther and Calvin were both Augustinians and believed his words unquestioningly—that church and state must work as one, uniting temporal and ecclesiastical power to suppress any disorder, even by force, if necessary. They seek to return us to the time of Augustine, not to the words of Jesus." He looked to Oporinus. His friend stared out the window, absorbed in the dark starless sky, once more fingering his beard.

A silence fell over the room. Sebastian knew they'd reached another crossroads. They could ignore all they'd discovered and turn back to safety. Or they could feel their way forward along what could only be a dangerous, precipitous path. The seconds ticked by, each waiting for another to speak. Sebastian glanced at Jan and observed his lips beginning to form a word. But before Jan could speak, the silence was split by a shriek of shattering glass and the sharp clang of falling metal.

Jan let out a frightened gasp. All four of them leaped to their feet. Nicholaas reacted fastest. He raced to the door and jerked it open. Standing there, with a look of utter shock on his face, was van Schlor. At his feet lay an upturned silver tray, a pool of red wine, and the shattered shards of glass.

"Nicholaas. Master van Brugge. I am so sorry. I was bringing some wine for you and your guests and the tray slipped from my hand as I reached for the door. Oh, so clumsy. I apologize."

Jan waved his hands in the air. "No matter, no matter!" Van Schlor bent down, using a cloth to sop up the mess. They left van Schlor to his work and reentered the room. Nicholaas locked the door behind him. He exhaled loudly. A round of nervous laughter rippled around the room.

"Well, then," Jan said. "As no one else will say it, I shall. It seems to me that we have more than enough material with which to write a book—and to try to save the life of Michael Servetus." Each word Jan spoke was like a new weight pressing down upon Sebastian's shoulders.

Oporinus slowly nodded his head. He looked from Nicholaas to Sebastian. "What other choice do we have?"

Chapter 24
Secrets Shouted from the Roof Top

For three weeks, Sebastian and his friends had been working around the clock, desperate to produce a book in a fraction of the time it usually takes. They had heard no news from Geneva and still clung to the hope they might save Michael Servetus.

Oporinus's print shop would be the platform from which the furtive text would be launched into the world. Jan and Sebastian had been working late into each night, collating material from Perna and Curione, reworking it into the semblance of a book. Given the haste and secrecy in which they worked, Sebastian knew it would not be the most eloquent prose ever penned. Rather it would be a simple assembly of reasoned arguments against the practice of persecuting "heretics," against the use of execution as a tool to silence them. It was Sebastian's idea to include words from Luther and Calvin, spoken in those tumultuous early days when their own ideas were considered revolutionary, when it was they who were accused of heresy by ecclesiastical powers. At first Jan struggled to see the advantage of this. Surely, they should argue against the current intolerance of Luther and Calvin?

"No. We need to let the world see how much they have changed," Sebastian said. "When they were small and vulnerable and persecuted, they argued for clemency and a fair hearing. But now that they have become powerful figures, backed by princes, cities and armies, it is they who persecute those holding ideas that differ from their own."

Jan shrugged. "You describe the history of our world. Was not Jesus also executed as a heretic by those in positions of power? Nothing has changed."

Early in the first week of November, just after dawn, Jan and Sebastian made their way to the print shop. Their plan was to compare pages of manuscript with typeface that Oporinus had set. They had barely begun work when someone pounded on the street-front door. Quickly, they gathered up the papers and crammed them into a cupboard, jamming it shut. Anxiously, Oporinus crept to the door. "Who is it?"

A low voice replied. "It is me, Curione. I have news from Geneva."

Oporinus unbolted the door and opened it just wide enough for Curione to slip in. His face was flushed. He looked from Oporinus to Sebastian to Jan, his eyes rimmed with sadness. "I am sorry my friends, but I have to tell you that Michael Servetus is dead. They have killed him."

Sebastian felt the blood drain from his face. Jan slid to the floor, burying his head in his hands. Anger twisted Oporinus's features, and a bitter exclamation exploded from his lips. "Those dogs. Those murderous, merciless dogs!"

Curione continued. "Three witnesses from Geneva arrived at my home very early this morning. Jean Colinet, Léger Grymoult, and Pieter Zuttere were all present at yesterday's execution. They are willing to speak against it to any who will listen."

"Then their story will be told. It *must* be told!" Oporinus turned to Sebastian. "Even if it means our present work is delayed, the obscenity these men have witnessed must be shouted till the whole world hears."

At Curione's home, they listened with horror as the three men described Servetus's execution.

Colinet spoke first. "A few days ago, we heard that the magistrates had reached a decision. Early the next morning—the twenty-seventh—they brought Servetus from his cell and led him to the front of the town hall, where we, like half the town, had gathered. One of the magistrates read from a long list of charges, two pages worth of 'crimes.' Servetus remained silent the whole time. Then they tied his hands and led him to the pyre."

"Farel was there," Zuttere said. "He'd come down from Neuchâtel to act as some kind of chaplain for the occasion."

"But Calvin was absent," Grymoult added. "Apparently, he felt unwell and had taken to his bed."

Zuttere proceeded with the account. "They walked to the stake, Farel reciting Geneva's catechism the whole way, urging Servetus to repeat it after him. But Servetus only prayed, quietly at first but louder as they approached the pyre. 'Jesus, son of the *eternal God*,' he said. 'Have mercy on me.' The more he said this, the more frustrated Farel became. 'No!' Farel shouted. 'You must pray, 'Jesus, *eternal son of God*, have mercy on me.'" But Servetus wouldn't say it, so Farel stalked off in anger."

Léger Grymoult took up the story again. "A couple of officers chained Servetus to a pole. They tied a copy of his book—the one he sent Calvin—to his leg. They also placed letters he'd apparently sent to Calvin at his feet."

"He said one more thing before they lit the fire," Colinet recalled. "He asked forgiveness from any he'd hurt during the course of his life. And then he resumed his prayer. 'Jesus, son of the eternal God, have mercy on me.' Then, after the theatrics of thrusting the flaming torch to his face, they started the fire."

"His death was not merciful," Zuttere added. "They made sure of that. Half the wood was green, selected just to slow things down. It took thirty minutes before the poor wretch stopped moaning and jabbering."

Léger's head shook, reliving the horror of the situation, as he concluded their account. "Farel ended it all with a homily for the '*edification*' of those gathered: 'If this heretic had repeated the catechism or confessed the true nature of Christ, he would have been burnt only in this world. Instead, he now burns for all eternity in the next.'"

When the three finished speaking, silence filled the room. Sebastian stared at the floor, sick to his stomach. Finally, Oporinus spoke up. "You must have made remarkable time to ride here from Geneva in what ... three days? Four?"

"We had incentive to leave as quickly as possible," Colinet replied. "I was supposed to appear before the consistory that very afternoon on my own charge of 'disrespecting Geneva's ministers.'"

Oporinus looked at Zuttere. "Pieter, I understand you have kept careful notes of this whole sorry episode—the charges, the trial, the execution?"

"I have," Zuttere replied.

"Sebastian and I would like to publish them, if we may. Are you willing?"

"More than willing, my friend. More than willing."

"Gentlemen," Curione asked, "are you willing to tell this story one more time? There are others in this city who despise such cruelty and oppression. They will wish to hear your words too." Curione waited as the three newcomers looked to one another.

Eventually Colinet replied. "I think I speak for all of us. We are willing, but we ask your protection. This is not a safe story to tell."

"Of course. Only our most trusted friends will be allowed to attend the gathering."

"My home, as always, is available," Jan said.

"Tonight?" Curione held Jan's gaze.

"Yes, tonight. Dirkgen and I will prepare for it."

Sebastian clasped Jan's shoulder. "We will bring only those we know support our cause. And we will urge them to be discreet, to share news of our gathering with no one else. Jan, you talk to the other Netherlanders. Celio, you invite the Italian brothers. But again, only those you can be sure of. I will go and see if Bauhin wishes to be involved." Sebastian held out his right hand, and Zuttere gripped it.

"We must be careful my friends," Curione said solemnly, "but not fearful. If God is a God of truth, once this story is told far and wide, justice will follow."

When they gathered that night, their numbers had been thinned to those whose loyalty and friendship they thought unquestionable. Jan and Dirkgen's table was once more dotted with food and drink, though far less sumptuously than at their previous meeting.

Grymoult, Zuttere, and Colinet each gave their accounts of what they'd witnessed. Each man's voice faltered as he recounted the hour of the Spaniard's death. By the time they'd finished, all heads were bowed, despairing at the tale they'd heard.

The three witnesses had begun to take questions when the sound of horses drawing near interrupted. Jan stood and raised his hand to silence the room. Within moments, three loud *thumps* pierced the silence as someone banged on the front door of the Rote Haus.

All eyes fixed on Jan, who stood rooted to the spot. Raised voices could be heard from the parlor, one locked door away from where they gathered. Sebastian made out the words "a private dinner" as the voices rose in argument. On the far side of the table, Jan stared at the doorway with a look of incomprehension. Then another voice, sharper and more authoritative sounded above the rest. "Open it!"

The sound of a key rattled in the lock, and chairs scraped as those closest to the door lurched to their feet. The door swung open. Several men entered led by a flustered Henrich van Schlor, Jan's secretary, who clutched an iron key in his hand. Behind him was Bernard Meyer, the city's Bürgermeister, flanked on either side by constables, swords strapped to their sides. Wolfgang Wissenburg, the university's professor of theology, followed, along with a sheepish-looking Simon Sulzer, Minister of Basel's Reformed Cathedral. Beyond them, still in the parlor, Sebastian could make out two more men whom he did not recognize—though from their weaponry, he assumed they were constables.

A fearful silence had fallen across the room. The Bürgermeister stepped forward. "Gentlemen." Then, noticing Marie and Dirkgen, he frowned and added "ladies" before continuing. "It has come to the attention of the council that you are meeting together to discuss a matter of some great importance—enough so that you hide behind a locked door. Surely a matter of this significance would be of interest to both the council and the church, and yet we were not informed." He looked directly at Jan. "Herr van Brugge, clearly you are hosting this meeting. Until now, you have been a good friend to our city, and our city to you. I do hope this accord will not be spoiled in any way, for that would be to our mutual distress."

Jan's face paled and his mouth opened, but he didn't speak. From the chair next to Sebastian's, Oporinus rose, his large frame bristling with indignation. Sebastian quickly placed himself between Oporinus and the Bürgermeister. Looking directly at Meyer, he spoke as confidently as he could. "Perhaps that is correct, my dear Bürgermeister. Perhaps it would have been a courtesy to have invited you to join with us. But by the same token, in gathering here we break no law. We commit no indecency against the city of Basel. We are simply friends gathered to dine and to greet our colleagues freshly come from Geneva. May I introduce them to you? This is Monsieur Jean Colinet, my successor as rector of the college in Geneva. And his companions, Monsieur Grymoult and Monsieur Zuttere, also upright citizens of that righteous city. However, they have been telling us of a most brutal event that occurred there but a few days ago: the execution of a man by fire, following a trial that many are convinced was full of judicial and theological errors. If you and your party would like to take a seat, I'm sure they will be willing to recount the facts of this sorry tale for you also."

Several present offered their chairs to Meyer's party. But Meyer stood unmoved, running his gaze over all those gathered around the table, as if committing their faces to memory. "I already have the facts. A known heretic was caught spreading his poisonous lies first in the city of Vienne and then in the city of Geneva. After a legally constituted trial before that city's council, he was found guilty and received the prescribed penalty for his perfidy. If you value the freedoms Basel grants you, I would advise each of you to leave the scrutiny of matters theological to the church and matters judicial to the councils. Cease from judging beyond your station. I will issue you a warning tonight: if any one of you does or says anything to threaten the accord between our city and our brethren in Geneva, the consequences for you will prove most severe. I warn you therefore"—his gaze turned back to Sebastian—"to be very, very careful what you say or what you write in relation to this case. Am I understood?"

Sebastian held Meyer's gaze and did his best to form an agreeable smile. "Perfectly, Herr Bürgermeister. Perfectly."

Van Schlor now stood beside Meyer, his head lowered, offering a tray with several small chalices of wine. Meyer frowned at the secretary before looking back at Jan with a forced smile. "Thank you, Herr van Brugge, but I think we have made our point. We will leave you and your guests to enjoy your dinner party." He exited the room, the others trailing after him.

Jan signaled for van Schlor to close the doors, then he and Sebastian moved to the large bay window and pulled back the edge of the thick drape. They remained silent and motionless. Only when the sound of horses' hooves striking the cobbles of the Rheinsprung faded did they dare to speak.

Sebastian turned to the room. "My friends, as you see more clearly than ever, we walk on dangerous ground. We must proceed with caution, but proceed we must. A great injustice has been committed. For us to stay silent would be tantamount to giving our approval. Yet once more I must plead for discretion, for I fear that one in our number has let slip something of our plans, and that news made its way to the ear of the council. How else could these men have known of our meeting here tonight? And so, I repeat the caution our own mayor has given us: guard your words. Be cautious who you speak to about this case." All heads nodded. When no one else spoke, Sebastian continued, eager to dismiss the group so he could confer with those he knew he could trust. "And now I think it prudent that we disband, that each of us returns to our own home. When it seems safe to meet again, we will get a message to each of you."

Nodding once more in agreement, the assembled filed out, their heads tilted in conversation, some reiterating the warning they had just heard, others speculating on how the council could have come to know their plans. One thing was clear: they had been warned, and only a fool would fail to heed such a warning.

After the other guests had departed, Colinet, Zuttere and Grymoult remained, along with Oporinus and Bauhin, Marie and Dirkgen. They moved their chairs to where Jan and Sebastian sat, all of them with expressions of deep concern.

Zuttere spoke first, clearly shaken. "You said we would be safe! How did the authorities know we were here? And Sebastian, why did you use our names so carelessly?"

Sebastian's face reddened. *He's right. How could I have been so reckless?*

Oporinus held his hands up, as if pleading. "If they knew we were meeting here tonight, I'm sure they already knew your names—all of our names. Their spies, whoever they are, will have told them that too, I'm sure."

Bauhin spoke next. "What do you suppose then? How *did* they find out we were meeting here?"

Sebastian pressed his fingers to his lips, his two hands forming a steeple. "I want to believe that one of us innocently slipped up and accidentally mentioned something to someone who, in turn, told someone who took it to the council. Yet ... that seems unlikely, for we each had only a few hours' notice of this meeting, hardly enough time for an innocent chain of gossip to have done its work. The alternative, however, is one I don't wish to believe."

He paused, considering how to form his next words. "I don't want to believe that one of our number has deliberately betrayed us." Every eye fixed on him, minds churning, no doubt, as they calculated how truly dangerous their situation had become if this were true. "But the Bürgermeister has been good enough to give us a warning. It could have been far worse. For if we were living in Geneva—"

Everyone knew exactly what he was thinking.

———

Beginning the next day, Sebastian and Oporinus set to work transcribing Zuttere's notes and getting them ready for publication. Wisely, the three men from Geneva had saddled their horses and ridden out before dawn, no longer feeling safe in Basel. At the back of Oporinus's shop, several of his most trusted staff worked diligently cutting letters, pouring metal into tiny molds, and preparing typeface for the print. Oporinus had a heavy bolt fitted to the door that separated the back of the print shop from its front, a barrier that could buy them time if they needed to flee through the courtyard at the rear of the building. It was clearer than ever how cautious they needed to be. As they discussed the best way to move forward, Oporinus assured them that he could obtain permission for this book's production from Martin Borrhaus, the university's head theologian and the city's chief censor. Jan and Sebastian voiced their skepticism, but Oporinus made it clear he believed he could talk Borrhaus around.

The next day, as they were dragging newly delivered bales of paper into the shop, Sebastian asked the question that had been worrying him all morning. "Your conversation with Borrhaus—when will you meet?"

Oporinus looked surprised, as if he had forgotten this detail. "Oh, that. Maybe tomorrow. Certainly this week sometime."

"And when you meet, what will you say? How will convince him?"

Oporinus frowned. "Don't worry. Martin is an old friend."

"Yes, but after this week's incident—surely Meyer will have talked to Borrhaus as well."

"As I said, don't worry, Seb. I know how to handle these people. Remember, in this same city I once printed copies of the Turk's holy book, the Koran." And then, in a slightly lower voice, "It only cost me two weeks in prison. So, by comparison, this should be easy!" He gave Sebastian a wink.

By mid-November, Oporinus's presses had produced several hundred copies of Zuttere's book, *A History of the Death of Michael Servetus*. Late on a Saturday, Sebastian and Jan helped stack the books into the bales that lined the rear wall of the shop. As they sewed shut the last of the bales, Oporinus clapped his hands together, halting everyone in the workshop.

"Well done, my friends, well done. You have worked with speed and prudence these past few days. I think fortune is favoring the brave, for tonight will be cloudy and moonless. There are men of my acquaintance arriving at our door tonight at midnight who will shift these bales to the river and onto a barge. From there, our books will travel to Mainz, Bonn, Cologne, Düsseldorf and Rotterdam, and from these ports, all across Europe." A satisfied grin split his bearded features. "But for now, I want to take you all down to The Hare for an ale or two. You have earned it."

A stifled whoop went up from the room.

Oporinus held up his hands "But my friends, do not let the ale loosen your tongues. There are some who would not understand the justice of our work, and it is best we don't give them cause to puzzle over it." As his men filed out the door, he lifted his doublet off a hook, struggling to pull it across his broad shoulders.

Sebastian stepped alongside him. "I thought you were getting Borrhaus's permission? If so, why are we smuggling these books out at midnight?"

"Sebastian, surely you know that the word *permission* is an elastic one. And yes, of course, I talked to Borrhaus."

"And what did you tell him?"

"I said you and I were working on a book of theology, with help from Pieter Zuttere, a printer from Geneva. I mentioned that we would be wrestling with the issue of capital punishment as a part of it. I assured him it was all very uncontroversial and that he didn't need to look at it before publication."

Sebastian winced. "So you misled him about the nature of the book? And you didn't really procure his permission?"

Oporinus shrugged. "I will ask his forgiveness."

Sebastian felt his stomach tighten. He gestured toward the bales of books. "Do you really think Borrhaus will forgive all of this?"

"Remember, he and I are old friends, and well acquainted with one another's foibles. He can sometimes appear gruff, as his role demands, but within, he has a generous heart and an open mind. He will forgive us."

Perhaps he might, Sebastian thought. *But what about Bürger-meister Meyer and Wolfgang Wissenburg? And the rest of the council?*

———

Within a few weeks, a letter had arrived for Sebastian from the city of Bern. Sebastian glanced to the signature at the foot of the second page: Nikolaus Zurkinden, a member of Bern's city council. *Interesting.*

Zurkinden's letter relayed how he had read the recently written book recounting the execution of Michael Servetus. Inquiries had led him to believe that Castellio had something to do with its production.

Sebastian's heart sank. *Have we covered our tracks that poorly?* But as he continued reading, his heart recovered.

The councillor desired Sebastian to know that the book's account was being widely read and much discussed, and in fact, he himself had been moved to write to John Calvin, a man he used to count as a personal friend. In his letter, Zurkinden said, he chastised Calvin for employing the same tactics as used by the detested Catholic Inquisitions. Calvin, he went on to say, informed him that he was already working on a defense to these slanders, a rebuttal.

Sebastian placed the letter on his desk. It was good of Zurkinden to reach out to him, but that he had so quickly and easily linked his name with this book about Servetus's death was concerning. He would need to be more careful from now on.

Sebastian became restless and anxious as he awaited Calvin's rebuttal. But he didn't have to wait long. By December, Calvin had produced his promised apologetic: *Defense of the Orthodox Faith against the Prodigious Errors of the Spaniard Michael Servetus*. When it reached Basel, Sebastian promptly obtained a copy. In it, Calvin insisted that Servetus was evil, a monster spewing blasphemies, and that he had saved the world from great danger by extinguishing this peddler of heresies.

By January 1554, Jan, Nicholaas, Oporinus and Sebastian resumed the work they'd begun prior to Zuttere's book. It would be titled *Concerning Heretics and Whether They Are to Be Persecuted*. Throughout January they spent night after exhausting night laboring over paper and type, assembling their treatise. Toward the end of the month, Jan brought them an invitation from Dirkgen to take a night off and come dine at the Rote Haus.

As the fire crackled behind her, Dirkgen lifted her glass to those sitting opposite. "I am proud of each of you. You are exposing works of darkness and bringing them into the light."

Opposite her, Sebastian felt abashed and shook his head. "No, we still have not done enough. I fear that Calvin may already have outflanked us. He is famous across the Continent and more will read his rebuttal than those who will read Zuttere's testimony. His following is great, and many hang on his every word."

Marie placed her hand on Sebastian's. "I know you are discouraged because you could not save this man, Michael Servetus, but I pray this book you are creating will save others. It is the future that you write for."

Jan looked defiant. "Sebastian, we are not finished yet. The book we are working on—I think even John Calvin will be silenced when he reads the beautiful and incredible words it will contain, yes?"

Sebastian smiled wryly. "I'm afraid that Calvin is not the type to be easily silenced. But you are right. What we are writing is powerful, and, I hope, persuasive."

Dirkgen spoke again. "Tell me of these beautiful and persuasive words. I want to know what it is you are saying to Master Calvin."

Sebastian had been working on them for so long now he could recite them by heart. "If Michael Servetus's words were in error, then you, John Calvin, should have fought against him with better words, not with chains and fire. For are we not followers of Jesus? Or do we follow some other god who still demands human sacrifice?"

"Oh, there's more!" Oporinus enthused. "Sebastian poses the question: 'Who is the greater heretic: the man whose thought is in error or the one who murders a man whose thought is in error?'"

Jan chimed in. "And Sebastian writes, 'What Jew or Muslim observing us would ever want to become a Christian?' And of course, he often reminds the reader that Jesus himself was executed as a heretic!"

Oporinus nodded. "No one has ever dared to write a book like this before, not that I know of anyway."

Sebastian's faced flushed. "The sections by Jan and Nicholaas are no less persuasive. Dirkgen and Tanneke, your men write with great skill and courage."

Tanneke leaned forward, eyes blazing. "Then make haste and print these startling words so that the world may read them."

Oporinus met her eye. "We are making as much haste as we can.

I have more paper and ink ordered. It arrives in a few days. But you are right. The world waits for this book."

Sebastian peered at Oporinus. "And what about Borrhaus? Despite your friendship, he was not happy with the furor that arose after Zuttere's book was circulated. When Calvin condemned Basel for allowing it to be printed, Meyer and Wissenburg turned on Borrhaus and criticized him most severely. He will not be so amenable to us next time, I fear."

"Yes, that's true. But we were wise to supply no name on the title page. Neither your name nor mine appears anywhere in the book. Meyer and Wissenburg suspected but were unable to prove it was connected with either of us. Borrhaus was not telling, and Zuttere and the others wisely left town before anyone could question them."

"Agreed, we came through that intact," Sebastian replied. "But with this book, will we be so fortunate a second time? Once it is printed, I expect John Calvin will heap even more pressure on the leaders of Basel to silence us. I am sure we are going to be severely tested."

"We will use the same tactic as with Zuttere's book, though with additional safeguards. I will create a title page that suggests the book was printed somewhere other than in Basel. And you two," Oporinus continued, "must think about what names you'd like me to put on that title page. Anything but Castellio and van Brugge."

Castellio looked at him askance. "What? We should lie?"

"I consider it artistic license rather than lying. It is a common enough strategy in the world of books for all kinds of reasons."

"But I have never knowingly used deception before. And this makes it seem as though we lack the courage of our convictions."

Oporinus leaned forward and locked eyes with Sebastian. "Sebastian, I hope you are not questioning my courage, for I would never question yours. There is a time when open battle is suicidal and prudence would suggest camouflage the wiser strategy. If this book is received as we suspect, there will be those calling for a fire to be built, and for you and I to be thrown into it."

"He is right Sebastian," Jan interjected as his cup descended to the table with a *bang*. "Listen to him. We must not use our names. Without any doubt, we must not use our names."

Taken aback by the passion in Jan's voice, Sebastian reached out and placed a hand on his friend's arm. "Of course, Jan. Yes, I hear you both. We will do as Oporinus has said. We will publish anonymously."

One evening in early February, Sebastian sat at his desk deep in thought, a blank page before him. The book was almost finished. Only the preface remained to be written. It needed to be something special, something that would arrest the reader. But his mind struggled. No words came.

Sebastian rubbed his eyes and stretched his arms above his head. He was tired, and if he were to be honest with himself, afraid. Anxiously, he began to pray. Soon his pen was moving, recording the words coursing through his heart:

O Christ, King and Creator of this world, do you see all these things that are happening? Is it possible that you have changed from what you once were and have now become cruel? When you walked upon the earth, no one was more compassionate, more gentle. Beaten, derided, spat upon, crucified, your retaliation was to beg forgiveness for those who scorned you. Have you now changed? Have you now ordered these drownings, these burnings, these beheadings, these tortures? Have you now become one who consumes human flesh? And if you have, Lord Jesus, then what is there left for Satan to do?

Later that same night, after supper had been eaten and the children cajoled off to sleep, Sebastian poured two cups of wine and passed one to Marie. He took a sip then cradled the cup in his hands as he stared at the embers that glowed deep in the fireplace.

Marie pried one of Sebastian's hands from his cup and held it. "You look pensive. Are you fearful about what might happen with this new book?"

Sebastian gazed at the fire for several more moments before he spoke. "Jan and I have prepared well and constructed lucid arguments. And Oporinus has shown that he can circumvent the city's watchdogs and keep our identities obscured. But this book will cause consternation for many, and I would not be human if I had no fear of where this all might lead. Yet what perplexes me even more is Jan. The emotion he brings to all this is immense; it drives him. We both saw his fear when Gribaldi spoke about Servetus's trial and mentioned the flames. You saw, too, his reaction when the Bürgermeister and the constables entered his house. He was paralyzed. More and more I find myself wondering if Jan has faced not only persecution but torture in the days before he came to Basel. Yet he never speaks of it."

"Would that be so unusual, Seb? Many who have suffered something terrible do not wish to speak of it."

"Yes, but there's more. After Gribaldi's speech, when Jan first pleaded with me to write this book with him, he described himself as a pastor. It was a small, fleeting reference, and he quickly hurried past it. But it struck me as odd, and I have puzzled over it ever since. To us, he has only ever described himself as a merchant and an artist."

"Then perhaps he meant he was *like* a pastor to the Netherlanders here. They all look up to him. He is kind and generous. He loves to write and contemplate on spiritual matters. Perhaps he just meant he is *like* a pastor."

"Perhaps, but that is not how it sounded at the time. And then there are the rumors we hear whispered about him and the other Netherlanders—"

"About them being Anabaptists?" Marie interrupted. "But what of it? The very reason you write this book is because you believe every person should be able to follow their conscience in matters of faith and not be persecuted. Would you abandon your friendship with him if he were an Anabaptist?"

"No, of course I wouldn't. But he and I have been friends ever since we first arrived in Basel, and we are working together on a project that could jeopardize many things, even our lives. I have shared with him all that befell us in Geneva, yet I feel he hides his own past, as if he has secrets he cannot trust me with. And if he does not trust me, then how true is our friendship?"

Marie bit her bottom lip, and joined him in staring into the fire. "So perhaps you should simply ask him about these things."

Sebastian pondered Marie's advice as he took a long, slow sip from his cup.

The following two weeks continued to be exhausting. Each day, Sebastian taught and lectured his way through his classes at the university. Each evening, he and Jan met at the print shop and helped Oporinus transcribe their writing for the presses. Finally, after four-teen long nights, the type was placed in the galleys and the sheets of paper into the tympan.

When Oporinus gave a signal, two of his staff set to work rolling the ink-coated balls of leather across the type, the sickly aroma of soot and linseed oil filling the room. Oporinus examined the press. Satis-fied the ink was consistent, he lowered the frame of the tympan and frisket down onto the type face, sliding the whole set beneath the plate and screw of the press. After a final check that everything was square, he called one of his men, a youth of eighteen, to come and pull the devil's tail, the lever that turned the wine press screw. The press was forced down onto the waiting paper and frame, kissing it with the soft *pomp* of wood on metal. When the youngster then pushed the devil's tail away from himself, the press lifted, and two more workers stepped forward to roll the frame outward again. They unclipped the tympan and frisket, revealing a page of monogram and text—the title page of the book.

As he always did with his most precious productions, Oporinus had cast the first title page. He freed the page from its frame and gently carried it to where a blanket lay draped across a bench. Sebastian and Jan followed him in a reverential silence. As Oporinus lifted his hands away, a gloss of shimmering black ink atop cream-colored paper appeared. Sebastian had witnessed this revelation many times, yet each was an epiphany, a new creation, a hidden treasure laden with hope.

All three men stared at the linen page which lay stark against the dark of the blanket, its bold, soot-black title proclaiming *Concerning Heretics: Whether They Are to Be Persecuted and How They Are to Be Treated: A Collection of Opinions of Learned Men Both Ancient and Modern.*

Oporinus had whittled down his staff to the ten men he trusted most. For the next week, they worked around the clock to print and bind the hundreds of books that would fill the waiting bales. Under the cover of night, they would be moved to a waiting barge to begin their silent journey down the Rhine. From there, they would be scattered like gunshot across the Continent.

Most of Basel was sleeping by the time the final book was sewn into its bale and the final bale loaded onto a wagon. The three men slumped down on a pile of empty sacks. The rough cloth felt like soft velvet to them. Oporinus laid back, as if to make his bed there. Sebastian though, had never felt more awake. His blood pulsed, exultant, as he watched the last wagon lumber off toward the docks.

Jan also looked awake, eyes shining, a broad grin refusing to leave his face. "Come my friends. Back to the Rote Haus. We will celebrate this beautiful moment. I have some fine wine recently purchased from France waiting for an occasion such as this. Come!"

Oporinus groaned. "I'm sorry, I just can't. I must sleep now. Perhaps in a few days, but not tonight. You two go ahead without me. You deserve it."

Jan looked at Sebastian, still grinning, his blue eyes twinkling, a look of expectation on his flame-bearded face. Sebastian laughed. "Why not? But only for an hour or two, mind you. I wish to wake in the morning lying next to my beautiful wife!"

"Lucky you," Oporinus murmured from his prone position. "And now I shall drag myself up to my cold and lonely bed. Come and wake me in a couple of days, if you can't find me."

"Certainly." Sebastian slapped Oporinus's back. "And in the meantime, we will keep our eyes peeled for a suitable wife for you."

"What?" Jan snorted. "For this crusty old widower? It will take us more than a couple of days to come up with that!"

In high spirits, the two men lurched down the dark and deserted streets, trading quips and jibes till they came to the Rote Haus. Jan unlocked the door and the two of them stepped into the parlor. A single lamp lit the room. One of the doors to the lounge stood ajar. They could see a figure seated at the table reading, silhouetted by the firelight and two thick candles.

"Nicholaas!" Jan exalted. "You are still up! Wonderful! Please, could you bring us some wine from the storeroom? The new stuff from France. And mugs—big mugs! Then come join us, for we have much to celebrate."

Nicholaas placed his book on the table and left the room. Sebastian spoke in a low voice. "May we talk freely in front of him?"

Jan looked back at Sebastian, almost wounded. "Yes, of course. As I've told you before, he is my son-in-law as well as my secretary. I would trust him with my life."

Jan threw a log on the fire, repositioning it with a poker.

Nicholaas returned, three mugs in one hand and three bottles clasped under his other arm, all of which he placed on the table. Jan pulled up a chair so that it faced the fire while Sebastian took a seat at the head of the table. Nicholaas resumed his place opposite Jan, with his back to the blaze. Jan eagerly uncorked a bottle and poured generous portions into each tankard.

"Nicholaas, we have done it! The book is printed and on its way down the Rhine. This night we have struck a blow for humanity and for freedom!"

Nicholaas raised his tankard, his craggy features shadowed and foreboding between the firelight that flickered behind him and the candlelight before him. "Then I offer a toast: to courage, to scholarship, and to truth."

Sebastian and Jan likewise lifted their mugs before draining the contents. Jan immediately refilled them and raised his aloft. "I, too, offer not a toast but a prayer—that with this book, the cruelty and violence of false faith will be exposed, and that men will learn that they must stop torturing and killing one another in the name of Christ."

Sebastian murmured amen and took another mouthful of the velvety red that made his tongue tingle and his head begin to float. Jan drank several lingering draughts from his own mug, clearly savoring the occasion. But as he stared into the darkness of the room, his mood seemed to change. "We sit here before a warm fire, drinking a sweet vintage, safe and full of hope. But all over Europe, men and women suffer, persecuted for their faith, brutalized for following their convictions. I want to believe that humanity is born for goodness, bearing the image of God, yet everywhere there is such cruelty. How can this be, Sebastian?"

"All my life, I have wrestled with this question, Jan. It haunts me too. All I know is this: that when Christ came, he too was misunderstood and persecuted by those who wielded power—the power of religion, the power of the state, it doesn't seem to matter which. He suffered what we suffer; he endured what we endure. Yet he never returned hate for hate. Till the very end, he offered only love and forgiveness to his enemies. This is what he teaches us, Jan."

"Yes, Sebastian. All of Europe claims to know this, but clearly they do not. They know the letter and betray the spirit." Jan took another long mouthful. After a few moments of silence, he turned toward Sebastian, a look of enormous grief on his face. "I have seen it, Sebastian. Men and women being dragged to the fire, tortured with pincers and screws. Men and women bound and bundled into sacks before being thrown into the river to drown while their good Christian persecutors laughed and mocked. 'You want a second baptism?' they said. 'Well, here you go. Plenty of water for you.'"

Sebastian's eyebrows arched and he leaned forward to listen more intently. He knew Jan was speaking of the mode of execution reserved only for Anabaptists.

"I've seen babies ripped from their parents' arms, and children forced to watch their mothers and fathers set on fire or drowned in a river. Hundreds have succumbed to this fate all across our enlightened Christian lands." By the firelight, Sebastian could see that Jan's eyes had filled with tears, but his words were angry ones. "I have seen it, and I have felt it. Innocent, good, and gentle people tortured, decapitated. My own mother, Sebastian. My own sweet, gentle mother"—he began to weep, his voice cracking with emotion—"taken by these brutes and bled and ... oh, dear Jesus. Dear, dear God."

Tears welled up in Sebastian's eyes. He took hold of one of Jan's hands, gripping it firmly. "And you, Jan? Did they torture you?"

Jan looked at him and blinked, trying to stem the flow of tears. "My torture was light compared to the others. They passed a drill through my tongue to try and stop me from blaspheming. But such wounds heal with time. Other wounds don't. I have lost so many loved ones Sebastian, so many."

Sebastian encased Jan's hand in both of his. "I have felt your pain for a long time, Jan. I have sensed that our struggle is a very personal one for you. You, too, are an Anabaptist, aren't you?"

Across the table, Nicholaas stiffened. Even in the dark, Sebastian could feel the younger man's glare. A look of confusion and fear crossed Jan's features. He glanced at Nicholaas before returning his gaze to Sebastian. His features softened back to grief, and he spent a long time weighing his answer.

Finally, Nicholaas leaned forward. "Father, please, be careful what you say. You give away too much."

Jan regarded Nicholaas with a look of infinite sadness and held up the palm of his hand toward him. The nearest candle threw curious shards of light and shadow across the flesh, and, for the first time, Sebastian noticed a series of scars on the underside of Jan's thumb—no doubt the work of a thumb screw. "Of all the men I have met in this world,' he nodded toward Sebastian, "this is the one I would trust with that which is most precious and most secret. Yes, Sebastian, I am what the authorities call an Anabaptist. All of us are."

From across the table, Nicholaas buried his face in his hands "Oh, dear God, no. *Stop*, Father!"

"No. Sebastian deserves to know. He, too, risks his life in the writing of this book. We should be honest with him."

"Thank you, Jan. And please know this: your secret is safe with me. I would never betray you to those who would harm you." Looking at Nicholaas he added, "I would never betray any of you. On my life I promise this. But I have questions I hope you can help me with. All I have ever heard said about the Anabaptists is that they are violent revolutionaries intent on overthrowing both church and state, and that what happened at Münster is proof of this. Yet all I have ever seen in you Netherlanders is tenderness and kindness and a yearning for peace. At every turn, you declare yourself to be opposed to violence. How then do you explain the atrocities of Münster?"

"Bah. Münster!" Jan spat out. "What an abomination. Those men violated every principle that Anabaptists stand for. Yes, they believed that adults should be baptized, but they embraced little else of that which we hold dear. They were an aberration, a sect, fools deceived and misled."

"But that is not what the rest of Europe believes. They say

Münster represented the true intent of all Anabaptists, which is to throw off authority and plunge the world into lawlessness and anarchy."

"No, no, no! Lies! Libel! And I can prove it to you Sebastian, I can!"

Sebastian sat back in his chair, puzzled, unsure how anyone could prove such a thing. Seeing the confusion on Sebastian's face, Jan rose to his feet. "Wait here. I have documents I will show you."

Again, Nicholaas spoke. "Father, what are you doing? Please, be careful."

"No, our people have been slandered for far too long. These must be seen. I want Sebastian to understand. Wait here. I will return shortly with something you must read."

Nicholaas looked aghast as his father-in-law walked from the room, pausing only to light another candle from one on the table. Sebastian's head spun from the night's disclosures—and the realization that even more were about to come.

Chapter 25
The Anabaptists Revealed

When Jan reentered the room, Sebastian and Nicholaas immediately looked up—Sebastian with expectation, Nicholaas with agitation. Jan took his seat and placed before Sebastian a folder constructed from thick linen paper. He pulled the two candles across the table so that both were in front of Sebastian.

Sebastian opened the folder. He found a page filled with writing set out like a constitution. It was broken into paragraphs, some of them numbered. At the top of the page, in bold cursive, was a title: *The Schleitheim Confession.* Below that lay a subheading: *The Brotherly Union of a Number of Children of God.* It was dated February 24, 1527, which meant the document had been composed ten years after Luther nailed his ninety-five theses to the door in Wittenberg, seven years before Münster, and nine years before Calvin published *The Institutes.*

As Sebastian studied it, he realized this was an Anabaptist confession of faith, a documenting of the beliefs these people held to be most precious and true. The very first article dealt, unsurprisingly, with baptism. It argued that baptism should only be for those who freely choose it, an expression of their desire to follow Jesus by reen-acting Jesus's death and resurrection.

The second article concerned how to deal with church members who fell into immorality. They were to be approached privately, twice, and if there was no change of heart, they were to be prevented from taking communion. But all of this was to be done in a spirit of brotherly love. *This sounds like a gentler approach than Geneva's consistory,* Sebastian thought.

The third article dealt with the rite of communion, which the confession spoke of as symbolic rather than as a mystical transforma-tion of the elements into Christ's actual flesh and blood. The fourth article urged true Christians to not participate in any form of evil and to flee from every institution that practiced evil—whether church or state. Believers, it went on to say, must never take up a sword or any other weapon. The next article concerned what manner of person could become a pastor: he must be a man of good reputation, supported financially by those in the church and never in the pay of the state.

In the shifting light of the candles, Sebastian leaned closer. The next clause began "Violence must not be used in any circumstance, for we learn this from Jesus himself." The sentences that followed advised Christians against becoming magistrates, for magistrates carried the state's sword and executed the death sentence. Sebastian frowned as he thought about how the rest of the church in Europe taught the exact opposite. For this was the very thing Calvin and Luther argued a Christian magistrate *must* do!

The final article counseled against the taking of oaths before a magistrate. It quoted Jesus, who had forbidden his disciples from making vows, telling them, "Simply let your yes mean yes, and your no mean no." *It's about honesty,* Sebastian thought. *Simply be truthful, with no caveats or obfuscation.* He ran his eyes over the full document. It was riddled with references to following Jesus and being a disciple. Most of its quotes were directly from the Gospels.

Sebastian looked up at Jan. "I grasp that this is an Anabaptist creed, but who wrote it, and why did those at Münster not follow it?"

"This is not a creed so much as a list of principles Anabaptists agreed to live by. It was put together by the earliest Swiss leaders in a meeting overseen by a man named Michael Sattler, a converted monk. Copies of this were sent to Luther, who rejected it, and later to those in Münster. But the people of Münster believed they could establish Christ's kingdom by the sword. Their dream was to force upon the world a theocracy, cobbling together ideas from the Old Testament, like polygamy and kingship. They forgot that Christ had said, 'My kingdom is not of this world.' And they forgot that when the people had tried to make Jesus king, he had walked away. You see, Sebastian? Our yearning has always been only for freedom, for peace, and for brotherhood."

'But did not those at Münster also insist on adult baptism?"

"Yes, but of the seven articles here, they rejected six. Had those fools followed this confession, that whole tragedy would have been avoided."

Sebastian stared at the frayed document before him. *Had all men followed this confession, a million tragedies would have been avoided.* "And this man, Michael Sattler—does he still live?" As soon as the words were out of his mouth, Sebastian regretted asking. He knew what the answer must be.

"Those gentle leaders in Zurich? Do you think they would let such a monster, such an utterer of blasphemies live? No, Sattler was arrested and tried before a panel of twenty-four Catholic theologians and judges. And can you believe it, Sebastian, they found him guilty of multiple heinous crimes: defying the emperor, debasing the Eucharist, rejecting infant baptism, dishonoring the saints, advocating against violence, and whatever other charge they could think of. Those in power could never allow such a man to exist. So they killed him. Not quickly, mind you, but with as much torture as their holy minds could conceive. He was dragged to the public square where they cut out his tongue. Then they tied him to a wagon and tore pieces from his body with glowing tongs. On the way to the site of his execution, they used those tongs over and over as he bled and writhed. They finally set him on fire, still living, at the edge of the town. Oh, and his wife, Margaretha? They were much gentler with her. She was tied in a sack and drowned."

Sebastian's stomach turned. *And so it continues: Each of us is made in God's image, yet sin crouches at our door. Beauty and barbarity wrestle for ascendancy.*

"Believe me, Sebastian," Jan continued. "Apart from those fanatics at Münster, we are not set on overthrowing the state or creating a theocracy. Rather, we desire to see a separation of church and state. We do not want the state to tell us how we must worship, and we do not wish to impose on the state how it should govern. We have no right to force our religion on others, and they have no right to impose their beliefs on us. Unlike the Münsterites, we have rejected the power of violence. If someone wishes to follow Christ's way, this must be freely chosen."

Sebastian nodded. His thoughts whirled. He was exhausted by all he'd heard this night. His world and all he thought he knew had been tipped upside down. Still, there was one more question he longed to ask. "Jan, were you a leader—a pastor—among these Anabaptists?"

Jan's brow creased and his lips trembled. He seemed to struggle to make a reply. As he began equivocating, Nicholaas interrupted. "No, Father! You have said too much already. It is late, and you have drunk too much. We should go to bed, and Master Castellio should return to his home before something is said that we all regret."

The sharpness of Nicholaas's voice—that he would speak to his father-in-law in such a manner—shocked Sebastian. But Jan didn't seem to notice. He stared at Sebastian, yet somehow beyond him, as if lost in the memories of another life.

For a full minute, the room remained excruciatingly silent. Finally, Sebastian rose to his feet. "Nicholaas is right. I should be going and should let you both find your way to your beds. Adieu, and sleep well my friends."

When Sebastian returned home, the candles had all been extinguished and everyone was fast asleep. He crept to the bedside and slipped off his outer clothes. He tried to slide between the sheets without waking Marie, but as soon as his weight moved the straw of the mattress, she turned toward him.

"Seb! It is so late. But is it done? Is it completed?"

"Printed, bound, baled and on its way down the Rhine."

"Thanks be to God. And have you come from Oporinus's just now?"

Sebastian took a deep breath. "No. Beyond the book, far more has happened tonight." Then, beginning from the moment he and Jan entered the Rote Haus and sat down with Nicholaas, he recounted everything that had unfolded over the course of the night.

Marie was quiet for a long time before she spoke. "He has trusted you with a great secret—and also a great burden. If he were to be exposed, it would go badly for him—and now also for us. We must guard this, Sebastian. We must keep it close and hold it tightly."

"I know. I assured Jan and Nicholaas that I would do so, on my very life."

"That is a sacred promise, and we *will* keep it. But the book! You have done it. Well done, my love!"

Sebastian leaned over and kissed Marie. "It is late. We should sleep now and talk more of this in the morning." He wrapped his body as close to Marie's as he could and murmured goodnight. After some time, came the deep rhythmic breaths that told him Marie had fallen back to sleep. But his own eyes remained open, and his thoughts continued to revisit all that had transpired that evening. His mind kept picturing the look on Jan's face when he'd asked him if he'd been a pastor. And in his head, he kept hearing Nicholaas's sharp words, which had prevented Jan from speaking further.

When morning broke, Sebastian forced himself to rise. The little sleep he had gotten had been fractured by fitful dreams. His day was filled with many classes, and he had to drag himself through each one. Late in the afternoon, he returned to his office and found a small note placed on his desk. It was in Jan's hand, inviting him and Marie to eat with them at the Rote Haus that evening. He quickly pulled his doublet on and made for home, wanting to prepare Marie for the possibility of more disturbing revelations.

With Alise and Katarina tending to the children, Sebastian and Marie pulled their capes tightly about them and set off for the Rote Haus. When they arrived, Dirkgen was in the parlor. She embraced Marie with both arms before turning and greeting Sebastian. They followed her into the dining room where the fire blazed, its warmth comforting. Jan and Nicholaas stood locked in conversation. Tanneke was seated at the table reading from a small leather-bound book.

As they worked their way through the meal an awkward silence spread across the table. Finally, Dirkgen summoned the courage to break it. "It sounds as if my husband was a little free with both his wine and his words last night, Sebastian."

Sebastian cleared his throat. "In Jan's defense, we were cele-brating a great achievement—our book freshly completed and shipped out. Perhaps we all lost a little of our usual decorum."

"And yet, Sebastian and Marie, I feel we must apologize to you. By saying those things, Jan has placed you in a dangerous position. As tolerant as Basel is, there are still those in this city who, if they knew of our convictions, would—" She hesitated.

"Would have us killed or expelled," Nicholaas cut in, a tone of exasperation in his voice. He was clearly unwilling to mince words.

"Please, Nicholaas," Sebastian replied. "As I promised you last night, I would never betray you. Marie and I are of one mind in this. Your secret is safe with us. We will tell no one."

"Even if they torture you? Burn your flesh? Even then?" It was Tanneke, her eyes shining with tears.

"You must forgive Tanneke," Dirkgen interjected. "All of us have watched as loved ones were dragged away by the authorities. We ourselves were forced to flee Holland on a barge, hidden beneath sacks."

"By some counts, thirty-thousand Anabaptists have been executed across Europe. And that is only a fraction of those who have been tortured and forced to recant." Nicholaas still sounded angry.

"But why so much hate? I don't understand it!" Marie's voice was almost pleading.

"We believe every individual is precious—called and gifted by God's Spirit. That threatens those whose position is based on hierarchy and power." Jan had entered the fray now. "We believe that we are called to live under the new law of Christ—the law of love—and that the Spirit of Jesus releases us from the old covenant with its harsh laws and its recourse to violence. Those who rule despise us because we refuse to offer our young men as fodder for their endless wars. We share our goods with one another, ensuring the poor among us always have enough. Those who hold on to power feel threatened by our way of life."

"Worse still," Dirkgen's voice dripped with sarcasm. "Some of our communities allow women to have positions of leadership and to teach and write. That, of course, proves that we must be witches and heretics, fit only to be burned or drowned."

Marie gasped. "What? Are these things true?"

Dirkgen's tone turned even sharper. "Margret Hottinger, Anna Jansz, Ursula Jost, Barbara Rebstock, Helena von Freyberg, Elisabeth Dirks. I can list many more women leaders if you wish me to."

Jan spoke again. "We believe that the calling to minister does not come from man but from God, based on the gifts he has given, not on a person's sex or social class or even education. Paul says that there is no longer Jew or Gentile, Greek or barbarian, slave or master, male or female, for all are one in Christ Jesus. This is how we read the New Testament. We don't believe in hierarchies."

Sebastian tried to make sense of these lofty ideas raining down on him. *Calvin always presents the Old Testament and the New Testament as a seamless whole, but these people are saying that the Old has been usurped by the New. And for Calvin, maintaining 'order' is one of the most crucial things in life. No wonder he fears and despises these Anabaptists.*

The van Brugges seemed spent. Once more, silence reigned. But eventually Jan spoke again, his voice even. "I am sorry if we have spoken too strongly, Sebastian. Because we trust you, we have unburdened ourselves. I apologize if this has been too much to hear."

"Please, don't apologize. We are not offended by your words." He glanced at Marie for confirmation. She nodded. "But it is late, and perhaps it would be best if we left now. I think we need time to reflect on all you have told us, for much of it is novel to our minds."

A look of concern crossed Jan's face. Sebastian stared straight into his friend's eyes. "Once more, I give you my promise that these secrets are safe with us. I may not agree with everything you believe, but I will never betray you."

Chapter 26
The Triumph of John Calvin

Tired from a day full of teaching, Sebastian returned to his office one afternoon to find a note on his desk from the cathedral minister, Simon Sulzer.

Sebastian,

These two small books have come to me from Lausanne, authored by Theo Beza. I waited here in your office as I wanted to speak with you about them, but after waiting as long as I could, I had to depart. I apologize that I could not stay longer. I don't know if Calvin and Beza are correct in naming you as the author of Concerning Heretics, but either way, I am sorry for the bitter tone used in these tracts. You deserve better than this.

Simon

Sebastian's heart sank. Somehow, despite all of their efforts to conceal his identity, John Calvin and his protégé, Theodore Beza, had rightly guessed that he was one of the authors of *Concerning*

Heretics. Heart thumping, Sebastian read his way through the two booklets, sighing deeply every few minutes. Clearly Calvin and Beza had either read *Concerning Heretics* very hastily or most maliciously, for they were constantly misquoting or twisting the things Sebastian had committed to paper. Beza's booklets ended with an attack on Sebastian's character, arguing that "Castellio's lack of dogma proves him to be an irreligious and impious man."

And yet, despite these smears, the influence of *Concerning Heretics* seemed to be expanding. Jan had written a shorter Dutch version now spreading across the Netherlands. Perna had penned an Italian version which dissidents had smuggled into Italy. There was even a version circulating through France.

But Sebastian knew there was no longer any hope of hiding his identity from the authorities. Not after both Calvin and Beza had named him as the author of *Concerning Heretics*. But rather than be cowed by that, he decided to respond directly with a defense entitled *Against Calvin's Book*. Throwing caution to the wind, he confronted Calvin by name and demolished, one by one, all of the arguments Calvin had used to justify Servetus's execution and his role in it. He concluded with a phrase, stunning in both its logic and lucidity: "When those Genevans executed Servetus, they were not defending a doctrine—they were killing a man."

While he was finishing his reply, Simon Sulzer found him in his office. Sulzer came with yet more worrying news. Calvin and Beza, he said, have been flooding Basel's ministers and city officials—including himself, Meyer, Wissenburg, and Borrhaus—with letters berating them for weakness and insisting they crackdown on the traitors who oppose the work of the Reformation.

"Be cautious, Sebastian," Sulzer urged.

Sebastian thought a minute, then turned defiant. "I thank you for your concern, Simon, but I think I have passed the point of no return. Before God and my own conscience, I cannot back down. These men have distorted my words and misrepresented my faith. I cannot and will not let this stand unchallenged." Once more he took up his pen, determined to counter Beza's assertions.

Beza had argued that orthodox doctrine is *crucial*, for without it, citizens cannot live good lives or refrain from evil. Sebastian shook his head, unprepared to let that go unchallenged. "Really, Beza?" he muttered to himself. "Can you prove that assertion? For in fact, the opposite seems true. By which I mean this: if the Genevans had been less certain of their doctrine of the Trinity, perhaps they would have been less certain that it was right to burn a man to death." He scratched the words onto his paper.

Late on a blustery autumn day, Sebastian arrived at the print shop and placed the manuscript, *Against Calvin's Book*, before Oporinus. Strangely, disquietingly, the big man hesitated.

"Things are heating up, Sebastian. Both Wissenburg and Borrhaus have come here instructing me to become more cooperative, insisting that if I don't, there will be consequences. Consequences for my name and consequences for my business. I think we should be more circumspect this time. Let me take this to Borrhaus and get his approval first. We need to get Borrhaus back on our side. I will visit him this afternoon, then tomorrow we can meet and begin to set up for the print."

Sebastian noticed the lines under each of Oporinus's eyes, deep and weary. His friend, who had always looked so brave and determined, today looked tired from the fight. "Of course, Johannes, of course. As you always say, you and Borrhaus are old friends, and you know how to talk him around. I leave it in your hands."

The next morning, Sebastian returned to the print shop. He made his way to the back and found Oporinus staring at one of his presses, the mechanism sitting idle. He turned to Sebastian, his face grave, his eyelids heavy. "I went to see Borrhaus. He was cold, distant. He wouldn't even look me in the eye. He flicked through the manuscript then told me to leave him alone so he could consider it. Early this morning, a note arrived." He passed the paper to Sebastian, who scanned the note. It didn't take long. It consisted of a single sentence:

The censors of Basel will not allow Sebastian Castellio's rebuttal to be printed.

A surge of anger welled up from somewhere deep within. "No! I refuse to accept this as a final answer, Johannes. If they will not let us print it, we will find another way."

"What alternative do we have, Sebastian? I'm afraid they have beaten us."

"Not yet, they haven't. I will make copies by hand and send them to those I know to be following this argument. I will not let Beza have the last word."

In the weeks that followed, Sebastian worked late into the night, furtively and laboriously, assisted by Marie, writing out duplicates of his booklet. Despite his new-found caution, Oporinus assisted him with the distribution, using trusted couriers to get the work to allies in the other Swiss cities.

That same year, 1555, news of growing political unrest in Geneva reached Basel. No one was surprised. The tension between Calvin's supporters and the older enfants de Genève had been building for years. The balance of the city had shifted with so many émigrés arriving from France coupled with the influence of a generation now reaching maturity that had grown up reciting Calvin's catechism. In May 1555, rumors swirled of an uprising, violence in the streets, and Ami Perrin driven from the city. The stories were chaotic, and from the distance of Basel, it was hard to piece together what had really happened. In early June, a letter arrived addressed to Sebastian. His heart leaped when he noticed the seal on the envelope—Perrin's. Part of him wanted to take the letter home and read it with Marie. But the longing for news of his friend's welfare proved stronger. He slid a knife under the wax and opened the envelope.

Dearest Sebastian,

The first thing I want you to know is that I and my family are safe. We have taken shelter in the city of Bern, as have some of our friends. We cannot return to Geneva. We have lost our home, our heritage, all we possess. As you know, the party of the enfants de Genève has held power on the council for many years, much to Calvin's disgust, for we denied he and his consistory the right to excommunicate any they please without the right of appeal to the council. But, cunning man that he is, he has been encouraging French refugees to come to Geneva by the thousands, and to buy themselves bourgeoise status as quickly as possible. Of course, this also buys them the right to vote, and to vote for the party of Calvin.

On May 15th, the new council elections were held. It was a narrow outcome, but the Calvinists gained control. There was shock and anger in the streets from those who had lived here for so many generations. There were skir-mishes. It threatened to become a riot. I felt I must do something to calm the people. The citizens know and respect me. To restore order, I realized I must take hold of the city's staff—the symbol of our authority—and hold it aloft as I commanded the crowd to desist from their agitations. As you know Sebastian, I am not a small man, and I have a very large voice! The councillor trying to control the crowd was a small man with a feeble voice, a man little known to the people. So I took the ceremonial staff from him and commanded the crowd to quiet. And quiet they did! But that pathetic little man—an acolyte of Calvin's—accused me of assaulting him and stealing the staff. Absurd! All I did was take temporary possession of it for the good of Geneva, as I have always done everything for the good of Geneva.

Sebastian paused and took a breath. How easily he could picture the melodramatic Perrin trying to take control of a mob in that way.

The next day, what do I hear? That Calvin's party is rounding up every member of the enfants de Genève and stretching them on the rack, forcing them to confess to crimes of sedition and revolution, making them say that my party was planning to slaughter all the French residents of the city! Four of my colleagues were dragged to Calvin's executioner and murdered. As our home was on the edge of the town, my family and I were able to flee on horseback. We received a kindly reception in Bern. Indeed, the city of Bern has issued a rebuke to Calvin and his cronies. But that has achieved nothing. On the contrary, Geneva has passed sentence on me in absentia, saying that my right hand should be severed from my arm should I ever return.

Oh Sebastian, you were right to leave when you could. It has all gotten so much worse. And now Calvin has finally attained his vision for Geneva: a theocracy, with himself as its pope.

There was more, another two full pages in fact, but Sebastian couldn't bring himself to read it. He folded the letter and placed it in his satchel. He would take it home and read it with Marie. Then they would pray for Geneva and for all those they knew and loved in that place.

Perrin's news provoked a renewed sense of despondency. When Sebastian had ridden out of Lyon in search of John Calvin all those years ago, he had been full of hope, full of faith. He had believed the Reformation would deliver the world from its darkness and savagery, into an age of light in which men practiced love of neighbor, as Christ had commanded. When he had left Strasbourg for Geneva, he was sure that, in John Calvin, he had found a man of truth, one who would lead Christendom out of superstition and into grace. Now as he looked about him, it appeared that Catholic violence and power lust had simply been replaced with a Protestant version.

He shared all of this with Marie. She did her best to comfort and encourage him. One evening after supper, they pulled their stools nearer the fire. Sebastian's thoughts wandered far away as he stared into the fire, lost in the movement of the flames.

"What's wrong, Seb? You look saddened. What are you thinking of?"

Sebastian sighed. "When I left France to find Calvin and then followed him to Geneva, I thought we were moving closer to the kingdom of God, that together we would be working for justice, for brotherly love, for that golden age spoken of by the prophets. I dreamed of honey but woke with a mouthful of ashes."

"No, Seb, don't say that. We have found so much that is good and beautiful here in Basel. God has opened a way for you to publish not one but two Bible translations. How many can claim such an achievement! God has used you. And look at the children we have been blessed with. All our children are beautiful and healthy! And

Nathaniel—have you noticed how much he grows to look like Euge-nie? There is so, so much we can be grateful for, surely?"

Sebastian continued to stare at the fire, but a hint of a smile played at his mouth. Finally, he turned to face Marie. "Yes, we have been gifted such beautiful children, and I such a beautiful wife!" Breaking into a full grin, he pulled Marie to her feet and wrapped his arms around her. "And I thank God for these gifts every day. It's just that I am so tired of going to war each time I take up my pen. It wearies me so."

"Then write about something else. Something that will lift you above the dirt of these squabbles. Another Bible translation perhaps? Maybe Italian this time?"

Sebastian chuckled. "Perhaps nothing quite as demanding as that. But you're right. I need to take up a project that will lift my heart toward heaven and by which I can lift others." He placed his lips on Marie's forehead.

That summer, Sebastian did finally have more joyful things to focus on. His family grew by another daughter, Sara, in whom he and Marie delighted. Around the same time as that birth came a literary one. Finally, after all the years of struggle, Sebastian's completed French Bible went to print. In its eloquent preface, Sebastian urged King Henri II, the French king, to protect and tolerate those in his realm being attacked for their beliefs, specifically the Protestant Huguenots.

The new translation was received with much acclaim, and for a brief period, Sebastian was able to ignore the torrent of abuse and disparagement that had been hurled at him. Soon after, more good news followed. That summer, the University of Basel awarded Sebastian his Master of Arts. Finally, it seemed a time of peace was dawning for them. Or so he hoped.

Chapter 27
The Honoring of Jan van Brugge

L ate in the summer of 1555, Sebastian began to ponder what his next writing project should be. Marie's earlier advice—that he focus on projects that cause his own heart to rise toward heaven—had proven to be sage counsel. So he thought back to those writings which had first inspired him to embark on this journey: the writings of Martin Luther. He had read everything Luther had ever written, though these days Luther's writings didn't move him the way they once had. There was, however, one exception. Hidden away in Luther's catalog was a mysterious little book called *German Theology*. Originally authored by an unknown mystic in the fourteenth century, Luther had rediscovered, reworked, and reprinted it. Calvin thought the book was too mystical, condemning it as satanic and poisonous. But, just as Luther had, Sebastian found its elegiac advice moving and helpful, urging readers toward union with God. This, he decided, would be his next project. He would translate *German Theology* into Latin and French.

For the rest of the year, he busied himself translating the little book's poetic counsel into phrases he hoped would inspire the hearts of a whole new generation. It proved to be just the tonic he needed.

Drop by drop, line by line, his faith in God's loving presence was slowly restored.

Sebastian had become totally absorbed in his new writing project and hadn't seen Jan for many weeks. If he had thought about it, it might have struck him as unusual that he hadn't received an invitation to dine with the van Brugges since that night following Jan's disclosures. And if he had bothered to inquire, others might have told him that all was not well in the Netherlander's camp. Oporinus or Bauhin, if asked, might have said that Jan, Dirkgen and Nicholaas somehow didn't seem as they were before. They might have commented that the joy had gone out of the van Brugges, that they seemed folded in on themselves. But immersed in his classes and in the thrill of translating *German Theology*, none of this came to Sebastian's attention. And then, one warm day in late August, a knock on the door of his office roused him from his work.

"Come in," Sebastian said. A moment later, a rangy Nicholaas entered the room. His face looked stonier than ever, his dark stubble standing out against his pale skin.

"Nicholaas! What a surprise. But you look ... troubled. What is it?"

Nicholaas remained standing. He took a deep breath, and his shoulders heaved. "Dirkgen and Jan are dead."

Sebastian gasped as he lurched to his feet. His blood seemed to run cold. His chest tightened, as if something was crushing his lungs, and his head began to swim. "Dear God! No! Nicholaas, what happened?"

"Among us Netherlanders, arguments and opposing camps have formed. For the past several months, both Jan and Dirkgen have grown more and more melancholy. I think perhaps their hearts were breaking. Last month, I made a trip abroad, but Jan did not come with me. He said he did not feel up to it. I got back a week ago to find both of them unwell. At first, it seemed no more than heavy colds, but it also plagued their stomachs with strange pains and made their chests heavy with fevers that would not break. Three days ago, Dirkgen passed away. And this morning, when we tried to wake Jan, he was gone too. They are dead. Sebastian." His grief-stricken face pierced Sebastian's heart.

"Did you call Bauhin? Did a doctor attend them?"

"We looked for Bauhin, of course, but he is in France on business at present. Fortunately, van Schlor found Gugliemo Grataroli, the Italian doctor, who came most willingly."

Sebastian hesitated. He knew that Bauhin disagreed with Grataroli's approach to medicine—and his commitment to alchemy and astrology. But with Bauhin away, it was good that the Italian had come to their aid.

"Grataroli spent many hours with both Dirkgen and Jan, administering his own medicines and letting blood, trying to break their fevers, but all to no avail." Nicholaas stared at the floor.

Sebastian rounded the desk and wrapped his arms around the stooped Nicholaas. "I am so sorry. This is devastating. I cannot believe it. Of course, we will come to see you all as soon as we can. Is there anything we can do for you?"

"As far as practical arrangements go, everything is in hand. This morning I visited Simon Sulzer at the cathedral. He will take the funeral. And he will inform the council, for he thinks they will want to be involved too."

"Of course. Jan has been a great benefactor to this city. They must acknowledge that. But please Nicholaas, let me know if there is anything Marie or I can do to help."

Nicholaas nodded and left without a further word. Sebastian stared after him, his heart breaking, unable to believe that Dirkgen and Jan had been snatched away so swiftly, and for their deaths to occur within days of each other. How very, very odd.

Over the next few days, the council and the church were unstinting in their effort to honor Jan. As Sebastian hoped, they had not forgotten his many gifts to the city, his help to the poor and his generous sponsorship of municipal projects. Using city funds, the council constructed within Saint Leonard Church a beautiful marble plaque of commemoration, and they gently placed Jan and Dirkgen's bodies side by side in a sepulchre in the chapel's cemetery. On the day of the funeral, Sulzer spoke movingly, reminding the congregants what a gentle, loving soul Jan had been, that the city of Basel had been honored to adopt him as a son. Yet, as poignant as the service was, Sebastian sensed something strange about the day. Anna van Berchem, her family, and the younger children belonging to Jan and Dirkgen all sat together, while Nicholaas and Tanneke, van Schlor and the rest of the Netherlanders formed a separate party on the other side of the church. Afterward, Sebastian noticed that they did not mix nor speak with one another. Marie noticed too. When they returned home, she asked Sebastian what he thought it meant.

"Grief manifests itself differently in all of us, I suppose. This will be a devastating shock for all of them, but I'm sure, in time, they will reunite and support one another as before." But even as he spoke the words, he failed to convince himself. Something very odd was afoot.

Marie cradled Sebastian's hand in hers, letting her head rest against his shoulder, and together they watched the flames dancing in the fireplace. "Of all the people I have known, no one emanated joy and sought beauty the way Jan and Dirkgen did. I pictured the two of them growing old together, and the four of us always being friends. I can't believe they are gone—and so suddenly. We never got a chance to say goodbye. If only we'd known, perhaps we could have done something. I don't understand why neither van Schlor nor Nicholaas ever came and sought us out for help."

Sebastian's brow furrowed. The same question was plaguing his thoughts too.

Chapter 28
Attack after Attack

Sebastian had never known anyone quite like Jan, and he knew there would forever be a void in his life where his towering friend had stood. Life in Basel appeared flatter and grayer without Jan.

Other things were changing in the city too, and not for the better. Oporinus's work was drying up and his business was struggling. Rumors swirled that the leaders in Geneva had come down hard on Basel's leaders, encouraging them to tighten their control. Those men had singled out Oporinus for particular scrutiny, refusing him permission to publish anything even remotely controversial. But the same scruples were not being applied by the censors in the other Swiss cities, for no questions were asked when, later that year, Theodore Beza sent his own Latin translation of the New Testament to a printer.

The day after he had obtained a copy, Oporinus arrived at Sebastian's office with the Testament under his arm. He sank into a heavy wooden chair. The morning sun streamed through the square panes of the mullioned window, highlighting flecks of gray pockmarking the big man's beard and temples. The lines around his eyes had deepened as well.

"I'm sorry, Sebastian. I don't come with good news."

Sebastian's heart sank. "What now? Another book banned?"

"The opposite actually. One published. Beza's New Testament." He placed his copy on the desk as he said it.

Sebastian shrugged his shoulders. "Beza and I have our differences, but I bare him no malice. If he has translated the Scriptures into words that bring comfort and insight to people, then we should thank him for it."

"I'm afraid your graciousness isn't reciprocated. You need to read his preface." He opened the Bible to its third page and slid it across the desk to Sebastian. "The middle paragraph."

Sebastian leaned over the desk and followed Oporinus's finger.

The reason this new version has become so necessary is as a correction to the recent proliferation of mischievous Bible translations that have abused the Word of God. Worst among these have been recent French and Latin translations, especially those by a certain man of gross impudence and ingratitude, a man so blasphemous that he reveals himself to be a tool of Satan, his words sent to confuse the faithful.

Sebastian slumped back in his chair. His cheeks flushed with fire, and he felt sick.

"Most who read this will know he is speaking of me. But why would he say these things? And to say them in the preface to a Bible?" Sebastian stared at the book, aghast.

"I think it is clear what is happening, Sebastian. On the one side, they exert every pressure to shut you up, to prevent you from writing or me from publishing. We are muzzled. On the other side, they heap up abuse and slander, making every attempt to discredit you and to present you as a fool who must be ignored. Or worse—as a blasphemer who must be punished."

Sebastian smiled grimly at the image that flashed through his mind. "I am a man with a pen, fighting a man with a city. A flea who attacks an elephant. They control the presses and have the ear of nearly all the councils. But perhaps even the flea can make the elephant turn around to see what bites him. We will continue to write. We will continue to publish where we can. And if that fails, we will copy our books by hand and give them to those who dare to read them. It is all we can do. But mark my words Johannes: I refuse to be bullied into silence."

That March was unusually cold, with snow followed by heavy rains. The Rhine became fast and swollen with logs from upstream. As usual, Sebastian gathered his grappling hook and went to the river to collect wood for the fire—anything to supplement his modest salary and to feed his growing family. After classes finished, he hurried to the riverside needing to get there before darkness fell, joining the other Baselers likewise fishing for fuel.

On one such evening, as twilight was descending into blackness, he could not shake the feeling that he was being watched. Looking around, he scoured the riverbank looming over him. *There! A lamp moves, and a shadowed face stares at me.*

But as he peered intently into the fading light, the lamp was extinguished. *Many people walk along the riverbank at this time. Surely it is nothing. You imagine it.* Chilled to the bone, he gathered his load and trudged home, hoping that Marie had their fire blazing.

The next day, after classes concluded, Sebastian sat in The Hare chatting with Bauhin and young Amerbach. His two friends were commiserating with him over the way Beza had attacked him in his Bible preface. Sebastian regarded his tankard of ale and slowly shook his head. "I never realized that spite was such a necessary Christian virtue until now. But it seems to be the foremost fruit our theologians possess." He sighed. "But enough wallowing. How are those remarkable boys of yours, Jean?"

At the mention of his sons, Bauhin puffed up with pride. "In love with God's creation. Their fascination is divided equally between medicine and botany. We can't take a walk anywhere without them stopping to collect a leaf or a root and sketching it in one of their notebooks."

"Goodness, I wonder where they get that from?"

"What about your brood, Sebastian? It must be a merry little houseful that you preside over these days?"

"It is, but the house is becoming a little too crowded. Marie is expecting again, and I am mustering the courage to ask Wissenburg for an increase in my stipend. If he grants that, we plan to look for larger accommodations."

"At the rate you and Marie are going, you'll soon need a castle and a very large raise!"

Sebastian gave Bauhin a sheepish smile. "We both love children. And it seems that God has blessed us with ... ah—"

"Fruitful loins," Bauhin added helpfully.

Amerbach intervened to rescue Sebastian. "I've heard that there are several houses for sale in the Steinenvorstadt district, some of them quite large. And the prices are reasonable. As you can imagine, not many gentlefolk wish to live in *that* neighborhood." Amerbach tilted his head in the direction of Steinenvorstadt.

Sebastian shrugged. "If it is a neighborhood filled with honest working men and women, that's good enough for us. We have no use for people who look down on those who labor with their hands. But wherever it is, I need to find somewhere large enough for my family and for me to tutor students after class."

"Then I suggest you go and take a look. You may well find a bargain from what I hear. And I will ask my father to have a word with Wissenburg on your behalf."

That Sunday, Alise watched the children while Sebastian and Marie walked from Saint Alban to the southern-most edge of the city.

Steinenvorstadt was a suburb of working men and women, artisans, weavers and the like, and generally thought of as a rough part of town. But what Amerbach had said was true—there were several large stone-block houses for sale. They had all seen better days, but between Sebastian's building skills and Marie's tailoring, restoring one of them was a challenge they would cheerfully accept.

Thankfully, Amerbach's intervention paid off. A small pay raise was secured, which enabled them to buy and move just in time for their baby to arrive. He came early—a healthy boy, named Bonifacius, after the benefactor whose financial help had been vital to their survival in Basel. But not long after the joyous event, they received a letter with tragic news. Sebastian's sister Jeanette and her husband, Evard, had both been overcome by sickness and taken from this life. A twelve-year-old niece named Jeanne had been orphaned. Could they take her? Given their love of children, they did not have to consider long. Sebastian procured a horse and rode south to collect the child.

Now they were a family of seven.

Over the next many weeks, Sebastian and Marie busied themselves setting up their house and welcoming the baby and the adopted Jeanne into their family. The last thing they were expecting was the pamphlet slid under their door one night as they slept.

Early that morning as Marie paced the kitchen, cradling Bonifacius, and Sebastian stoked the fire, she noticed the leaflet. Balancing Bonifacius against her, she bent to pick it up. Sebastian whirled at her cry of anguish. She looked up at him, her face crumpled in disbelief.

"What is it? What's wrong?" He stepped closer, but before he could reach his wife, she held the tract out to him at arm's length, as if it were something fetid.

Cautiously, Sebastian took it from her. It bore the title *The Calumnies of a Scoundrel*. As his eyes scanned the page, they widened in disbelief. A tumbling maelstrom of words, vicious and unrestrained, that opened by naming the said scoundrel as Sebastian Castellio. The author went on to pillory him as a liar, a thief, a traitor, an ungrateful reprobate who had turned on those who once sheltered him and who now sought to destroy the work of the Protestant Reformation. From there, it launched into an extraordinary series of accusations. He was, among other things, a pilferer of firewood, someone so beggarly as to steal driftwood that rightly belonged to the city of Basel. Several more paragraphs of malicious venting followed.

The lump in Sebastian's stomach grew heavier with each line. Finally, as he neared the end of the missive, his eyes rushed to the conclusion, longing for the abuse to be over. But the last sentence was the most hurtful of all: "May God bind you up, Satan!" It was signed by none other than John Calvin.

Sebastian looked up at Marie, his face hot with anger. Tears rolled down both her cheeks, her lips pressed against the top of Bonifacius's head. "Why are they doing this to us? Why? They call you the devil's servant and now this. Why, Seb, why?"

Sebastian enfolded them in his arms, holding them tenderly. He tried to think of something reassuring to say, some answer that would make sense, but he could think of nothing. Not a single word of comfort for them or for himself.

By the afternoon, the lump curdling in his stomach had calmed. That day's teaching had been difficult, and he'd returned home as soon as he could. He sat in his study wondering how he should respond to this latest bizarre attack or if he should hold his tongue. But he was growing convinced that to leave these accusations unanswered might be seen as conceding that Calvin's charges were true. Besides, Calvin and Beza's accusations had only been increasing in frequency. Several times now, they had falsely accused Castellio of authoring other publications. If an anonymous tract, pamphlet or book was critical of Calvin's theology or reforms, then surely, in their minds, Castellio was behind its publication.

As he glanced around the room, his eyes fell on the coiled rope and four prongs of iron nestled in the corner. It was the very device he used to fish lumber from the water, the lumber he was now accused of stealing. A smile played across his lips as he dipped his quill into the inkwell. In a careful hand, he titled his response to Calvin's accusations *The Grappling Hook*.

In its opening stanza, he categorically denied being the writer of the tract intercepted at the gates of Geneva some months past, the one attacking Calvin. He also castigated Calvin and Beza for making public accusations without proof. He then refuted the charges of thievery, explaining the process by which Basel's council permitted citizens to dredge the river for wood. Once these rebuttals were laid down, he allowed his heart to flow out through his pen.

> Perhaps you can no longer bear to think of me as a friend or as a brother. But I am. And now you have no qualms about calling me the devil. But I am not. I am a human being created in the image of God. I am a Christian, and in Christ I have dignity, a dignity that you can never take from me. Be careful, for you and I will both one day have to give an account to God for every word we speak or write. We are each fallible and make many mistakes, but let us remain friends, for our first duty as Christians is to love one another. If we think we have wisdom, let us show it by our humility, for the Lord has said, "I will raise up the humble and cast down the proud." And so I pray this—that by the blood Jesus shed, you would let me live my life in peace and cease persecuting me, for I am entitled to the freedom to hold onto my own beliefs just as I grant you the freedom to hold onto yours.

He'd written with restraint and respect. Surely Borrhaus would allow him to make this reply, to answer the slanders that had been heaped upon him. Tomorrow he would go to Borrhaus directly and plead his case for publication.

—————

The next morning, he strode purposely to Borrhaus's office. The door stood ajar. The thickset man sat at his desk reading through a pile of papers. Sebastian knocked gently. Borrhaus glanced up, a look of wary surprise on his face.

"Sebastian. I didn't realize we had an appointment this morning."

"We don't, but I have come to make a personal appeal to you concerning a publication."

Borrhaus stiffened. "What kind of publication?"

"Martin, I'm sure you are aware that for many months I have been under constant attack from John Calvin and Theodore Beza. Their denunciations of my character and my scholarship pile higher and higher, but I have been denied the opportunity of defense. This does not seem just, and so I come to you seeking permission to publish a response. I have written a short text, tempered with moderation." He slid the papers across the desk.

Hesitantly, Borrhaus picked up the pages and began reading. After several minutes, he put Sebastian's reply down. He held his silence, his jaw moving as if chewing on the words he'd just read. Finally, his jaw firmly set, he looked at Sebastian. "No."

"But why? You see how they abuse me with insults, and here I answer them with mildness. Can you not even allow me to do that?"

"I want an end to this trouble between Basel and Geneva. If I allow you to print this, it will set off yet another round of accusations and recriminations. Then I will have Wissenburg and Meyer barking in my ears, and Calvin and Beza berating me for my weakness. It shocks me that you don't recognize how powerful these men are and where this could all end if you don't back down. I'm tired of being in the middle of it all. I will keep the peace. I forbid this to be printed."

"But surely, in the name of justice, I must be allowed some dignity, I—"

"I said *no!* That is the end of this matter. There is nothing more to discuss." His voice was sharp, sharper than Sebastian had ever heard.

Sebastian reached across the desk and regathered his pamphlet, folding it into his satchel. As he strode down the corridor and toward his own office, he contemplated the long night that lay ahead of him. He would be up late writing out copies to distribute, including to Geneva. One way or another, John Calvin would read his reply.

Two weeks later, a letter arrived at their home, sent from Geneva. He recognized the handwriting immediately—it was from his sister, Etienne. Nervously, Sebastian broke the seal while Marie hovered at his shoulder. As was his practice, he read the missive aloud.

The first few lines inquired after everybody's health, especially Jeanne's, hoping she had settled in well and was a blessing to their family. But as he reached the letter's second page, its tone grew more grave. Etienne and her husband, Pierre, had been visited by members of the consistory several times. Their home had been searched for "heretical literature." They had, of course, found several pieces penned by Sebastian. These items were seized and burned, and their owners threatened. Etienne ended the letter with a plea for Sebastian to be more cautious, and to be careful who he trusted. In Geneva, whispers and rumors abounded about a plan to silence those critical voices emanating from Basel.

The next day, Sebastian arrived at the university to find a large envelope, sealed with the city of Basel's imprimatur, sitting on his desk. He broke the seal and read the single page within.

Sebastian Castellio
Chair of Greek
Basel University

The gravest of all charges has been brought against you: that of heresy. Within one week, you must supply the city council and the university senate a full and truthful account of your creed so that it might be established that you truly hold to the orthodox Reformed Christian faith. You will appear before a panel appointed by the city's magistrates to defend your position and answer any questions put to you.

By order of Bürgermeister Meyer
City of Basel

A flush of cold sweat seeped across his body, the sensation in his stomach turning to stone. It was a sense of dread he knew all too well. It was that darkness he had first seen in the streets of Lyon. It was the oppression he had fled in Geneva. Here, in the city of Basel, he thought he had found a place of refuge. Was that now being stripped away?

Shaken, he found a sheet of paper and began making notes describing his understanding of the central doctrines of the Christian faith. But after a few minutes of struggle, he put his quill down. *How can I answer their charges when I don't even know what those charges are?* He stood and moved toward the door. *Perhaps some fresh air will clear my head.* As he stepped into the corridor, he very nearly collided with the cathedral minister, Simon Sulzer.

"Simon! What are you doing here?"

"I've come to see you, Sebastian."

Sebastian hesitated, searching Sulzer's face for a clue as to where the man stood. *Are you one of my accusers too?*

Sulzer glanced around, then asked, "May I come in? I have information I think will be helpful to you." Cautiously, Sebastian gestured for Sulzer to enter his office.

"I know about the accusations that have been brought against you, Sebastian. Actually, Borrhaus and Wissenburg asked me to join them in interrogating you on those charges."

"And will you?"

"No. The opposite in fact. I have come to offer you my support. If I can help you in any way, I am willing to do so. I am appalled by these witch hunts, by the spectacle of Christians attacking one another. And not just I. Amerbach has also offered to assist with your defense. I think it will help to have a legal advocate of his stature on your side."

A sense of relief swept over Sebastian. "Thank you, Simon. Your arrival is timely, for I've been trying to compose a defense, but it is impossible when I don't even know the nature of their accusations against me."

"And this is where I can help you. Borrhaus and Wissenburg spent a long time trying to convince me of your errors, so I am now very familiar with what they believe them to be. I can also tell you this: the origin of these charges is not in Basel but Geneva."

Sebastian grunted. "Of course. But tell me: what heresies am I accused of?"

"Believing in free will and denying the doctrine of predestination. They also say that you deny the divine inspiration of Saint Paul's letters in the New Testament."

"What? I have never once said or written anything against the inspiration of Paul's letters. How can they accuse me of that?"

"They say that it is Paul who first proposed the doctrine of predestination. Therefore, by questioning this doctrine, you question the truth of Paul's words."

"This is absurd. One can easily construct an argument for free will from Paul's teachings. This is not an argument about inspiration but about interpretation."

"Yes, I agree. They are grasping at straws in order to shut you up —and to appease Geneva."

"I see that. But thank you, Simon. The information you have just given me will help immensely in preparing a defense. May I meet with you and Amerbach tomorrow to discuss what I have prepared? You can point out any weaknesses in what I write and advise me on how to strengthen it."

"It would be an honor. I will talk to Amerbach. I'm sure he will agree. Let's meet in his office tomorrow at this same hour."

Chapter 29
A Trial for Heresy

Three days later, Sebastian stood outside Borrhaus's office waiting for the command to enter. Once given, he walked straight to Borrhaus's desk and laid his defense down. Borrhaus picked it up and flicked through the pages. He paused at the final page and lingered there before he spoke. "This will be submitted to the city's ministers and magistrates. They will examine it to discern whether you have contravened the city's laws or its confession of faith. Wissenburg and I will also study this document, then you will appear before us in the professorial lounge to make a defense. Gathered to hear you will be Basel's ministers, her teachers of theology and her magistrates. You may bring an advocate with you, if you so choose."

Sebastian nodded. There seemed to be nothing more to say.

On the appointed day of the defense, Sebastian and Marie walked hand in hand to the university, up two broad staircases, and along a tiled corridor till they came to the professorial lounge. Sulzer met them at the door.

Sulzer cleared his throat. "I'm sorry, Marie, but women are not permitted to enter. Of course, I will bring a chair and you may sit out here. As soon as things are concluded, we will let you know what has transpired." Marie's face clouded with anger, but Sulzer had already turned away to speak to Sebastian. "Do you feel prepared for this, Sebastian?"

"Simon, had you not come to me I would have been caught blind, as if in a trap. But now, armed with this document that you have helped me create, I feel more than able to answer any accusation they may bring."

"Good. But I also have another idea, one that I believe will throw them off guard. When you take your place before them, I will join you, and I will make a statement in support of your faith and your interpretation of the Scriptures."

Sebastian's throat tightened. He could barely choke out, "Thank you, Simon."

Just as they were about to move into the room, a hand fell on Sebastian's shoulder. He turned to find both the older Amerbach and his son Basilius behind him. The senior Amerbach winked. "I would like to sit with you too, and to testify in your support if I may. I very much want these men to know where I stand."

Sebastian's eyes misted as gratitude flooded through him. He regarded his old friend and mentor, Bonifacius. He was elderly now, his beard and mane quite silvered. "Yes, of course, Bonifacius. I would be very glad of that."

He kissed Marie before turning to follow the others into the room. It was an ornate chamber lined with panels of oak. Across from where they entered, thick velvet curtains framed mullioned windows. At the front of the room resided a long wooden table, rather like a bench. Thirty or so chairs had been set out to face it. Dozens of Basel's leading citizens already occupied those chairs. In a corner, off toward his right, he noticed Oporinus, Curione and Platter.

At the front of the chamber stood a row of empty seats. He followed Sulzer and the two Amerbachs toward them. They had only just sat down when a side door opened and Borrhaus and Wissenburg entered. They took their places behind the table.

After surveying the room, Wissenburg rose to his feet. "Gentlemen, we are gathered here because one of the gravest charges that exists in our laws, civil or ecclesiastical, has been brought against one of our colleagues: the charge of heresy. But we live in a free and just city and will not condemn a man without hearing his defense. Therefore, we wish to invite our chair of Greek, Sebastian Castellio, to stand and give an account of his beliefs before us all. Following his defense, there will be the opportunity for any of us to question him further." He gestured for Sebastian to move to a chair that had been placed directly in front of the large table, facing it. "Master Castellio, you may take your seat."

As Sebastian stood, an audible gasp rose from the assembled crowd. Sulzer and Amerbach had risen as well. They followed Sebastian, carrying a chair which they placed next to his. They returned to the front row and repeated the process with a second chair. Then Sulzer sat in one chair and the elderly Amerbach in the other.

Wissenburg, Borrhaus and Meyer stared at them in bewilderment. Then Sulzer stood. He surveyed the room before turning back to face the men at the front. Clearing his throat, he spoke. "It is my understanding that Master Castellio was permitted to bring an advocate with him. Myself and Master Amerbach both wish to be advocates for him today."

An excited murmur rippled around the room as Wissenburg's brow knitted in irritation. "Yes, that is allowed. But I think it would have been more respectful if you had informed us before today who those advocates were to be."

Amerbach now stood and spoke. "No doubt. Just as it would have been respectful to Master Castellio if you had informed him of the *exact* nature of the charges leveled against him before today."

Wissenburg's cheeks flushed. He looked to Meyer, whose face was clouded with anger. Borrhaus shuffled papers on the table in front of him. He finally chose one and began to read.

Sebastian Castellio is charged with speaking and writing against holy doctrine found in the inerrant Scriptures, namely the doctrine of predestination as proclaimed by the apostle Paul in the letter to the Romans, chapter nine. In defiance of Paul's writings, Sebastian Castellio has shown himself to be a believer in free will and an arch supporter of those who propagate this false doctrine. We conclude from this that he does not hold the Scriptures to be inerrant and that he believes the apostle Paul's writings are not truly inspired by God.

Borrhaus looked directly at Sebastian, waiting for a response. But it was Sulzer who stood again. Stepping to the side of the chamber so that he could address both Borrhaus and those seated across the room, he testified as to Sebastian's sincerity of faith and integrity in the time they had known each other. Personally, he believed Sebastian Castellio to be a Christian in every sense of the word. When he'd finished, Bonifacius Amerbach slowly rose. In his deep, senatorial voice he recounted the legacy of scholarship, inquiry and tolerance the great Erasmus had bequeathed to the city of Basel and how admirably Sebastian Castellio had continued that legacy.

For the next half hour, Sulzer and Amerbach took turns reading from Sebastian's written defense, adding references from Scripture to show that an argument for free will could be made just as convincingly as one for predestination. Quoting Sebastian, they conceded that God might *possibly* preordain some to heaven, but it was *impossible* for any of them to believe that a loving and just God could or would ever preordain anyone to eternity in hell. Using Sebastian's notes, they cited church fathers in their support and argued that the New Testament reveals Christ to be merciful and loving, not vindictive and cruel.

When it came time to conclude, Sebastian rose to his feet. Astutely, he cited passages from Basel's confession of faith which supported his views. Bible in hand, he opened it to the place of Paul's letters. Turning to face his accusers, he read aloud, "'For God desires *all* people to be saved and to come to know the truth; that there is a mediator, Jesus Christ, who gave his life as a ransom *for all.'*" He paused and looked at each of his three judges before continuing. "Like Paul, I believe this with all my heart. How you can sit there and say that I deny Paul's inspiration is beyond me. Why, I might just as well accuse you of not believing Christ's words to be authoritative and divinely inspired, for certainly they are barely being followed by—"

He stopped there, midsentence, and sat down. A silence fell across the room. Meyer glared at him with fire in his eyes. Wissenburg, again flushed, stared straight ahead. Borrhaus shuffled his papers once more but couldn't seem to find what he was looking for. Finally, Borrhaus rose to his feet and addressed the audience, asking if any had further questions for Sebastian Castellio.

No one spoke or moved. Sebastian glanced across to Oporinus, Curione and Platter. Each of them grinned back at him. It was obvious to everyone in the room that the accusations brought against Sebastian Castellio had been utterly demolished.

As soon as Sebastian stepped out of the chamber, Marie jumped to her feet, her eyes dancing with questions. Sebastian broke into a wide and triumphant smile. She surged forward and threw her arms around him.

Oporinus and Curione filed out of the room next. Curione wrapped an arm around Sebastian's shoulders, pulling him close, then reached for Sulzer's hand followed by Amerbach's, pumping them hard. "Well done, my friends. So, so very well done! Did you see? By the end they had nothing more they could say. You silenced them!"

"I couldn't have done it without Sulzer and Amerbach. Did you see my accusers' faces when these friends first stepped forward to speak for me?"

Curione let out a peal of laughter. "It was priceless. What a victory! This evening, we should celebrate. Perhaps a small ale or two at The Hare?"

"Why not?" Oporinus answered. "Sulzer, Amerbach—you will come too?"

Simon Sulzer gave a little cough. "As much as I would like to, perhaps not. There are many who would consider it ill-fitting for the minister of Basel's cathedral to be seen supping ales in the local tavern. I have probably risked my reputation enough today."

Marie reached out and touched his hand. "What you did today, Simon, was very courageous. You are a good man." She pecked him on the cheek. Sulzer's boyish face flushed.

Sebastian glanced at Amerbach, then at Curione. "The Hare you say, Celio? Actually, I'm not much given to frequenting public houses either. But—oh, hang it all. Of course, I'll come."

It was a merry walk home for Marie and Sebastian, holding hands and exchanging laughter like a newly courting couple. They found a plaza and sat watching the late afternoon sunlight dance across a fountain, their own conversation bubbling like water, recounting how blessed they felt. Sebastian had defeated the blasphemy charge. Their income was more secure. Jeanne, their adopted niece, was loving and helpful. And their larger house in Steinenvorstadt was proving a godsend.

After a while, a breeze from the north picked up and clouds obscured the sun. They rose to their feet again. They ambled past storefronts where goods were sold and looms worked, finally arriving at the cherry-red door of their home.

Inside, Susanna and Jeanne were readying the younger children for a walk to Saint Peter's Platz. Alise entered the kitchen holding little Bonifacius, both of them wrapped in a shawl. Alise smiled at Marie and Sebastian. "I hope you don't mind. They've been begging for a walk all afternoon. I'll have them back within the hour. I promise."

"That's a lovely idea, Alise. But I think the weather may be turning, so you should hurry. And don't let Sara climb too high in the trees."

"I won't. Oh—I almost forgot. A messenger delivered two letters for Master Castellio while you were out. I've put them on the table."

As Alise and the children shuffled out the door, Sebastian and Marie sat at the table. Sebastian picked up the letters and examined their insignia. One he recognized immediately as from André Zebedee, sent not from Orbe but Lausanne. The wax seal on the second envelope had a few words in German, thus suggesting its place of origin. There was also the image of an eagle and the initials P. M.

"P. M. from Germany. Who could that be?" Marie wondered.

"Let's find out." Sebastian slipped his knife under the seal and began working the envelope open. "I can't think of anyone I know with those initials. Let's see." He pulled the letter out and ran his eyes down to the foot of the page. "No! Good Lord. Marie, you won't believe this. It's from Philip Melanchthon."

"Philip Melanchthon?" she repeated uncertainly.

"Philip Melanchthon! Martin Luther's right-hand man! After Luther, surely the greatest German thinker in the field of theology." *And also,* he thought with a shudder, *one of those who agreed with Calvin that Michael Servetus should be executed.* He swallowed hard.

"What does he say?" Marie's voice quavered.

Nervously, Sebastian's eyes moved to the start of the letter, and he began silently reading. After a few moments, he looked up with a feeling of amazement, which he felt sure showed on his face. "He says ... he says he has been following my trials and tribulations closely, and he ... he laments the divisions and the slandering of good people that preoccupy all sides, which causes him great pain to witness. He says he finds much that he admires and respects in my writings, and he offers me his best wishes and eternal friendship, as he hopes we may one day meet in person to discuss the things we hold in common." Eyes brimming, he looked at Marie, whose tears mirrored his own. She leaned against him and rested her head on his shoulder.

"You see, Sebastian? Your words touch the hearts of many. Even men like Simon Sulzer and Melanchthon hear your wisdom and see your goodness." Sebastian embraced her. They remained that way until Marie finally asked, "What about André's letter?"

Sebastian let go of his wife and returned to the letter on the table. "Oh, yes. Dear old André. It's been a while, hasn't it?"

Using the knife, he loosened the seal and unfolded the paper. As he read, he summarized for Marie. The first page consisted of a string of questions asking after Sebastian, Marie, and the children. The second page followed up with questions as to what Sebastian's current thinking was on the elements of communion, the use of musical instruments in church, and the creed they used in Zurich. Sebastian smiled as he ruefully shook his head. "Some things never change, do they?"

But then Sebastian gasped with surprise. André had long sought a teaching position in the city of Lausanne, but he'd been opposed at every turn by Calvin's followers. Yet he'd finally triumphed and won an appointment! "'Furthermore,' he writes, 'aware as I am of the damage Beza and his clique have been inflicting on you, I am now trying to land some blows of my own.'"

Marie laughed. "Good for him! And here I thought he'd forgotten us!"

Toward the bottom of the page, Zebedee's tone shifted again, and he posed a question that Sebastian thought very odd. He cleared his throat and read aloud again. "'Have you heard about our old friend Guillaume Farel and the scandal he has caused?'" That page ended, so Sebastian quickly turned to the next one. "'A month ago, the old man finally ended his bachelor days and married himself a maiden.'" Sebastian looked at Marie, both their eyes wide.

"Goodness me," Marie gasped. "Farel must be quite elderly by now."

Sebastian looked back at the letter and continued reading, finding it easier to summarize this unsettling news. "According to this, he is sixty-nine years old. And"—Sebastian reread the sentence before him

—"and his bride is a maiden not yet twenty years." Sebastian glanced at Marie. She swallowed hard.

When he'd finished reading the letter, Sebastian laid the pages back on the table. "Well. What to say about that?"

Marie shook her head. "Poor girl is all that comes to my mind."

"Indeed. But let's put that thought aside and rejoice that André still fights in my corner, and at those unexpected words of encouragement from a man as famous as the great Philip Melanchthon. What a day this has been! I propose we have a celebratory meal tonight. Let's go to the market and purchase some sweet pastries—a strudel perhaps? I think the children would enjoy that. As will I!"

"But I thought you told Curione you'd meet him at The Hare this evening?"

"Days as victorious as this come too infrequently. And so, we shall do both!"

Chapter 30
The Desecration

At the end of that year, Bürgermeister Bernard Meyer died unexpectedly and was replaced as mayor by a gentler man named Caspar Krug. But if Sebastian thought Krug's appointment might bring a relaxing of the scrutiny Basel had fallen under, he was mistaken. Johannes Sphyractes, who taught law at the university, had recently been appointed the school's new rector. Upholding the law was Sphyractes's singular passion. He took pride in being a relentless hunter of heretics and an unapologetic hater of the Anabaptists. He was a man on a mission: to root out dissenting thought and destroy unorthodox literature.

It was only a few weeks after their triumph before the senate that Simon Sulzer tapped on Sebastian's office door. As soon as Sebastian opened it, he could see that Sulzer looked troubled. "Simon, what is it?"

Simon stepped inside. "Ever since our defense and their failure, Wissenburg and Borrhaus have been determined to strike back. Now Sphyractes has joined them. The scolding they received from Geneva makes them even more determined to try again to expose the sedition they believe dwells in this city. Once more, they are trying to provoke both the senate and the council to take action. To find the heretics, charge them, and this time make the indictment stick."

"Who has told you this?"

"People are whispering in corners, and I see much plotting and planning going on. Something is afoot that makes me afraid. Two days ago, Borrhaus and Wissenburg cornered me and asked a litany of questions about Jan van Brugge, his family, and what I knew of their beliefs."

"Jan has been dead for two years. Why would they ask these questions about him now?"

"I have no idea. It seemed very odd to me. But their questions were insistent, and they seemed angry. Have you spoken with Nicholaas in recent days?"

"Not really. Since Jan's death the whole group of them have become somewhat withdrawn from the rest of us. Almost reclusive."

"Well, something strange is going on. I just don't know what it is. But if I hear anything more, I will let you know. And I ask that you do the same for me."

"Of course, I will."

Once Sulzer had left, Sebastian tried to return to the pile of documents he was working through, but his mind kept flashing back to the night when Jan had confided in him that they secretly held to the faith of the Anabaptists. He had kept his promise to never disclose this to anyone. But had someone else?

After repeatedly trying—and failing—to return to his work, he laid his quill down. He lifted his doublet off a hook and pulled it on, for despite the season there was a crisp breeze coming off the Rhine. If that breeze could help clear his head, that would be welcome. He descended the stairs from his office and crossed the tiled entrance that led toward the street. As he did so, he spotted Curione entering the building. "Celio! Where are you going?"

"To see you, Sebastian. I have terrible news."

"What is it, Celio?" Sebastian asked in a low voice.

Curione looked at the students milling about them. He took hold of Sebastian's arm. "Not here. Outside. We should find a spot where we cannot be overheard."

Curione led him out into the bright sunlight. As he had expected, a cool breeze hit him as they rounded the corner of the building and moved toward the river. They continued through the university garden till they came to the low stone wall that marked the top of the steep riverbank. A few paces to their left, an opening led to flagstone steps. They descended till they came to a wooden bench which afforded them a view of river. They seated themselves there.

"I have already had an odd start to the day," Sebastian said. "Simon Sulzer came to tell me that Wissenburg and Borrhaus have been asking many questions about Jan van Brugge and the other Netherlanders. What do you think it could mean?"

Curione shook his head, his face pale and drawn. "Things are even worse than that, Sebastian. I have a friend on the council who came to me this morning to warn that all the Netherlanders are being rounded up and taken in for questioning."

"Then we must warn them!"

"No. My friend said the constables have already been dispatched. Interrogations will begin this afternoon."

Sebastian groaned. "Has it come to this even in Basel now?"

"It has, and you and I must be more vigilant than ever, for they know we worked closely with Jan in the past. If you have any writings in your office or in your home that you wouldn't want the authorities to see, you should go now and hide them. Or destroy them."

Sebastian nodded. "I will return home as soon as I can, but via Oporinus's. We must warn him, so he can clean out his print shop and ready it for any such visitors. Could you pass this news on to Pietro? I promised I would tell him as soon as I heard anything new."

Curione agreed. Both men stood and shook hands. Then Sebastian bounded up the stone steps as quickly as he could, past Saint Martin's Church and along the road that led to Oporinus's print shop.

He arrived as Oporinus and his men were unloading paper from a wagon. Out of breath, he paused. Oporinus came to his side, eyeing him quizzically. "What's happening?" he asked in a low voice.

"Curione told me that the authorities have arrested the Netherlanders. All of them are to be questioned today."

"Has the whole world gone mad! Why?"

"Sulzer says, one way or another, they are determined to find a heretic." Oporinus swore under his breath. Sebastian continued. "Curione told me to return home and destroy anything that might incriminate me or link me to Jan or to the book. I have come to warn you to do the same. I don't know how much time we have."

Oporinus glanced back at the print shop, frowning. "I have some copies of *Concerning Heretics* hidden in the back of a cupboard. A thorough search might well find them. But upstairs I have a cavity beneath my floorboards, below my bed. It is a much more secure place."

He started to enter the shop, but Sebastian caught him by the arm. "Perhaps it would be safer to destroy them than hide them?"

Oporinus swung around, his eyes blazing. "Never! I'd rather be dragged before one of their pig-circus Inquisitions than destroy good books!" As Oporinus disappeared inside the print shop, Sebastian turned in the direction of Saint Leonard's Church and briskly moved toward his home.

Bursting through the front door, he almost collided with Marie who was carrying Bonifacius in her arms. Behind her, Alise was stirring a pot of something on the fire. Both women looked up at Sebastian with surprise. Taking hold of Marie's arms, he backed out of the house. His voice was low and grave. "They have rounded up Nicholaas, Tanneke and all the Netherlanders and taken them in for questioning. Curione believes this is the start of a wider sweep through the city. He has warned me to cleanse our house of anything that could prove incriminating."

Marie's eyes widened with alarm. "I don't understand. So many years have passed since you and Jan worked together. And Jan died so long ago. What is happening?"

"I don't know exactly, but it won't be long till we find out. They are being interrogated as we speak, so time is short. You need to send Alise away so we can go through the house and get rid of everything that ties us to Jan and the book."

"I'll ask her to go to the market and then to the fish market after that. Will that give us enough time?"

Sebastian grimaced. "When she leaves, we will bolt the door. If she returns before we get everything done, we'll just send her on another errand."

Marie nodded. She returned to the kitchen and gave Alise a list of things to buy from the two markets, while Sebastian slipped up the stairs to his study.

Behind the door to his office, he lifted an iron key from a hook. With it, he opened the bottom of the three drawers on the left side of his desk. From the open drawer, four copies of *Concerning Heretics* stared back at him. He lifted them out and placed them on the floor. He was about to slide the drawer shut again when he noticed the sheaf of loose papers that had been under the books. These pages were old and well worked, covered with handwritten notes that sprawled across the pages and into the margins—the manuscript of the book itself. He retrieved them and flicked through the pages, remembering how many sleepless nights he had spent creating them. What he was about to do was grievous, but he steeled himself and placed the pages on top of the books. He pushed the bottom drawer shut and rifled through the other two, looking for anything that, if read through vindictive eyes, could be seen as heretical. He pulled out a dozen or so more pages and placed them with the others. Then he scooped up the whole pile and headed downstairs.

In the kitchen, the children were seated around the table where Marie nursed the baby at her breast. Susanna was helping Sara take spoonfuls of the vegetable pottage that Alise had been preparing before she left. Without speaking, Sebastian walked to the fireplace. One by one, he committed the pages of his manuscript to the flames until they were fully consumed. Then he picked up the first book, opened it, gripped both sides, and twisted hard till the binding broke. Repositioning his hands, he pulled at the pages until they came free. Handful by handful, he fed them into the fire. Taking up the poker, he stabbed at them till the flames fully devoured the book he had worked so tirelessly to produce. By the time he'd begun on the second book, all of the children were staring—Nathaniel more closely than the others. "Papa! Why are you burning those books?"

"Shh. Don't be alarmed. These are my own books."

"But why? You have always told us that books are precious and that we should never damage them. Why are you doing this?"

Sebastian could think of no explanation to give his son. Marie intervened. "When Papa writes, he writes about the truth. He writes about how we should love each other, and how we should treat each other as Jesus taught us to do—with mercy and forgiveness. But there are those who hate these words, so your father's books make them angry. If those people found these books, they would call your papa a bad man and say that he must be punished. It's very sad that the world is like this, but this is why he must burn these books."

Nathaniel looked more confused than ever. "But ... but I don't understand."

Sebastian found his voice. "Shh, my little one. It is very hard to understand, we know. For now, this is the world we live in, but it won't always be this way. God promises that one day he will build a better world for us all, where no one will train for war anymore, where he will settle the disputes even between nations. But this world has not yet come, and so we must be patient." He gave Nathaniel a small, sad smile and turned back to the fire, stirring it with the poker till the last of his books had turned to ash.

A few days later, word spread that the Netherlanders had been released. Curione arrived in Sebastian's office with the news. As soon as he heard it, Sebastian threw on his doublet and made for the Rote

Haus. It took several minutes of rapping on the heavy wooden door before anyone appeared. Nicholaas finally opened the door. He looked even more pale and unshaven than when Sebastian last saw him.

"Nicholaas! Thank God you are safe. May I come in?"

Nicholaas hesitated for a moment before stepping back so Sebastian could enter. They stood awkwardly in the parlor, Nicholaas with his head down staring at the pattern of tiles on the floor.

"Is there somewhere we may talk privately so you can tell me what has happened? I need to know."

Nicholaas nodded and led him to a door opposite the one that led to the dining room, one Sebastian had never passed through before. As Nicholaas pushed the door open, it revealed a small study with shelves full of books and a desk placed under the single leadlight window. Nicholaas pulled out a chair and sat, indicating for Sebastian to sit in another near the wall.

"Your study, Nicholaas?" Sebastian asked as he surveyed the room.

"It is," Nicholaas replied tersely.

For several seconds, silence hung in the air. It soon became obvious that Sebastian would have to be the one to break it. He took a deep breath before plunging in. "Nicholaas, I know you were all rounded up and taken in for questioning a few days ago. But I don't know why, nor what has transpired since. Curione fears this has something to do with the book we all worked on, *Concerning Heretics*. He, Oporinus, and I have been busy these past few days disposing of any evidence. But I need to hear from you what the authorities are after, and if the rest of us are in danger."

"You are wise to dispose of anything that connects you with my father-in-law. The truth about him has come to the ears of Borrhaus, Sphyractes and Wissenburg, and they are furious that he deceived them, that he was able to live a false life under their noses for so many years. They are determined to make someone suffer for their humiliation."

"They want to punish him for concealing that he was an Anabaptist? But he died over two years ago! Why are they overreacting like this?"

Nicholaas's eyes fixed on the floor again. He appeared to be struggling to find words, but eventually they came. "Not just that he was an Anabaptist, but a leader of the sect."

"What?" Sebastian asked, perplexed.

"I expect you know, Sebastian, that there are two men seen as leaders of the Anabaptists here in Europe, both of whom the authorities desperately seek to find. They are Menno Simons and David Joris. The authorities have placed a heavy price on both their heads and hunt them relentlessly." Nicholaas sighed deeply. His shoulders rose and fell. His hands shook, and his head still faced the floor. "Sebastian, my father-in-law's true name was not Jan van Brugge." He paused, taking in a slow, deep breath. "My father-in-law's real name was David Joris."

Sebastian felt like he was falling, as if the floor beneath his chair had suddenly collapsed. His mind raced, full of confusion. *No! This is impossible! How could my friend have been David Joris?*

He swallowed hard as he tried to gather his thoughts into words. "I knew Jan had secrets. When he confessed that you were Anabaptists, I was willing to keep that secret till the day I died. But now you tell me this! How could—this just doesn't make sense. For one thing, how could he have lived such a completely different life here in Basel, as a man of prominence and standing? None of what you say makes sense."

Nicholaas continued staring at the floor, his hands trembling.

In the moments that followed, Sebastian tried to remember everything he'd ever been told of David Joris. He was said to be a charismatic orator who had assumed leadership over the disillusioned revolutionaries who survived the siege of Münster. A mystic who wrote books detailing his visions and insights into Christ's kingdom, books regarded as bizarre and dangerous by most. A character far, far different from the gentle and wise friend he had known as Jan van Brugge.

Nicholaas raised his face and met Sebastian's gaze. An expression Sebastian found hard to read clouded his features. "He was able to live such a prominent life and hide his identity by lying, and by forcing the rest of us to lie with him." Sebastian was taken aback by the sharp anger in Nicholaas's words. "He lived a lie. And because of him, we all did."

"But surely you can see he had no choice? The authorities would have killed him had they known who he really was. Even I can see that."

"You don't know how terrible it was to watch him change, to give away God's calling on his life. When I first met him—in the early years—I'd never met anyone bolder or braver. He heard God's voice, and he obeyed it! He was a prophet, full of fire and unwilling to compromise the words of Jesus. God gave him visions and the gift of speaking in tongues. He—and we—believed he was another leader like the biblical David, sent to further God's kingdom on earth. We were prepared to face death to follow him. But after we'd fled here to Basel, he changed. The fire disappeared. The prophet disappeared. He was content to stay hidden, to live the life of a gentleman— feasting and drinking and playing with his paints. Whenever I challenged him on this, he would say, 'The kingdom of God is in our hearts, not in our outward actions. What church we go to, what ceremonies we practice, what words we use are all of secondary importance. So long as we love God and love one another, nothing else matters.' Do you know that by the end, he didn't believe that the devil was real or that hell had an objective existence?" Nicholaas winced as he said the words.

"But he and I used to talk about the reality of evil. He used to speak of men's worst actions being devilish! I remember this well."

"By which he meant that sin, hell, and the devil himself were things to be found within the human heart, not outside of it. He came to believe that those things had no real existence beyond that. But I'm not surprised you misunderstood. He was skilled at mincing his words so others would be fooled by them."

Sebastian blinked as he tried to take in this information. "But Nicholaas, even if what you say is true, I think your father-in-law was a good man, a gentle man. You are being too harsh."

"A good man? You don't understand Sebastian. Many people laid down their lives for him—to protect him, to hide him, to follow him—because we believed he was anointed to usher in God's kingdom on earth. But what was it all for? So that he could lie and hide and pretend to be someone he was not? That he could make a mockery of all our sacrifices?"

Sebastian tried to understand what could be behind Nicholaas's torrent of anger. And then, a terrible, terrible thought lodged itself in his mind and refused let go. "Dear God, Nicholaas. Was it *you* who betrayed Jan's identity to the authorities?"

Nicholaas's gaze dropped to the floor once more. When he eventually spoke, it was barely above a whisper. "When the magistrates came, they took van Schlor first, myself a day later, and then the rest after that. As they questioned me, it was obvious they already knew many things. Someone had tipped them off. They made it clear that someone must suffer for the humiliation my father-in-law's deception had caused the city of Basel. And not just his deception but his immorality. They accused him of having affairs and bearing children by Anna van Berchem. And other women too. They said if we came clean and told them the truth, they would treat us with clemency. They said any punishment and shame would fall on David Joris alone. But if we refused to cooperate, all of the Netherlanders and all those who had been associated with Joris would be treated most severely. As they already seemed to know my father-in-law's true identity, I decided we should confirm what they already knew and protect the living. Including you, Sebastian."

"Then was it van Schlor who betrayed Jan?"

"I thought that too, but he denied it repeatedly. He said they already knew the truth before they started questioning him."

Sebastian nodded. But then a new wave of confusion crashed through his thoughts. "What do they mean by the punishment and shame falling on David Joris? Your father-in-law is long dead and buried."

Nicholaas shrugged his shoulders. "I'm sorry, Sebastian; I can't answer that. I have no idea what it means. But I think you should go back to your home and search it a second time. Keep nothing that could in any way link you to my father-in-law."

Sebastian headed west from the Rote Haus, wanting to warn Oporinus of this latest development. When he entered the print shop, one of the young printers pointed toward the ceiling. "He's upstairs."

Sebastian bounded up the steps two at a time, calling Oporinus's name. His big, bearded head appeared, craning around a half-open door at the top of the stairs. "Sebastian. Come in. Curione is here too."

Sebastian entered the book-lined room, in the center of which was a table surrounded by chairs. Curione sat in the nearest. "I have unsettling news," Sebastian began. "Oporinus, you should be sitting too. I have just come from meeting with Nicholaas." Once all three of them were seated, he took a deep breath and relayed everything Nicholaas had told him, pausing often to answer their questions, which were many, given their shock and confusion.

"David Joris, the arch heretic? I don't believe it!" Oporinus shook his head. "Jan was the perfect citizen of Basel. The leaders of this city loved him! And the perfect church member. He was loved there too."

"The perfect Nicodemite," added Sebastian.

"The perfect what?" Curione looked confused.

"It's the term Calvin uses for those who hide their true religious beliefs in order to escape punishment or execution—like Nicodemus in the Bible, who came to speak with Jesus by night. Calvin despised them. He regarded such people as the worst kind of cowards."

"Oh." Curione sounded only a little less confused.

Sebastian arrived home as Marie was preparing dinner. Once they had eaten and the children were in bed, they sat at the table while Sebastian recounted the extraordinary twists and turns of the day—and the new dangers they faced because of it.

"If you're an Anabaptist, the authorities call you a heretic. Unless you recant, they will drown or burn you. Now we know that Jan used to be much more than that—a leader, a teacher, perhaps even some kind of prophet in their movement. Everyone he had contact or friendship with now falls under suspicion. It is probable that they will search our home, not just for evidence that we wrote that book but for any evidence that we shared ideas or that I helped him hide his true identity. I know I have some letters of his that I must destroy."

"What about the glass painting he gave you? Must we destroy that too?"

Sebastian's head dropped. "If they see it, they'll recognize it as his work. And so, even though it's all I have left to remember our friendship by—" Sebastian didn't finish the thought. Instead, he stood and walked to his study. The beautiful glass disk, which shone with an image of Lady Veritas, hung in the window. He unhooked it, balancing it in his hand as he admired it. He then knelt down beside his desk and began to rifle through a drawer till he found what he sought: a small leather pouch. He slipped the glass into it.

When he returned to the kitchen, he held the pouch aloft to show Marie. Her eyebrows rose in question. "To be sown in the garden," he said. "Between the rows of cabbage." With a wry smile he added, "I've noticed that most magistrates and theologians dislike manual work, so it should be safe there."

He went out the back of the house, to the little space where they kept their garden, and he began to dig.

When he returned to his office from a class the next day, a knock sounded at the door. Before he could give an invitation to enter, Wissenburg stepped inside. He threw a sheaf of papers onto the desk in front of Sebastian, three or four pages of tightly written script. The front page was titled *Testimony against the Arch Heretic David Joris*.

Sebastian looked up at Wissenburg for explanation. It came swiftly. "This is the evidence that myself, Borrhaus and Sphyractes have collected from witnesses. It proves that Jan van Brugge and David Joris were one and the same man. It catalogs all the lies, crimes, adulteries and blasphemies this man committed. Every minister in the city, every teacher in this university will be required to sign it and give their approval to his punishment. Only you and Curione remain to sign."

Sebastian flicked to the last page. A list of names stretched from the top to the bottom. He scanned down the signatures and winced at the sight of Sulzer and the two Amerbachs.

Wissenburg must have noticed his reaction. "Bonifacius Amerbach's legal advice has been very helpful to us in pursuing this matter."

A coldness filled Sebastian's chest. "But when you speak of punishment—what punishment? He is dead already. What more can you do to him?"

"This wretch was—is—a heretic. An arch heretic, in fact. Therefore, he must receive the punishment due his deceit and vileness. He corrupted Basel with his presence, and now he corrupts the very earth in which he lies. His cadaver will be dragged from its sanctuary and publicly burned until nothing remains but ash. Those ashes will be scattered to the four winds, so that he should never find rest. This man shamed the Word of God and deceived multitudes. His name, his very memory, must now be shamed, and the land purged of his presence."

"And if I don't agree to sign this document?"

"Then our suspicion that you are either this man's enabler or follower will be confirmed. As a fellow heretic, you will share his fate." Wissenburg's jaw was set hard and his gaze was icy.

"I ... I need time to read carefully through these charges. You can't expect me to sign it now."

"You have a day. At this time tomorrow, you will return it to me with your signature attached. Then I will take it to Curione. And you should know that, as we speak, officers of the council are searching your house, looking for evidence that you aided and abetted this man in his perfidy. You should pray that they don't find any."

As soon as Wissenburg left, Sebastian gathered up his things and made hastily for home. Marie greeted him at the door, her face grim. The officers had gone. The search had been brief and perfunctory. Nothing had been found. A shiver of relief passed through him.

He ascended to his study with the document and began to read it carefully. With each paragraph, a new calumny was attributed to David Joris / Jan van Brugge. Lying and deceiving, of course. A litany of blasphemous utterances made against the church, against the Holy Trinity, against the Bible, against the state, against right thinking. And then came the accusations of sexual immorality—that he had advocated and practiced polygamy and adultery, had multiple affairs and children by many women. On and on it went, describing a man that Sebastian was certain he'd never known. Either Jan was one of the greatest deceivers the world had ever seen, or this document exaggerated his crimes beyond recognition. He needed to find Curione as well as talk through with Marie about what his response should be. But then what? Even if this document was a fabrication, he would have no option but to sign it.

The next day, as ordered, Sebastian returned the sheet of accusations to Wissenburg. After verifying Sebastian's signature, he handed him another sheet of paper with his name at the top. A single paragraph followed.

> Saturday, the 13th of May 1559, at 10:00 a.m., you will attend the public burning of the wicked deceiver, blasphemer and adulterer, the criminal Anabaptist arch heretic David Joris. This sentence will be conducted before God and before man beyond the city walls at the Steinentor gate.

It was signed by all the members of the council.

As the days passed and Saturday approached, the wait became agonizing. Much as he tried, Sebastian could not focus his mind on any other task. He and Marie would begin conversations and then not be able to finish them. Marie suggested they go see Nicholaas and Tanneke to offer their sympathy, but they immediately realized this would only incriminate them further. Marie fell back into silence. Each time they left the house, they were sure that eyes followed their every move and ears strained to hear their every conversation. Sebastian found excuses not to go to the university. He even canceled classes. Basel had become a different city. A sense of fear and mistrust seemed to haunt the streets like a malevolent spirit.

When Saturday finally came, Sebastian dressed in silence then sat in his study watching the hands of the clock above his desk as they crawled toward the appointed hour. At exactly half past nine, he descended the stairs. The children were gone. They'd arranged for Alise to take them for a walk toward Saint Peter's Plaza. Marie sat at the table with her head in her hands, but as Sebastian entered the room, she rose and embraced him. For a long time, the two of them simply held each other for comfort. Eventually, Sebastian whispered, "It's time."

Marie released him.

As Sebastian entered the plaza, it looked to him as if every man in Basel had been summoned there. And yet the square was silent. Just beyond the gate, he saw the Platters, father and son, and he made his way toward them. Both acknowledged him with a glance as he took his place next to the younger man, Felix. He noted how tall and strong Felix stood, and he wondered if his keen interest in medicine and human anatomy had somehow inured him against what was about to unfold. He turned his head. A few rows back, he saw Nicholaas and van Schlor, their faces pale and drawn, both refusing to meet his glance. At the front of the plaza, to the left of the gate, a stage had been erected and twelve chairs placed upon it—the tall, high-backed thrones favored by magistrates and church elders.

Movement caught his eye from the edge of the plaza. A procession of robed figures filed in and ascended the stage, led by the Bürgermeister. Members of the council fanned out on both sides of him, each taking a seat. Last came Wissenburg, Borrhaus, Sphyractes, and Sulzer, whose face said that he'd rather be anywhere else in the world but here.

Borrhaus was the first to address those assembled, spitting out words full of recrimination and wounded pride. This man they knew as Jan van Brugge, he snarled, had deceived them all with his lies, worming his way into their affections even as he propagated false doctrines, bringing shame on the city that had given him refuge and succor. Wissenburg spoke next, reiterating the long list of crimes he claimed had been proven against this monster of a man. Sphyractes followed, focusing on the many dark doctrinal errors that belonged to David Joris and the terrible, terrible danger those ideas posed to society.

Finally, it was the reluctant Sulzer's turn. He spoke in a voice so low the already quiet crowd fell completely still, straining to hear. Unlike the others, he did not enumerate the dead man's many sins but focused instead on the mercy the city showed to the living by not prosecuting Jan's family or friends, letting justice fall on the dead man alone. When he finished, Simon Sulzer shuffled back to his seat, and the eyes of those gathered on the stage turned toward the Steinentor gate.

The air about them seemed to thicken. Breathing became laborious, and movement took effort. Then Sebastian heard it—the sound that heralded all he had been dreading. A low rumbling noise approached from beyond the thick stone wall. The sound had grown louder and closer, a dysrhythmic *clack, clack, clacking* of a wagon's solid wheels struggling over cobblestones. Then came a flicker of movement within the shadow of the archway.

The cart emerged into the sunlight. One man was before the cart, pulling the load. The other behind it, pushing. Both wore handkerchiefs wrapped around their faces. The clumsy wooden wheels lurched over cobblestones and threatened to shake apart their pitiful burden. It seemed to take the men an age to pass completely into the paved courtyard. On either side of the archway, the rock walls extended north and south. Above rose a squat clocktower and a turret that brooded grimly over the unwilling city.

In horror, Sebastian watched the grotesque struggle as the workmen wrestled the corpse of Jan van Brugge onto the woodpile. For the first time, he noticed that the fuel gathered around the stake had been constructed not just of kindling but also of books, papers, canvas and painted glass. It appeared as if they had dragged here everything they'd found that had been created by Jan. A wave of grief swept through Sebastian. He fought to hold back tears.

As the hooded torchbearer approached Jan's body, Sebastian dropped his gaze to the ground. Someone near him gasped as, from the front of the plaza, came the sound of crackling wood. As that noise grew louder, a pall of smoke began to spread through the plaza, stinging his eyes and forcing tears. As the sickly aroma of burning flesh grew stronger, Sebastian rifled through his pocket, found a cloth and crushed it against his nose and mouth. From behind him, the sound of retching was followed by the acid scent of vomit.

A loud *crack* forced him to look up. The blaze burned fiercely, eating its way through Jan's shriveled corpse. A wave of nausea swept through him. Sweat ran down his face, his arms, his torso. His shirt clung to him like a wet sheet. He began to sway, a low buzz ringing in his ears, growing louder. Young Platter grasped his arm, holding it with an iron grip. Through the haze, Felix whispered, "Master Castellio, are you well?"

Sebastian glanced up. He could just make out Felix's worried eyes staring into his own. He nodded, and wordlessly planted his feet more firmly on the plaza's stones, begging God to keep him upright.

After what seemed an eternity, his nausea faded. When the crowd began to stir, he looked up once more. Those on the stage were filing off one by one. Where the pyre had stood, only a heap of smoldering charcoal and bone remained, the thick stake reduced to a blackened rod. The last one to file off the stage was Simon Sulzer, and as soon as his feet touched the plaza's cobbles, those nearest the Steinentor gate turned and made quickly for home.

Chapter 31
Sebastian Castellio, Satan's Tool

Despite Sulzer's assurance that those still living would be safe, the bitter winds of oppression only blew stronger. Borrhaus, Sphyractes and Wissenburg were watching van Brugge's former friends like hawks. Oporinus was denied the opportunity to print anything other than the blandest of documents, thus crushing his business. Clearly Jan's burning had not satiated those looking on from Geneva. Instead, it had emboldened them. Their demands became ever more strident. There were days Sebastian was sure he was being followed. Other days, new students would appear in his class only to disappear again, making him wonder if they had been placed there to report on the content of his teaching. Basel, once a city of freedom, had become a place of suspicion.

Early in January 1560, Sebastian and Curione had agreed to meet at Oporinus's shop to share new information and to encourage one another to stay strong. It was a gray winter's day with skiffs of sleet blowing in from the north. As Sebastian approached the print shop, he pulled his cloak tighter, but it did a poor job of keeping the chill at bay. He went inside and ascended the stairs. Oporinus greeted him with an embrace at the top landing, then ushered him into his study. Curione was already there. A book lay open on the table before him. Sebastian and Oporinus took a chair on either side.

Sebastian reached for the book, letting out a small *ah* as he scanned the cover. He had known for months that Calvin, with Beza's help, was working on another French New Testament. It had now arrived. He had been bracing himself for this moment, sure it would heap more condemnation on him.

"Another attempt to paint me as a villain, I presume?"

"Worse than before, Sebastian." Oporinus slid the Bible toward him. "Last time, they insinuated. This time, they have abandoned any pretense of subtlety. They identify you by name and call you 'Satan's tool.' Clearly there is no slander these two won't stoop to in their war against you. They have no shame."

Sebastian's eyes went to the page Oporinus had indicated. It was part of the Testament's foreword. As he read, he came to the line Oporinus's finger had indicated. His heart pounded hard as his mind absorbed the words.

This new translation has been necessitated to counter the heresies and falsehoods of recent mistranslations that the devil has inspired to create confusion, first and foremost among them being the error-ridden Latin and French translations made by Sebastian Castellio, that impudent and chosen tool of Satan.

Sebastian placed the Bible back on the table and stared straight ahead for several seconds. "This will not end till they see me burned like Servetus and Joris, will it?"

"Or until we are driven out of Basel. Or we publish an apology saying we have sinned and that Calvin and Beza are right in all they say and do." Oporinus shook his head.

"Pff!" Curione interjected. "Then we might as well say the Catholic Inquisitions are right, for they use the same methods to silence those who question them."

Sebastian glanced out the window as a fresh flurry of sleet lashed the pane. "I am not a dogmatist. I have always admitted that my translations are imperfect. With everything I publish, I invite others to correct me. I believe my heart is teachable, so to say that everything I have written is satanic and filled with lies ..."

Oporinus filled the gap as Sebastian trailed off. "Calvin and Beza are cut from the same cloth. If you challenge their interpretation of Scripture, they are sure you must speak for the devil. Their instinct is to then silence or destroy you."

Curione placed a hand on Sebastian's shoulder. "Sebastian, you are one of the humblest men I have ever known. I believe you would happily be corrected if anyone showed you where you were in error. But God is *always* on the side of the humble and of those who speak truth, is he not?"

Oporinus grunted. "Believing that meekness and standing for truth will always triumph is a comforting thought, but I have seen too many exceptions. The real question is how best can we fight these lies? With the exception of Bern, Calvin and Beza have the ear of every council, every censor, and virtually every press in the Swiss Confederation—and beyond."

Sebastian looked wistful. "I have to keep faith and believe. 'Love always trusts, always hopes, always perseveres.' Perhaps I am being pig-headed, but I can't back down. I won't."

That night, Sebastian began work on his latest rebuttal to Calvin and Beza, a slim booklet that would outline the principles of translation he had followed and why, before moving on to address, one by one, each accusation Calvin and Beza had leveled against him over the years. He cited parts of the Bible that supported his understanding of free will and the role conscience played in seeking God's guidance. He then spent another few days revising his words, making certain his writing was free from invective, that it was a calm, reasonable response. Determined to be beyond accusation, he once more took his work to Borrhaus to be approved for publication. Borrhaus seemed deeply surprised to have Sebastian hand him a booklet for approval. The two men shook hands, then

Sebastian returned home to await the outcome of Borrhaus's scrutiny.

By the week's end, the work was returned by a messenger. Retreating to his study, Sebastian tore open the package and began flicking through the booklet. But he was immediately confronted by thick bands of ink drawn across each page. It seemed as if every third or fourth sentence had been ruled out. He leafed through to the end of the work. Every single page was the same—thick black bands covered whole sentences, and in some places, entire paragraphs. Stunned, Sebastian sank back on his chair. He glanced back at the packaging and noticed a note that had accompanied the booklet.

> *Dear Master Castellio,*
>
> *As you well know, it is vital to the harmony of the Swiss cities and our churches that we maintain unity in matters of religion. To this end, it was necessary that I delete from your manuscript anything that might create further friction or controversy between the city of Basel and the city of Geneva. I have removed passages that could be interpreted by John Calvin or Theo Beza as attacks upon their scholarship, or which could reignite needless debate over questions of doctrine. The version of your work here contained in this envelope, I will allow to be printed.*
>
> *Yours in God's service,*
> *Martin Borrhaus*

Sebastian read through the version that had been returned to him. It was insipid, stripped of any real defense or rebuttal of Geneva's accusations. The logical arguments he'd developed were now broken and difficult to follow. The biblical citations he'd chosen, that spoke of free will or the role of conscience, had been removed.

The study door creaked open. He looked up to see Marie smiling at him. Her smile faded as she registered the look of disappointment on his face. "Seb? What has happened?"

He held the little booklet aloft then let it drop onto the desk. "My reply to Calvin and Beza, with my explanation of the principles of translation I employed, has been returned. I made the mistake of giving it to Borrhaus to read first. Now all I have left is a tissue, and an unconvincing tissue at that."

Marie stepped behind Sebastian and rested her hands on his shoulders. "What will you do now?"

Sebastian sighed. "Half an answer is better than none, I suppose. That Borrhaus has even allowed me this much is a small victory. So ... I will have it printed and ensure that copies are sent to Geneva." He stood, stretched, and embraced Marie.

Marie looked at him tenderly. "Don't ever give up, Sebastian. One day God will vindicate you. I know it."

Sebastian stared into her large hazel eyes, the flecks of green and brown luminous in the room's lamplight, her pupils dark and wide. "Thank you. I know I couldn't do any of this without you. I thank God for you every day, Marie." He leaned closer, felt the warmth of her lips as he brushed them with his. He ran one hand slowly down to the small of her back and with the other pulled her even closer till both their bodies were one. Where his hand rested on her back, he felt the line of little buttons that fastened her dress. One by one, he began to unfasten them. Marie reached behind Sebastian, toward the desk. Finding the knob of the wick raiser, she turned it counterclockwise till the room was cloaked in darkness.

Chapter 32
Bent on War

A few months later, Beza penned another vicious tract aimed directly at Sebastian. It made little attempt to address Castellio's theological beliefs and instead was filled with ad hominem attacks on his character. It pleaded with Basel's council to remove Castellio from his position as chair of Greek, "an undeserved office from which this tool of Satan corrupts the minds of your city's youth."

Sebastian sat in his office and stared out the window, watching boats pulling out into the current and on toward the Low Countries. He stood and paced around the little room, reflecting on his predicament. No matter what he said or wrote, it was twisted and used as a weapon against him. If he lifted his eyes beyond his own circumstances, events unfolding across Europe gave him no greater cheer. Everywhere things seemed to be descending into vitriol and hatred. From France the news was increasingly dark. All attempts at brokering peace between Catholics and Protestants had failed, and both sides were growing more strident and more militant. A report had arrived of dozens of Huguenots slaughtered during a church service in Vassy. Other reports spoke of priests and nuns being attacked and beaten by Protestants. The powder keg which was France seemed ready to explode.

Wearied by the never-ending accusations against him and by his apprehension that a religious war in France was growing closer, Sebastian once more sought solace beyond the edge of the city. Rising early one morning, he left Saint Alban's cottages and mills and walked on till he found himself surrounded by the orchards and fields overlooking the Rhine, channeling its inexorable flow. He spent an hour in stillness, meditating on the early chapters of Matthew's Gospel, going over and over in his mind Christ's words in the so-called Sermon on the Mount. As he reflected on Jesus's words of mercy and forgiveness, he felt them sinking deeper into his soul. But the longer he sat, the more an aching sadness also enveloped him as he pondered the widening gap between the teachings of Jesus and the actions of those across Europe who claimed to follow Jesus. By his second hour near the river, as the sun rose higher and the river rolled on, a measure of peace began to return, almost as if the water's flow had washed away some of the ache from his heart.

As he continued reflecting on Jesus's mountainside sermon, his thoughts turned to perhaps the most radical command contained in it: love your enemies. *No follower of Jesus embodied this ethic better*, Sebastian thought to himself, his musings now flowing as freely as the Rhine, *than the saint from Assisi, whose life has often been a source of inspiration for me.* Saint Francis had also lived in violent times. And Sebastian found himself thinking back to one of his favorite stories about the man. At the height of the Fifth Crusade, Francis had journeyed to Egypt to try and persuade the crusaders not to kill their Muslim neighbors. When they ridiculed him, he journeyed on through the battle lines and met with the Sultan, al-Kamil, who heard him out, treating him with great respect. Francis had been unable to stop the killing, but at least he'd had the courage to try. Sebastian's new peace gave way to resolve. An idea had formed. A daring one. Swinging his legs off the ancient stump he had been sitting on, he set off through the fields and back toward the city.

As he passed back through the town's gate, Sebastian knew he must visit Oporinus. He needed to run this new project idea past his friend. He walked north along the riverfront until he neared the Rathaus. From there, he bore west toward the print shop. The place was quiet. Twenty men once rushed between these presses; now only a few remained. Even so, Sebastian pulled Oporinus aside.

"May we go somewhere private?" he asked. Oporinus nodded and led him upstairs to the study. Once seated, Sebastian laid out, piece by piece, his idea for a new book, one that would sound a gospel warning to both Catholics and Protestants, pointing out the ultimate futility of war, the mayhem and evil that violence creates. It would be a book that pleaded with all the protagonists in France to look to Christ and re-sheath their weapons—and their words—before it was too late.

Oporinus heard him out, then exhaled with a soft whistle. "Sebastian Castellio, you just can't help yourself, can you?"

"What do you mean? This will be a plea for peace, not an attack on anyone."

"Come on, Sebastian. You know that's not how such a book will be seen. The French Protestants will feel betrayed because you don't unequivocally take their side. As will Geneva. As will the Catholics."

"I promise there will not be a single word about Geneva or Calvin or Beza. I will say nothing to antagonize them."

"Are you being deliberately naive? Calvin's party not only controls Geneva, they provide leadership to the Huguenot movement in France. They send Calvinist ministers there to lead the Protestant churches. But they have gone far beyond simple missionary work now. Calvin and Beza encourage the French Calvinists to take up arms and to unite behind the Huguenot general, Louis de Bourbon, prince of Condé. Beza has taken on the role of military treasurer and is currently traveling across Europe raising funds that will enable the Huguenots to buy weapons and build forces great enough to defeat the Catholics. Your call for peace and toleration will be seen as a direct criticism of Calvin and Beza, even if you don't mention their names."

"But that is not my intent. I only wish to appeal to the teachings of Christ. To read the New Testament and compare it with how we live now. Surely, I am not the only one who can see this? And aren't we to warn others when we see them staggering toward a cliff?"

"What do you think you can achieve, Sebastian? Even the Queen Mother, Catherine de' Medici, and the Chancellor, de l'Hôpital, called together a grand colloquy last year, desperate for Catholics and Protestants to reach an accord. But neither side was willing to compromise a single jot. Since that colloquy, the violence has only grown worse. Huguenot troops are on the march capturing Catholic cities and destroying Catholic churches. Meanwhile, Catholic troops and street mobs are slaughtering Protestant neighbors. Across France, blood flows in the streets, each act of violence sparking a fresh round of retribution.'"

"And so that cycle must be broken! Jesus said we no longer live under the law of an eye for an eye. We exist under a new law: the law of love, the rule of forgiveness. If we claim to be Christians, we can't in good conscience just fold our hands and watch. We must say something! Surely you will help me do this?"

The fingers of Oporinus's right hand tapped rhythmically on the table, while his other hand fidgeted with his beard. "It is surely too late."

"So we should do nothing? Close our eyes and look away?"

An anguished growl erupted from Oporinus. "Ah! Of course, I will help you! But you and I have been warned so many times. If we are caught once again calling into question the wisdom of those who wield power—" The big man paused. Sebastian could see him struggling to get control of himself. "Well. We must not be caught. As we did with *Concerning Heretics*, this book must be anonymous as to the author, printer and place of publication."

"I agree, Johannes. I absolutely agree."

After a month of intense and secretive writing, the new book was ready for publication. In it, Sebastian pleaded for tolerance from all sides. He encouraged Christians, both Catholic and Protestant, to follow Jesus's Golden Rule, that injunction to do unto others that which you would want done to you—that is, to treat each other with grace, forgiveness, and mercy. He concluded his book with a radical plea: "My counsel to you, France, is that you cease the oppression, the persecution, the murder of conscience, and that you allow everyone who believes in Christ to do so in his own way." He added a cover page. In large script, he penned what he believed the most appropriate title for such a plea: *Counsel to a Desolate France.*

When he brought the manuscript to Oporinus, the printer again stressed that the process of publication must proceed with the utmost secrecy. No one could hear a word about this book until it had well and truly departed his shop and arrived in their hands. Once more, Oporinus selected those he most trusted to work with him. They labored as quietly as they could under the cover of darkness. Finally, multiple bales of the book were loaded onto a barge and sailed down the Rhine. The finished work contained only white space where the name of the author, printer, and place of publication usually appeared.

Of course, despite all his precautions, what Oporinus could not ensure was the silence of those who had driven the wagon to the docks or those who had loaded the cargo onto the barge.

Sebastian breathed freely for a few weeks until, one day, he arrived home to find Marie in tears at their table. "Marie, what has happened? Tell me what—"

He noticed pamphlets fanned out in front of her. Picking one up, he read the title: *A Response to the Reprehensible Sebastian Castellio* by Theo Beza. Flipping through the copy, it quickly became obvious that, not only had Beza berated him throughout, but he had also repeatedly shamed the city of Basel for harboring him. His eyes stopped on one particularly egregious sentence: "Castellio is a liar, a blasphemer, an Anabaptist, a Papist, a stinking sycophant, a desecrater of the sacred, a befriender of criminals, adulterers, and heretics."

Gathering up all the pamphlets, he threw them into the fire. "Shh, my love, be still. These mean nothing. No one who truly knows me will believe anything Beza has written."

"But what about those who don't truly know you? Alise says these are all over town and everyone is reading them."

"Even among those who don't know me, if they have any sense, they will see that this abuse is nonsense. It contradicts itself. Did you read how he accuses me of being both a Papist and an Anabaptist? Why, that's like describing a creature as being a cat and a dog at the same time—an impossibility. People will remember how he and Calvin once accused me of stealing firewood, and thus they'll realize that once more these accusations flow from malice, not from fact."

Marie ran the back of her hand across each of her eyes. "You plead with them to follow Jesus's teachings, and they accuse you of blasphemy. Why are Christians so cruel to one another? Why are these two men so cruel to you?"

Sebastian wrapped his arms around her where she sat. "For some men, the mark of true religion is to always be right and to feel like they've proven everyone else is wrong. Even I believed that once. It took me a long time to understand that the mark Jesus set for his followers is not that of being correct. It is rather that we live a life of faith and trust that expresses itself through love—for real faith is only made manifest in love. One day, perhaps, Beza and Calvin will come to see this too. It is what I pray for, anyway."

"Perhaps there is another reason for my tears, Sebastian."

Alarmed, Sebastian took a step back from his wife. "What is it? What else has happened?"

"Nothing bad. It's just that, well, when I'm pregnant I always find tears come more easily."

It took a second for her words to sink in. Then Sebastian threw his arms around her once more. "My clever, beautiful Marie! You are full of miracles!"

"I think you might have had something to do with it too."

Sebastian looked up at the ceiling, calculating. "We have five girls living in this house and only three males. We're quite outnumbered. Fairness dictates that this one must be a boy."

Marie rolled her eyes. "As if we have any control over that."

Chapter 33
Who Should We Imitate?

A storm was blowing in from the north, a cold wind cutting its way across the Rhine and through Basel's streets and alleyways. Sebastian huddled with Oporinus and Curione above the print shop as the storm battered the room's single window. The door rattled each time a fresh draft spiraled up the stairwell. They could feel the chill spreading through the room. Below them, the presses were quiet. Little work was coming Oporinus's way. The big man looked unusually solemn. "I'm sorry to say this, but perhaps this book has inflamed your enemies more than anything else you have written, Sebastian."

Curione nodded in agreement. "From now on, you must be very cautious, Sebastian. I hear reports from Italy that the Catholics have joined the Reformed in saying you harm their cause and you should be silenced. I have spoken with Amerbach, and I know he also counsels greater caution. The council seeks greater unity with Geneva and Zurich, even if it means embracing their intolerance. And both those cities urge our council to expel those Geneva identifies as heretics."

Sebastian shrugged his shoulders. "Should I give in to fear, or should I trust in Christ?"

Oporinus snapped. "Think of your wife and children, man! You may be willing to die a martyr's death, but how would they survive if you do?"

"I have no wish to be a martyr, I can assure you of that."

"Be more circumspect then. And perhaps—perhaps it is time to consider an escape plan."

Sebastian startled. "What do you mean?"

Oporinus looked awkward, clearly unsure whether to continue.

Curione intervened. "There are other parts of Europe that would welcome a scholar of your quality, Sebastian. There are other places that tolerate a wider range of religious ideas than the Swiss cities do. Many are finding refuge in Poland even as we speak."

Sebastian stared at them, shocked. "Are you suggesting I uproot my family and flee to Poland?"

His voice softer, more reassuring, Oporinus answered. "No. But it is good to have a plan should—should things deteriorate further here in Basel."

Curione nodded. "Do you have any contacts in Poland who could help you, if needed?"

Sebastian's mind whirled. *I have fled two cities and lived eight years as a pauper. Basel is my home. I have good work here. These are my friends. Must I once more run and start over?* Yet he knew Oporinus and Curione were simply trying to help him see a reality he hadn't fully acknowledged—that the powers that controlled the city of Basel were more and more turning against him.

He turned his mind to their question and spoke his thoughts slowly. "Over the years, many of my best students have been from Poland. Through them, my writings have spread there. So, thankfully, I do have supporters who hold significant roles in that land."

"Good. Very good. Nobody is saying you should flee now, but it would be wise to cultivate those contacts should you need them. I would write to them if I were you." Curione's gaze fixed on the room's small window, as if contemplating the gathering storm beyond its pane. "It is clear we have enemies in this city, those who plot against us. At times it feels as if someone in our circle betrays our confidence, one who would send us to the stake if they could. It would be good if we knew who."

Oporinus cast him a quizzical look. "What are you suggesting?"

"That we act with caution, of course. But also, that we keep our eyes open and look for clues as to the identity of the Judas amongst us."

Another fresh gust of wind rattled the window and sent a zephyr of chill air up the stairwell and into the room. Sebastian shivered as Curione rose to his feet. "I have business I must attend to, my friends. But I think it would be useful if the three of us met regularly and shared any insights or clues we've noticed concerning things we have seen or heard."

Sebastian wandered home, his head thick with unwelcome thoughts. But he knew Oporinus and Curione were right. The tide was turning, and he might not be able to live out his days in Basel. As he neared home, he wondered how he would broach all this with Marie.

He found Marie in the kitchen preparing vegetables for a pottage. Sebastian stepped behind her and wrapped his arms around her stomach. Or at least he attempted to. Now in the ninth month of pregnancy, she was large, finding it difficult to sit or lie comfortably, desperate for the baby to be born. There had been some spots of blood too. This was a delicate and anxious time for them both. Sebastian decided he would not raise the subject of Poland until after the baby was safely born.

In the last week of March, the first contractions began. Sebastian sent a messenger to fetch Bauhin and Éleana, the midwife. Marie took to her bed with Alise watching over her. Ever since the day Eugenie had died, Bauhin had made it his mission to learn all he could about childbirth. He had studied *The Rose Garden* by Rosslin and *On Human Generation and Conception* by Jacob Rueff. He had attended several complicated births in Basel, and learned a little more each time. Sebastian and Marie were reassured to have him so close. Until now, giving birth seemed to happen more easily for Marie than it had for Eugenie. But today there was a deposit of fear in their hearts.

When Bauhin arrived, he insisted that Sebastian and Katarina take the children to the garden near Saint Peter's. He would send a messenger for them when the child had safely come into the world. Nervously they set off, walking two by two.

It was a warm day, and Sebastian found the exercise unaccountably taxing. At the park, he found a bench where he sat and regathered his breath. Midday rolled around with still no news. Sebastian fished for some coins in his pocket and sent Susanna to buy bread for them all.

The children sat around the edge of that plaza's fountain chatting excitedly, the water dancing behind them. They speculated on whether they were about to gain a new brother or sister. All the while, Sebastian and Katarina exchanged worried glances, peering back the way they'd come for any sign of a messenger.

Finally, they recognized Alise approaching quickly. She got within a few steps before she smiled. "You have a boy; a beautiful little boy."

A squeal of joy erupted from beside Sebastian. Katarina grabbed his hand and shook it. But Sebastian still felt worried. "And Marie? How is Marie?"

"Marie is fine, Master Castellio. Sore and tired, of course, but full of happiness. The midwife and Doctor Bauhin did a fine job."

Sebastian turned to the children. "Quickly, each of you take another's hand and let's return to see this miracle!"

They named the child Thomas, in honor of the disciple Sebastian admired for his willingness to ask questions of Jesus. The Castellio household had never been fuller—eight children, Sebastian, Marie, and Alise, who was now living with them. Katarina, Bauhin, and the midwife were frequent visitors, and Sebastian's students regularly dropped by, of course. The house was crowded and lively, which filled Sebastian and Marie with immense gratitude.

As always, the arrival of a new child seemed to spark a fresh burst of creativity for Sebastian. More than a hundred years earlier, a Dutch monk by the name of Thomas à Kempis had written a beautiful little book called *The Imitation of Christ*. There were many—like Erasmus—who had been inspired by it.

What if I could update the antiquated Latin that Kempis used, Sebastian thought, *and produce a fresh version, one that could inspire a new generation to meditate on the life of Christ and on the path of following him? What if I could redirect the reader's eyes away from the creeds and confessions that are causing so many conflicts and help them gaze instead at Jesus himself? What if I could turn their attention to simply following Christ?*

Of all the works of translation Sebastian had wrestled with, none came to him more easily than this one. Old fashioned as Kempis's words were, they were a joy to work with, pointing the reader to a life of humility and purity of heart. A life where deeds mattered more than words. Kempis had written, "On the day of judgment, a good and pure conscience will give more joy than all the philosophy one has ever learned." Sebastian had grown to share this conviction. Kempis had a way with words that Sebastian found enchanting. He loved how the Dutchman had paraphrased Jesus's words *I am the Way, the Truth, and the Life.* "Without the Way," Kempis had written, "there is no going; without the Truth, there is no knowing; without Life, there is no living."

There were several passages in Kempis's book that Sebastian knew his generation would find difficult or baffling, written as they were out of medieval Catholic thought. He would use a lighter, more contemporary Latin. And the final section—which focused on the sacraments, particularly the Eucharist—he would omit entirely. With

Catholics, Lutherans, Calvinists and Zwinglians all warring over these doctrines, it was a battle he had no interest in wading into. Europe seemed obsessed with the death of Jesus, while he longed to help his readers focus on the life of Jesus.

Surprisingly, when Sebastian showed Borrhaus the manuscript, he liked it. In fact, once the book was printed, nobody in Protestant Europe seemed to have any problem with it. Indeed, the new edition proved to be very popular, especially in Kempis's birthplace, the Netherlands. But if Sebastian thought he'd finally published something that wouldn't see opprobrium heaped on his name, he was mistaken.

Now it was papal Europe's turn to be outraged. Soon every Inquisition had banned the book and issued vehement denunciations of its translator. Castellio had, they said, maliciously corrupted Kempis's words and, by removing the final section on the sacraments, was attempting to undermine the holy Catholic faith. Everything Sebastian had ever written was now placed on each Inquisition's list of blasphemous publications. Having been banned, the author and his books were to be burned.

Chapter 34
The Arrival of a Stranger

In 1563, joy once more permeated Sebastian and Marie's humble home. They had recently welcomed their eighth child —ninth if you counted Jeanne, whom they had adopted. But there was anxiety too. Bonifacius Amerbach, their close friend and benefactor, had died. His estate passed to his son, Basilius. Without the older Amerbach to protect him, Castellio felt more vulnerable than ever. He sensed the increased danger.

Though it didn't come naturally, Sebastian worked hard to be more cautious. Early in the year, he began work on another book—his most definitive work yet, one that would summarize all he'd come to believe about conscience, tolerance, and using the Bible for good not ill. He wrote secretively in the night, telling no one of the book's existence, keeping the manuscript far from prying eyes.

Yet he could feel himself tiring. Were all the years of grinding conflict catching up with him? Perhaps he was just growing older. There were times he set out to walk to the beech grove overlooking the river, but had to stop and wait for the burning in his stomach to pass. He turned to Bauhin for help. His learned friend prescribed fresh milk to drink, alternating with a tea of mint leaves steeped in steaming water. He found that the milk did usually help ease his discomfort.

Once, however, he was crippled by an especially bad attack when Bauhin was abroad. The pain was so severe that he turned to Gugliemo Grataroli for advice. Grataroli kindly sent him a vial of a tonic he himself had distilled. Sebastian used it but afterward felt even worse, so abandoned the bitter elixir.

Within a few weeks, Bauhin returned from France and brought with him the root of a plant called ginger, insisting that Sebastian take it instead of the mint. Sebastian had to force it down, for just as with Grataroli's elixir, it tasted awful. But he said nothing, for he was sure Bauhin must have parted with a bag full of coins in order to obtain for him such an exotic medicine.

As the year progressed, religious persecution spread like wildfire throughout Europe. Thousands of people were on the move, trying to escape sectarian violence. Each week, new travelers would enter Basel in search of refuge.

One morning, Sebastian was sitting at table with Marie and the children. They had just given thanks for their breakfast when a knock came at their door. When Sebastian opened it, Curione pulled him out onto the doorstep. "Please, Sebastian," he spoke in a fierce whisper. "Come with me to Oporinus's. I need to tell you of things I heard this night just passed."

Sebastian blinked, wondering if Curione had gone mad. "What things? What are you talking about?"

"Not here. Not in front of your children. Come with me. Please."

Sebastian recognized the fear and confusion in Curione's voice. Anxiously, he returned indoors to Marie. "I am sorry, but it seems I must go with Celio immediately. We are going to Oporinus's, but I will return as soon as I can."

They arrived as Oporinus was preparing his few remaining men for the day's work. Curione motioned to Oporinus that the three of them should take the stairs to the apartment above.

As they reached the top of the stairs, Sebastian could contain himself no longer. "What on earth is going on, Celio? What news do you bring?"

"I have news, yes, but news I can make no sense of. Last night as I was walking home, I followed two men into a tavern called The Boar for no reason other than one looked familiar—and yet strange, by which I mean there was something curious about him. No, about both of them. I tried to stay hidden. So, though I sat near them, I could only hear snatches of their conversation. Much of what I heard was incomprehensible, but I did hear the names Calvin, Beza, and Joris clearly enough. Also Occhino's name—our friend in Italy. And something about heresy and a trial ... and then ... then I heard your name, Sebastian."

Sebastian leaned back in his chair and let out a long breath. Awhile back, Occhino had asked him to translate a small book he'd written, taking it from Italian to Latin. In it, Occhino had raised controversial questions about polygamy in the Old Testament and about the lack of specific reference to the Trinity in either Testament. Sebastian had been hesitant at first to take on the project, but for the sake of his friendship with the Italian pastor, he had finally agreed. Perhaps it had been a mistake.

Oporinus leaned forward impatiently. "Who were these men, Celio? Who was doing the talking?"

"One I did not know, and I missed his name. He appeared tall and blond is all I can tell you. The other, the one I thought I recognized? I am sure it was Hendrich van Schlor."

"Van Schlor? Jan's servant?" Oporinus shook his head in puzzlement. He looked at Sebastian. "Do you know what happened to him after Jan's burning? He seemed to disappear. Have you seen him since then?"

"I haven't seen him," Sebastian answered. "After Jan died, the Netherlander community dissolved into camps. Jan and Dirkgen had not left a will, so there were arguments over how the money and property should be divided. The money used to buy all those houses had come from many purses in the Dutch group, but mostly from the van Berchems. Things seemed even more divided and acrimonious after the burning of Jan's body. Some of their group blamed Nicholaas, but even more van Schlor, saying it was he who had betrayed Jan's identity. They drove van Schlor out of their community. From what I've heard, he wandered for a time among the Swiss cities, looking for work, seeking noble families who would take him on as a secretary or valet. They say he moved around a lot."

"Well, he's back in Basel now," Curione chimed in. "At one point last night, he seemed to be describing his new employer's work, but I didn't catch the master's name. He talked about alchemy a lot. And astrology. Something about Saturn and Jupiter and 'perilous times.' I didn't understand much of it, but enough to know they spoke of something strange and dangerous."

"If we can find out who van Schlor is working for and what they are planning," Oporinus said, "that may help us to head off the danger—or at least to prepare a defense. Sebastian, are you still in touch with Nicholaas? He may know more about van Schlor's situation."

"Like van Schlor, Nicholaas has kept moving. He has lived in many places since the incident with Jan. He studies theology and keeps very much to himself. But for the past few months, he has been back in Basel and staying in the Spiesshof with Tanneke. I do still see him occasionally. I will make a point to look him up and ask what else he can tell us about Hendrich van Schlor."

It was noon when Sebastian arrived at the door of the Spiesshof, the spacious mansion where they had often dined with Jan and Dirkgen, which now belonged to Nicholaas and Tanneke. Frustratingly, Nicholaas was able to add little to what Sebastian already knew. Van Schlor, he said, had been expelled from their circle and wandered about seeking employment wherever he could. Nicholaas was surprised to hear that van Schlor was back in Basel, but he could shed no light on who his present master might be.

During the long autumn of 1563, bitter storms stripped the leaves from the city's trees. When the first winter weather arrived, it fell hard. The cruel winds dropped away, but hoarfrosts drifted across the Rhine, coating buildings with layers of frozen crystal. It was on one such icy morning, late in November, that Sebastian returned home from the university extremely tired. He went to the bedroom to rest. But a few minutes later, a knock on the bedroom door disturbed him. The door opened and Bauhin entered, greeting Sebastian with a smile.

"I wanted to let you know that in a few days I will be returning to France for another visit. I will endeavor to be back here by the middle of December and shall bring with me more ginger when I come."

Sebastian propped himself up on his elbows. "As always, you show yourself more than generous, Jean. I think the ginger does help a little—certainly more than the mint did. But it is the milk that helps more than anything else. When I feel the burning, a cup of that does bring some relief. Marie and I will continue to try to keep a good supply of it on hand."

Just then Marie entered. Sebastian wondered if he should tell them both that he was convinced his stomach problem was growing worse. The pain came more frequently now, accompanied by great sweats. And he was so tired most days. He looked at Marie, her eyes regarding him with great tenderness, and decided he would say nothing, for it would only add to her anxiety over him.

But, he now wondered, *if I should need help while Bauhin is away, who would I turn to?* He thought of young Felix Platter, recently returned from medical studies in Montpellier. There were rumors that Felix had developed a fixation with dissecting cadavers to the point that, back in France, he'd even been involved in the robbing of graves. He liked Felix, but the thought of being treated by one who plundered corpses was not a pleasant one. Then a more agreeable idea entered his head: the Italian physician Grataroli would still be here. Grataroli had shown him kindness in the past. He glanced up at Jean, who was giving instructions to Marie. He would not mention this to Bauhin. For reasons he hadn't yet fathomed, Jean disliked the Italian doctor and disapproved of his methods.

His reverie was broken by Jean's voice issuing a final instruction to Marie. "And find a way to stop this man working day and night! The stress he puts himself under is not helpful." He turned to Sebastian. "There's no commandment that says you have to produce a new book every year!"

Marie gave Bauhin a look of resignation. "I try. I really do. But every night, he's in his study scribbling away—and he won't even show me what he's working on! But now, Sebastian, you've heard what the doctor has ordered, haven't you?"

Sebastian gave an embarrassed smile. It was true; he was writing in secret and had described his work to no one, not even Marie. "You're a good man, Jean, and we thank you for how much you have helped us. I shall do my best to stay out of controversy while you are away."

"If you can manage that, Sebastian, I will be very pleased. And it will renew my faith that the age of miracles has not passed!"

When Bauhin left for France, a strange sense of melancholy crept over Sebastian. Jan and Dirkgen were gone. Oporinus, once so fiery and determined, seemed lost these days. By crushing his business, the city's leaders had also successfully crushed his spirit. And as for Zebedee—they hadn't heard from him for a long, long time.

As November passed and December dawned, winter grew deeper and colder. The days were short and dark, the sun more and more absent. Along with the melancholy, a strange sense of foreboding formed, growing like a lump in Sebastian's stomach, a hard ball of fear that he could not dislodge.

Chapter 35
The Accusations

I t was Wednesday, the 18th of December, a week before Christmas, and winter darkness had fallen like a heavy drape across the city. Already the frost had formed a slick layer on each cobblestone and window pane. The Castellio family gathered in the kitchen, taking dinner by the fire, feasting on a catch of fresh carp. The thought of the approaching Christmas filled the room with merriment. Laughter and teasing rippled around the table. Even Sebastian found his spirit lifting, warmed by the fire and the food. Nathaniel launched into a story about a huge fish he had almost netted. Sebastian egged him on. "No, Nate, even bigger than that! Tell us the whole story. It was enormous!"

Then *Thud!*

The whole room seemed to shudder. Again *Thud!*

The window panes rattled from the force. A third time. *Thud!*

Their banter fell silent. Every head turned to face the door. Sebastian stood and cautiously moved toward it. Slowly he turned the latch and inched it open. Peering into the darkness, his eyes watered against the chill of the night air. He fought to make sense of a large shadowy figure, its fist raised and hovering inches from his face.

A shock of fear coursed through Sebastian's chest. He tried to shove the door closed again, but the man—bigger and stronger—thrust his hand forward, forcing it back open. Sebastian tried to focus. Now he could see that the raised fist held the hilt of a sword, which had been poised to thud against the door a fourth time.

As his eyes continued to adjust, Sebastian thought he could make out the silhouette of a second man behind the first. That one carried a struggling lamp. By its dim light, Sebastian saw that the second man also carried a sword, this one strapped to his hip.

Blocking the door, the closer man spoke, his voice hard and gravelly like a snarling dog. "Are you Sebastian Castellio, chair of Greek at the University of Basel? Are you this man?" he demanded.

Sebastian's throat tightened. He strained to reply. "Yes. Yes, I am."

"We have been sent by the council. We bring you a summons." The man thrust a thin stack of papers into Sebastian's hands. Sebastian stared at the top-most page. He recognized the city's crest followed by his own name. Below that was written a single line: "Against whom has been brought the charges of heresy and abuse of office."

The night air bit at him, pressing against him. His extremities shivered.

The thickset man continued. "You will meet with Basel's censor, Martin Borrhaus, at nine o'clock tomorrow morning, in his office. If you do not appear, we will come back for you, and we will take you there."

Sebastian had never met these men before, yet they glared at him as if he were the foulest of criminals. "Yes, yes. Of course, I will appear. I promise you."

The men regarded him a few moments more, their eyes contemptuous. Then, silently, they turned and melted into the night.

He closed the door and moved back into the kitchen, dazed. Marie and the children watched him, their faces pale. They had heard the whole conversation. Alise, fussing over Thomas and Frederic, was pretending she hadn't. Tears formed in Marie's and Susanna's eyes. The younger children started whimpering. His mind slowed to a crawl. He worked to pull his thoughts together, searching for words.

He looked at Marie, her eyes damp and wide. Finally, his words came. "This has happened before, and we survived, remember? These are false charges, and God will not allow a false witness to prosper. He will deliver me from their accusations, just as he has in the past." He pulled Marie into an embrace, then Susanna, Anna and Barbara too. He looked around the table at the ring of anxious faces before him. He knew he should say more, sit down and offer further reassurance, but his thoughts, while numb a few moments ago, were now a storm. He turned back to Marie, his eyes apologetic. "I'm sorry, but I must go to my study now. I must read these documents and prepare a defense. I must familiarize myself with these charges so that I know what absurdities await me tomorrow."

She bit her bottom lip and lowered her head.

Sebastian turned back toward the children. "We mustn't be afraid. Papa needs to go to his study and write a letter to answer these men, then all will be well. Nathaniel, will you lead the Bible reading tonight? And Susanna, you will say the prayers, won't you?"

Nathaniel and Susanna had both stood when he called their names. Now both nodded mutely and retook their seats.

Sebastian left the kitchen and climbed the stairs, ascending toward his study as if a great weight resided upon his shoulders, as if he were scaling a mountain. After reaching his desk and reading the charges, he wanted to begin writing his refutation immediately, but no words would come. Instead, he found himself writing a letter to André Zebedee, pouring out on paper all that had befallen him in this latest twist of the knife. Something inside him needed to reach out to his old friend and pull him close.

Chapter 36
Refuting the Charges

The frost that had begun the night before was now fully formed. Sebastian carefully edged his way across the slippery cobbles and flagstones as he made his way to the university. He'd somehow forgotten his gloves, but not wanting to be late, he pressed on. By the time he arrived at Borrhaus's office, his hands were so cold he could feel nothing as he tapped on the door. After a command to enter, he cautiously pushed open the door and stepped inside. He blinked as he took in the arrangement of the room. He had expected to see Borrhaus behind his desk. But he hadn't expected to find Wissenburg and Sphyractes seated in front of Borrhaus, all three eyeing him coldly as he entered. Borrhaus indicated a seat next to the other two theologians, but there was no greeting from either man. As soon as Sebastian was seated, Borrhaus began.

"I take it you have read the charges against you?"

"They were delivered last evening, and I have."

"And you realize the seriousness of these charges?"

"Of course. But you must tell me who has brought these charges. I will face my accuser soon enough, but I have a right to know who that will be."

Wissenburg wouldn't meet Sebastian eyes. "Adam van Bodenstein," he said quietly.

"Adam van Bodenstein?" Sebastian echoed. He pictured van Bodenstein in his mind: a tall young blond man; a physician, astrologer, and alchemist; someone he'd met a few times who had always seemed friendly enough. "Why on earth would ... what connection does he have with ...?" He stopped, unable to fit the pieces of the puzzle together.

Wissenburg cleared his throat. "His father was a good man and a great theologian. Likewise, his son is a good and honest man and, what's more, a staunch patriot." He peered intently at Sebastian. "A man loyal to his superiors, loyal to Basel, and loyal to the Reformed Protestant cause."

Sebastian sat dumbfounded. *Why would Adam von Bodenstein bring such accusations against me? I know his father, Andreas Bodenstein Karlstadt, was once Martin Luther's right-hand man. And after having a falling out with Luther, he pastored Saint Peter's Church here in Basel and befriended Wissenburg. But why would his son—*

Borrhaus's words cut through his swirling thoughts, and they were thick with frustration. "I have always tried to treat you fairly, Sebastian. For many years I have done my best to prevent things from reaching this point. But I can no longer protect you. I have warned you and warned you, but you have allowed your pride and stubbornness to get the better of you. You have dared to write and translate material you knew would offend. Zurich and Geneva are furious and lay the blame at our feet. Now the council and the university have no option but to act. Of course, as always, we will follow the letter of the law. You will be given a week to prepare a written answer to the accusations brought against you. If the council and senate believe there is still a case to be made against you after reading your reply, you will appear before the city's magistrates, along with your accuser, at which point you both will be heard. After that, judgment will be passed and a sentence given."

Sebastian nodded slowly, his stomach churning. "I understand."

Wissenburg leaned forward and cleared his throat. "We have consulted with the council and are all in agreement. You are to be suspended from your position at the university until your trial and this second accusation of blasphemy is decided one way or the other. You have become an embarrassment to the university. Your salary will be suspended until that time."

Sebastian startled in his seat. "But I have a wife and eight children to feed! Please—think of them!"

Sphyractes's face reddened and his voice rang with anger. "It is you and no one else who has created this ugliness, Castellio. It is your problem to solve."

The twisting in Sebastian's innards knifed its way up from his stomach to his chest. Fighting a wave of nausea, he tried to stand. Slowly, unsteadily, without looking back, he walked away.

After leaving Borrhaus's office, Sebastian struggled his way home across the ice, panic gripping him without release. *I must try to resolve this quickly. I must complete the work on my defense and submit it as soon as possible.* He winced, wondering how to tell Marie about the loss of his salary. He thought of those who had helped him in the past, and how he would have to humble himself and approach them again. But Jan was gone. Oporinus was virtually penniless. Bauhin was away on business, though he hoped his friend would return soon. Once more, he would have to turn to his old patrons, the Amerbach family, their estate now having passed from the deceased Bonifacius and into the hands of his son and Sebastian's former student, Basilius. He'd also have to use his grappling hook and net to gather wood to keep their fire burning and food to fill their plates. He would have to divide his time between writing his defense and going to the river to work. At least he had Nathanial to help him.

As he neared home, he tried to clear his head and push down the fear, but the churning in his stomach only worsened. When he reached the door, he realized he'd forgotten his key. Feeling pathetic, he thumped on it with gloveless hands that ached from the cold.

Marie gasped as she opened the door. She pulled Sebastian into the room and toward a stool near the fire. "What's wrong? You look unwell."

"My stomach complaint, but it's gotten worse."

"Is Bauhin back yet? We must call for him to come see you."

"Jean is still in France. I need to keep drinking the milk he prescribed."

"I will send Sara to the market to bring back some fresh milk, and there is still a little mint behind the house. The meeting with Borrhaus—what happened?"

Sebastian couldn't meet her eye. "I have been suspended without pay. I must prepare a written defense to the charges brought against me by a man called von Bodenstein, then face him in a trial. I need to do this as soon as possible so I can get back to work and start earning money for our family again."

When he looked up at her, Marie's eyes brimmed with tears, though she fought to hold them back, biting hard on her lip. She knelt and drew Sebastian close, slowly stroking his back with her hand. "We mustn't fear. God will provide for us." It sounded to Sebastian more like a plea than an assurance. After a few moments, she added, "Who is this man, Bodenstein, who comes against you? And why?"

"It is a mystery. But Curione did come to Oporinus and me some nights ago with an odd story. In a certain tavern on the far side of town, he said he was sure he'd seen Jan's old secretary, van Schlor, deep in conversation with a blond stranger. I feel certain that that stranger must have been Bodenstein. That gets us no closer to an answer, but I'll wager that Bodenstein is simply a straw man, a stooge for Calvin and Beza. Nothing more. This is an old tactic. They prefer to use a proxy in order to not get their own hands dirty." Sebastian looked at Marie sadly. "With all that is happening, I'm afraid it will not be a lavish Christmas for us this year."

She shook her head. "Neither of us has ever concerned ourselves with that. Why should we start now? We'll send Nathaniel to catch more carp. And for these past months, I have been keeping aside a little sugar to make a bread pudding. I have sewn clothes for the children, and you have made toys. They will be happy with all of that." It was true. Each time he had dredged an odd-shaped piece of wood from the river, Sebastian had fashioned a plaything from it—a bear, a dog, a horse, or a spinning top. The younger children loved these keepsakes.

When he had warmed enough to move, Sebastian dragged himself up the stairs to his study. The day was so dim that he placed a lamp on his desk. He periodically cupped his hands around it, warming his fingers enough to hold a quill. Eventually his fingers moved freely and words spilled across the page.

Methodically, logically, he addressed each of Bodenstein's charges. Taken one by one, they were, in fact, easily refuted. Indeed, he had answered most of them many times over these last few years. He reminded the senate and council—who would be the ones reading his defense—that past accusations against him had often been bizarre, such as when Calvin and Beza accused him of thieving the city's wood. Having refuted each accusation, he then lobbed a charge of his own:

> It is obvious that the real author of these charges against me, he wrote, is not Adam von Bodenstein but Theodore Beza and John Calvin. If these men have the courage of their convictions, let them step out of the shadows and into the light. Come to Basel to confront me in a public trial and dispute before the eyes of all.

He read over what he'd written. Satisfied, he signed off with a final quotation from Saint Paul.

> "If I have all knowledge, and can speak in the tongues of men and of angels, yet have not love, I am nothing."

As he folded the paper into an envelope, a fearful sense of urgency gripped him once more. He pushed to his feet, wanting to get this to Borrhaus as quickly as he could. But as he stood, the room began to spin and a wave of nausea engulfed him. He gripped the edge of the desk, holding it hard as he struggled to stay upright. Eventually—when his heart had slowed and his head had cleared—he carefully picked his way down the stairs.

When he arrived in the kitchen, Marie hurried to him. "Seb, you're so pale. Are you *sure* you are well?"

Sebastian wafted his hand as if to wave the question away. With his other hand, he held aloft the paper he had been working on. "I have answered the charges against me. I need to take my reply to Borrhaus and ask him to take it before the council immediately."

"Must you go right now? I think you should rest."

"No, no, I must return this now. And then I will take Nathaniel to the river so we can dredge for fish and wood. We are almost out." He glanced at the small pile of sticks beside the fireplace.

Marie's eyes, however, were fixed on Sebastian's face, pleading. "And we need to ask young Amerbach for his help."

Sebastian dropped his head and nodded. "Yes, I know. I will do it. I promise. But the priority is to get this to Borrhaus." He turned for the door.

"Seb," Marie said softly as his hand touched the bolt. "Can we pray over what you have written—and for God's protection over us?"

Sebastian looked chastened. "Of course."

They joined hands. Marie leaned into him, pouring herself out, pleading with God to keep Sebastian and, indeed, all of them safe from those who would do them harm. When she'd finished, Marie picked up Sebastian's gloves from the table and handed them to him with a mock scowl. He looked at her, chastened a second time, and mouthed a silent *thank you* before gently kissing her on the cheek.

As he willed himself out of the house and down their alleyway, the wind dropped and its bite abated. A small winter sun appeared. When he reached Borrhaus's office, Basel's chief censor and Old Testament scholar looked shocked to see him back so quickly, rebuttal in hand.

Sebastian passed him the document. With an imploring note in his voice, he asked, "Please, Martin, as much as it is in your power, schedule this trial as soon as is possible."

Borrhaus regarded him carefully. Then his face softened. "That isn't up to me, but I will advocate for it. I do realize that these circumstances must be very difficult for you and Marie."

Chapter 37
The Art of Doubting

As the 24th of December, Holy Eve, approached, the younger children's excitement grew. Days earlier, Sebastian and Nathaniel had cut down a small spruce and carried it home. In a custom Sebastian had learned from Martin Bucer's family in Strasbourg, the children attached little candles to each of its branches. Later that evening, they would light these to welcome the birth of the Christ child.

After their dinner of carp—and the promised dessert—they gathered round the fire, the older children reading nativity stories from the Gospels, the younger ones listening with eyes wide and luminous. Soon Sara and Thomas began to shuffle restlessly, standing on their tiptoes and peering around the room. They knew what was coming and couldn't wait any longer.

Sebastian regarded them with a smile, waiting for the right moment. When he knew they could contain themselves not a moment longer, he gave the word and they were off, searching the house for the gifts he and Marie had hidden. Exclamations of surprise and laughter punctuated the next few minutes as each child discovered something upon which a piece of paper had been laid and their name written—an item beautifully sewn by Marie or a toy Sebastian had carved. Soon they were all back in the kitchen, flurries of joy bursting forth each time a garment was tried on, a top spun, or a hobbyhorse ridden.

Sebastian reached for Marie's hand. It was soft and warm. Her eyes sparkled in the firelight. He savored this moment of grace. It was as if this evening—and the act of handing in his defense a few days before—had lifted some of the weight from his shoulders. That night, he slept more peacefully than he had for many a month.

⸻

The next day, Christmas Day, Sebastian rose feeling stronger. In fact, he felt the best he'd felt in a long time. He even felt well enough to cross the river to visit Basilius Amerbach, a task he'd been putting off for a week. He would pass along his Christmas greetings, a gift, and his request.

A biting wind from the north grew stronger as Sebastian crossed the Mittlere Bridge and walked uphill toward Amerbach's grand home near the old Carthusian monastery. The brass knocker echoed against the hardwood door. As Sebastian waited for an answer, he jiggled, moving from one foot to the other, hugging himself in an attempt to ward off the cold. Amerbach's cheerful valet soon opened the door and ushered Sebastian into the drawing room, where a great fire roared. Leaving Sebastian to warm himself, he hurried off to find Basilius.

As he looked around the room, Sebastian's eyes drank in the ornate wooden cabinet filled with paintings, books, and other curiosities. Then he turned his attention to the middle of the room where there sat a chest filled with hundreds of coins collected from around the world. Sebastian stepped closer and circled the elaborate box, a series of trays that could be pulled out in multiple directions. The artistry was a welcome distraction from the threats that had preoccupied him these past few days.

The valet returned with young Amerbach, once Sebastian's

pupil, now his friend and colleague on the university faculty. As Basilius entered the room, his face lit up. "Sebastian! Merry Christmas!"

"Merry Christmas to you too, Basilius. I trust you had a wonderful Holy Eve?"

"Indeed. My sister Faustina came. Some cousins too. We banqueted on roasted goose and parsnip and enjoyed one another's company greatly. And you, Sebastian?"

"Yes, we had a merry time with all the children. We enjoyed a feast of carp pulled from the Rhine! But your mention of Faustina—is it true what I hear? That Oporinus is courting her?"

"Yes, it is true, and I am not opposed. Both have lost those they were married to and will be a great comfort to each other, I think. And perhaps we can help keep Johannes's business afloat. But tell me: to what do I owe the honor of your visit on this auspicious day?"

"Of course, it is always good to see your face, and"—Sebastian reached into his satchel and extracted a small leather-bound book— "I'd like to give you this. It's a collection of poems I once translated from Greek and for which Oporinus arranged the calligraphy. I think you might enjoy them."

"Thank you. How very thoughtful. And now I am embarrassed as I have nothing for you. But perhaps ..." The man's eyes roamed the room looking for something to give Sebastian in exchange.

"No, Basilius. You and your father have given me so much over these many years. The debt is very much mine. And, well, there is another reason I have come today. I'm ashamed to say I need to call on your family's assistance once more."

Basilius's face crinkled with concern. "Is everything well with you, Sebastian? You do look thinner and paler than last we met."

"Things are not so well, I'm afraid. Once again, the council wishes to try me on charges of heresy. A man called Bodenstein has built a case against me. As a result, the senate has suspended me without pay from the university."

"What!" Basilius exploded. "How dare they treat you like that!

You are a better scholar than all those clods put together. Suspended without pay? That is designed to cause your family suffering. Where are their hearts? Sebastian, I assure you, this estate will be pleased to support you until your position is restored. There is no shame in this for you. My father and I have always believed in your scholarship and your integrity. But this must be a terrible time for your family. Is there any other way we can assist you in your work? You're always working on some writing project or other. Is there a current one?"

Sebastian looked sheepish. He had intended to tell no one about the book he was working on, but given Basilius's kindness and his question, he felt obligated. "Actually, yes. One that will serve to summarize all I have thought and written previously about conscience and toleration and why mankind keeps falling into the evil of persecuting those with differing opinions and beliefs. I wish to explore the underlying reasons why this happens and how it may be prevented."

Basilius was listening intently. "That sounds impressive. And risky. But tell me: why indeed *does* this happen? What is your theory?"

"I believe it has everything to do with power, pride and false certainty. I intend to entitle the book *The Art of Doubting*." He glanced at Basilius to observe his reaction.

"*The Art of Doubting*," he repeated uncertainly. "By which you mean what exactly?"

"That there is an art in knowing who and what to believe, and an art in knowing who and what to doubt. Much harm has been done by those who believed what they should have questioned and doubted what they should have believed. Look around and observe. Those who are certain that they alone possess the truth and that any who doubt or question them do not—they become tyrannical. And this holds true whether in the realm of religion or of statecraft."

"You are, of course, thinking of John Calvin and Theo Beza when you say this."

"Not only them but also Catholicism and Protestantism in

general. Both claim to possess all truth and thus accuse the other of apostasy and heresy. They inflame us to hate and kill one another. Yet the Jesus we read of in the Gospels calls us to live with mercy, humility, and, above all else, love for one another. As to truth, we should all admit that none of us is able to read the Bible without prejudice or with perfect understanding. And if we are honest, we will even admit that parts of it are obscure, ambiguous even, and cannot sustain the weighty doctrines we build upon them."

Amerbach looked at him anxiously. He'd picked up a small cushion from a chair and began fidgeting with it.

"Take the doctrines concerning the Trinity or the Eucharist, for example," Sebastian continued, overlooking his friend's nervousness. "We persecute and kill men for having wrong doctrine in each of these, even though Scripture never defines either very clearly. We see deviance in these doctrines as great errors, worthy of death or torture, yet deem it no sin to hate and murder one another! How is such a contradiction of Christ's teaching possible? And so we come back to the need for humility. Attempts to attain absolute certainty lead to self-righteousness and enmity; we become imitators of the Pharisees whom Christ condemned. If we have humility, we will allow doubt as to whether we have understood the Bible rightly, thus making room for the possibility that another person's interpretation—or even another sect's interpretation—is more accurate than our own. I have come to believe that doubt is not a *fault*, but a *virtue*. And even more than that, doubt is a partner to *genuine* faith. For what is faith other than an act of trust?"

"But is not religion the search for perfection—and for perfect truth?"

"Yes, *the search*. But great danger comes when we believe we have captured the truth so completely that no other understanding is permissible except for our own."

"But we must do our best to grasp and hold on to God's truth, surely?"

"Yes, but *how* do we 'grasp' it, as you say? Truly, I am convinced that it is only by *love*! Jesus says that all the words of the prophets and the law are fulfilled in a twofold command—*love* the Lord your God and *love* one another—nothing more than this. Saint Paul says that *all* of God's laws are fulfilled by one single injunction—'love your neighbor as yourself.' Later, Paul explains that 'love does no harm to its neighbor.' Thus, if our interpretation of Scripture ever leads us away from love and toward harming our neighbor, we know we are in error, that we have read the Bible wrongly. This is the true test of biblical interpretation: that it should make us better followers of Jesus and more like him. But—" He looked at Basilius. His former student's fingers were still working their way around the cushion's edges, as if it were some kind of rosary. Sebastian drew a breath. He'd said too much to turn back now. And more than that, it was a relief to finally entrust someone with the thoughts he'd been hiding away for so long.

"Basilius, I've come to see that *doubt* and *questioning* are vital to the Christian faith. It is through doubt and questioning that we come to exercise *reason*, and reason is crucial. If we abandon reason, terrible, terrible danger awaits us. 'Come let us reason together,' God says. And that, surely, is an invitation to reason, to question, and to debate."

"Are you saying we have an invitation to question and debate *with God*?" Basilius sounded incredulous.

"Is that not what Abraham did when he tried to argue God down from destroying Sodom? And Moses when he interceded for the Israelites about the golden calf? Does Jesus not do the same when he allows the Syrophoenician woman, against his first instincts, to persuade him to heal her daughter? The Jews have always debated with God!"

Basilius looked troubled. "Are you saying there is no place for dogma or doctrine? That there's nothing the church can say is absolute truth? I have always been taught that the goal of Christian theology is to make faith certain."

"The apostle says we may possess 'all knowledge'—or absolute truth, if you prefer—but that without love it means nothing. We may have the faith to move mountains, but without love it is meaningless. Love listens to one another. Dogma refuses to listen. I believe we are to seek and follow the one who is neither theory nor dogma but a living Word—wisdom. *Logos.* Reason itself! He who came *before* all ceremonies and rites and sects and doctrines. Perhaps then we will finally be able to rise above this enmity that destroys us and beat our swords into plowshares, like the prophets dreamed one day we would."

Basilius had taken a seat and now stared at his cabinet full of art. For a long time, the only sound in the room was the ticking of the clock on the mantel over the fireplace. Eventually he spoke. "These ideas are new to my ears, Sebastian, and very ... challenging. I need to think more on them." His face looked troubled, and Sebastian could see he wanted to change the subject. "Of more concern to me now is the news that you face another heresy trial, and my father is not here to support you. But you have escaped their conniving twice, surely you will again."

Sebastian hesitated. "Each time, they come at me with greater accusations and new accusers, though—of course, Calvin and Beza lie behind each." Sebastian looked at his former pupil sadly. "I may not be able to stay in Basel much longer. I have written to friends in Poland and made contingencies in case we must flee there in haste."

Basilius looked shocked. "With Marie and all your children? Across Europe in the dead of winter?"

Sebastian shrugged. "If our choice comes down to battling snow or battling flames—" He could not bring himself to finish the sentence.

Chapter 38
Another Letter

On the way home, Sebastian dropped by his office to collect some necessary papers. Atop his desk, someone had propped a large envelope with his name on it, sealed at the back with a disk of black wax.

He broke open the seal and glanced to the signature at the bottom of the page. To his surprise, it was from Gugliemo Grataroli, the Italian doctor. He went back to the top of the page and began to read.

Dear Master Castellio,

I write this to you out of deep concern for your life. We live in perilous times and I have become aware that you have many enemies in this city.

No doubt you have heard of all that has befallen Bernadino Occhino, your friend and my compatriot? The Council of Zurich moved harshly against him after that book you and he produced. Are you aware that Occhino was removed from his position as pastor and given 48 hours to depart Zurich? Poor man—seventy-six years old and recently widowed! Occhino took only what he could carry, forced to flee in the midst of winter snows. Even crueler, Bullinger sent messengers ahead, warning every Christian town and every Christian person to refuse shelter to a heretic. I heard he could find no rest in any town of Switzerland, nor of Germany, finding shelter only in hedgerows and barns until finally he came to Poland, sick and penniless.

Sebastian, I fear that this too—or worse—will be your fate.

I have also heard the news of your continued sickness. Soon I will send you the right medicine for your disease.

Gugliemo Grataroli

Sebastian knew that Zurich had expelled Occhino, but he'd not heard the rest of the story until now. A wave of panic rose up in him. Was Grataroli right? Was this—or worse—to be his fate as well?

A pain radiated across his chest and stabbed at his stomach. Dampness spread beneath his arms and around his torso. He tried to push away the growing sense that a net was closing around him. He knew that the kindly Grataroli had sent him this letter out of concern, but it had made him feel far worse. Sebastian slipped the note from Grataroli into his pocket. It was best if Marie never saw it—or heard what had become of Bernadino Occhino. He stumbled his way out of the office and into the teeth of a wind so cold it cut at his skin like the edge of a blade.

Chapter 39
Fire and Ice

By the time he arrived home, Sebastian's whole body was shaking. Marie pulled him to the fire. As he slowly warmed, she gathered an envelope from the table and held it out to him. Fingers trembling, he tore at the seal, its gray wax bearing the mark of Basel's council. He read the letter, then swallowed hard, hesitating before he spoke. "The council and senate have reached a decision. A date has been set for my trial—this coming Monday, December 30th, at the university." He blinked at the words on the page, as if they might change before his eyes. When he looked up, Marie gazed at him through tears.

He glanced at the dwindling stack of kindling beside the hearth, noting how small it had become. "Nathaniel and I will take the grappling hook and head to the river before this wood is exhausted."

"But you're so cold," Marie said. "You should warm yourself before you go out again."

"The light will fade from the sky soon, and if we don't catch any fish or find wood before dark falls, it will be a cold, hungry night for us all."

Marie nodded with resignation. Sebastian forced a smile and tried to make his next words sound defiant. "Amerbach has promised to support us again. He will get some funds to us in the next day or two. Not just for food but to purchase a horse and a wagon if need be."

Marie did not meet his eyes. She stared at the sparse pile of kindling, still nodding.

Sebastian made his way slowly up the stairs and collected the grappling hook and net from a cupboard in his study. Soon he and Nathaniel were back in the kitchen, Marie bundling them both into scarves and hats. She studied them, worry etched on her face. "Take care. Please take care. And get back before it grows too dark."

They each hoisted a basket onto their shoulder and made their way out the door, closing it as a flurry of sleet swept across the road before them.

As the door closed, Susanna and Sara descended the stairs and entered the kitchen. "Where are they going, Mama?" Sara asked.

"To gather wood and fish for our supper."

"But it's freezing out there!" she cried.

"I know." Marie hated that her own voice sounded so sad and flat.

Susanna stepped forward and embraced Marie, speaking softly. "What is going to happen to us? What will happen in this trial? I'm so afraid Mama."

"Me too." Marie couldn't prevent a small sob from bubbling up in her throat.

Susanna held her more tightly. "Will they put Papa in prison?" she asked.

Marie knew the outcome could be far worse than that, but she wasn't willing to talk of it. "We may have to move cities again if things go badly."

Susanna pulled away. She and Sara both looked alarmed.

"We haven't said anything to you before now, but Papa's been writing letters and asking friends in Poland if they will receive him— us—there."

Susanna straightened. "Poland? But that is so far away!"

"If we can find safety there, then it is a journey we must take."

It was nearly dark when Sebastian and Nathaniel returned. As they neared the door, Sebastian could see that a sheet of paper had been pinned to the wood. Puzzled, he reached for it. But to read it, he had to step to where a faint light emerged from the little kitchen window. Slowly his eyes adjusted. He began to make out the lines of a sketched picture. After a few moments it became clear. The paper bore the image of a fire, a stake, and a man being burned. Underneath, the word *heretic* had been penned. Sebastian crumpled the paper into a ball.

"What is it, Papa?" Nathaniel asked.

"Nothing, Nate. Nothing good or useful anyway."

The two of them struggled through the door, their baskets crammed with wood and half a dozen perch strung from a line. Sebastian pulled off his gloves and unwound the scarf from his face. He spoke quietly to Marie. "Shall we have some of these fresh tonight and smoke the rest?"

Marie, who had been tending a pot over the fire, turned and took the fish from him. Her hand touched his. "Your fingers feel like ice!" She cupped his cheek and gasped. "Your face. It's burning up. Sebastian, you have a fever."

"Papa got quite wet at the river," Nathaniel said. "And then on the way home, we had to stop several times because of his stomach." He looked at his father, who was shaking. "Pa, please take some rest now. I'm worried for you."

When Sebastian saw the compassion in his son's eyes, a wave of emotion swept over him. *How like Eugenie you look and sound.*

Marie looped her arm under Sebastian's. "We are going upstairs, and you are climbing into bed right now. Susanna will gather extra blankets, and Nathaniel will go for Bauhin."

"Bauhin might not be back from France yet."

"Or he may. We will call for him anyway."

As they started climbing the stairs, Sebastian doubled over. Marie staggered under his weight. They paused until he recovered the strength to keep going. Once in their room, she helped him strip off his outer garments and climb into the bed. Sebastian complained of feeling nauseous, so Marie placed a pail next to him. His hands and feet felt frozen, but the rest of him burned with fever. Sweat ran down his torso and soaked his undershirt.

Marie pulled a small glass vial from the pocket of her apron. "A messenger came this afternoon while you were out, a man sent by Gugliemo Grataroli. He said Grataroli had prepared this for your stomach. He advised that you take one sip each day until you are healed."

Sebastian examined the little glass bottle. It was thick and viscous, the color of mustard, and when he moved the bottle, the contents were sluggish, sliding along the inside of the glass. Sebastian placed it on a small bureau beside the bed.

Marie spent the next hour periodically wiping sweat from Sebastian while he lay clutching his stomach. But upon hearing a loud knock on the downstairs door, Marie leaped to her feet and descended the stairs as fast as she could. When she got to the kitchen, Susanna had already opened the front door and ushered Nathaniel and Bauhin into the house.

"Jean, you came!" Marie threw her arms around their friend. "Thank God."

"I only just returned from France this afternoon, but as soon as Nathaniel arrived, I gathered my things and came. I have heard about the new charges brought against Sebastian, too. I am so sorry, Marie. The men who bring these charges are the ones who would be on trial if it were up to me. Sebastian is upstairs?"

"Yes. His stomach is worse than ever, and he is burning up with fever. He looks bad, Jean."

Bauhin bounded up the stairs, Marie following. When he

entered the room, Sebastian was lying soaked in sweat and holding his stomach. But as soon as Sebastian saw Bauhin, his face animated and he tried to sit up. Grimacing from the pain, he managed a faint greeting. "Jean! You are back. Wonderful!"

Bauhin placed his hand on Sebastian's forehead. He began to undo the buttons on Sebastian's undershirt and examine his torso, his groin, under his arms, and his throat and neck. "Where is the pain?"

"Just the stomach, but it has gotten worse. Not just burning now, but also stabbing."

"Have you been drinking the milk and the mint-leaf brew?"

Sebastian shook his head. "I have felt nauseous these past few days and have struggled to eat or drink much of anything. In front of the children, I force myself to eat and drink a little."

Marie looked shocked. "Why didn't you tell me?"

Sebastian gave her an apologetic look. "I didn't want to worry you."

Bauhin stared at Sebastian's torso, then he crouched and put his ear to Sebastian's chest. "Your heart is racing, and so is your breathing." As he spoke, Sebastian winced and clutched at his stomach, half curling into a ball. Bauhin frowned. "I think we should try some more milk, for it has helped you in the past. I have brought some dried ginger back with me also. We will add that to the milk."

With a tilt of his head, Sebastian indicated the bedside bureau. "Grataroli has also sent some medicine for me. That vial there."

Bauhin looked puzzled as he picked up the little bottle and shook it. He removed the cork and sniffed at the medicine, wincing and shaking his head. "I smell sulfur and nightshade, certainly. And"—he shook the bottle again—"and I think I perceive the presence of mercury."

"Should I take some, Jean? He recommended one sip per day."

"With sulfur and mercury in it? This would burn a hole right through your stomach. Is Grataroli's intention to transform you into a bar of gold through his sorcery? No, please. Take the milk and ginger, not this." He held Grataroli's vial aloft a second time, and his face darkened. "Didn't you once tell me that Grataroli attended Dirkgen and Jan just before their deaths?"

"Yes, that's what Nicholaas told me."

Bauhin looked back at the vial, his brow creased. "This should be thrown into the nearest privy. Marie, can we try more milk now?"

Marie went to the door and called for Sara, asking her to fetch a jug of milk and a cup from the kitchen. A few minutes later, Sara returned to the room with both items. Bauhin took a small knife and began to carefully flake slivers of dried ginger into the bottom of the cup; then he poured the milk over that, stirring it with his knife until the ginger was well suspended.

He passed the cup to Sebastian, who took it with trembling hands. Lifting the cup to his lips, he began sipping it ever so slowly, though he seemed determined to drain the whole draft. Eventually the cup was empty. He passed it back to Bauhin. But as Marie watched, his breathing grew more rapid and his shoulders arched. His eyes widened and he lurched to the side. With a deep groan he retched, a stream of dark vomit exploding out of him. He collapsed back onto the bed, his chest heaving.

Bauhin stared at the vomit in the pail, so Marie followed his eyes with her own. Apart from the milk and ginger, it was the color of pitch with a ring of red at its edges. Sebastian groaned and rolled to the edge of the bed a second time. This time a small stream of bright red fluid flowed from his mouth.

He rolled back onto the bed and closed his eyes, still groaning. His breathing had slowed, but he looked spent. Bauhin took hold of Marie's hand and led her out of the room beyond the doorway.

"What is happening, Jean?" Her voice shook. "Has the plague returned?"

"No. There are no boils or swellings, and besides, no one else in Basel has this sickness."

"What came out of his stomach was black then bloody. What is happening to him?"

"The first, dark fluid was old blood; the second was fresh. His stomach is bleeding."

Marie's skin went cold. "What can you do? Can you stop it?"

Bauhin looked her fully in the face as he placed his hands on her shoulders. "I can't. I can only give herbs and medicines, but he'll throw them up again. The only hope is rest, and for the stomach to heal itself."

Marie's face crumpled. "*Will* it heal?"

"We will pray for this. But his condition is grave. We must allow him to rest as much as he can. In the meantime, give him nothing to eat or drink."

When they reentered the door, Sebastian had collapsed into a fitful sleep.

"I will return later tonight," Bauhin told her. "But if anything changes, send someone to fetch me. I will come immediately." He gave Marie a brief embrace. She stood rooted to the spot while listening to his steps descend the stairs and exit through the kitchen door.

As promised, Bauhin returned a few hours later. Sebastian had been dozing the whole time. Though the stomach pain remained, he'd rallied a little and was propped up in the bed. When Bauhin entered the room, he greeted him with a wan smile.

"Jean! I'm glad you're back. I am feeling a little better than when you left." He turned to Marie. "There are things I must tell you, but I wanted Jean to hear them also. A few days ago, I prepared my will. It sits in the top drawer of my desk." He took hold of Marie's hand. "I'm sorry I have accumulated so little to leave you and the children. I own little more than a clear conscience and loyal friends."

"Shh." She stroked his hair from his forehead. "Your love and faithfulness have brought me more joy than all the riches in the world, Sebastian."

A wave of tenderness washed over him as he gazed at Marie. It seemed to soften the fear the past week had etched into his heart. "Thank you for loving me. After Eugenie was taken, I could have wasted away in loneliness, in bitterness, but you saved me. I have been so blessed."

Marie's eyes welled with tears. Silently, softly, she let her hand brush Sebastian's cheek.

Bauhin took a step back toward the door. But Sebastian noticed and turned his attention to his friend. "Jean, in my will I have asked you to be the guardian of my family should I die. Would you do this for me, my friend?"

Bauhin nodded. "Of course. It would be my greatest honor in all the world."

Sebastian turned back to Marie. "In my will, I leave a plea for the children to always support you, to apply themselves to study hard, to learn a trade and how to work with their hands so that they may support themselves. And I ask them to learn to speak German well, without an accent, seeing that has caused me so much trouble here in Basel." He produced a faint smile. "But more than that, I want you to tell them how much I have loved them. And how much I have loved you."

"Sebastian!" Jean took a step closer to the bed now. "It might not come to this. I am heartened that you look stronger this evening. The key is rest. And to protect you from attack and from worry."

"Protect me from attack, Jean? Today I received the council's letter informing me that my heresy trial will begin in four days."

Bauhin cleared his throat. "I spoke to Amerbach when I left here earlier. In the morning, he will go to the council to demand the trial be postponed until you are well."

"And yet it was I who begged them to make it happen soon." He sighed. "What have I done to deserve friends like you and Amerbach? I give thanks to God for you both."

Marie spoke up. "Sebastian has also made contact with friends in

Poland who say they would welcome us there. We intend to buy a wagon in case flight is necessary."

Bauhin frowned. "You are wise to make such a contingency. Justice is never guaranteed in cases of religion."

———

Bauhin stayed on for another couple of hours, until Sebastian seemed more comfortable. When Sebastian finally slept, Bauhin took Marie by the arm and led her outside the room. "He seems stable now, but he must rest as much as possible. And one more thing. If Grataroli sends any more medicine for Sebastian, please refuse it."

"But why? Surely he is only trying to help us?"

Bauhin hesitated. "I believe these witches' brews he concocts do more harm than good. There is something about that man that makes me afraid. I don't think he is to be trusted. Please do not allow him— or any of his so-called medicines—anywhere near Sebastian."

"Should I tell Sebastian about this?"

"When he is stronger, I will explain my theory to him. Perhaps in a few days. But for now, we must simply let him rest. I must go, but call me *immediately* if anything changes."

Chapter 40
Days of Rest

The next day, Sebastian did as Bauhin advised. He rested. Marie kept him company. With food and drink off the menu, they spent their time reflecting on all that God had brought them through over the years and what might await them beyond this trial, whether in Switzerland or Poland. The children came and went, holding little conversations and reciting portions from books they'd read which they thought might cheer their father. Susanna, now twenty, and Nathaniel, fourteen, lingered longest. Both of them had inherited Eugenie's raven hair and chestnut eyes, but of the two, only Susanna had any memory of Eugenie, and even those were terribly faded.

Several other visitors came and went. The first was Oporinus, these days gray and stooped yet still having to bend to fit his tall frame up the narrow stairs. He clasped Sebastian's hand and sat on a stool by the bed.

"It's so good to see you, my friend," Sebastian said. "It has been too long."

"I'm sorry. I have been so busy trying to scrape up work just to keep my business alive. These days I am forced to search high and low and scratch around for something to print."

"What they have done to you is reprehensible. You must always be proud of how you have fought to share knowledge and give people access to books that contain it."

"I am indeed proud of that. And of the fact that I got to work with those who sought understanding ahead of wealth or comfort or power. Men such as yourself." His face carried a small smile, but it seemed to Sebastian to be an expression of sadness more than joy. Oporinus got to his feet, promising to return in the morrow.

Later in the day came Amerbach, his look worried as he surveyed Sebastian lying there.

"Basilius! Thank you for coming. Bauhin told me you were going to visit the senate and the council and seek to have the trial postponed till I am well. Were you successful?"

Basilius looked stricken. He stared only at the bedcover. "These men have hearts of flint. Their lack of compassion sickens me. They refused to budge, saying that the date set for the trial—the early date you insisted on—still holds. But I'm not finished with them yet. I shall visit them again—every day, if need be. In this case, I *will* get blood out of a stone."

Sebastian forced a smile. "You're a good man, Basilius. I do thank God for you often."

———

Friday provided another day of rest, with Sebastian moving little and sleeping much. His fever ground on, but he had begun to take a little thin soup, just a few spoonfuls at a time. Still, he was successfully keeping that down, which buoyed everyone's spirits. Three or four spoonfuls seemed to be the limit. Beyond that, the nausea and burning ache in his stomach would return.

Chapter 41
The Reunion

That Saturday began with another visit from Amerbach. He entered the room looking defeated. Sebastian could guess his news before he spoke. "They won't budge," Amerbach said with a sigh. "They say you must attend on Monday as scheduled, as everything is arranged. It is almost as if they suggest you are hiding behind this illness to avoid trial."

"Pff," Sebastian huffed, wondering if the indignation flashing through him was showing in his eyes. "Then I shall be there, even if I have to crawl my way to the university!"

Amerbach didn't linger long.

About noon, the sound of a horse's hooves stopped outside the house, followed by a pounding on the front door. Loud, animated conversation rose to the bedroom from the kitchen below. He sat up, trying to discern what was being said. Within a few seconds, he heard the clomp of riding boots marching up the stairs, their leather soles heavy on each wooden tread.

The handle of the bedroom door turned. It inched open. A face appeared. A familiar face. A face sitting above the square shoulders of André Zebedee. He stepped inside, followed by a grinning Bauhin.

"André! What are you doing here?"

André's face broke into an even more expansive grin. "You did write to me suggesting I come, so why are you acting so surprised? When I got your letter, I rode like the wind. I must have covered the distance from Nyon to here in record time."

"Yes, I heard of your move to Nyon. But what prompted you to go there?" Sebastian's face crinkled.

"I got tired of constantly battling Beza's carping theologians in Lausanne, so I'm back to pastoring a flock of God's people—ordinary, humble, unpretentious folk—in Nyon."

"I am so glad! It is so good to see you again, my friend. Have you seen Marie? She will be glad too. Look! The three of us together again, just as in Lyon.

"Lyon! But we will never be that young again. Nor so full of hope."

"Except perhaps for this man," Bauhin interjected, pointing at Sebastian. "Despite everything, he has managed to keep his courage and his ideals intact, though it has cost him dearly."

"Yes, yes, you are right. Sebastian has proven himself braver than any of us." André's expression turned sad. "But Jean tells me that you are quite unwell, and that he believes it is the unrelenting persecutions by Calvin and Beza that have carried you here."

Sebastian gave a little shrug. "Perhaps. They have many supporters who carry out their work for them in Basel. They are determined to convict me of heresy. We are thinking about fleeing to Poland if the situation does not resolve."

"Poland? Yes, I can understand. While liberty erodes everywhere else, they seem to grow in tolerance there."

"Many of my students have returned to Poland, taking my writings with them. I'm grateful my books are proving helpful there, for between Calvin and the Inquisition, they have banned and burned my works just about everywhere else in Europe."

Over André's shoulder, Bauhin studied Sebastian, an odd expression on his face. He finally stepped forward, his gaze intent on Sebastian. "I want to tell you something about your writings, Sebastian. I know much heartache has come to you through them. Most have been suppressed or destroyed, and your name has been reviled. But I believe—I have a firm conviction—that one day your writings will be viewed as godly and prophetic. One day all you have written will be regarded with the honor it deserves. As will you. One day books will be written *about you* and all you have stood for." Tears trickled down Bauhin's cheeks as he spoke.

Sebastian had never seen his friend so emotive before. His own cheeks felt flushed and his eyes stung. "Those are kind and generous words, Jean. But I think if even one small syllable of Christ's mercy and love have been spoken or written through me, that would be reward enough."

By early afternoon, Sebastian was feeling so hungry that he ate a whole bowl of soup—as they all did. The long-delayed reunion of Bauhin, André, Sebastian and Marie carried on into the evening, until finally they could see that Sebastian was tiring.

André stood first. "We should leave now and let you rest." But then his eyes flashed. "What if we part with the bread and the wine? I brought some in my pack."

Bauhin looked dubious, his brow furrowed. He seemed on the verge of saying no, but Sebastian had pushed himself up on his elbows and smiled. "What a splendid idea. There is healing in the Eucharist, isn't there, André?"

André cocked one eyebrow, as if unsure of his meaning. But then he shrugged and reached down into his pack. He produced a bottle, which he uncorked, a small loaf of bread wrapped in linen, and a little platter. Marie rushed down to the kitchen and retrieved four cups. André then poured the wine into the cups and broke the bread onto the wooden plate.

Bauhin leaned forward. "Not too much for Sebastian. His stomach should still be resting."

André nodded and passed the platter of bread to each person, followed by a cup. A holy stillness had descended on the room. The four of them, bound together by a history of love and pain and loss, remained still for several long moments. Then André began to pray quietly.

"God of mercy and deliverance, thank you for these rich lives you have given us and for the love you have shown us. You are a God of grace and compassion. Right now, we lift Sebastian before you and ask that your love would protect him, hold him, and heal him. In Jesus's name we pray. Amen."

They each partook of the bread then drank the wine slowly, all of them lost in their own memories, hopes and fears.

When they had finished, each eye shone, each face caught somewhere in the arc between sorrow and joy. Bauhin broke the stillness. "We should let Sebastian rest now. Let's return in the morning."

After his friends left, Sebastian sank into a deep sleep. Marie lit several candles, placing them on the bureau near their bed, then gently got into bed next to him. Near midnight, Sebastian groaned. She felt him rolling sideways, as if in search of the bedside pail. As he began to retch, she pushed herself out of bed and hurried to his side. Frozen with horror, she watched as a stream of red liquid spilled from his mouth, followed by another, and then another. She stumbled backward, calling Nathaniel's name over and over, yelling for him to run to Bauhin's house and bring him back immediately.

By the time Nathaniel and Bauhin returned, the vomiting had slowed a little. But every few minutes, Sebastian still reached for the bucket. His whole body was soaked with sweat and his heart raced as if it would burst. Bauhin watched as Sebastian drew breath in shallow gasps. Gradually the gasps began to slow, and Sebastian fell back into another fitful sleep.

Both Marie and Bauhin kept watch until the small hours of the morning had arrived. As the hours passed, they could see Sebastian's breathing grow ever shallower, punctuated by little groans. Every half hour or so, another bout of vomiting blood would occur. Finally, the vomiting turned back to retching, then slowed, then ceased.

Sebastian descended into sleep, this time so deep they could not wake him. Marie and Bauhin spoke his name, trying to coax him back to wakefulness. But his face grew more and more masked, more and more phantom-like, as if his spirit were departing.

As dawn approached, his breath slowed to the point of imperceptibility. Bauhin leaned forward and began to rub Sebastian's chest above where his heart resided, while Marie called his name over and over. He responded to neither. He lay motionless. Once more, Bauhin placed a hand on Sebastian's chest and leaned forward to place his ear there too.

Bauhin slowly sat back onto his stool by the bed, silent. He turned to Marie, his face a picture of grief. He shook his head. A burbled cry welled up from Marie's throat, and she collapsed on top of Sebastian, sobbing. Ten minutes passed as she cradled him and wept.

Eventually Bauhin placed a gentle hand on her arm. "His heart has given out. Such a huge heart, but it has given out. In the end it was quick. That is a mercy, Marie. Really it is." Tears coursed down his face.

In his forty-eighth year, early on Sunday morning, the 29th of December 1563, Sebastian Castellio had breathed his last.

Chapter 42
The Triumphant March

Marie sat in the house and received their friends. It had still been early when Bauhin sent a message to André to tell him Sebastian had died just before dawn. André immediately mounted a horse and came to comfort Marie and farewell one of his oldest, dearest friends.

As the morning sun struggled to climb the winter sky, Marie felt the sorrow of the whole city. Many were rocked by the news of his death, for few knew he'd even been ill. While some claimed it was God's punishment for his heresy, others assured Marie that God had rescued him out of the hands of those who had accused him of heresy. At the university, she was told, his students wept at the news, gathering in little groups, talking about how they should farewell their beloved teacher. Some of the Polish students, with whom he had been especially close, sent a message begging Marie to let them assist with the funeral.

Amerbach came next to see Marie. He'd gone angrily to the university to thump on the doors of Borrhaus, Sphyractes, and Wissenburg. He also made a point to speak with Ulrich Coccius—Simon Sulzer's brother-in-law and the university's newly appointed rector—confident he would surely listen. He presented them with three demands, he told Marie. He ordered them to restore Sebastian's salary indefinitely and pay it directly to her in support of the family, to contribute toward the funeral, and to farewell Sebastian with the honor he deserved.

"'Or so help me God,' I said to them, 'I will use my family name to make your lives a misery.' And so, my dear Marie"—he covered her hands with his—"all the costs of the funeral are covered, and you and the children will be provided for. Now I must say my farewell to Sebastian."

The day of the funeral, wisps of mist lifted off the languid Rhine. An assembly of teachers and students along with a cast of townspeople gathered before the university. The cohort of Polish students had begged for the privilege of carrying Sebastian's casket. This granted, they lifted it proudly onto their shoulders.

Marie and the children stood behind them. Then came Bauhin, Zebedee, Oporinus, Amerbach, Perna and Curione, followed by Felix and Thomas Platter, then Simon Sulzer. Behind those came Nicholaas and Tanneke and the whole Netherlander community—all but van Schlor.

Parallel with the river, moving in a direction opposite to its flow, they set out on their slow walk to the cathedral. As the church came into sight, the students broke into a hymn of triumph, their words drawn from the New Testament:

> *In a moment, in the twinkling of an eye,*
> *The dead shall be raised, and we shall be changed.*
> *The corruptible must put on the incorruptible,*
> *The mortal must put on the immortal.*
> *When He appears,*
> *We shall be like him.*
> *Then we shall say,*

"Death is swallowed up in victory!"
And then we shall say,
"O death, where is thy sting?"
And then we shall say,
"O grave, where is thy victory?"

As they entered the cathedral cloister, their voices rang off the walls and columns and galleries, up to the vaulted ceiling, the volume growing ever louder until they reached the sepulchre of marble and stone that Simon Sulzer and Ulrich Coccius had insisted be built. As they lowered Castellio's body into his resting place, a second wave of singing swelled, reaching a crescendo just as they slid the tomb's marble carapace into place.

———————

The students hadn't yet exhausted their passion to honor their mentor. Later that week, a young man, a certain Paul Cherler, wrote a long, poetic hymn of praise to his teacher and hero. Oporinus had gathered his few remaining resources for one final paean. Though warned by Borrhaus not to do so, he printed Cherler's poem with the most beautiful calligraphy he could design, distributing copies far and wide. From the words of the poem, a silver plaque was fashioned and affixed to the marble sepulchre. It served as a eulogy, a message that spoke of a man of intellect, of piety, of integrity. A man who believed in freedom. A man who believed that the godliness of love exceeds that of any single creed.

Afterword

As Sebastian Castellio had prophesied, France's religious conflict soon descended into civil war marked by appalling butchery. Killing between Catholics and Huguenots had been ebbing and flowing since the 1530s, punctuated by savage massacres at Mérindol (1545), Vassy (1562), Michelade (1567), and the truly horrific Saint Bartholomew's Day Massacre of 1572 in which up to thirty thousand Protestants were slaughtered. Several colloquies and negotiations were attempted, but finding compromise between the two sides proved impossible. Calvin and Beza had thrown themselves behind the cause of recruiting and arming the Huguenot forces, convinced that military victory rather than negotiation was all that could secure a future for France's Protestants. Castellio's book—which called for tolerance and peacemaking in the name of Christ—had been banned and burned by both sides. His cry in the wilderness had fallen on deaf ears.

In the years between 1562 and 1598, between two and four million French citizens perished in the religious battles and the famines that followed. In 1568, a savage war of independence erupted in the Low Countries between occupying Spanish Catholics and Dutch Calvinists, with an estimated 600,000 deaths. Terrible as these numbers are, they pale in comparison to the ten to twelve million people who died in the Thirty Years' War (1618-1648) that occurred half a century later between Catholics and Protestants across Germany, Bohemia, and surrounding states. Another half million or so people perished in the religio-political violence that rocked Britain and Ireland from 1639 to 1651. The Protestant Reformation, which had dawned with the promise of freedom and enlightenment, had now descended into some of the worst bloodletting Europe had ever seen. In the 154 years from 1561 to 1715, Europe only saw thirty years of freedom from significant warfare.

After Castellio's death, there was an ongoing effort by Beza and his followers to deride Castellio's name and suppress his writings. In fact, not long after his death, Castellio's tomb was opened and badly damaged. Some sources say it happened accidentally during cathedral renovations. Other sources say it was an act of deliberate desecration by Beza's followers.

In 1564, Beza wrote a hagiographic biography of John Calvin in which he presented him as a man of extraordinary saintliness, even to the point of claiming that Calvin and Idelette had had a celibate marriage. (In fact, in 1542 the couple had had a baby son, Jacques, who sadly survived only two weeks.) Throughout his life, Beza continued to slander Castellio, urging Reformed believers to not engage with the man's heretical writings. Beza's influential biography shaped opinions toward both Calvin and Castellio for centuries afterward. Calvin became an orthodox hero; Castellio, a dangerous heretic.

In 1559, Beza became head of the academy in Geneva. A few years later, when Calvin died in 1564, Beza succeeded him as head of the Company of Pastors. Beza was determined that Reformed churches and ministers should pursue pure doctrine—"changing nothing"—just as Calvin had urged. Beza continued to raise resources in order to arm the Huguenot forces in France. He engaged in heated arguments with Lutheran scholars over doctrines such as the Eucharist and predestination. When Beza died in 1605, he was laid to rest in a simple grave in one of the cloisters of Saint Peter's Cathedral in Geneva.

Late in the sixteenth century, Castellio's writings gained a foothold in the Low Countries, particularly among Dutch Christians who grew tired of endless religious conflict. Several of his works were translated and printed there. The foremost supporter of Castellio in the Netherlands was Dirck Coornhert, a hero of the Dutch resistance against the Spanish Catholic forces. Coornhert spoke out against the persecution Dutch Calvinists were inflicting on the other religious groups in the Netherlands. In the late sixteenth century, the Netherlands, alongside Poland and Bohemia, gained a reputation as one of Europe's most tolerant nations.

Castellio's final book, *The Art of Doubting*, was to be the summation of his life's thought but was never completed. Only a rough manuscript survived him. Though portions were printed in the following years, it was only in the late twentieth century that the manuscript was printed in full. In this work, Castellio reflects on the nature of faith, reason, and experience. As always, he advocates for freedom of conscience and belief while decrying those who hold that there can only be one right interpretation of Scripture—theirs. Castellio argued that we must approach the Bible with humility, with an awareness of our fallibility, and with the honesty to admit that some parts of it are ambiguous and opaque. This, he proposed, will help us to see that persecuting those who hold differing ideas is both hypocritical and absurd. "Christ," he wrote, "calls his followers to a life of love and mercy, not to a life of dogmatic certitude."

The major characters in *Fire and Faith* are, indeed, based on real people whose lives played significant roles in the period covered (see the List of Historical Characters and Events section below). I have tried to stay true to what we know of those characters' thoughts, actions and personalities as revealed through their writings or what others wrote of them. However, *Fire and Faith* is a novelized version of events in which I speculate on motivations and invent otherwise unrecorded interactions and conversations between characters. Some of the characters in this story have had much noted about them in the historical record, others very little.

For example, of Eugenie (actually spelled *Huguine*) and Marie almost nothing is known other than their names, so I have invented much. The exact manner of Eugenie's death is not recorded by history, but we do know that Nathaniel was born in March of 1549 and that Eugenie's death occurred that same month. I have also been creative toward the end of the story concerning Sebastian's death. It is believed that he died of a perforated stomach ulcer, perhaps accompanied by heart failure. It was believed by his friends that the stress of persecution and the immanent heresy trial were major factors in his premature death. Could he have been poisoned by Gugliemo Grataroli? None of his contemporaries ever suggested this. In *Fire and Faith*, this insinuated plot device was created by me. But what we do know is that Grataroli disliked Castellio intensely, seeing him as an enemy of "the true faith" (i.e., Calvinism).

Grataroli was indeed in correspondence with Calvin and Beza, advising Calvin on his many health ailments. And he did act as an informant for them concerning the "traitors" in Basel. Adam van Bodenstein was indeed the man who brought the final heresy charges against Castellio—and was quite possibly in conversation with Grataroli, for they had much in common. It has always been a mystery as to why Bodenstein turned on Castellio, for when he first returned to Basel, he was friendly toward him and seemed supportive of the idea of tolerance. Nobody has been able to explain why he turned so dramatically hostile.

The remarkable story of David Joris living in Basel under the assumed identity of Jan van Brugge is largely as I have written it. Concerning van Schlor, it is widely accepted that it was he who betrayed Jan van Brugge's identity to the authorities, and he was indeed driven out of the Netherlander community as a result. However, the collaboration between him and Grataroli/Bodenstein is my creation.

As I have written, Grataroli and Bodenstein were both physicians, alchemists and astrologers. Both continued to write books and practice their esoteric disciplines following Sebastian's death, but not without controversy. In 1564, Adam von Bodenstein was expelled from the faculty of Basel University and from the city's Council of Medicine for promoting and practicing alchemy without permission. In 1567, Gugliemo Grataroli was appointed Dean of the University's Medical Faculty—a contentious appointment. At the end of that year, he was rebuked by Rector Simon Sulzer for criticizing Basel's church and for speaking words that denigrated the memory of Sebastian Castellio.

Apocalyptic fever was rife in the sixteenth century, and it came with an astrological twist. Conjunctions of Saturn and Jupiter occur every twenty years, but the conjunction of 1563 was the last in the water signs (Cancer, Scorpio, Pieces) and that of 1583 was to be the first in the fire signs (Aries, Leo, Sagittarius). This was seen by many as heralding apocalyptic calamity, the end of the age and the coming of the Antichrist.[1] John Calvin would not have agreed with Grataroli's (or Bodenstein's) belief in astrology. In his writings, Calvin decries the use of "judicial astrology" for prognostication. However, Calvin was willing to believe that astrology could be useful in the diagnosing and treatment of bodily ailments, thus his openness to Grataroli's medical advice.

John Calvin has always been a figure who divides. To many, he is a theological genius and a hero of the Protestant Reformation. To others, he was a tyrant willing to use any means to silence those who opposed—or even questioned—his ideas. To some, Geneva was a paradise of Christian order and discipline. For example, John Knox, the founder of Scottish Presbyterianism, visited and wrote that Geneva "is the most perfect school of Christ that ever was on earth since the days of the apostles." To others, however, Calvin's Geneva was a place of oppression and dark intolerance. According to historian E. William Monter, between 1559 and 1569, one in fifteen citizens was summoned before the consistory, and around one in twenty-five excommunicated.[2]

Born in 1509, Calvin lost his mother when only six years old. A precocious intellect, he left home at fourteen to attend Paris's College de la Marche. The schools and colleges he attended were austere and disciplinarian, and Calvin was extraordinarily studious. Fellow students nicknamed him "the accusative case," as he was known to chastise less studious peers for their laziness.[3] His father, Gerard, an abrupt, argumentative and controlling man, often found himself at odds with the local Catholic hierarchy for whom he worked. In fact, he was excommunicated by the local bishop shortly before his death. The family had to argue for their father's right to be buried in consecrated ground.

John Calvin's intense study of the Bible steadily drew him in the direction of Protestantism. In the face of rising persecution, he slipped out of France and made for Basel, where he flourished in the intellectual freedom he could never have found in his homeland. At this stage, Calvin had his heart set on a life of scholarship. But in the year 1535, traveling near Geneva, he was to have a fateful encounter with the iconoclastic Guillaume Farel. The Farel that confronted John Calvin that day was every inch the Old Testament prophet. He argued with Calvin that he was not born for a life of quiet study, but was meant to support him, Guillaume Farel, to bring the fullness of the Reformation to Geneva and beyond. Taken aback, Calvin resisted, insisting that his gift was to assist the church through a life of scholarship. At that, Farel broke into something between a prophesy and a threat. "I call upon God to curse your studies and damn the work of your pen. I warn ye: if you abandon his church, God will abandon you." Perhaps this was the real moment of Calvin's divine call, that moment that would give him such confidence in the face of all future opposition.

By September 1536, the two had relocated to Geneva. Their work was feverish, stripping churches of every vestige of idolatry, the city of every hint of Catholicism or heathenism. For a tumultuous two years, they battled with Geneva's council over who had the right to enforce public morality and excommunicate sinners. By April 1538, this had spilled into a fiery argument over how the upcoming Easter communion should be administered. The council ordered the two to follow the ceremony they shared with the city of Bern. Calvin and Farel refused, believing the unleavened bread they were being asked to distribute was too Catholic. As a protest, they served no communion at all. The tumult resulted in them being expelled— Calvin to Strasbourg, Farel to Neuchâtel. However, Geneva remained in such a fractious and dissolute state that Calvin was called back there (with Ami Perrin leading the charge from the council and de la Mere from the pastors) in September 1541.

Calvin passed away on May 27, 1564, five months after his former protégé Sebastian Castellio. For years, Calvin's health—never great—had been deteriorating. He was in constant pain from hemorrhoids, constipation, kidney stones, migraines, malarial fevers and tuberculosis. Ulcerated veins and crippling gout made walking near impossible in his final year. Despite this, he insisted on being carried to Saint Pierre, where he preached to the congregation from a chair even in his final months. On April 27, Calvin called the magistrates to his bedside. He asked them to forgive him for his quarrelsomeness and vehemence, and enjoined them to remember that he'd always meant well. On April 28, he called the Company of Pastors to his bedside. He urged the pastors to hold tightly to all that he had taught them. "Change nothing, make no innovations ... because all changes are dangerous."[4]

One of Calvin's greatest fears was that his resting place would become a site of veneration among his followers. To avoid this happening, he begged Beza to have him buried without ceremony among the unmarked graves of the Plainpalais, between the plague hospital and the place of execution. The plan was successful. Within a year, visitors and locals alike were unable to locate Calvin's final resting place.

Concerning the fascinating and tragic story of Michael Servetus, I recommend the works listed below by Marian Hillar. Servetus was a prodigy who, by age sixteen, had mastered Latin, Greek and Hebrew. He studied the Bible, the Koran and the works of the church fathers. Apprenticed to notable Doctor of Theology, Juan de Quintana, he grew disillusioned with the opulence and political maneuvering he witnessed among the Catholic Church hierarchy. He became convinced that the Christian faith had been made not more accurate but more erroneous by the church councils Emperor Constantine and his successors had convened from the fourth century onward. He also sought to make the Christian faith more plausible to the Jewish and Moorish communities he'd grown up with in Spain.

In 1532, he published *Dialogues on the Trinitarian Error* and was promptly placed on the Spanish Inquisition's list of heretics, ordered to be arrested and burned. He adopted a new alias, Michael Villeneuve, and traveled to France. At the University of Paris, he studied anatomy as well as mathematics, astrology and geography, and was the first European to describe the system of human pulmonary circulation. While at the University of Paris, he encountered another young man on the rise, John Calvin. He found Calvin's theology intriguing and his blazing intensity matched Servetus's own.

He took it upon himself to befriend Calvin and offer him the benefit of his biblical insights—much to Calvin's annoyance.

Hunted by the French and Spanish Inquisitions because of his writings, Servetus traveled to Lyon and then in 1542 to the town of Vienne, where he lived under an assumed name as a highly regarded physician. Still intrigued by his French college-mate, John Calvin, he began a correspondence with him. He sent Calvin a copy of his book *The Restoration of Christianity*.[5] In his letters, he argued that both Catholics and Protestants had adopted many nonbiblical ideas. His letters were also critical of Calvin's book, *The Institutes*. Outraged, Calvin (via the cousins Trie and Arneys) sent letters and pages from Servetus's *The Restoration of Christianity* in order to betray him and his identity to the Catholic authorities in Vienne. Calvin wrote a letter to Farel in which he promised to have Servetus executed should he ever come to Geneva.[6]

Servetus was arrested and imprisoned in Vienne and interrogated by the Dominican Grand Inquisitor, Brother Ory. Ory was infamous for having said, "If dead books may be committed to flames, how much more live books, that is to say, men?" Servetus pulled off a daring escape. Using the prison's outdoor privy, he climbed on its roof and leaped over the adjoining wall. Almost inexplicably, he then made his way to Geneva.

———

Of Castellio's surviving children, only one leaves an extensive historical record.[7] His youngest son, Frederick, showed some of his father's talent for music and poetry. In 1589, Frederick was promoted to the Chair of Rhetoric at Basel University and, in 1595, to the Chair of Eloquence. He indeed exceeded his father's ability to speak fluent German.

We know little more of Nathaniel, other than that, in 1564 or 1565, he devoted himself to painstakingly making copies of his father's letters and pamphlets. By so doing, he helped ensure their survival.

Three letters survive from Sebastian's youngest daughter, Sara, written in the late 1570s through 1580, penned in a neat hand and eloquent German. The first letter was to her guardian, Jean Bauhin, describing her work in the household of a certain woman of Duisburg and how she and Bonifacius had traveled there via Strasbourg, where they had searched without luck for their brother Thomas. Thomas was apparently working in Strasbourg as an assistant to a local artisan.

Sara's second letter was an affectionate missive to her mother, Marie, who was now living in the Bauhins' family home. She describes her happiness in Germany, her confidence in God, but also her homesickness. She longed to be reunited with her other siblings and, above all, with her mother. She reported that her brother Bonifacius was doing well working as a tailor. She begged Marie to write to her soon, as she missed her terribly.

The third letter from Sara was written to Basilius Amerbach in 1580, informing him of her and Bonifacius's intention to return to Basel. Sara did indeed return. In 1594, she married a Basel printer by the name of Georg Müssner.

Historically, how important was Sebastian Castellio's life and work? As far as we know, he was one of the first Europeans to write and argue for freedom of conscience and thought, and for the importance of religious toleration. In a period of extraordinary religious hatred and violence, he advocated for peacemaking and dialogue. Sebastian Castellio is one of those rare figures who had the courage to stand against the prevailing tide of his time. Some writers trace a line of thought from Castellio's writings to Dirck Coornhert, Baruch Spinoza, Roger Williams, John Milton, John Locke, Pierre Bayle, and eventually Voltaire, thinkers deeply engaged in the fight for freedom of conscience and, eventually, for human rights. The English philosopher Locke was known to possess several works by Castellio and to use Castellio's Latin Bible for study. It was Locke's writings that were so deeply influential on the shaping of the American Declaration of Independence.[8]

Why then are Castellio's name and writings so relatively unknown? Largely because Calvin and Beza were extraordinarily successful in linking his persona and his words to the fearful concept of heresy. For the next three centuries, it was considered too dangerous to risk one's reputation by referencing Castellio's writings. In many ways, Sebastian Castellio's name and work were not rehabilitated until 1892, when French scholar Ferdinand Buisson published *Sébastien Castellion, Sa Vie Et Son Œuvre*. And more recently, in 2016, the city of Basel placed a plaque to the memory of Sebastian Castellio close to Saint Alban's Church in a lane renamed Castellio's Way. In five languages, the plaque repeats Castellio's simple words: "To kill a man is not to defend a doctrine, but to kill a man."

---

1. E.g., see Aston, M. *The Fiery Trigon Conjunction: An Elizabethan Astrological Prediction.*
2. See, Monter, W. The Consistory of Geneva, 1559-1569, *Bibliothèque d'Humanisme et Renaissance,* 38 (1976): 467-484.
3. See, Stockwell, *The Cities of Calvin,* p. 22.
4. See, John L. Thompson, "Patriarchs, Polygamy, and Private Resistance: John Calvin and Others on Breaking God's Rules," *Sixteenth Century Journal* 25, no. 1 (1994): 3.
5. After Servetus's burning, an intense hunt took place to make sure every copy of *The Restoration of Christianity* was destroyed. In fact, only three copies remained in all of Europe. Nancy and Lawrence Goldstone tell the remarkable story of these three books' smuggling and survival down through the centuries in *Out of the Flames* (Broadway Books, 2002).
6. *"Should this man ever come to Geneva, as much as it is in my power, I will make sure he does not depart this city alive."* Calvin's letter to Farel, 13 February 1546. See *https://www.gutenberg.org/files/45463/45463-h/45463-h.htm#Page_31*
7. On the legacy of Sebastian and Marie's children. Much here is drawn from Hans Guggisberg, *Sebastian Castellio 1515-1563*, pp. 206-209; and from Schaff, Philip, *History of the Christian Church*, (Oak Harbour, WA: Logos Research Systems, Inc.) 1997, chapter XV, section 126.
8. On Castellio as a pioneer of religious toleration, author Perez Zagorin calls Castellio "the first hero" in the long and costly fight for the toleration of those with differing beliefs. Zagorin, Perez. *How the Idea of Religious Toleration Came to the West*, p. 93.

Acknowledgments

To my manuscript group—Ken, Jennifer, Janean, Jo, and Christine—for all their helpful feedback, and to Diane Brown for her guidance in the art of writing. To my early readers: Brett Knowles, Christian Auer, Markus Meury, Neville Walker, and Janet Cornwall. To Jason Porterfield (*Fight Like Jesus*) for all his wisdom and encouragement; to Dr. Michael Bruening (the Castellio Correspondence Project; *Refusing to Kiss the Slipper*) for his encouragement and suggestions. To Dave Andrews for his inspiration, passion and Castellio-like life. To Sonia and Claude Corneille for being wonderful hosts and guides around Strasbourg. To Jérémy Kohler of the Médiathèque Protestante for allowing me into the archives to see Castellio's writings. To Christian and Janice Auer (along with Gudrun Ahlers) for being beautiful hosts and guides around Basel, including into the archives with Castellio's handwritten notes at the University of Basel Library. To the staff at Calvin College in Geneva for their help and suggestions. To my editor D'Ann Mateer for her oh-so-careful eye and expert guidance. And of course, last but not least, to Susan for her patience and support on this whole adventure!

List of Historical Characters and Events

Amerbach, Basilius – The son of Bonifacius (see below), he followed in his father's footsteps as a jurist and teacher of law at Basel University. Upon his father's death in 1562, he inherited the family's "cabinet of curiosities," expanding it with more art, antiques and novel pieces. He had an ornate wooden box built to house thousands of coins, which was a wonder in itself. (These are now housed in the Basel Historical Museum). Sebastian Castellio became Basilius's tutor shortly after arriving in Basel.

Amerbach, Bonifacius – A leading jurist and scholar in Basel. Amerbach was the son of the pioneering Basel printer Johannes Amerbach. Bonifacius taught at the University of Basel from 1525. During the Protestant iconoclasm of 1529, he was able to save works of art (including Holbein's) from destruction, and established a large collection in his famous "cabinet of curiosities." A close friend of Erasmus, he inherited his collection of books and became trustee of his estate following his death. Amerbach became a close friend and supporter of Castellio's.

Anabaptism – Like Lutheranism and Calvinism, Anabaptism was a sixteenth century Protestant breakaway from the Roman Catholic Church, though many regarded them as neither Catholic nor Protestant. Originating in Switzerland in 1525, their distinctives were voluntary adult baptism, building community, separation of church and state, and New Testament discipleship. Most branches of Anabaptism developed a very strong commitment to nonviolence based on Christ's Sermon on the Mount (the Gospel of Matthew, chapters 5–7).

Augustine of Hippo (St. Augustine) AD 354–430 – The most widely read and followed theologian of antiquity, whose influence on the shape of Catholic, Orthodox and Protestant theology is immense, even today. Outstanding in eloquence, Augustine was a brilliant Latinist but not proficient in Greek (the language of the New Testament). Augustine's (mis)interpretation of Luke 14:23 and Matthew 13:24–30 led to his infamous line "There is a righteous persecution which the church inflicts upon the impious. ... Moreover, she [the church] persecutes in a spirit of love." His explanation legitimized the use of religious force and violence for centuries to come (see, Augustine, *Letter 185 to the Tribune Boniface*, 2:11).

Bauhin, Jean – An outstanding French physician. Prior to fleeing France, he was personal physician to Jeanne d'Albert, Queen of Navarre (sister of Francis, King of France). He married Jeanne Fontain, and fled to Basel after his conversion to Protestantism. Their two eldest sons (Jean and Gaspard) went on to become famous physicians and botanists, writing pioneering books full of sketches on plant typology. They taught at Basel University. Jean Bauhin was one of Sebastian Castellio's closest friends and became guardian to the Castellio family following Sebastian's death.

Berchem, Anna van – Wealthy heiress and close friend of Jan van Brugge. She followed him into exile to Basel.

Beza, Theodore – A Latinist, poet and jurist, Beza converted to Calvinism and journeyed to Geneva to work with John Calvin in 1548. Thereafter, he spoke of Calvin as his "spiritual father." Beza was appointed Professor of Greek by Viret at the Lausanne Academy in 1549. By 1558, due to conflict with the city council over his attempts to establish a Genevan-style consistory in Lausanne, he returned to Geneva. As Calvin's right-hand man, apologist, and defender, he inherited leadership of the movement when Calvin died. He was deeply opposed to everything Sebastian Castellio stood for.

Blesdijk, Nicholaas – Son-in-law and secretary to Jan van Brugge and husband of Tanneke, but also a gifted linguist, thinker and writer in his own right.

Bodenstein, Adam von – Medical doctor and alchemist with a deep interest in astrology. Having grown up in Basel, he was the son of Andreas Karlstadt and family friend of Wolfgang Wissenburg.

Borrhaus, Martin – German theologian who, in 1544, became professor of Old Testament at Basel University and was the city's chief censor. In 1546, 1553 and 1564 he served as the University's rector.

Brugge, Jan van – Dutch artist, business man and thinker who fled to Basel to escape religious persecution in the Netherlands. Married to **Dirkgen**, father of **Tanneke** (married to **Nicholaas Blesdijk**) and **Clara.**

Bucer, Elisabeth – Wife of Martin Bucer (see below) and a remarkable woman who Bucer credited with making both himself and his theological writings what they were. On her deathbed (from the plague), she urged a distraught Martin to marry her close friend Wilbrandis Capito.

Bucer, Martin – A German Reformer based in Strasbourg, who sought reconciliation between the Catholic and Protestant churches. An early Protestant theologian and thinker, he wrote extensively. A fatherly character, he took Calvin under his wing following the latter's expulsion from Geneva to Strasbourg. In 1549, when Catholic powers retook Strasbourg, Bucer was exiled to England. Married to **Elisabeth** (see above) and then **Wilbrandis**.

Bullinger, Heinrich – Swiss Reformer, successor of Huldrych Zwingli as head of the Protestant Church of Zurich. A staunch opponent and polemicist against Catholics, Lutherans, and Anabaptists. Over time he drew increasingly closer to the views of John Calvin.

Calvin, John – The French Reformer whose systematic theological writings (particularly *The Institutes of Christian Religion*) were extremely influential on the later development of Protestantism. In the first edition of *The Institutes,* Calvin pleaded with the king of France to show clemency toward all those the Catholic Church persecuted, even toward Turks and Saracens! Yet, in a move indicative of his ever-increasing intolerance, Calvin deleted this passage from all subsequent editions of *The Institutes* (see, Hans Guggisberg, *Sebastian Castellio 1515 – 1563*, p. 82). Calvin married the Anabaptist widow, Idelette, who had two children from her former marriage. Calvin's brother, **Antoine**, features in the Strasbourg phase of this story.

Calvinism – Sometimes called Reformed Christianity, Calvinism is a major branch of Protestantism which follows the theological practices set down by John Calvin, Theo Beza and the generation that followed them (particularly in the Netherlands). Calvinism emphasizes the absolute sovereignty of God and the inerrancy of the Bible. Worldwide, Calvinism is made up more than one hundred million members across more than two hundred denominations (Presbyterian, Dutch Orthodox, Congregational to name but three). Calvinism is often defined by the five core tenets extrapolated in the seventeenth century, under the acronym TULIP:

Total depravity (fallenness) of mankind.
Unconditional (unearned) salvation of the elect (the chosen), and the unconditional damnation of the lost.
Limited atonement (Jesus died only for the elect and not for all).
Irresistible grace (an internal call to salvation which the elect are power-less to resist).
Perseverance of the saints (the assurance that the elect cannot lose their salvation no matter what they do or don't do).

Many later Calvinist thinkers did argue for greater religious tolerance. For example, Pierre Bayle (1647–1706) who was familiar with Castellio's writings (Zagorin, p. 271). In the year 1903, representatives of the Reformed Church erected a monu-ment in Geneva at Champel, on the corners of de la Roseraie and de Beau-Séjour avenues, on the spot where Michael Servetus was executed exactly 350 years earlier. The inscription reads:

As reverent and grateful sons of Calvin, our great Reformer, repudiating his mistake, which was the mistake of his age, and according to the true principles of the Reformation and the Gospel, holding fast to freedom of conscience, we erect this monument of reconciliation on this 27th of October 1903.

Over time, most Calvinist denominations have grown increasingly collegial and democratic in their leadership.

Capito, (Wil)brandis – The erudite Brandis was married and widowed four times. She first married scholar and humanist Ludwig Keller (died 1528), famous Protes-tant theologian and Reformer Johannes Oecolampadius (died 1531), Oecolampadius's friend Wolfgang Capito (died 1541), and finally Martin Bucer (died 1551). Brandis herself died from the plague in 1564.

Capito, Wolfgang – A German Protestant Reformer with a reputation for kindness, he sought to reconcile the Calvinist, Lutheran and Zwinglian factions. He also held talks with the Anabaptists. In 1523, he settled at Strasbourg, where he remained until his death. In 1532, Capito married Wilbrandis (**Brandis**) Rosenblatt, who, after Capito's death from plague, married Martin Bucer.

Carafa, Gian – Archbishop of Naples, future Pope Paul IV, Prefect of the Holy Office, he became known as "the father of the Roman Inquisition." Violent, austere and uncompromising, he was responsible for creating the first index of forbidden books. He confined Rome's Jews to a ghetto where they were required to wear yellow for identification. Later, as Pope, he helped ferment a ruinous war between France and Spain.

Castellio, Sebastian – Savoy-French thinker, classicist, philologist and Bible translator, he converted to the Reformed movement as a student and went in search of John Calvin. Initially a colleague and friend, Castellio risked his life to care for Calvin's family during the plague that tore through Strasbourg in 1541 (see, Guggisberg, *Sebastian Castellio, 1515–1563*, p. 26). Castellio later became a fierce critic of Calvin, becoming one of the first Europeans to write arguing for religious tolerance, freedom of conscience and—on biblical grounds—the immorality of persecuting those with heterodox beliefs.

Castellio's Children – Susanna, Nathaniel, Anna, Barbara, Sara, Bonifacius, Thomas, Frederic, and Jeanne (niece, adopted in 1558 at age 12).

Cherler, Paul – A student of Sebastian Castellio's at Basel University.

Church of England (Anglicanism) – One of the major branches of the sixteenth century Protestant Reformation, though it includes features of both Protestantism and Roman Catholicism. Under Henry VIII the Church of England broke with Rome largely because the pope would not grant Henry a divorce (from Catherine of Aragon). Wishing no great reform, Henry simply intended to replace Rome's authority over the English church with his own. After Henry's death, Thomas Cranmer (Archbishop) began changes that took the Church of England in the direction of the Reformation.

Colinet, Jean – Successor to Castellio as Rector of the College de Rive in Geneva. A supporter of Sebastian Castellio, he believed Calvin had treated his predecessor very badly. He spoke out against the mistreatment of Michael Servetus in Geneva before escaping to Basel.

Coornhert, Dirck – Dutch loyalist and patriot, theologian and a follower of Castellio's writings, he spoke out against the harsh treatment of religious dissenters by the Dutch Reformed church. He was responsible for having a number of Castellio's work translated into Dutch and printed from the 1580s onward.

Cordier, Mathurin – French-born theologian, teacher, humanist, and pedagogian active in Geneva before moving to the Academy in Lausanne, where he became the director. Both Calvin and Castellio regarded him as a mentor.

Curione, Celio - An Italian humanist, grammarian, editor, publisher, historian, and professor who wielded considerable influence upon the Italian Reformation. He had a controversial career, moving frequently to avoid denunciation and imprisonment. He finally settled in Basel, where he was admired as a publisher and editor of theological and historical writing and for his innovative teaching. He became Chair of Rhetoric at Basel University.

De la Mere, Henri – A rural pastor based outside Geneva (Foncenex). He led Geneva's Ministers in inviting Calvin back to Geneva, but despite this, Calvin disliked him and allowed his parish to fall into neglect. Married to Helene.

Erasmus, Desiderius – Dutch philosopher and Catholic theologian, he is considered one of the greatest scholars of the Renaissance (known as the "Prince of the Humanists"). He translated pioneering Latin and Greek editions of the New Testament, which raised questions which would be influential in both the Protestant Reformation and Catholic Counter-Reformation. He argued passionately for peace and brotherhood and for Europe to become a commonwealth of Christian love. The Reformers, particularly Luther, tried furiously to recruit him to Protestantism, but after initial openness, Erasmus came to see the Reformation as a source of division and enmity rather than peace or Christian love.

Farel, Guillaume – French evangelist, Protestant Reformer, and a founder of the Calvinist Church in the Neuchâtel and wider Geneva region, he was an iconoclast fanatically opposed to all things Catholic. He is famous for his fiery encounter demanding that Calvin join him in establishing the Reformation in the Geneva area, lest God's wrath descend.

Francis of Assisi – Born in 1181 into a wealthy Italian family in Umbria, Francis initially lived a pampered life as a military adventurer and playboy. After a series of mystical encounters, he began to distribute his family's wealth to the poor, leading to a breakdown in his relationship with his father. Soon after, he completely renounced "worldliness" and committed himself to following the teachings of Jesus. He began to gather like-minded followers. In 1210, he founded the Order of the Franciscans. In 1219, he followed the crusaders to Egypt and attempted to mediate between them and the Sultan al-Kamil.

Grataroli, Gugliemo – Medical doctor, alchemist, astrologer, spiritualist and physiognomist, he fled severe persecution in Italy and came to Basel. A prolific and well-known author on the above subjects, he briefly became Dean of Basel University's medical faculty in 1567.

Gribaldi, Matteo – An outstanding Italian legal scholar who taught and wrote extensively throughout Europe, he came to question the logicality and biblical basis of the Trinity, defending Michael Servetus's view and opposing Calvin's dogmatism and persecution of Servetus.

Grymoult, Léger – A former Augustinian monk who, after his conversion to Protestantism, fled persecution in France to Geneva. During a time of study in Basel he developed a friendship with Sebastian Castellio and a deep admiration for his writing, some of which he later helped edit and translate. He was again in Geneva at the time of Michael Servetus's burning, after which he fled back to Basel.

Huguenots – The name (of uncertain origin) given to French Calvinist Protestants by French Catholics in the sixteenth century. Initially a derisive term, Calvinist Protestants soon adopted and used it for themselves.

Joris, David – Mystic, artist, songwriter, he was also an important Anabaptist leader. A glass painter by trade, he practiced this work in the Low Countries and in England (1520-22). As a charismatic leader, he sought to unite the post-Münster Anabaptist factions, both militants and pacifists, under his authority (1536-1539). As a key Anabaptist leader, he was denounced as an "arch-heretic" and had a price placed on his head. He was hunted by Catholic and secular authorities while also being denounced by Lutherans and Calvinists. In the last period of his life (1544 onward), Joris became increasingly focused on an internal spirituality, seeing doctrine, ceremony, and externals as unimportant, with the state of one's heart being all that mattered before God.

Karlstadt, Andreas Bodenstein – An early Reformer, he was initially a close colleague of Luther's in Wittenberg. After Luther opposed him due to his iconoclasm and other idiosyncratic ideas, he fled to Zurich and then Basel. In 1534, he become minister of the Basel Cathedral, Professor of Hebrew, and University Dean. He remained in Basel until his somewhat odd death in 1541. While preaching his final sermon—and possibly feverish—he observed a demonic-figure roaming the cathedral and mocking him. Karlstadt was the father of **Adam Von Bodenstein.**

Luther, Martin – An Augustinian monk influenced by Erasmus's writings, Luther set the Protestant Reformation in motion by nailing his ninety-five theses of protest to the door of the Wittenberg Cathedral in 1517. (Whether this was a literal or figurative nailing is disputed.) Chief among his complaints was the church's sale of indulgences for forgiveness of sins along with a raft of other corruptions and misuses of the Bible. He challenged the authority of the pope, instead teaching that the Bible was the only authoritative source of divine truth. He taught that every vocation is sacred because all Christians are, in effect, priests. He translated the Bible from Latin into the German vernacular, making it more accessible to people, which had a tremendous impact on both the German church and German culture and encouraged multiple vernacular translations to follow.

Lutheranism – One of the largest branches of Protestantism arising in the sixteenth century and identifying with the teachings of Martin Luther. During the Reformation, Lutheranism became the state religion of numerous areas of northern Europe, especially Northern Germany and Scandinavia. Lutheran clergy often became civil servants, and Lutheran churches came under state sponsorship. Unlike Calvinism, Lutherans retain many liturgical practices and sacraments close to those of the Catholic Church. It is estimated that today there are over seventy-four million Lutherans in the world.

Melanchthon, Philip – German Reformer and a close colleague of Luther's, he is regarded as one of the four most important sixteenth century Reformers, along with Luther, Calvin and Zwingli. Regarded as gentle and conciliatory, Melanchthon emphasized grace and sought healing between various religious groups. As a result, he was often attacked for lacking firm convictions.

Meyer, Bernard – From a wealthy and influential family, he served as Bürgermeister (mayor) of Basel from 1548 to 1558. He also held key positions on the council and with other leading institutions in the city. From 1529 onward, he was committed to the Reformed denomination of Calvin.

Münster Rebellion – In 1534–1535, the German city of Münster was seized by a breakaway Anabaptist sect who, based on visions and prophesies, believed they were living in the last days. They believed that violence was necessary to establish a theocratic state in Münster prior to Christ's return. During their reign, polygamy and redistribution of goods was practiced—often by force. The city was retaken by combined Catholic, Lutheran, and mercenary forces in June 1535, and the rebellion's leaders were imprisoned or executed.

Müntzer, Thomas – German preacher and theologian in the early stages of the Reformation who opposed both Luther and Catholicism because he saw Luther as compromising too much with feudal authority. He was a leader in the peasant uprising of 1524–25 (see below), where he was captured, tortured and executed. Müntzer believed that the world was living in the last days, and it was the work of true believers to assist God in ushering in a new era of history.

Myconius, Oswald – Initially a teacher in Zurich and a close follower of Zwingli (who he witnessed die in battle), he moved to Basel following Zwingli's death and became professor of New Testament at Basel University. A conciliatory man, he sought the union of all Protestant groups.

Occhino, Bernadino – In 1538, he became Vicar General of the Catholic Capuchin Order, but increasingly his beliefs moved toward Protestant doctrine. In 1542, Cardinal Carafa demanded he come to Rome to answer charges made against him. On route, he found his friend (Cardinal Gasparo Contarini) dying, having been poisoned by inquisitors. He fled across the Alps to Geneva, eventually becoming pastor to the Italian refugee community in Augsburg. When that city was overrun by Catholic forces, he fled to England to pastor an Italian refugee community there. When the Catholic Queen Mary ascended the English throne, he fled to Basel in 1553, and later became pastor of an Italian refugee community in Zurich. A believer in free will, he wrote the book *Labyrinth,* undermining Calvin's idea of predestination. With the writing of *The Thirty Dialogues* in 1563 (which Castellio translated into Latin), he was charged with blasphemy and driven out of Zurich. He died in poverty in Moravia at the end of 1564.

Olivétan, Pierre-Robert – John Calvin's cousin, he was the first to translate the Bible into French from the Hebrew and Greek sources, for which Calvin wrote a Latin introduction.

Oporinus, Johannes – A brilliant man, the son of an artist, Oporinus initially worked as a proofreader for Froben, one of Basel's most celebrated printers, before later inheriting that mantle himself. He taught Latin and Greek at the university, and completed medical studies before resigning to focus on producing books. He was married and widowed three times before marrying Faustina Amerbach, daughter of Bonifacius, sister of Basilius. A devoted friend and supporter of Castellio's, he sadly died deeply in debt.

Ory, Brother Matthieu – From the Dominican Order, Brother Ory was appointed Grand Inquisitor for France in 1534. He is believed to have said, "If, then, dead books may be committed to flames, how much more live books, that is to say, men?"

Peasants' War – The peasant uprising in Germany (1524–25) was inspired by changes initiated by the Reformation. The poor of the land invoked divine law to demand agrarian rights and freedom from the oppression of landlords and nobles. The revolt was supported by Thomas Müntzer and Huldrych Zwingli but condemned by Luther, which contributed to its defeat by the armies of the princes. It is believed 100,000 peasants were killed by the princes.

Perna, Pietro – A leading Renaissance printer, editor and independent thinker who had fled from the Catholic Inquisition in Italy to Basel.

Perrin, Ami – From an old, wealthy, and noble Genevan family who had fought for its independence, Ami Perrin was a councillor and member of the *enfants de Geneve*. Initially an enthusiastic supporter of Calvin, he and the other *enfants* became opponents over many issues, notably increasing religious legalism and loss of liberty.

The Plague – Also known as the Black Death (or Pestilence, or Great Mortality), this was a vast pandemic caused by the bacteria Yersinia pestis, usually found in small mammals (mostly rats) and their fleas. It first swept across Eurasia and North Africa in the sixth century then again in the fourteenth. Thereafter, smaller outbreaks continually erupted in various parts of Europe and Africa. The second pandemic (1346) was the deadliest in human history, causing an estimated 75–200 million deaths. It was known as Black Death because of the gangrene that blackened flesh and as the Bubonic Plague because of the grossly swollen lymph nodes (buboes) it produced. Victims could be infected by flea bites, contact with contaminated body fluids, or by inhaling the respiratory drops of an infected person.

Platter, Felix – Son of **Thomas Platter** (see below), he was a talented botanist, physician, and anatomist. Felix eventually became one of the most distinguished physicians of Switzerland, leading a celebrated academic career at the University of Basel. As a student, he was indeed involved in stealing fresh corpses from a graveyard in Montpellier. He also wrote an early text on psychiatric ailments and the causes of hand-tendon disorders (Dupuytren's disease). Felix Platter's diary (still in circulation) describes witnessing the burning of David Joris while standing next to Sebastian Castellio.

Platter, Thomas – Like Castellio, having grown up in poverty, Thomas Platter went on to master several languages including Hebrew, Greek, and Latin. He was a gifted teacher. Along with Oporinus, he founded a notable early printing house in Basel.

Sattler, Michael – Formerly a German Benedictine monk, Sattler was one of the very earliest Anabaptist leaders and thinkers. He was particularly influential in the writing of the Schleitheim Confession. He was tortured and executed in 1527.

Schlor, Hendrick van – A Secretary to Jan van Brugge, he fled with van Brugge's entourage from the Netherlands to Basel. He was later expelled from the exiled Netherlander community.

Servetus, Michael – A brilliant and eccentric Spanish physician, cartographer, anatomist, linguist and polymath, he abandoned Catholicism in 1530 and moved toward Protestantism. But he held an unorthodox understanding of the Trinity which brought him into conflict with several Reformed leaders, particularly Calvin. As a result of his anatomical studies, he became the first European to describe the pulmonary circulation system in the human body (some seventy-five years before William Harvey).

Simons, Menno – A Roman Catholic priest from Friesland in the Low Countries, he became deeply disturbed by news of "re-baptizers" being persecuted and killed. This led him to search the Scriptures and come to agree with most Anabaptist beliefs. In 1536, he left the Catholic Church and joined the Anabaptists. Shocked by the violence at Münster and a subsequent sectarian battle in which his brother was killed, Menno renounced violence as incompatible with the gospel. By 1540, he was regarded as the most influential Anabaptist leader, after David Joris disappeared from public view. He was hunted by the authorities and had a price on his head. The movement he founded—the Mennonites—continued to be savagely persecuted. They went underground, becoming known as "the quiet in the land." Today the Mennonites have around 2.13 million members in 86 countries. The Mennonites, like the Quakers, are known as a "peace tradition" church, continuing to practice and advocate for peacemaking, nonviolence, and reconciliation.

Sphyractes, Johannes – A Professor of Law, he was Rector at the University of Basel in 1545 and again in 1563. Zealous in rooting out unorthodox beliefs, he wrote a virulent booklet in 1559 that condemned David Joris's many errors, a text widely circulated and read across Europe and as far away as England.

Sulzer, Simon – Head of the cathedral in Basel. Though the city was officially Reformed or Calvinist, Sulzer held Lutheran views and tried to mediate between the two factions. Opposed to religious persecution and the use of coercion, he defended Sebastian Castellio.

Sturm, Johannes – German Reformer and educator, he founded the Strasbourg Academy (or Gymnasium).

Villeneuve, Michael – A brilliant Spanish student, he studied medicine at the University of Paris at the same time in which John Calvin was studying law there.

Viret, Pierre – Viret was very instrumental in Lausanne's embracing of the Protestant faith. He was chief minister of the city and founder of the Lausanne Academy, where he taught theology. He was a friend and colleague of Calvin's.

Wissenburg, Wolfgang - Professor of New Testament at the University of Basel from 1541, he succeeded Andreas Bodenstein Karlstadt as pastor at the Church of Saint Peters in Basel from 1543 to 1548. He was elected rector of the university in 1536, 1549 and again in 1557.

Zebedee, André – A lifelong friend of Castellio, they first met in Lyon (according to Guggisberg, p. 120), possibly during 1536-38. He taught at the College de Guyenne 1533-34. In 1538 he was appointed pastor in Orbe. He taught at the Lausanne Academy from 1547-49. In 1552 he was appointed Pastor in Nyon. A fierce opponent of Calvin's doctrine of predestination, he held firmly to a Zwinglian (non-Catholic) understanding of the Eucharist.

Zurkinden, Nikolaus - From 1561 to 1565, he served as the town clerk of Bern. He worked to reconcile conflicts between Bern and Calvinist Geneva and between churches. Formerly a friend and supporter of Calvin, he was heavily influenced by Castellio's writings and later rebuked Calvin over the Servetus affair. He campaigned for tolerance toward religious nonconformists and allowed Anabaptist and Catholic preachers to teach openly and publicly in his jurisdiction. He denounced the use of violence between religious factions.

Zuttere, Pieter – A Dutch printer and writer who was in Geneva at the time of Servetus's execution, he helped author *A History of the Death of Michael Servetus*.

Zwingli, Huldrych – An early leader in the Reformation in Switzerland, Zwingli began to preach ideas to reform the Catholic Church in 1519. He was iconoclastic and attacked Catholic teaching (for example, on the Eucharist) at every opportunity. He was also fiercely critical of the Anabaptists and encouraged their persecution. In 1531, he launched an armed attack on Catholic cantons near Zurich and was killed in battle.

Select Bibliography

Aston, M. *The Fiery Trigon Conjunction: An Elizabethan Astrological Prediction.* Isis Journal (of the history of science, medicine and technology), Volume 61, No. 2, Summer 1970. University of Chicago Press, 1970.

Baber, John. *Luther and Calvin on Music & Worship.* Reformed Magazine, Volume 8, No. 26, June 25-July 1, 2006.

Balserak, J. *Geneva's Use of Lies, Deceit, and Simulation in their Efforts to Reform France, 1536-1563.* Harvard Theological Review, 112 (1), 76-100. https://doi.org/10.1017/S0017816018000354. University of Bristol, 2019.

Blacketer, Raymond A. *Blaming Beza: The development of definite atonement in the reformed tradition.* Chapter 5 in *From Heaven He Came and Sought Her: Definite Atonement in Historical, Biblical, Theological, and Pastoral Perspective.* Edited by D. Gibson and J. Gibson. Wheaton: Crossway, 2013.

Bonnet, Jules. *Project Gutenberg's Letters of John Calvin,* Volume II (of 4), compiled from the Original Manuscripts and Edited with Historical Notes. April 23, 2014 [eBook #45463]

Bruening, et al. *Castellio Correspondence Project* (an online, open-access, collaborative critical edition of Sebastian Castellio's correspondence). https://web.mst.edu/~bruening/Castellio%20Project/Index%20Page.htm

Bruening, Michael W. *Refusing to Kiss the Slipper - Opposition to Calvinism in the Francophone Reformation.* Oxford Studies in Historical Theology, 2021.

Burnett, Amy Nelson. *Simon Sulzer and the Consequences of the 1563 Strasbourg Consensus in Switzerland.* University of Nebraska – Lincoln. Originally published in Archive for Reformation History 83, pp. 154–179, 1992.

Burnett, Amy Nelson. *Teaching the Reformation: Ministers and Their Message in Basel, 1529-1629.* Oxford University Online, 2006.

Burnett, Amy Nelson (Editor). *John Calvin, Myth and Reality.* Papers of the 2009 Calvin Studies Society Colloquium. Cascade Books, 2009.

Calvin, John. *Institutes of the Christian Religion, Vol I & II.* Edited by John McNeill, translated by Ford Battles. The Library of Christian Classics. Westminster, 1960.

Castellio, Sebastian. *Concerning Heretics: Whether They are to be Persecuted and How They are to be Treated; a Collection of the Opinions of Learned Men, Both Ancient and Modern; an Anonymous Work. 1554.* Translated by Roland Bainton, Columbia University Press, New York, 1935.

Castellio, Sebastian. *Advice to a Desolate France. 1562.* Translated by Wouter Valkhoff. Introduction by Marius F. Valkhoff. Journal of Markets & Morality, Volume 19, Number 1 (Spring): 155–218, 2016.

Christie-Murray, David. *A History of Heresy.* Oxford University Press, 1989.

Coffey, John. *Scripture and Toleration between Reformation and Enlightenment.*

Published in Eliane Glaser, ed., *Religious Tolerance in the Atlantic World: Early Modern and Contemporary Perspectives;* pp 14-40. Palgrave, 2014.

Coggins, James R. *Toward a Definition of Sixteenth-Century Anabaptism: Twentieth-Century Historiography of the Radical Reformation. Journal of Mennonite Studies* Vol. 4, pp 183-207, 1986.

Cottret, Bernard. *Calvin: A Biography.* Translated by M. Wallace McDonald. William B. Eerdmans Publishing, 2000.

Curley, E. *Sebastian Castellio's Erasmian Liberalism.* Philosophical Topics, Vol. 31, No. 1/2, Modern Philosophy, pp. 47-73, SPRING AND FALL, 2003.

Cuthbertson, David. *A Tragedy of the Reformation.* Oliphant, Anderson & Ferrier, 1912.

Dickson, John. *Emperor Constantine.*https://podcasts.apple.com/us/podcast/undeceptions-with-john-dickson/id1478239058?i=1000554638385

Erasmus, Desiderius. *Querela Pacis/The Complaint of Peace,* 1521. Translated by T. Paynell (1802 edition). Available from https://en.wikisource.org/wiki/The_Complaint_of_Peace

Erdozain, Dominic. *A heavenly poise: radical religion and the making of the Enlightenment.* Intellectual History Review, 27:1, 71-96, 16 Jan 2017.

Erdozain, Dominic. *Jesus and Augustine: The God of Terror and the Origins of European Doubt.* Journal of Religious History, Vol. 41, No. 4, December 2017.

Fournier, É. *Persecuting Heretics in Late Antique North Africa: Tolerant Vandals and Intolerant Bishops?* pp 147-166 in *Inclusion and Exclusion in Mediterranean Christianities,* 400-800, ed. by Yaniv Fox and others. Turnhout: Brepols, 2019.

Freeman, C. A.D. 381. Heretics, Pagans and the Christian State. Pimlico, 2008

Funk, John F. *Menno Simon, The Complete Writings (Translated from the Original Dutch).* John Funk & Brother, 1871.

Gordon, Bruce & Marshall, Peter (Eds). *The Place of the Dead: Death and Remembrance in Late Medieval and Early Modern Europe.* Cambridge University Press, 2000.

Gordon, Bruce. *Calvin.* Yale University Press, 2009.

Gordon, Bruce. *To Kill a Heretic: Sebastian Castellio against John Calvin.* Censorship Moments: Reading Texts in the History of Censorship and Freedom of Expression. Ed. Geoff Kemp. London: Bloomsbury Academic, pp 55–62, 2015.

Graham M.F. *The Uses of Reform: 'Godly Discipline' and Popular Behavior in Scotland and Beyond,* 1560-1610. Brill, 1966.

Greene, Ainsworth. *Ecclesiastical Organisation of Geneva in the Time of Calvin.* Journal of the Presbyterian Historical Society (1901-1930), October, 1923, Vol. 11, No. 8, pp. 305-367.October, 1923. http://www.jstor.com/stable/23323403

Greyzel, S. *The Jews and Roman Law.* The Jewish Quarterly Review, Vol. 59, No. 2, pp. 93-117. October 1968. https://www.jstor.org/stable/1453726

Guggisberg, Hans Rudolph. *Sebastian Castellio, 1515-1563, Humanist Defender of Religious Toleration in a Confessional Age.* Translated by Bruce Gordon. Routledge Taylor & Francis, 2003.

Guggisberg, Hans Rudolph. *Basel in the Sixteenth Century: Aspects of the City Republic Before, During and After the Reformation.* Wipf & Stock, 2010.

Hillar, Marian. *Sebastian Castellio and the Struggle for Freedom of Conscience.* Published in the Essays in the Philosophy of Humanism, eds, D. R. Finch and M. Hillar, Vol. 10, pp. 31-56, 2002.

Hillar, Marian & Allen, Claire. *Michael Servetus: Intellectual Giant, Humanist, and Martyr.* Published by University Press of America, 2002.

Horsch, John. *Menno Simons; His Life, Labors & Teachings.* Mennonite Publishing House, 1916.

Jenkins, Gary. *Calvin's Tormentors – Understanding the Conflicts that shaped the Reformer.* Baker Academic, 2018.

Johnson, Keith L. *He Descended into Hell.* Institute for Faith and Learning at Baylor University. https://www.baylor.edu/content/services/document.php/217609.pdf. 2014

Jones, Rufus. *Sebastian Castellio, A Forgotten Prophet.* Kessinger Legacy Reprints, 2010.

Kingdon, Robert M. *Adultery and Divorce In Calvin's Geneva.* Cambridge: Harvard University Press, 1995.

Kingdon, Robert M. *Registers of the Consistory of Geneva in the time of Calvin, Volume 1: 1542-1544,* 2000.

Koeppler, Daniela. *The Art of Doubting: A Christian Perspective.* European Judaism (Vol. 53, Issue 1). Berghahn Books, Inc. Spring 2020

Kreis, Georg. *550 Years of the University of Basel. Permanence and Change.* Christoph Merian Verlag, 2010.

Kvicalova, Anna. *Listening and Knowledge in Reformation Europe: Hearing, Speaking and remembering in Calvin's Geneva.* Palgrave Macmillan, 2019.

Lavatera, Hans Rudolf. *Calvin, Farel, and the Anabaptists: On the Origins of the Briève Instruction of 1544.* Trans. by John D. Roth. MQR 88, July 2014.

Linton, Marisa. *Citizenship and Religious Toleration in France,* in Ole Peter Grell and Roy Porter (eds), Toleration in Enlightenment Europe (Cambridge University Press), 157-74, 2000.

MacGregor, K. *Nonviolence in the Ancient Church and Christian Obedience.* Themelios, Volume 33 - Issue 1. https://www.thegospelcoalition.org/themelios/article/nonviolence-in-the-ancient-church-and-christian-obedience/ May 2008.

Manetsch, S. *Calvin's Company of Pastors – Pastoral Care and the Emerging Reformed Church, 1536-1609.* Oxford University Press, 2013.

McTernan, Oliver. *Violence in God's Name – Religion in an Age of Conflict.* Orbis Books, 2003.

Miles, Margaret. R. *Theology, Anthropology, and the Human Body in Calvin's "Institutes of the Christian Religion."* The Harvard Theological Review, Vol. 74, No. 3 (Jul., 1981), pp. 303-323. Cambridge University Press, 1981.

Monheit, Michael. *Word Against Image: A Reconstruction of Calvin's View on the role of art in worship.* In 'Calvin, Beza and later Calvinism. John Calvin and the Interpretation of Scripture. Calvin Studies Society, 2005.

Monter, William. *Calvin's Geneva.* John Wiley & Sons, 1967.

Monter, William. "The Consistory of Geneva, 1559–1569," *Bibliothèque d'Humanisme et Renaissance* 38 (1976): 467-484.

Moss, Christina and Waite, Gary K. *Argula von Grumbach, & Katharina Schütz Zell, Anabaptist and Jorist Women.* Chapter 8 in: Protestants and Mysticism in Reformation Europe, St Andrews Studies in Reformation History, Volume: 14. Editors: Ronald Rittgers and Vincent Evener, 2019.

Mullet, Michael. *Radical Religious Movements in Early Modern Europe.* George Allen Unwin, 1980.

Naphy, William G. *Baptisms, Church Riots and Social Unrest in Calvin's Geneva.* The Sixteenth Century Journal, Vol. 26, No. 1, pp. 87-97. Spring, 1995. https://www.jstor.org/stable/2541527

Naphy, William G. *Plagues, Poisons and Potions – Plague Spreading Conspiracies in the Western Alps, 1530-1640.* Pp 44-59, 2002.

Ocker, Christopher. *Calvin in Germany.* Politics and Reformations: Histories and Reformations—Essays in Honour of Thomas A. Brady, Jr., pp. 313-344, 2007.

Ployd, Adam. *For Their Own Good: Augustine and the Rhetoric of Beneficial Persecution.* Chapter 6 in *Heirs of Roman Persecution,* eds. Éric Fournier and Wendy Mayer. Pp 95-111. Routledge, 2019.

Porterfield, Jason. *One Hundred Early Christian Quotes on Not Killing.* https://jasonporterfield.com/freebook/100-quotes/, 2021.

Schaff, Philip. *History of the Christian Church.* Oak Harbor, WA: Logos Research Systems, Inc, 1997.

Schirrmacher, Thomas. *Advocate of Love – Martin Bucer as Theologian and Pastor.* "World of Theology Series." Studies published by the Theological Commission of the World Evangelical Alliance. Volume 5/30. Bonn, 2013

Schmidt, S. *Church and World – Eusebius's, Augustine's, and Yoder's Interpretations of the Constantinian Shift.* Princeton Theological Monograph Series, 2020.

Selderhuis, Herman J. (Ed). *Calvin – Saint or Sinner?* Studies in the Late Middle Ages, Humanism and the Reformation. Mohr Siebeck Tübingen, 2010.

Shantz, Douglas H. *David Joris, Pietist Saint: The Appeal to Joris in the Writings of Christian Hoburg, Gottfried Arnold and Johann Wilhelm Petersen.* MQR 78, July 2004.

Smeeton, Donald D. *Calvin's Conflict with the Anabaptists.* The Evangelical Quarterly, Volume: 54, Issue: 1, Pages: 46-54, 1982.

Spellman, Ched. *I Wait Upon My God: Exploring the Life and Letters of Michael Sattler.* Southwestern Journal of Theology, Volume 56, Number 2, Spring 2014.

Spelman, Leslie. *Calvin and the Arts.* In the Journal of Aesthetic and Arts Criticism, Vol 6, No 3, pp 246-252, March 1948.

Stockwell, Clinton E. *The Cities of Calvin (The Background of Calvin and the Swiss Reformation).* Dordt College, Calvinism in the 21st Century, 2010.

Tuggy, Dale. *History of Trinitarian Doctrines.* Stanford Encyclopedia of Philosophy, 2020.

Tweddie, Rev W.K. *Calvin and Servetus. The Reformer's Share in the Trial of Michael Servetus.* Cross Reach Publications, 2017.

Valkhoff, Marius. *Sebastian Castellio and his 'De Haeriticis A Civil Magistratu Non Puniendis ... Libellus.'* In Acta Classica, Vol 3 No. 1, pg 110-119. https://doc-slib.org/doc/2089979/sebastian-castellio-and-his-de-haereticis-a-civil-magistratu-non-puniendis-libellus-by-marius-valkhoff-university-of-th

Veen, Mirjam van. *Contaminated with David Joris's Blasphemies - David Joris's contribution to Castellio's de Haereticis an sint Persequendi.* Bibliothèque d'Humanisme et Renaissance. T 69, No. 2 (2007), pp. 313-326. 2007. https://www.jstor.org/stable/20681109

Waite, Gary K. *Writing in The Heavenly Language: A Guide To The Works Of David Joris.* Renaissance and Reformation / Renaissance et Réforme, XXVI, 4, 1990.

Waite, Gary K. *The Anabaptist Writings of David Joris.* Herald Press, 1994.

Waite, Gary K. *The Anonymous Biography.* Waite, Editor and Translator in *The Anabaptist Writings of David Joris, 1535-1543.* Vol.7 of the Classics of the Radical Reformation Series, Herald Press, Waterloo,1994. New edition: *The Anabaptist Writings of David Joris, 1535–1543,* 2d edition, edited by Gary K. Waite. Walden, NY: Plough, 2019.

Waite, Gary K. *The Reception of the Dutch Spiritualist David Joris in 17th-Century English Polemics. The Devil of Delft in England.* In Church History and Religious Culture 101, pp 429-495, 2021.

Wallace E. Gregory. *Justifying Religious Freedom: The Western Tradition.* Penn State Law Review. Vol. 114:2, 2009.

Warfield B.B. *John Calvin: The Man and His Work.* From The Methodist Review, Quarterly, October 1909. https://www.monergism.com/thethreshold/sdg/warfield/warfield_calvinmanwork.html

Watt, Jeffrey R. *The Consistory and Social Discipline in Calvin's Geneva.* University of Rochester Press, 2020.

Webstr, Noah. *A brief history of epidemic and pestilential diseases; with the principal phenomena of the physical world, which precede and accompany them, and observations deduced from the facts stated. : In two volumes.* 1758-1843. Hartford: Hudson & Goodwin, 1799. https://collections.nlm.nih.gov/catalog/nlm:nlmuid-2576058RX2-mvpart. Public Domain.

Willgren, David. *Women, Power, and the Bible in Early Anabaptist History.* SJLT 4; *Woman, Power, and the Bible in Early Anabaptist History,* 2017. https://www.academia.edu/35937666/Women_Power_and_the_Bible_in_Early_Anabaptist_Academy of Leadership and Theology, Sweden.

Willis, Robert. *The Project Gutenberg eBook, Servetus and Calvin.* February 23, 2017. [eBook #54226]

Wills, Gary. *Augustine's Hippo: Power Relations (410-417).* In *Arion: A Journal of Humanities and the Classics,* Vol. 7, No. 1 (Spring - Summer), pp. 98-119, 2019.

Witte, John, in *Great Christian Jurists in French History,* ed. by Olivier Descampes and Rafael Domingo; Chapter 7, *John Calvin,* pp. 117-133, 2019.

Witte, John, in *Oxford Handbook of European Legal History* Dubber, Markus &

Godfrey, Mark Eds. Oxford: Oxford University Press. *Chapter 25, Law and the Protestant Reformation, pp* 583-610, 2018.

Witte, John, *Calvinist Contributions to Freedom in Early Modern Europe.* Published in Timothy S. Shah and Allen D. Hertzke, eds., *Christianity and Freedom: Volume 1: Historical Perspectives,* pp 210-234. Cambridge: Cambridge University Press, 2016.

Wursten, Dick, Review: *Sebastian Castellio, Annotationes in Pauli Epistulam ad Romanos ex Cap. IX.* Critical edition and English translation by Michiel Op de Coul and Mirjam van Veen, 2020, in CRMH – Journal of Medieval and Humanistic Studies, 3 August 2022.

Zabel, Gary. *All Things in Common: Spinoza and the Collegiant Letters.* Undated. https://garyzabel.academia.edu/research#papersandbookchapters

Zachman, Randall. C. *John Calvin as Teacher, Pastor, and Theologian: The Shape of His Writings.* Baker Academic, 2006.

Zagorin, Perez. *How the Idea of Religious Toleration Came to the West.* Princeton University Press, 2003.

Zweig, Stefan. *The Right to Heresy, Castellio Against Calvin.* Plunkett Lake Press, 1936.

About the Author

Kristin Jack lives in Dunedin, New Zealand, where he runs a mentoring program for vulnerable young people. Prior to 2010, he and his wife Susan (along with their children, Kaleb and Emma) spent sixteen years in Phnom Penh, Cambodia, starting health and development projects among the city's poorest residents.

In 2004, Kristin's coursework at the Oxford Centre for Mission Studies led him to ask the question: why is church history so full of violence, when Jesus spoke so much of love? A few years later, Kristin learned about Sebastian Castellio—a courageous sixteenth century reformer whose life and writings addressed the very same question. Castellio's advocacy for peace and tolerance in an age of violence and tumult resulted in the church trying to silence him.

Over the last four years, while battling lymphoma, Kristin has been forced to slow down and reflect on what is truly important about a life of faith. He's reached the same conclusion as Castellio came to: In life, there is nothing more important than love (1 Corinthians 13:13). And in faith, there is nothing more vital than mercy, forgiveness and forbearance (Galatians 5:6).

You can learn more about Kristin Jack at www.kristinjack.co.nz. And if you enjoyed this book, help others discover it by posting an honest review wherever you bought your copy.